Also by Tanaz Bhathena

A Girl Like That

The Beauty of the Moment

The Beauty of the Moment

tanaz bhathena

FARRAR STRAUS GIROUX
NEW YORK

Farrar Straus Giroux Books for Young Readers
An imprint of Macmillan Publishing Group, LLC
175 Fifth Avenue, New York, NY 10010

Printed in the United States of America
Designed by Elizabeth H. Clark
First edition, 2019

1   3   5   7   9   10   8   6   4   2

fiercereads.com

ISBN 978-0-374-30844-5 (hardcover) / ISBN 978-0-374-30848-3 (ebook)

Library of Congress Cataloging-in-Publication Data

Names: Bhathena, Tanaz, author.
Title: The beauty of the moment / Tanaz Bhathena.
Description: First edition. | New York : Farrar, Straus and Giroux, 2019. |
    Summary: Sixteen-year-old Susan is the new girl in her Canadian high
    school, striving to meet her parents' academic expectations, missing the
    friends she left behind in Saudi Arabia, dreaming of pursuing her passion
    for art, and secretly meeting with troublemaker Malcolm.
Identifiers: LCCN 2018009361 | ISBN 9780374308445 (hardcover)
Subjects: LCSH: East Indians—Canada—Juvenile fiction. | CYAC: East
    Indians—Canada—Fiction. | Dating (Social customs)—Fiction. | Family
    life—Canada—Fiction. | High schools—Fiction. | Schools—Fiction. |
    Canada—Fiction.
Classification: LCC PZ7.1.B5324 Be 2019 | DDC [Fic]—dc23
LC record available at https://lccn.loc.gov/2018009361

Our books may be purchased in bulk for promotional, educational, or business use. Please
contact your local bookseller or the Macmillan Corporate and Premium Sales Department
at (800) 221-7945 ext. 5442 or by email at MacmillanSpecialMarkets@macmillan.com.

To the real Manchershaw Ek-Dus—
expert swordsman and late great-grandfather.

To my parents—
For believing in me and my ~~im~~possible dreams.

To Aditi, Priya, Purva, Shachi, and Sweta—
For your friendship and the laughter
and the monkeying around.

The
Beauty
of the
Moment

Susan

My mother talks about love in extremes. A Bollywood sort of romance, with a hero and heroine, villainous parents, and a coterie of smart-mouthed siblings. That these love stories, repeated film after film, are strikingly similar to her own is pure coincidence.

"Do you know I ran away to get married?" Amma declared once, to a group of my awestruck cousins in India over a Skype call. "My poor parents nearly had a heart attack!"

With the air for drama that storytellers and convincing liars have perfected, she opened her brown eyes wide, tossed her long black braid behind her, and played with the edge of her cotton sari, increasing the tension in the moment. Seconds later, she segued into the climax that led to her perfect Ever After as a doctor's wife in the Arabian Gulf.

"First India. Then Saudi Arabia. And now you are in Canada," one of my father's sisters said, her smile not quite hiding the envy in her eyes.

Amma smiled in response. Her hand went to the minnu that my father had fastened around her neck on their wedding day—a delicate gold pendant in the shape of a leaf, seven gold beads forming a cross at its center. It was a necklace she never took off—one that told the world that she was married. Loved.

She did not tell my aunts about the hours she spends waiting next to her laptop, signed in to Skype, for the call that my father makes once each afternoon from Jeddah, Saudi Arabia. The call that he sometimes forgets about completely. She did not tell them about the anger, the fights, the despair—the gray, messy side of her love that gets turned off by the very mention of my father, that still blames me for the distance between them.

———————————

What people back home know about Canada: It's cold and terrible for highly qualified immigrants, especially doctors like my father. *Haven't you read the stories? Men and women with four degrees each, bagging groceries at the supermarket or working as cashiers at gas stations?* Amma always says.

What people back home do not know: Appa never really tried for a job here.

We arrived in Mississauga at the beginning of April as permanent residents. Within two whirlwind months, Appa moved us into a new condo, enrolled me in a new school, registered me for driving lessons, *and* bought us a new car. By the first week of June, he was gone, flying back to Jeddah five days before he needed to report back for work at the clinic.

"You know your father," Amma said, when I asked her why he didn't stay longer. "Busy, busy, busy. But he has promised to sort things out at the clinic within the next two or three months. He will be with us again before we know it."

Initially, apart from Appa not being here, I didn't mind the move to Canada so much—especially since my father's cousin, Bridgita Aunty, who lives an hour away from us, came over to visit a few times in the summer with her family. Also, after months of slogging at school in Jeddah, I was enjoying myself, almost feeling like I was on an extended vacation.

As August rolls to an end, though, I grow restless again, nervous about starting my final year of high school in a different country. Amma becomes tense as well—especially when my father postpones his arrival from late August to the end of September.

I sense it in the careless way she adds spices to her sambhar, the tone of her voice now, in early September, at the time of her usual Skype call with Appa.

"Hi there, Rensil is on the other line. He'll be right with you."

The voice is gentle and sweet, the video at my father's end disabled.

"And who might you be?" My mother's voice is equally sweet. Deadly.

"Aruna!" my father's voice booms, seconds before his face appears on the screen. It brings warmth to Amma's otherwise frosty expression and a smile to her pursed lips.

"Rensil, who was—"

"That was Mrs. Kutty, my new neighbor. Mrs. Kutty, please come here and say hi."

Another person peeps into the screen. Mrs. Kutty waves, her skin softened with age and wrinkles, her silver hair shimmering in the overhead light. "I'm sorry, dear. I didn't know how to turn on the video."

"That's okay." Amma's skin, several shades lighter than mine, turns pink. "I didn't recognize the voice, so . . ."

There's a knowing look on Mrs. Kutty's face, an understanding familiar to women who have grown used to their men leaving them behind in other countries. For work. For children. For other, unspoken reasons. If Amma sees the look, she doesn't acknowledge it. She turns into the mother I knew before our move. The impeccable hostess and social butterfly. Dr. Rensil Thomas's wife. Even though she's dressed in an old flowered nightgown and no makeup, I can feel the glamour dripping off her.

"I am not meant for weather like this." Amma launches into her usual complaints after Mrs. Kutty leaves. "I nearly froze to death waiting at the bus stop yesterday morning."

An exaggeration. It wasn't that cold and she had her coat on.

"It's a matter of adjustment, dear." Appa uses what I think of as his Doctor Voice. Careful, melodic, soothing. "I will come there as well soon enough."

"You said that when you left." Eighteen years of marriage have immunized Amma against the Doctor Voice. "I don't see why it's taking you so long to move here. Suzy had another driving lesson yesterday—"

I slip into my bedroom and shut the door quietly, cutting her off midsentence. I decide to Skype my best friend, Alisha Babu, in Jeddah, sighing with relief when she answers after a few seconds.

"Hey, what's up?" Alisha's had a haircut since we talked last week, her formerly long black curls cut into a messy chin-length bob and held off her forehead with a thick blue headband. The tightness in my chest unravels on seeing her familiar wide-spaced brown eyes, round face, and broad grin. For a minute, I almost believe that I never left Saudi Arabia, that she's still only a few buildings away from me on Sitteen Street.

"How was the driving lesson?" Alisha asks before I can reply. "You never answered the text I sent you yesterday!"

A cardinal sin as far as my best friend is concerned, even though there are days when Alisha herself doesn't reply to my messages, citing excuses such as schoolwork, head-girl duties and *general busyness*. (Her words, not mine.)

"I'm sorry, I forgot. And the driving lesson was terrible." I tug the elastic out of my ponytail, feeling it pull out a few long strands of my black hair with it. "As usual."

"Come on. You said that the last time as well. What was this now—your fourth lesson?"

"Fifth."

"Then it probably wasn't as bad as you think. And it's not like it was a *real* test."

No, it wasn't. A real test, that is.

In April, shortly after we arrived, Appa and I headed to the nearest DriveTest Centre with our passports and landing papers to begin the process of getting our driver's licenses. Appa was able to immediately take a road test and obtain a full driver's license thanks to his Saudi license and international driving experience. However, the rules for me are different. As a new driver with a G1 license, I need to wait a full year before taking my road test and making it to the next level of Ontario's graduated licensing program: the G2. A G2 license isn't permanent (I will need to take *another* road test before it expires), but it will allow me to drive independently on all roads, including highways, with few restrictions.

And this was where my driving instructor Joseph Kuruvilla

(a.k.a. The Tyrant) came in. Not only did Joseph convince my parents to enroll me in his driving school, but he also explained how finishing a government-approved driving course with a certified instructor will allow me to attempt the road test after only eight months—in December—instead of waiting for a whole year. The idea seemed great at the time.

Five lessons with Joseph, however, have managed to change my initial enthusiasm into dread. His voice, sharp even when saying hello, echoes through my head now: *Don't steer so hard! Reverse! Reverse! Use the brakes, will you! Why is it taking you so long to catch on to the most basic instructions!*

The last comment—made yesterday after I botched my fifth attempt at parallel parking in a row—had stung the most.

"What if I fail the road test, Alisha?" I ask now. "What if I can't get my license?"

Alisha laughs. "Don't be silly. You're not going to *fail*, Suzy. You never fail at anything!"

When I say nothing in response, the grin on her face fades. "Holy falooda! You're serious."

Fish. Fudge. Falooda. On a normal day, Alisha's swear word replacements make me laugh. Today, the back of my throat burns and I have an awful feeling that I'll burst into tears.

"Listen, you had a bad lesson, okay?" she says gently. "That could happen to anyone. Worst case scenario, if you do fail your test, you can give it again, right?"

Right.

Except, at my house, failure isn't an option. When I was little, my mother drilled the word *excellence* into my brain, pinning the letters one by one on an old corkboard in our house in Jeddah.

And excellence was what I had delivered year after year, by acing every subject, by ranking first in my classes at Qala Academy, no matter what curveballs the teachers threw at us during exams. My parents haven't even planned for the possibility of me failing my road test; they've taken it for granted that I will get my license in December.

"Once you pass the test, maybe your mother will get over her silly fear of driving as well," Appa joked once—a comment that made Amma roll her eyes.

I am too embarrassed to tell him about the nerves that hit me whenever I get into the driver's seat of my instructor's twenty-five-hundred-pound Toyota. About the clammy sensation that seeps up my back and down my shoulders and arms whenever Joseph shouts at me, making me freeze behind the wheel.

"Can we change the subject?" I ask now, unwilling to answer Alisha's question.

She shoots me a concerned look and then complies. "Hey. Do you know what happened with Verghese Madam yesterday?"

A funny story about my old physics teacher in Jeddah follows and soon I'm cracking up at Alisha's exaggerated imitation of Verghese throwing a temper tantrum when she caught two girls talking in class that morning.

"I thought she was going to send them to the headmistress." Alisha's hands make accompanying gestures, her nostrils flaring exactly the way Verghese Madam's did. "But she fumed a bit, said a few more things, and went on with the lesson."

"I can't believe I'm saying this, but I miss old Verghese." I don't mean this literally. Verghese Madam had a tendency to call me "Soo-sun," a pronunciation that made my name sound like

9

soo-soo, the Hindi word for urine. But I do miss being in class with Alisha and the feeling of holding back a laugh until my stomach aches.

"Right. You really miss the taunts about how a single lost mark in a board exam makes you a total failure at life. Besides, forget about that." Alisha's mouth spreads in a wide, evil grin. "You're in *Canada* now."

I roll my eyes. "Not this again!"

"I'm serious! Suze, you're so lucky. You can do whatever you want there. You can go to *art school*. What options do we have here in Jeddah or even India once we graduate? My parents are already talking about enrolling me in an engineering college in Trivandrum and having me talk to suitable Jacobite boys from Kerala. The types who'll judge everything from my 'slim figure' to my 'shiny black hair.'"

She rolls her eyes, while I laugh at the reference to the horrible matrimonial website Alisha's parents want her to create a profile on the year she turns eighteen.

"*You*, on the other hand, can play the field," Alisha says. "See greener pastures. Boys, Suzy! All those boys!"

"Um, hello? Have you forgotten how *my* parents want me to marry someone from our community as well? And art school? Seriously, Alisha?"

"First off, you've never even *talked* to your parents about art school. Who knows? They might actually say yes! And who's talking about marriage? It's just dating!"

But it's never just dating—not with my family, at least. While Amma and Appa are less conservative than Alisha's parents, I highly doubt they'll give me free rein when it comes to matters of the heart. Whenever the topic of boys comes up, they always talk about it in matrimonial terms—key phrases including *good Malayali Christian boy* and *degree in medicine or engineering*, with bonus points for *North American or European citizenship*. Alisha seems to have forgotten this or maybe she no longer cares.

"It's my first day of school tomorrow. I'll be lucky if I can find my way around, let alone find myself a boyfriend," I tell her.

"Then get yourself a boyfriend who can show you around!"

Alisha's obsession about me getting a boyfriend isn't a surprise. Neither of us has been out on a date before. That we lived in Saudi Arabia (where dating was forbidden by the law) was secondary; our parents wouldn't have allowed it. Also, we were too shy to approach anyone back then, in spite of having crushes on them.

"This way, I can live vicariously through you." Alisha has a look on her face that's so dreamy, it's comical. My fingers itch to sketch her as she is now: starry-eyed, with hearts popping all over her head.

Through my earphones, I hear a *thump* from the other side of my bedroom door. I take one earpiece off and hear Amma's voice rising in argument with Appa—a sound that I've grown more and more familiar with over the past month. I pop the earpiece back on.

"Boyfriends are overrated," I say.

I don't want to end up like my mother, with an Ever After that consists of perpetual fights and disagreements, mostly about her only child. Amma likes to pretend it never happened, but I haven't forgotten what she said to my father during our first week here: *If it wasn't for Suzy's education, we wouldn't have to even be here.*

"Says the girl who's never—oh, crap, I've got to get back to work."

From Alisha's end, I hear a mosque's sonorous call for prayer. It officially marks the beginning of her evening study session and the end of our chat. She grimaces. "I have to go. Want to chat later? Same time tomorrow?"

11

"I'll be at school." I've memorized the timings—8:20 a.m. to 2:40 p.m. instead of 7:00 a.m. to 1:00 p.m. the way it was in Qala Academy. Even if I take the bus, I'll still only be home by 10:00 p.m. Jeddah time—which will be too late for Alisha on a school night. "How about the morning, my time? Like around 2:00 p.m. in Jeddah?"

"I have biology tutoring then." Alisha frowns. "Never mind. Text me. I really have to go now or my mom will blast me off into outer space. Bye!"

"Bye."

Instead of going back to the living room, where my mom is still arguing with my dad, I head to the window and push aside the curtain to let in more light. The fabric is navy—a shade that perfectly matches the bedspread and pillows Amma picked out for this room. There are days when I'm tempted to change things around with splashes of orange paint, followed by teal, purple, and gold. I imagine doing a replica of Basquiat's skull or Dalí's melting clock or a creation of my own. I squint, picturing my latest sketch: a caricature of a man's open mouth forming the entrance of a subterranean tunnel, the insides teeming with butterfly fish, sea urchins, and sharks. For effect, I could add multihued coral creeping up the sides of his teeth and mouth.

I snort, imagining Amma's outraged *Aiyyo!*, followed by her punishing me for *spoiling the furniture*, the way she did when I had, at age five, decided to redecorate the stark white walls of our Jeddah living room with a bright green marker.

I don't look at the two paintings hanging on the wall next to the window—the only two I've done that have met with Amma's approval in all these years. A detailed depiction of a Kathakali dancer's green face done in oils sometime last year, and above that,

12

a watercolor of the sun setting over the Red Sea, King Fahd's Fountain white against the sky.

Nice! Look how they brighten up your room, she had declared when we were decorating the place in May, in that casual tone grown-ups use to describe hobbies they think have no potential to turn into careers.

I grip the curtain, my knuckles turning pink and yellow. Alisha does not know about the times I've screwed up the courage to ask about attending art school and failed. How, every time the topic of my career comes up, Amma and Appa get into an argument about what I'll be—a doctor (Appa) or an engineer (Amma).

I lean out the window and breathe in the cool September air. Unlike our neighborhood in Jeddah, where buildings were clustered more closely, interspersed by a mosque every couple of blocks, the nearest building over here is half a mile away, separated by an iron fence and a neatly trimmed lawn, the last of the summer flowers wilting now that fall is slowly setting in, the grass so green I wonder if it's even real.

Trees are slowly turning color—hints of russet and gold interspersing pointed evergreens. I revel in the difference for a few moments, in the absence of the brine and humidity that makes up Jeddah air.

The sound of bells under my window distracts me, a series of *clings* accompanying a pair of girls who weave across the street, dodging cars, pedaling in the direction of a park a few blocks away.

Are you happy there, Suzy? Appa often asks when we talk on Skype. *Do you like the new condo?*

Yes, Appa, I always tell him. *I love it here.*

He does not want another answer. He does not want to know that sometimes, when I Skype him, I try to time it so that I can overhear the muezzin calling for prayer from the mosque next to our apartment in Jeddah. He does not want to know how every night, after Amma falls asleep, I scroll through Qala Academy's secret student group on Facebook and read the messages there, feeling a pang go through me whenever my friends plan a trip to the beach or joke about a new teacher.

A red car screeches up the driveway, a rap song blasting from its speakers, startling an old lady walking her poodle on the sidewalk. I watch it zoom up the ramp and then smoothly, flawlessly reverse park into one of the numbered slots to the side of our building. This person probably had no trouble during their driving lessons, I think resentfully.

Moments later, a group of boys stumble out, the rough sound of their laughter rising in the air. I instinctively cringe. Boys. Another element that my parents expect me to adapt to after growing up with no brothers, after next to no male interaction in an all-girls school for most of my life.

I have a year to do it before university starts, they keep reminding me. A whole year to take advantage of the free high school education every immigration agency and lawyer touts in the Gulf. A year I will spend with strangers instead of my best friend and the girls I grew up with. At Qala Academy, I would have been arts editor for the school yearbook this year. The headmistress had promised me free rein to do what I wanted, including comics. But that was before the Class XI finals. Before Appa came home, declaring that our application for permanent residence had been approved.

When I look at the parking lot again the boys from the red car have disappeared. I am about to turn and reluctantly go back to the living room, to Amma, when I catch sight of a figure standing near the building entrance, right under my window.

The boy, probably seventeen or eighteen years old, is looking right at me, his eyes wide and curious, his spiked hair shimmering in the fading afternoon light. A desi boy, I think initially—though I can't be sure without speaking to him—his skin the same shade of brown as mine. When my gaze meets his, his chest rises and falls quickly the way a runner's might after a couple of laps around the park.

I feel my cheeks grow warm. Under normal circumstances, I would step back or simply close the curtain, embarrassed to be the center of a boy's attention. But something feels different today—maybe because of Alisha and her constant prodding. It's ridiculous, I tell myself. Silly to be nervous over boys just because I haven't interacted with them before.

So I do the unthinkable. I draw up my courage and look back at the spiky-haired guy who stands on the pavement three floors below.

It's easier, perhaps, because he isn't looking right into my eyes when I decide to look back, his gaze resting on my hair which is lying loose over one shoulder. Easier because when he does look at me, I decide that he isn't handsome in the traditional sense. His head is disproportionately large compared to his small, lean body, his nose flat and somewhat off center. But there are parts of his face that I like as well: the strong, square jaw, eyes that shimmer with warmth in the fading light, even from this distance. He takes out a hand from the pocket of his shorts, grins at me, and waves.

What I want to do is smile and wave back. It's what my brain urges me to do. But then Amma calls for me and I remember why this is a bad idea, why dating and boys and marriage have been bad ideas all along. I retreat into the shadows again, waiting for a long moment until I hear the door below open and shut.

Malcolm

When I see her again the next day, the new girl's hair is in a ponytail. It brings her features into sharp relief, the small, triangular jaw, the too-high forehead, the nervous, somewhat cynical look in her dark eyes.

She's so different from the curious girl I saw yesterday at Ahmed's apartment building that I am tempted to look around and check to see if she has a twin. But I'm pretty sure she doesn't. Ahmed, Steve, and I are smoking by the ramp outside the school cafeteria when I see her getting off a bright yellow school bus and I am pretty sure there's only one of her. A wave of ninth graders rumble past, fresh-faced kids with new backpacks over light fall jackets. Many wear eyeglasses and look nearly as confused as the new girl.

A hand rises from the rear of the pack, a familiar bracelet tied to the wrist. My sister, Mahtab, grins when she sees she has caught my attention. Her long brown hair shields her face when she looks down at her phone and jabs at the screen. Seconds later, a text pings on mine.

Can I come talk to you? Or will you be embarrassed by your little sister's presence?

I grin and wave back hard. Mahtab weaves around the lost-looking ninth graders, completely unaware of the way jaws drop when she passes some of the boys. I glare at them and take a step forward.

"Malu. Stop it," Mahtab admonishes.

If I wasn't glaring at the boys, I would glare at her. Mahtab knows how much I despise that nickname.

"Hello, Mahtab. How was your summer?" I see Steve scan my little sister from head to toe, observe how his eyes widen a little, as if he's surprised by how much she has grown. I jab him with an elbow. He grins at me sheepishly.

"Boring," Mahtab says, cheerfully unaware of what passed between me and Steve. She stretches her hands over her head and I frown at the shortness of the crop top she wears under her denim jacket, the stud in her belly button that she got on her fourteenth birthday this summer.

"You're not wearing your sudreh," I say, referring to the sacred undershirt we both are supposed to wear for religious reasons, day in and day out, come life or death. "Or your kusti," I add, which is the sacred thread tied around the sudreh.

"It's a crop top." She slips into pidgin Gujarati, the way she always does when she wants to keep our conversation private. "Who'll wear a sudreh-kusti with that?"

I make note of the warning embedded in her tone: *Back off, and don't be a chauvinistic jerk, big brother.*

"Hey, *I'm* not the religious one." I raise my hands. "How do you think Ronnie will feel? Doesn't he want you to cover up head to foot like those old Parsi widows back in India?"

"Ronnie is not like that!"

Mahtab's face turns pink with guilt. Not many people know about the ancient religion of Zoroastrianism or its followers, the Parsis, who migrated from Iran to India centuries ago, but a single conversation with my sister on the topic usually changes that. She has always been more Zoroastrian than I'll ever be, with her daily prayers, her involvement in the ZCC Youth Committee, and that whiny Rohinton "Ronnie" Mehta, the Parsi boyfriend she brought home last month at a family dinner. Ronnie is the guy who will stop a speeding car to let a group of ducks cross the street, the sort of guy who will do anything for the betterment of the world. Me, on the other hand? You'd be lucky if you caught me praying, let alone found me with any one of Mahtab's or our father's uptight ZCC friends.

"Just because you spent the whole summer moping over You-Know-Who—"

Steve coughs, cutting Mahtab off. "Wait, so your ex is Voldemort now? We can't mention her by name?"

My face heats up.

Mahtab's mouth, pursed tight, softens into a smile for Steve. "He has been grouchy all summer. I couldn't wait for school to start."

I give her a stern look. Or try to.

The trouble is, I can't hold on to my anger, not around Mahtab. She wrapped her hand around my heart as surely as she got me

18

wrapped around her finger, ever since the day Mom first put her in my old crib, a brown-haired, brown-eyed cherub who always laughed more than she cried.

Steve blows a line of smoke to the side. He watches me warily, as if expecting me to break down and collapse on the pavement the way I did a couple of months ago, after my breakup with Afrin. The swoon was more from heatstroke than anything else, but Steve and Ahmed still think it was because I saw Afrin kissing a random guy outside the mall. I drop my cigarette butt to the ground and stub it out with my sneaker, watching the ash smear over the concrete, and then kick the butt into the bushes nearby.

"Don't do that!" Mahtab gives me an annoyed look and picks up the cigarette butt. She walks over to the trash can a few feet away and drops it in. "If you *insist* on ruining your lungs, at least don't ruin the environment in the process."

"He's already doing that with the smoke," Ahmed points out before taking a drag of his own cigarette. Next to him, Steve rolls his butt between his fingers. If Mahtab was not around, I know he would have done exactly what I did and tossed it into the bushes.

My sister rolls her eyes. "Fine. Whatever. I need to go now or I'll be late."

"Do you know where your homeroom is?" I ask. "Want me to go with you?"

"Don't worry." She wraps me in a hug that smells of the sandalwood incense of our prayer room at home. "Text if you need me," she whispers in my ear.

I close my eyes. I hate the sound of worry in her voice. Hate how she was forced to grow up over the past two years because of my mess-ups.

"I promise."

"Really?"

I flick her nose with my finger. "Really."

I watch her make her way to the front doors, the sun in her hair as she merges into the crowd of backpacks, jackets, and jeans, the flash of a neon sole as she skips up the stairs, her silver bracelet glinting as she waves at me one last time.

I ignore the faint twinge of worry in my chest and tell myself that Mahtab will be okay. She has always been the stronger one out of the two of us, sticking to the straight and narrow, even after Mom died. Unlike me.

First days, unlike other days at school, smell of waxed floors and artificial air freshener. Sounds gather and disperse in pockets: the metallic squeal of lockers opening and closing, the *thump* of a basketball on the floor, the high melody of a girl's laugh. Hallways shrink with the added crush of students milling about and teachers in every corner, wearing pasted smiles, on the lookout for anyone breaking the school dress code. Last year, a guy from the basketball team came in wearing a neon-orange bikini top and jeans, and sang an old Queen song at the top of his voice while a couple of teachers escorted him to the principal's office.

Nothing that exciting seems to be happening today. In the crowd gathered around the guidance counselor's office, I catch a glimpse of the new girl again, standing at the very back, a puzzled expression on her face as she glances at the bright pink schedule she holds in her hands and then at the kids waiting outside the doors.

A boy swears, kicking a nearby locker, and the new girl jerks back slightly, even though the comment isn't directed at her. Body language says a lot about a person and, unlike my sister, who looks like she has been going here forever, the new girl is clearly out of her element. Glancing at her schedule one last time, she shakes her head and turns to leave, her eyes averted from everyone else around her, her lips straight and unsmiling—signs that point to extreme shyness or extreme snobbery, though for the moment I can't tell which.

I think I like her better with her hair all loose, hanging over her shoulder like a perfectly cut sheet of ebony, like those old-school Bollywood heroines, her face perked up with a secret smile—the kind that happens when you think no one's watching you. The best kind on a face like hers.

"Hey." Ahmed nudges me out of my attempt at telepathically communicating with the girl. "Are you listening? There's this party tonight at Justin's place. Wanna go?"

Justin and I go back. Way back to when I was raising hell as a fifteen-year-old and my old man was making my life a living one. But things are different now. I don't drink as much, don't smoke as much. I definitely don't take any pills anymore and that's what we'll find at Justin's: a candy bowl of pharmaceuticals that he gets from God knows where.

"You know I don't do that anymore, Ahmed," I tell him.

"You don't have to take anything." Ahmed shrugs his broad shoulders. "I don't."

"Not all of us are Muslims with balls of steel."

Ahmed laughs.

But the truth is that I'm simply not strong enough. Not like Ahmed, who's so secure in his faith that the peer pressure to drink or get high never gets to him the way it does with me and Steve. Cigarettes are Ahmed's only vice and, even then, he usually stops after one.

"Besides, Mahtab will kill me."

My sister and my mother, the two best people in my life. Only one of them remains with me now.

"By the way, Voldemort—I mean, Afrin was asking about you," Steve says.

"Oh yeah?" I try to sound disinterested.

"She was saying she misses you."

Sure she does. Several times she missed me so much that she didn't know or care who she made out with or hooked up with when she got high. When I broke up with Afrin earlier this year, she kept crying, saying that she hadn't meant it, that the guy she'd slept with looked exactly like me after she'd taken Justin's favorite blue pills. Except for that time at the mall, I didn't see Afrin for the whole summer. I want to pretend I'm over what she did, but even now the thought of her sleeping with some random, faceless guy pricks the inside of my chest.

"I don't want to get into that anymore, Steve. If you want to date her, you have my blessing."

Steve snorts. "And take away your only opportunity for a true Zoroastrian girlfriend?"

"Says the guy who drooled all over the floor when he first saw her at the ZCC."

"She has great boobs! Where else was I supposed to look? Besides, you know I don't date desi girls. No time for them— especially not another Patel!"

"What's wrong with desi girls? They're hot." Ahmed grins and passes around a pack of gum. I pop two pieces into my mouth and sniff my jacket to make sure it doesn't smell like cigarettes.

"I could be dating some long-lost Hindu ghotra cousin," Steve explains. "Besides that's what my *parents* want. For me to marry some good Patel chick."

22

"Maybe that Patel chick won't want *you*," I tease him. "Ever thought of that, Sma—"

Steve shoves me before I finish the sentence, almost knocking me into Vice Principal Han.

"Sorry, sir," we chorus. No one wants to get on Han's bad side on the very first day of school. I did that in grade eleven and ended up in detention, with Han breathing down my neck every five minutes, lecturing me about how lucky I was that corporal punishment was banned by the government.

Today, however, Han does little apart from giving us dirty looks and telling us to behave ourselves. You'd think we were the high school's biggest troublemakers the way Han keeps his eye on us. At least I know I deserve it for mooning him last year from the window of the bio lab. But Ahmed and Steve only get into trouble for being my friends. For sticking with me through all my phases, including the bad ones.

Ahmed Sharif, the stud. With a beard as thick as a grown man's even though he's only seventeen, tall and muscular with a face that has been drawing girls since the ninth grade, even though he has dated only one girl briefly in the time I've known him.

Steve Patel, the class clown. Stork-like and skinny, with a smile that perpetually borders on a smirk. A guy who has been friend-zoned by more girls than both Ahmed and I can count, even though Steve always jokes about them getting intimidated by his (nonexistent) good looks.

Then there's me. Malcolm Vakil, hell-raiser. The One Without a Future, according to every adult in his life.

As I walk down the hallway to my locker, I see the new girl again, staring at a locker like it's some sort of math problem.

I watch her pull out a lock—slender and gold, the three-digit kind that's super easy to crack. I am partly tempted to call out and warn her about this when she smiles slightly and slides it into the metal holes, closing it with a *snap*.

I was right about that smile. It changes her face, lingers when she lifts her head up and her gaze clashes with mine. Her eyes, rounded with recognition now, are deep and brown, the fine lines of the irises visible even in the dull fluorescent lights.

My tongue sticks to the roof of my mouth and my palms bead with sweat the way they did yesterday afternoon when I saw her leaning out of her window, brown skin aglow, black hair falling over her shoulder. A faint bit of color tints her cheeks before she awkwardly twists her head around, turning this way and that before heading down the math and science hallway, without another glance in my direction.

Behind me, Steve laughs. "Whoa."

"Shut up, Steve."

"Come on, man. She's cute."

"Whatever." I bury my face in my locker.

Steve raises his hands. "All right, all right. With my luck, she's probably a Patel anyway."

"Don't think so," Ahmed says. "She was wearing those tiny gold chandeliers in her ears. South Indian girls wear those."

"How do *you* know?"

"Remember my old girlfriend, Noorie? She was from Kerala. She's the one who told me."

I continue watching the new girl, the slender curve of her neck as she raises her head to check the room number, the unconsciously graceful sway of her hips.

"Wonder if she lives near Square One, like Noorie. Maybe I should ask around," Ahmed teases.

"She lives in your building," I say without thinking.

"What? How do you know that?"

I bite my tongue. "I don't. Forget I said anything."

Ahmed grins the way a cat might right before it eats a mouse. "Aww, come on. Don't be like that. If she does live in my building, I can hook you up."

"It's fate," Steve says. "You have a thing for her; looks like she has a thing for you—*ow!*" he shouts when I punch him in the arm.

As embarrassing as it was to be caught salivating over a girl—that's Steve's thing, not mine—I am not ready yet to get into a relationship like the one I had with Afrin. Afrin wasn't only the first Zoroastrian girl I ever dated, but also the first girl I felt something for that was more than lust. I've faced disappointments with girlfriends before, but Afrin was different. She taught me the meaning of heartbreak.

Ahmed and Steve think that hooking up with other girls will change that. But whoever these fictitious girls are, I know that the new girl isn't going to be one of them. She's way too shy, for one thing. It'll be a miracle if she says hi to me by the end of the semester, let alone allows me to slip my hand into the back pocket of her jeans.

"Malcolm. Come on." Ahmed's face is a little more serious now. "Don't you think it's time? I know what Afrin did was awful, but—"

"I don't want to talk about Afrin."

I ignore the look Ahmed and Steve shoot each other, ignore my heartbeat, which has gone from a steady canter to a gallop.

"In any case, it looks like she's taking calculus along with the rest of the nerds," I say, pointing toward the room the new girl disappeared into. "It's not like we're going to have any classes in common."

Or *any*thing in common.

Pretty as she might be, I know that girls like her do not go for guys like me. Heather Dupuis. Elle Fernandez. Preeti Sharma. All straight-A students with crushes on star athletes like Vincent Tran and Sergio Garcia.

I look up at the new girl's locker which, as luck would have it, is right next to mine.

"Should we leave you here?" Ahmed asks.

"Yeah, maybe you can practice talking to her locker," Steve says.

"Shut up," I tell them, and head to class as the warning bell goes off.

———————————

I don't see her again for the first half of the day. Not in college-level math. Nor in accounting. Not even during lunch, when the guys and I go out (with everyone else who knows better than to eat the cafeteria food) to inhale giant gooey cheese slices from Joe's Pizzeria across the street.

Before the start of the third period, a part of me relaxes, thinking that maybe I won't see her, when I suddenly do, right at the back of the room, in a university-level course I would never have enrolled in had it not been for my surprisingly good performance during eleventh-grade English and the insistence of the teacher, Mr. Kristoff, who thought I had "great ideas" and a "way with words."

The new girl is sitting right at the back of my English class, in the second-last row, inches away from where Ahmed, Steve, and I usually sit when we have the same classes together. I can already hear Steve suppressing a laugh behind me. I school my face into its usual indifferent mask and scan the rest of my classmates, familiar faces I know by name, but barely talk to. Then I see *her* and feel my mask slip again. Godafrin, a.k.a. Afrin, Irani. Long hair. Longer legs. Settled in the lap of some guy, her high giggle unmistakable, painful to my ears.

I walk to the back of the room, nodding at a couple of guys I recognize from basketball, and then, casually, without thinking too much about it, slide a hand over the new girl's desk. I don't miss the way her head jerks to watch my hand, or the slight blush on her brown cheeks.

She stares at the three-ring binder in front of her, already opened to a freshly lined page, the date and course code neatly written down in the upper-right corner in blue ink. An HB number 2 rests right next to the pen, the point fresh, sharpened.

A perfectionist. So not my type.

My fingers slide off the desk.

I begin chatting with Ahmed and Steve, ignoring the girl's presence, or at least pretending to, seeing her shoulders slowly, infinitesimally relax into a slouch. She picks up a pen again and flips to the back of the binder where she begins scribbling something.

Probably math equations. Maybe she'll be the one to finally discover a solution to world peace through numbers. I turn to face the front when I hear the door closing, the level of noise in the classroom growing subdued, announcing the arrival of the teacher.

The man—an awfully familiar man—clears his throat and adjusts his tie, probably still a clip-on, from what I remember from ninth grade.

Crap. What's Zuric doing here?

I check my schedule, wondering how I managed to miss this,

but the bright pink paper still only says *TBA* in small black letters next to *Instructor*.

"He's the only one teaching twelfth-grade English this year," Ahmed says, and I realize that I've spoken my question out loud.

"I'm dropping."

"Don't be an idiot. You can't. You won't graduate otherwise. Come on, man. It's only a dumb teacher."

I curse again.

When I signed up for this course last year, still doped up on Mr. Kristoff's praise, I completely forgot that he would not be teaching English this year, that he *never* taught the senior class. Clearly there's only one teacher for university-level English this year and that is my old nemesis Emil Zuric. The man who you'd think was a nervous wreck from the way he conducted class, from the way no one took him seriously, until the day he called my normally MIA father in the ninth grade to tell him I would fail English that year if I didn't wise up. I never lost the scars from the caning I got after that. Or forgot the role Zuric had to play in them.

"Good afternoon, everyone. Hope you're having a great first day back to school." Zuric's teeth flash a dull yellow; the classroom lights aren't doing him any favors.

His eyes move in that practiced way teachers have, scanning the room for old favorites, picking out new faces. Narrowing when they land on me, his smile slipping slightly.

"I heard some of you did really well in your English exams last year."

Afrin's highlights shimmer when she tosses her hair behind her back. She turns to look at me. I roll my eyes at the ceiling and ignore both her and Zuric.

"This is a good thing. Because let me tell you that this course

28

won't get any easier. We have a play and a novel to cover this semester, not including your independent study, along with several short stories and poems. This course is heavily focused on analyzing literary themes and will be more challenging to some of you than to others."

Zuric fumbles with the bulldog clip holding a stack of course outlines together. He splits the stack in four, one for each row of desks, and hands the outlines to the kids sitting in the front row.

I pull out a pencil from my binder and spin it on the desk like a compass. As the outline makes its way to the back, I tune out Zuric's mumbling monotone and once more find myself staring at the back of the new girl's head. I spy a thin strand of silver peeking from the hair tie at the center of her skull. A blessing from a loved one, Mom used to call them when they appeared on anyone younger than thirty.

I ignore the stabbing sensation in my chest that always comes with thoughts of my mother and force myself to smile for the crowd. The fake smile remains on my face when the new girl finally turns in her seat, holding out the last couple of outlines. She does not smile back, but this time looks me in the eye again.

Five seconds. Ten. Fifteen. She does not look away and this amount of time is pretty much an eternity when it comes to engaging a guy's attention according to those teen girl magazines Mahtab keeps reading. Despite my vow not to get involved with anyone this semester, I find myself leaning forward, reaching out to grab the papers and brushing her fingers in the process.

My skin tingles in a way it never has before, not even with Afrin, and I pull away, startled. The new girl turns quickly, tugging her long ponytail over one shoulder, exposing her nape and the tiny birthmark there, a dot placed right where her spine begins.

I roll my fingers in, accidentally crushing the paper's edge in the process. I am so distracted by what happened that I don't hear the announcement Zuric makes about class introductions. But he must have made one because I see a couple of girls in front stand and recite their names, favorite books, and hobbies to the rest of the class. Normally I couldn't care less about class intros, but I am now desperate to know who this new girl is, to put a name to the mystery, solve it and be done with it. Names classify things, make them familiar, easy to understand. Ordinary.

It takes a long time to get to the last few rows. The girl finally stands, a wrinkle in the back of her lavender shirt from sitting all day.

"My name is Susan Thomas. My favorite book is *Macbeth*. I like drawing things." Her voice is smooth and clear, the Indian accent unmistakable.

Mr. Zuric's face glows in the way it always does when someone mentions one of the classics or Shakespeare as a favorite book. "Thank you, Ms. Thomas. That's one of my favorite books, too."

Susan Thomas sits down, her shoulders hunching from the attention.

Steve is next: "Steve Patel. Favorite book—the *Kamasutra*." I grin as the class bursts into laughter. "And ladies . . . I'm available!"

More laughter, and claps, as Steve bows.

Zuric's face is a nice even shade of tomato. He squints beadily at Steve. "Thank you, Mr. Patel."

Zuric has got to be the only teacher at Arthur Eldridge who still refers to us by our last names. It's ridiculous, considering how he mispronounces every name that isn't European.

When Ahmed's turn comes, he winks at me. "Ahmed Sharif. Favorite book—*Sports Illustrated* swimsuit edition." (A lie; Ahmed's real favorite is *Crime and Punishment*.)

Zuric's complexion deepens in color as the class laughs again.

"I like cars," Ahmed adds. (The truth.) "The faster the better." (Also true.)

A guy whistles from the front. A couple of girls giggle, one of them Afrin, who flashes Ahmed a flirty smile. I feel a sense of relief when Ahmed doesn't smile at her but only settles down, winking at Susan Thomas, who looks scandalized. There is a brief moment of silence before Zuric finally looks at me and nods. I don't stand up. I am never this disrespectful during other classes, but Zuric and I have a history. I know how to tick him off. I want to.

"Call me Vakil. Malcolm Vakil," I mock, part Ishmael, part James Bond.

"Mr. Vakil, will you stand up so that everyone else can see you, please?" Zuric says.

I give him a wide, fake smile. "I'm happy right where I am."

"Stand up." Zuric's hands are shaking. "Right now."

Unlike all the others, who have turned to look at my reaction, Susan Thomas is facing front. Her back is ramrod straight. I slip out of the chair and stand.

"Malcolm Vakil. Favorite book—*Moby-Dick*." Predictably this makes a few people giggle.

"I like drawing things, too."

Giggles turn to loud laughs and this is when Susan turns around to glare at me. I raise an eyebrow, tilt my head to the side, and smile. I can feel Afrin's stare from the front of the room, examining both Susan and me. When I sit down again, Susan's facing the front of the room where Zuric is now going over the course outline.

The phone in my pocket vibrates. It's Steve.

so you DONT have a thing for her, eh? 😊

I look up again, pretending to watch Mr. Zuric write something on the board, before turning my phone off.

Susan

BENEFIT CONCERT FOR SYRIAN REFUGEES
Volunteers needed to help organize a special
fund-raising concert to spread awareness about the
war in Syria and the refugees struggling to make lives
for themselves outside their homeland.

WE ARE CURRENTLY LOOKING FOR:
Fund-Raising Directors—4 positions
VIP Liaisons—2 positions
Secretary—1 position
Treasurer—1 position
Art Director—1 position
INTERESTED? COME TO THE FIRST MEETING:
Friday, September 25, 2015, School Cafeteria, 4 p.m.

QUESTIONS IN THE MEANTIME? IDEAS?
Contact chairs Ronnie Mehta and Mahtab Vakil at
BenefitConcertExec@arthureldridge.ca

Printed in bold black, the posters are everywhere: on the bulletin board outside the guidance counselor's office, on the insides of the doors of the girls' bathroom stalls, flyer versions being handed out by a pair of boys at the door next to the cafeteria during lunch. One morning, a boy and girl show up during physics to talk about the concert as well.

"If you've been watching the news recently, you probably know about what's been happening in Syria." The boy who addresses the class wears glasses, pressed trousers, and a button-down shirt. I half expect him to carry a briefcase in one hand. "Many have been forced to leave their homes and seek asylum in other countries. Canada is one of those countries."

He looks to the girl, who's dressed more casually, in jeans and a green sweater. Her wide smile reminds me of Alisha—a younger version of Alisha with long, shoulder-length brown hair.

"We're looking for volunteers to help set up a concert in January to raise money for Syrians forced to leave their homes," she says. "Proceeds raised from the concert will go to the Red Cross."

"Where do we volunteer? Here?" Someone asks the question that suddenly pops into my head.

"Friday the 25th, in the cafeteria," the girl says. "Everything's on the poster. If there are multiple people trying out for the same position, we'll do interviews."

I take one of the flyers being handed out and fold it in half before placing it neatly into my binder. *Art Director.* The words have a nice ring to them. I think back to what Alisha told me last week. What if I *do* tell my parents about art school?

"What if?"

I sing the words under my breath, feel them add a skip to my step as I walk out the door at the end of the period. Daydreaming does me no favors: instead of the stairs that lead to the cafeteria, I reach a dead end, an entire wall of lockers and—my cheeks flame— two students making out.

I double back, wondering if I'll ever get used to scenes like this or even to attending a coed school. Relief floods through my veins when I finally locate the stairs leading down to the cafeteria. I take a deep breath and tell myself to stop being silly. They're *boys*, not aliens. I, on the other hand, might as well have come from another planet.

My first week at Arthur Eldridge passed in a haze of rooms and hallways, a surprising maze of confusion for a building so small. At Qala Academy, our classes were static, which made sense as it was ten times larger. Over there, I would never have been able to make it from one end of the building to another on time, even at a dead run.

The schoolwork isn't nearly as bad. Calculus is a breeze, the syllabus almost equivalent to what I already studied last year in Jeddah, except for the functions, which are a lot more complex. English isn't difficult either; unlike Alisha and a few of my other friends, I've always liked reading. Art is pure joy—by far the best course I've taken at *any* school, I admit to myself, even though it feels like a minor betrayal of Qala Academy.

Physics is the most challenging of all my courses. I never really liked physics at Qala Academy, but I didn't exactly find it difficult to follow. However, unlike at my old school, at Arthur Eldridge the assignments are not a matter of rote learning. Not only does my new school have bigger and better laboratories, but here, class time is devoted to actually performing the experiments and drawing conclusions from our results—even if they don't match what we know of the theory. Our teacher, Mr. Franklin, may crack jokes in class and smile all the time, but when it comes to marking our assignments, he's even tougher than Verghese Madam.

Bridgita Aunty said kids who come from educational backgrounds like mine face similar issues with lab work. "You can't get away with *mugging* here, Suzy," she teased me last night over the phone, using the South Asian colloquial term for memorizing large sections of textbooks and spitting them out word for word.

I join the flow of bodies pouring into the cafeteria, dodge elbows, skip over stretched-out feet. The air is thick with the smell of grease. French fries are the only item the cafeteria sells hot, in red boxes filled constantly by a woman with pale blond hair. No one asks for the pizza, and it took me only one bite on my very first day to figure out why. I can still recall the taste of the burned cheese and too-sweet sauce, the paste-like texture of the crust.

A pair of girls from my homeroom pass by and find seats at a nearly full table. Spotting an extra chair at the table, I head in the same direction. As if sensing my approach, one of them drops her bag into the empty seat. "Sorry. This one's already taken."

I smile back stiffly and nod before turning and facing a sea—no, a veritable ocean—of tables, nearly every chair taken by a body or a bag. On my second day, I sat at a table full of ninth graders who appeared so intimidated by me that they gave me nothing more than monosyllabic replies or shy smiles when I tried to make conversation. Today, the only free spot appears to be at a table

36

where a group of boys wearing the school's basketball team jerseys are cheering on a teammate's attempt at inhaling soda through a pair of straws in his nostrils.

"Forget it," I mutter. I slip out of the cafeteria and walk rapidly in the opposite direction—past the brightly decorated art and music hallway where I have class fourth period, past the flowcharts and staid brown stencils marking the business studies wing, and through a pair of heavy green double doors—a side entrance that directly opens into the school's now-quiet parking lot.

It's here, atop a small set of stairs, that my lungs finally begin filling with air. A moment after I settle down, I hear the doors open again. I brace myself for a teacher or the stern vice principal, Mr. Han, who often lurks the halls in search of truants. But it's only a group of students who amble past, talking among themselves, paying me no attention.

It is an excellent spot for watching everyone without being noticed. Most students use the main doors to exit the building and cross the street to the tiny pizza parlor on the other side. Moments later, they emerge again, carrying big slices on cardboard trays. Though I can't see the pizza from here, I guess by the happy expressions on their faces that it's a lot better than the cafeteria's unappetizing version.

Though the canteen at Qala Academy is little better than the Arthur Eldridge cafeteria, no student is allowed to leave campus for lunch over there, especially not the girls. Alisha often grumbled about the double standards surrounding this decision—"At the boys' section, the seniors are allowed to go out with permission! Admin acts like we can't even cross the road alone because we're girls!" In this particular instance, I understand why she keeps calling me lucky to have moved to Canada.

I look at my lunch for the day—cucumbers and cream cheese on brown bread. "I'm tired of eating dosa all the time," I told Amma last week. With the stress of settling in, I didn't have the heart to tell her the truth. How on my first day here, when I opened my plastic box to the mouthwatering scent of a paper-thin rava dosa and coconut chutney, I heard a girl behind me complain about the "stinky curry smell" in the lunchroom.

I bite into the sandwich, wondering what it would have been like if I had screwed up the courage to turn around and educate the girl about the difference between curries and chutneys, to point out that if it was made in France, the dosa would be called a savory crepe. But in that moment my body simultaneously grew hot and cold, cheeks burning with embarrassment, jaw frozen shut, the way it always does in these situations. The comeback, as usual, came long after, when I was home in bed.

The cream cheese sticks to the roof of my mouth. I crumple the aluminum foil I packed the sandwich in, molding it into a hard silver ball.

To distract myself, I pull out my sketchbook and draw the beginnings of a face: an elderly Indian woman I saw on the city bus this morning. She wore a sari and coat, her socked feet stuffed into Crocs. I outline her mouth, the gentle slope of her nose, the small, bright eyes that twinkled when she saw me looking. Once I have the basic shapes done, I add texture and shadow: crosshatching the arch of her feathery brows, rounding out the lower half of her right cheek, emphasizing the slight indent in her chin. I'm drawing from memory, which means I'm likely getting some of the details wrong, but my new art teacher Ms. Nguyen said it's good practice to draw faces to scale—even as a caricaturist. "You need to learn the rules first if you intend to break them," she told me.

After a few moments, I'm stretching my arms out, trying to relieve them, when I spy a shadow from the corner of my left eye.

It's him. The boy from English. Malcolm Vakil or the Troublemaker as I think of him, with his spiky hair, baggy jeans, and thick silver chain around his neck. Up close, his nose is flatter and even more off center than I first perceived. Earlier this week, I tried to draw a caricature of him, focusing on the nose and that terrible porcupine hairstyle. *Caricature* comes from the Latin *carricare*, which means to load or exaggerate. By its very essence, it should have allowed me to focus on his imperfections, reminding me that he isn't as attractive as I once thought. Instead, I found myself outlining his strong jaw and the scar on his chin that could almost be mistaken for a cleft. I spent nearly an hour with my watercolors trying to match the exact shade of his eyes, which are unlike any I've seen before: brown with gray circling the pupils.

His stares make me nervous. Then there's that jolt I felt in the classroom when his hand brushed mine. I don't know what to make of it, what to make of him. When Alisha and I envisioned a boyfriend from my new school, we went the usual unimaginative Prince Charming route. Blond hair. Blue eyes. A younger Duke of Cambridge lookalike without the British accent and the bald head. Only, in the time I've been here, no white boy has ever caught and held my attention for longer than a few beats.

I watch the tall bearded boy next to Malcolm—Ahmed Sharif, I think his name is. I've seen Ahmed several times in my building. He lives a couple of floors above mine and each time we run across each other in the elevator, he nods at me and smiles. I've now slowly begun to smile back. Ahmed does not intimidate me the way the other boys at school do, does not make my skin break into goose bumps every time he's in my presence, the way Malcolm does.

As if sensing my thoughts, Malcolm turns, his eyes finding mine. A side of his mouth curves up. A smile. I snap my book shut and tear my gaze away, pretending to look for something inside my bag. I don't look up. Not when they approach the staircase I'm sitting on. Not even when the toe of Malcolm's sneaker lightly nudges mine on the way in.

I do nothing until their voices disappear, contained once again by the door behind me clanging shut. My breath rushes out, as if I've been holding it for too long, and I feel like an idiot because of it.

I pick up my phone and scan it for texts and emails. A forwarded message from Appa with a link to the Aga Khan Museum in Toronto: You should go with Amma. Picture texts, mostly quotes from the Bible and jokes in Malayalam from family members in India. Nothing from Alisha even though I can see she read the long text I sent her last night.

"Come on," I mutter. "What kind of friend are you?"

It's two weeks into September and the trees are ablaze with yellows and reds. September is mock-exams prep month at Qala Academy, when everyone from Classes X and XII starts studying for the central board exams set in New Delhi, India. Unlike regular school exams for other classes, which start and end in February, the boards start in March and can go all the way up to April, depending on which subjects you've taken. Brutally designed and unforgivingly marked, these exams decide the fate of every Indian who graduates from a CBSE-affiliated school anywhere in the world and plans on applying to colleges in India. Alisha told me once that the most competitive colleges evaluate your board exam results from *both* Classes X and XII, making the process even more challenging.

The memory of this makes me feel simultaneously relieved and guilty. Of course Alisha hasn't forgotten me. She has exams to deal with. Also, as head girl, she has more work piled on her than before. I now feel silly over my jealousy about the Instagram video she and my old classmates posted about their visit to the art museum in Al-Balad. It's not Alisha's problem that I haven't been able to make a friend at school yet. Rationally, I know this.

But Alisha isn't here. In a country where, in spite of speaking the same language as others, she would be judged on the South Indian lilt to her accent rather than on her words. Buffered by the same girls she grew up with since kindergarten, my best friend does not feel the sting of being snubbed outside classes or the bone-deep loneliness that settles in at seeing groups of kids chatting together at recess. I'm about to go back into the school building, when a voice calls out my name.

"Hey, Susan! Wait up!"

A girl I recognize vaguely from physics appears from somewhere in the middle of the parking lot, her bright blue jacket capturing my attention first and later her eyes: a pale azure tint that matches the September sky behind thick, black, square-framed glasses.

"Heather Dupuis," she says, holding out a hand before I make the attempt at recalling her name. "We're in physics together."

"I know. I mean, I've seen you."

I clamp my mouth shut. Two weeks of not speaking at length to a classmate and I automatically lose the ability to form sentences. But Heather only smiles. She wears skinny jeans ripped at the thighs and knees, a soft white sweater, and the lightest traces of lip gloss and liner. Her freckled cheeks are free of makeup and her curly red hair is braided neatly over one shoulder.

I force myself to not look at my own outfit: jeans bought to spite my mother who called them "elephant-legged" and the oversize red polo I carelessly dumped into a handcart at Walmart without even trying it on.

"I'm sorry for interrupting your lunch," Heather says, even though I'm clearly finished and she is not interrupting anything. "But do you happen to have this weekend's physics homework on you?"

"Sure." I unzip my bag to pull out the strange three-ring-binder that I use now instead of actual notebooks and pull out the sheet where I scribbled down the homework. "You can keep this if you want."

"What?" Her eyebrows shoot up. "Won't you need it as well?"

"Page 42. 1a, 2c, 5d, e, and f." I recite the assigned problems from memory. "I think I'll be okay."

Heather grins, impressed. "Wow! That's amazing. Do you have a photographic memory or something?"

I shrug, partly pleased, partly embarrassed. "I'm good at remembering things."

The sort of memory that's both a blessing and a curse because I remember everything I read. Word for word.

"Wow, I wish I was that good at remembering things. I can barely remember my locker combination most days." Heather tucks the paper into her binder. "Thanks so much! You're the best."

"You're welcome," I say, smiling at the genuine gratitude in her tone. At Qala Academy, all I would've received for any kind of help I gave out was a nod and a quick *Thanks*—like nothing less was expected from the Smartest Girl in Class. As Heather leaves, my phone buzzes, the screen lighting up with a text.

Alisha: hey! sorry didn't write back before! wanna chat this weekend?

I grin. Yes! I text back. I feel like we haven't talked in WEEKS!

Alisha: MONTHS

Alisha: NO YEARS

Alisha: WHY'D YOU GO TO CANADA AND TAKE MY BFF WITH YOU????

I text back a series of heart emojis, my world temporarily restored.

I drew a caricature of my physics teacher at Qala Academy in Class XI, during an especially boring chapter on relative velocity. While Verghese Madam stood by the blackboard and lectured, I added details to the sketch in my notebook. A flaring nostril. A curl matted to the forehead. An extra layer of flab under the starched folds of Verghese's gold-bordered kanjivaram sari.

It took thirty minutes for Alisha to give the game away, the snort lodged in her nostrils bursting into the air like a fart in the middle of a eulogy. It took another thirty seconds for Verghese to locate the culprit—*Soo-sun!*—before throwing a piece of chalk at my head and telling me to report to the headmistress for *disrupting the class.*

At Arthur Eldridge, it takes a grand total of two weeks for our English teacher to scold Malcolm for snickering with Ahmed in the back row. On the other hand, it takes about three seconds for Malcolm to smile in response and tell Mr. Zuric to *screw off.*

Mr. Zuric, with bachelor's degrees in arts and education and a master's in English literature, according to the biography in my course outline, a man twice as tall as Malcolm, blinks like an animal caught in the headlights of a van. His thick, pigmented hands fumble with the clip-on tie at his throat.

"What did you say?"

"I said, screw off," Malcolm repeats calmly. "Sir."

Giggles erupt in the classroom. Beside me Steve begins mumbling gibberish the way Mr. Zuric does when he's talking out loud to himself or writing something on the blackboard. It makes Ahmed slam a hand on the table before covering his face, shoulders shaking.

"You shouldn't say such things," Mr. Zuric says, his face pink, his humiliation as palpable as the dried gum on the underside of my desk.

Our English teacher can recite yards of Shakespeare without looking into a book. But he is incapable of handling a rowdy class—especially a boy like Malcolm, who'll walk out, whistling, before Mr. Zuric even thinks of throwing him out.

After class, I've often seen Malcolm mimicking Mr. Zuric's unintelligible responses for his friends. He usually performs the acts right in front of my locker, leaning against the metal door, rotating the numerals of the sleek gold, single-digit combination lock Dad sent me from Jeddah. It's my lock that interests him, I suppose: the only gold one in a row of round double-digit steel combination locks with fat bellies and dark blue dials. Whenever I approach, he moves away with a grin on his face—the same grin he gave me the day before school started, when I was looking at him from my bedroom window, still thinking about stupid things like being able to talk to a boy.

I no longer want to talk to Malcolm. And I think he senses that from the way he smiles whenever I hurry away, preferring to lug my four-pound textbooks in a backpack rather than putting them away in a roomy metal cabinet.

"Malcolm Vakil? He's not even handsome," I overheard a girl say in physics class this morning.

"Yeah, but he's so . . . cool." A giggle. "That don't-care attitude of his? It can be a turn-on."

"He's still giving old Zuric a hard time. It was funny at first, but now it's only getting disruptive."

"Malcolm wasn't always like this," Heather Dupuis said. "I still remember him from middle school. He was really nice back then. Friendly. The teachers thought he would be on the honor roll. But everything changed after his mom . . . well, you know. One day he came to school with bruises over his face. He told the teacher it was a biking accident, but everyone knew he was in a fight of some sort. He always is."

The conversation remains at the back of my mind, bubbles to surface in English class, when once again Mr. Zuric calls Malcolm to the front to pick up his assignment and the latter deliberately aggravates him by taking more time than needed.

On the way back, Malcolm slides his fingers across my desk. When I look up, he raises an eyebrow and winks. I glare at him wishing that Mr. Zuric could, like Verghese Madam, throw a piece of chalk at that spiky little head and hit the mark with painful accuracy.

On Saturday morning, Amma and I go shopping at the Indian grocery store about ten blocks away from our condo, Amma muttering all the way about how inconvenient it is to lug our groceries back home on a crowded bus and how awful the transit system is over here. She's talking so loudly on the way back home that, at one point, a couple of other passengers on the bus turn around and watch us with raised eyebrows.

"Amma, please!" I finally snap, feeling embarrassed. "People are staring. Also, I don't see what the big deal is. Other people take the bus, too!"

It's only when I finish that I register the silence around us, the smirks on the faces of some of the passengers, the fury and shame in my mother's eyes before she turns away from me.

When we get back to the condo, Amma and I are no longer talking and I'm more than ready to lock myself in my room with my homework.

Can't wait for our call, I text Alisha, wishing I didn't have to wait another whole hour to Skype her. The message remains unread and, after a few minutes, I decide to get a head start on my calculus problem set.

An hour passes by. I log on, figuring Alisha will be here in a few minutes. When I finish the calculus, I look up: ten minutes gone. I send her a text—waiting for you—and decide to check Facebook. Another four minutes. By the time Alisha finally pops online, another whole hour has passed by, interspersed with a slew of missed calls and unread texts from my end.

"I'm so, so sorry, Suzy! I turned off my phone and my headphones were plugged into the computer!" Alisha lets out a *whoosh* of air. "With that badminton final against Abu Dhabi and that English debate on Monday, it's so *busy* right now, I've barely any time to breathe!"

I'm tempted to tell her that I'm busy, too. The time I spent waiting for her could easily have been spent working on the *King Lear* essay that Mr. Zuric assigned us this Friday, five minutes before class ended. But seeing Alisha's frazzled face now, her hair a mess the way it usually is after studying long hours, I feel my annoyance dissipate. "It's okay."

I tell her about my new school and classes, pleased when she laughs at my commentary about the cafeteria food. I also bring up the locker situation, finally admitting that it—*Malcolm*, a voice in my head corrects—bothers me more than I expected.

"Ignore him," Alisha says. "What's the point of having a locker if you don't use it? I'd kill to have a locker!"

"I'm not used to it." This is partially true. There are, after all, no lockers at Qala Academy. "Alisha, he . . . he stares at me. It makes me uncomfortable."

"What do you mean, he stares at you?" A frown mars Alisha's forehead. "Is he like, being perverted or something?"

"No," I say slowly. "It's not like that."

Malcolm does not leer at me or block my way when I need to use my locker. He always looks me in the face, as if mapping its contours, those too-pretty eyes of his clouding over with disappointment when he doesn't find what he's looking for.

"You know what, forget it. Forget I said anything."

"Hmmm."

"What's *that* supposed to mean?"

"What you're not used to is boys hitting on you."

"He's not hitting on me!" I clap my hands over my mouth and whip my head around to make sure Amma is nowhere near my room.

Alisha rolls her eyes. "Chill, no one's there. Let's go back to this Malcolm dude—"

"Let's not," I interrupt, regretting having brought up the topic in the first place. "He's not important and it doesn't matter in any case. I barely use that locker. I don't have gym or a class where I'd need it to store clothes or stuff like that."

"What about art? Don't you need to store supplies?"

I say nothing.

"You *are* taking art, aren't you?"

"Yes, yes, I am. But we don't need to. Get supplies, that is. The teacher provides everything here."

The teacher, Ms. Nguyen, who is only a few years older than us, squealed with delight when she saw my caricatures. "This is *so* good!" she said, holding up the one I made of Verghese Madam. "Almost professional." She even asked me to do something with them for my final project, worth 30 percent of the class grade.

"Thank God." Alisha looks relieved. "You have real talent, Suzy. And the great part is that you can do something about it. Not like the rest of us here who are stuck with the option of doctor, lawyer, engineer, or accountant."

"I doubt it. When I first signed up for art, Amma said, 'Oh, why art? Why not French? That'll be more useful!'" Alisha and I roll our eyes. "She only gave in when Appa backed me up, saying I needed to have some fun with my other courses."

The irony of my father classifying a school course as *fun* did not escape me, but in this case, I didn't mind the comparison.

"But your dad is still a little more flexible than your mom, right?" Alisha insists hopefully. "Maybe you should ask *him* about art school."

It isn't a bad idea. Appa has always been more receptive of my art than Amma. It's probably why he's my favorite parent—even though I would never tell Amma that. When I was little, he'd often put up the drawings I made for him on the fridge. In Class VII, when one of my sketches—a portrait of my youngest cousin from India—placed third in Qala Academy's art exhibition, he took a picture of it on his phone and sent it to all our relatives in India.

"Or better yet, rebel, dummy!" Alisha says, when I don't respond. "What's the point of being a teenager otherwise?"

"Yeah, well, sorry I don't meet your expectations," I joke.

But the comment stings. I wonder if this attitude of mine—this lack of rebellion—stands out to my new classmates as well, driving them away from me. *Who, Susan? Oh, she's no fun. She only studies all the time.* I'd heard the comments before, even in Jeddah.

". . . and I need to . . . Susan? Susan! Soo-sun!" Alisha shouts into the mic, Verghese Madam–style, jerking me back into the conversation.

"Sorry," I say. "I zoned out."

"It's okay. I need to go. Studying. Again." She groans.

I sigh. "Bye, Alisha."

"Bye, Suzy."

I watch Alisha blip offline—after fourteen minutes of conversation—and turn back to my binder, to the neat pages of physics and calculus homework I've already completed. I could get started on the *King Lear* essay, a thousand-word literary analysis. But with the deadline two weeks away, it suddenly no longer feels like a priority.

It would not be like this in Jeddah. In Jeddah, I would be reading ahead like Alisha and the others, trying to prepare myself for my classes the next day. It was almost mandatory over there, especially during your final year, with the Class XII board exams hanging over your head like a guillotine.

It's one of the few things about my old school that I do not miss. Here, classes are more relaxed. Even before a quiz, I often hear students discussing other things—crappy bosses at work, the latest *Game of Thrones* episode, younger and older siblings, boyfriends, girlfriends, unrequited crushes. No one is squeezing their eyes shut and muttering prayers; no one is feverishly going over their notes.

Heather Dupuis smiles and says hi now whenever she sees me in physics. I smile and greet her back. This is usually the extent of our conversation—Heather has other friends she normally talks to during class—but it's nice to be acknowledged when I'm still miles away from fitting in with the other kids at school.

Amma and I might not stand out for being brown-skinned in this new city, but assimilating into the culture is another story. My father does not get this. He talks about *becoming Canadian* like it's a destination: a utopia of privilege that comes with a first-world citizenship, a house instead of an apartment, two cars, and a dog in the backyard. "That's what so many people did before us," he told me when we first talked about moving. "That is what we will do as well."

We, as in all three of us, not just me and Amma.

In Jeddah, Indian expats joke about a whole street of buildings across from the Mississauga Civic Centre, where new immigrants buy apartments to deposit their wives and kids in, and then return to their tax-free, high-paying jobs in the Gulf. Begumpura, they call the place: the City of Wives. "Now the City is expanding thanks to your father," Amma told me sarcastically, and I knew she wasn't referring to Mississauga.

Thoughts of Amma remind me of our argument this morning. I sigh, knowing I shouldn't have blown up at her like that. I find her in the living room, her nose buried in a romance novel, completely ignoring me even when I clear my throat.

50

"Amma, I'm sorry."

Silence.

"I shouldn't have yelled at you like that."

Amma's mouth purses ever so slightly at one corner. She turns the page, saying nothing.

"Please, Amma."

I'm thinking of the numerous ways I've groveled before my mother in the past and which ones have worked, when Amma replies, "Sorry doesn't make a dead person alive."

Okay, she's talking. A good sign.

"Oh?" I walk casually to the sofa and sit down. "Has my amma been replaced by a ghost? Maybe I should check and see."

Amma's eyes shoot daggers at me. "Don't you dare!"

I lunge, letting out my best horror-movie laugh. It cracks through my mother's stern facade, makes her burst into laughter as well, even though she grabs hold of my fingers before they reach her ticklish left side. Her arm wraps around my neck and draws me close, cloaking me with the smells of my childhood: steamed rice and jasmine oil, spices and coffee.

"I'm sorry, too," she says now. "I shouldn't be so critical of everything."

"It's okay."

"By the way, your Yvonne Chechi is visiting her parents for the weekend," Amma says, referring to Bridgita Aunty's daughter, who is also my second cousin. "Bridgita told me she's arriving this afternoon and that she wants to speak to you and *catch up on all the gossip* before she goes."

I laugh, a small weight lifting off my shoulders. Yvonne isn't really my older sister, but I've always called her chechi. During large family gatherings in India, Yvonne and I always ended up together at the same end of a table or side by side on a sofa, mostly ignored by the rest of our cousins. "The two non-resident outcasts," Yvonne liked to joke.

Yvonne is the only one apart from Appa who is capable of deflecting my mother's attention from me when I'm being criticized, the only person in our family who saw—and fully approved of—my art.

"Can Yvonne Chechi come visit?" I ask, making a mental note to call her tonight.

"She goes back to Hamilton tomorrow night for university. Next time we'll tell her to stay longer, yes?"

Amma gives me a squeeze and, for a moment, I'm thrown back into the past. To a time when my feelings for her simply ranged between love and more love.

"Amma, what if I want to take art at university?" The question floats out, hovers multihued in the air like a bubble.

What if?

My mother squeezes tighter. "Come, kanna." Her arm slides off. "It's time for lunch."

I follow her to the kitchen, even though my heart has sunk to somewhere around my knees. "Amma, I really think—"

"Be serious, Suzy." She lifts a lid off the pot of sambhar and turns on the stove. "It's one thing to paint as a hobby, but as a career? You'll only be stuck with a liberal arts degree that will leave you unemployed or married too early." She undoes the lid of the Crock-Pot holding idlis, and ladles a few of the steaming rice cakes onto a plate. "Look at what happened to me."

"It's not the same thing!" Not this again.

"Isn't it? I thought I was following my dream as well, marrying your father before I even got my degree. He said I would be able

52

to combine both—my love for him and my love for science." Her laughter is as rich as coffee, and as bitter. "I thought it was the most romantic thing he ever said to me. It probably was."

This is the part of her love story that Amma never tells our relatives: the bit where her Happy Ever After turns into a Lifetime of Drudgery. In me, Amma sees a way to live the future she could have had if she'd stayed in college in India, busy with Bunsen burners, instead of spending the last sixteen years behind a kitchen stove in Saudi Arabia.

"I'll ask Appa," I say defiantly. "I'll see what he says."

"Fine." There's an oddly pitying look on my mother's face. "Come, now. Let's set the table for lunch."

Malcolm

I see the drawing by accident, thanks to a stray breeze flipping a page in Susan Thomas's binder, leaving the sketch unguarded while she stands at the front in English next to Zuric's desk, asking him a question she probably already knows the answer to.

It's one of those rare classes when everyone is supposed to be working on some sort of group project, which is pretty much license for anyone and everyone to talk as much as they want to without doing any real work. Beside me, Ahmed and Steve are cracking jokes about some kid who fell flat on his face during basketball practice yesterday, their copies of *King Lear* lying untouched in front of them.

I lean out farther, my nose nearly brushing the chair in front.

Zarin Wadia, the caption reads. *In Memoriam.* A pretty girl with a smile on her lips, a scarf loosely covering her cropped black curls. She's wearing one of those black cloak-like things some Muslim girls wear with their hijabs. Only I know she isn't Muslim—or not entirely anyway—because of her surname. Her undoubtedly Parsi surname.

At the knee, where the cloak flies open, I see the loose trousers of a salwar, white like the one Mom sometimes wore when I was younger, and black sneakers. I blink a couple of times, as I look closer: the girl is holding a cigarette in one hand. A shadow falls over the page and the binder shuts with a thump.

I look up into Susan's angry eyes. "Nice drawing," I say.

There's a long pause before she answers. "Thank you."

"She's pretty." I grin.

"She's dead," she says flatly.

"Whoa. I'm sorry," I manage to say, after a pause. I look at Susan a little more closely and add another bit of what I know of her to the list in my head: Susan Thomas, smart girl who keeps to herself, and draws dead Parsi girls.

"What school did you go to?" I ask. "It wasn't here, was it?"

"Qala Academy. And you're right. It's a school in Saudi Arabia."

Saudi Arabia. The name instantly conjures up images of deserts, camels, and veiled women—images that my maternal uncle, Mancher, told me once were as stereotypical as the Parsis Bollywood depicts in its movies.

"Where in Saudi Arabia?" I ask.

"You've been there?"

"No, my mama—uh, I mean my mom's brother worked there for four years. I was born here."

"Oh."

The interest in her eyes dims. It's the disappointment on her face that gets to me, that urges me to continue the conversation when I normally would have stopped.

"What about you?" I ask. "Did you live there?"

"Yeah. In Jeddah. Grew up there."

"What was it like?" Truth is, I'm kind of curious. "I mean, I've heard things about it." From Mancher Mama, who hated it and said we were lucky we never had to live in a place like it.

She looks at me for a long moment. "We didn't go to school on camels, if that's what you're wondering."

I feel my face heat up.

But then Susan laughs—a funny sort of laugh that's almost a wheeze. She covers her mouth, cheeks flushing.

"It's not your fault. It's . . . I always get that look from people when I tell them I lived there. Like I was living in some primitive magic-carpet land and not a cosmopolitan city with beaches and highways and malls and a population of nearly three million."

"Can you blame us after the things we see on TV?"

But Susan doesn't seem amused by my joke. If anything, she looks pissed off.

"Kidding." I wonder how I've managed to put both feet in my mouth in my very first conversation with this girl.

The silence between us grows thick, awkward.

She's settled back in her chair when I speak up again. "Hey, Susan. Feel like eating a shawarma? My brain might be clueless about most things, but my stomach never fails to sense greatness." I rub a hand over it. Partly to suppress the rumble that comes with thoughts of sliced beef and pickles on pita.

Susan's smile is less frosty this time, making me wonder if her lips are as soft as they look. "Is there a good place here?"

"Probably not as good as the ones back there. But this place that

I know of isn't too bad. If we skipped last period, we could take the bus there and get back before school lets out."

Her smile slips. Her hand hovers in the air almost as if debating someone inside her head. It lands on my desk, about four inches away from my fingers. "I can't skip school. My mom would kill me."

"How about after school, then?"

She goes red, mutters something about homework. Her hands, those strangely expressive hands of hers, fidget, as if searching for something to hold on to.

For the most part, I'm pretty good at reading people, a skill that Mahtab says I got from our mom. But Susan's expressions are hard for me to decipher. Such as the fine line between her brows, which could be a synonym for anything from hating my guts to having overprotective parents who don't want her going out with boys to really having homework.

Her eyes flicker to my lips and back up again. I'm pretty sure she does not mean it the way I think she does, but it throws me off for a second. It's moments like these that confuse me about this girl, that make me wonder if she secretly thinks of me the way I think of her. Late at night, when there is no one trying to read my face. Ahmed has said that Susan watches me sometimes, and for the most part I've always blown off his theory with a laugh.

But now . . .

I lean closer, until our faces are nearly as close as our hands. "It's not that far. I'll even bring you back in time for your homework."

"I really do have a quiz." There's a hint of regret in her voice. Her lashes are long and slightly uneven. But when she wrinkles her nose and smiles at me, I barely notice.

Ahmed mutters something about my face cracking in two from

57

the goofy grin on it. Susan must have heard him as well because her face grows pink. I, on the other hand, keep my attention fully focused on the girl in front of me.

"It's okay," I tell Susan, trying to sound cool even though I've just been rejected. "Another time, then."

I don't say when or prod her to set it up. It's probably the right thing to do because she relaxes at my statement, her eyes far warmer than I've seen them before.

"Okay, then," she says.

"Okay."

She turns to face the front again and I lean back into my seat with a sigh.

Nothing fazes me for the rest of the class.

Not when Zuric bumps up the midterm exam to a day before it was supposed to be, to a chorus of loud groans and protests.

Not when Steve and Ahmed blow spitballs at me, point at Susan, and make kissy faces.

Not even when Zuric unfairly puts all three of us in detention for Steve's tone-deaf rendition of some song by the Weeknd, interrupting his last-ditch attempts to give us homework.

"You like her," Steve says later, when we walk to my locker. "That Susan girl."

I shrug, saying nothing, instead focusing my attention on undoing the lock and pulling out the copy of *King Lear* that I didn't take to class, just to annoy Zuric. Today, though, it was useless as he gave us a group assignment. I reluctantly pull out the list of essay topics he gave us last Friday. Might as well *try* to do something useful in detention.

Especially with Mahtab on my case about volunteering for her latest fund-raiser—some sort of benefit concert for Syrian refugees. Another one of those flyers she designed falls out of my locker. I sigh, tempted to leave it lying there, but then pick it up again.

"I don't see why you keep saying no," my sister said irritably the night before. "Ronnie says you're so good at presentations and talking in front of crowds! We could really use your help!"

Used to be good at presentations, I wanted to retort. Back when I was still thirteen-year-old Malcolm and not a potential nominee for Most Detentions Served Last Year. Right now, I doubt I can string together a coherent speech, let alone convince some big-shot corporate exec to sponsor a high school concert. As for Ronnie—I want nothing to do with him. Perfect Ronnie Mehta: a fixture at school assemblies, Terry Fox Runs, and every charity event bannered by the ZCC; a shoo-in for valedictorian this year.

While I'm not surprised that he and my sister started dating, Ronnie is seventeen, three whole years older than Mahtab. Mahtab says I'm narrow-minded and that a three-year age gap won't make a difference in the long run. And maybe she's right. But that doesn't mean I have to like or trust the guy. Especially when he comes over to our house and sucks up to the old man, always talking in fast, indecipherable Gujarati, cracking jokes that go over my head.

"Come on, stop pretending," Steve tells me now. "I know what I saw and heard last class. 'Feel like eating a shawarma?'" he mimics, in a voice that isn't mine but high and squeaky.

"She lived in Saudi Arabia. I figured she might like it." I toss the flyer back inside and slam the locker shut.

"So you're like her personal Tour Guide with Benefits? Do you get a tip at the end?" He starts making kissing noises, which I ignore.

My hand automatically goes to the gold lock that holds Susan's locker closed. I've gotten used to playing with it, rotating the numbers, feeling the delicate ridges and cool metal against my skin. I don't expect the soft *click*, the sudden pop of the lock against my fingers and into my hand.

I look at the combination: 1-2-3. I frown, wondering why in the world she made it so ridiculously easy. Or maybe she doesn't care, considering how little she uses her locker. Arthur Eldridge hasn't had many cases of locker theft from what I know, but there have been a couple times when a wallet was taken or a necklace disappeared. And those kids had regular locks, not flimsy little gold things like this one.

"Look at that. Now he's breaking into lockers," another voice calls out from behind me. "What are you gonna do, Malc? Leave your heart in it?"

I snap Susan's lock back in place and scatter the numerals before facing my old friend Justin Singh, who's arm in arm with—surprise, surprise—my old girlfriend.

"Making your way around the group are you, Afrin?" Steve says sarcastically. "Weren't you sitting on Jerry's lap in English?"

"Stop being a hypocrite, Stevie," Afrin replies with a toss of her silky hair. "You'd never say that to a boy, would you?"

The answer is trademark take-no-guff-from-anyone Godafrin. The sort that would've made me push her up against her locker when we were dating and press my mouth to her clavicle.

Afrin watches me now, as if hoping for a similar reaction and then, after getting nothing, plays with Justin's collar.

To Afrin, there was nothing more thrilling than to pit one guy against another, to see which one would get pissed off on her behalf

60

and get into fights for her. For a long time, I used to be that guy. It was how we met the first time. At one of Justin's parties, when Afrin's ex-boyfriend began calling her every insulting name he could think of. Tipsy from my first few beers and a little belligerent, I stepped in, bent on rescuing her from a guy who looked like a reincarnation of the Hulk. I still have old scars on my arm from that fight, though it didn't make Afrin fall for me.

It took several more months and a couple more girlfriends in between before Afrin finally agreed to go out with me in eleventh grade. Back then, I thought she was the best thing that ever happened to me, the one girl I'd chosen to go out with for myself and not to spite my old man.

Ahmed said that what happened with Afrin was bound to happen at some point. "You gave her too much of yourself," he said. "And she gave you nothing in return."

I can feel his gaze boring into the side of my head now, can almost hear him warning me: *Don't take her bait.*

"We hooked up this summer," Justin tells me. His hold on Afrin tightens. "Sorry, man. But it looks like you're moving on already, aren't you? With that new girl."

I still say nothing, not knowing why they both are here. There's a hard glint in Afrin's brown eyes. I saw it a couple of times in the past, once while we were playing beer pong with Justin's nineteen-year-old university friends, once when a girl at a party showed up looking prettier than her.

Only now it makes no sense. Afrin moved on after we broke up. She doesn't love me. I don't think she even liked me as much as she liked the idea of me fighting some other guy over her. I pull the strap of my backpack higher over my shoulder.

"Gotta go," I say. "Detention with Han."

Fingers latch on to the elbow of my jacket, hold me in place before I can leave.

"Hey." Justin smells of Pall Malls and mint gum and Afrin's powdery perfume. "We miss you, man. You never show up. You always showed up before. Always."

There's a hint of sincerity in his voice and I feel guilt creeping up on me, even though I know my decision to cut ties with Justin was the right one and I no longer want to spend my Friday nights passed out on a couch or the floor of his basement, smelling like vomit, vodka, and weed.

"I've been busy."

"Busy doing what? Studying?" He sneers. "Looks to me like you're just hanging around with these two losers. You think you're too good for the rest of us now, eh?"

"Justin, go easy, man." Ahmed's deep voice is as soothing as balm on injured skin. "You know I'll be at your party next week. And so will Steve. Malc's got work and everything. He's busy now. That's it."

Justin raises an eyebrow and snorts. "Looks like Tweedledumb and Tweedledumber are still rescuing you, Malc. You're a sissy, aren't you? You always have been. No wonder Afrin left you."

I feel the words under my skin, boiling along with my blood. I am about to respond with my fist when Steve grabs hold of my arm. And just in time.

"What's this?" a voice calls out. "Why are you loitering in the hallway?"

Vice Principal Han stands a few feet away, the fluorescent light shining on his bald head, arms folded over his chest. "And you three." His beady eyes zero in on me, Ahmed, and Steve. "Have you forgotten you have detention?"

Behind me, I hear Steve heave a sigh of relief.

"See you losers." Justin turns his back to Han and gives me the one-finger salute. "C'mon, babe."

But instead of following, Afrin stays a moment longer. I feel her gaze on my back, all the way down the hall, where Han waits, and into an empty classroom.

"Where were you?" The voice that greets me when I step back into our house doesn't belong to Mahtab.

I ignore it and kick off my sneakers without bothering to untie them.

"I asked, *where were you?*"

My old man always tends to boom when he's angry, his voice echoing impressively in the small hallway. It would've scared me when I was younger. But I'm not eleven anymore.

"In detention," I say calmly, looking right into his face.

Mom always used to call our father handsome. Freddie Mercury handsome with high cheekbones, broad forehead, thick mustache, and strong chin. Age has done little to change that reality except add silver to his eyebrows, a layer of fat to his belly, and a receding hairline.

Physically, Tehmtun Vakil and I have nothing in common, except for our matching height and eyes. Dark brown with gray shooting from the pupils. *Centrally heterochromatic*, he taught me when I was nine. A tiny gold Asho Farohar pendant hangs around his thick neck on a delicate gold chain. It's the only thing he wears from his past with my mother, and probably only because it's twenty-four karat.

Red shoots up the pale skin of his neck and curls around his ears. A sure sign that he'll raise a fist or two if I get close enough, the way he did when I was fifteen. I inch forward. My knuckles strain against my skin. Let the old man try. This time Mahtab isn't here to stop me.

But maybe he sees something different in my eyes today, something that makes him take a step back and cross his muscular arms in front of him. Physically, I am no match for my father, who is built like a wrestler and fought professionally as one for the Indian Railways team in his twenties. But he does not have my anger, built up over years of waiting for him to come visit me and Mahtab, over the years of seeing my mother waste away from bone cancer and the complications that came with the surgeries, while he stayed in Detroit, wrapped up in work and the arms of other women.

Now that Mom's gone, he's back here with one of them: a woman he expects Mahtab and me to eventually accept as a replacement. Like anyone could be.

Mahtab says that I should give our stepmom a chance. That Freny isn't as bad as I think. I've never cared to find out. My father likes to pretend otherwise, but I know my mother didn't die of a broken body so much as she died of a broken heart. Tenth grade was the year I first met Justin Singh. It's also known as the Year Mom Died, Freny Cama Moved in, and the Universe Collapsed Around Me.

The old man now switches over from anger to calculation. "Are you still going to work?"

"Every day. But you should know. You keep checking in with my boss."

So much that Jay wanted to know if I was planning to die on him and leave him short one barista at the coffeehouse.

His mouth tightens. "I'm only doing what a father should do."

"The way you should have when it mattered? Well, guess what? Time's up. Only a year left before I turn eighteen and get out of here."

Something flickers across his face, an expression that another person might have mistaken for sadness. I twist my shoulders to the side and slip past, leaving him in the hallway as I head up to my room.

Susan

My father says no to art school, which shouldn't surprise or disappoint me. Theoretically.

"Susan, do you know why we decided to immigrate to Canada?"

My stomach begins to fold inward. I don't want to hear this. Not now, when all I can see of him is on a computer screen, from thousands of miles away in another country. But before I can say yes and cut him off, Appa continues: "We came here so that you can have the chances we never did."

By *we* Appa means himself—the impoverished son of a municipal clerk in Kochi. A man who had little to no chance of finishing school, let alone of becoming a doctor and marrying the daughter of a district magistrate.

"I was working from the age of ten—delivering tea and snacks to office buildings to make some money and help my family. There were so many days when we had no electricity. I still had to study for my exams." His face softens and then hardens a moment later. "Here, you will never have to pay some bureaucrat under the table to get admission into a university; you will never have to prove anything except your own merit. And you have so much of it! Art is a hobby, kanna. Not a career."

From the background, I can feel Amma watching.

"Suzy, are you listening to me?"

"Amma wants to talk to you." I hear my voice coming from a distance, as if it doesn't quite belong to me. I reach up to take off my headphones, belatedly realize I'm not wearing any, that I never wear any when we Skype my father, that my mother has heard every word he's spoken, and probably even co-written half the speech.

I ignore her indignant "Say bye to Appa, at least!" and head to my room. There's a strange feeling in my throat, like I've swallowed a fish bone. It's not until now that I realize how much I was counting on Appa. How I expected him to back me up in this one big thing the way he often did for me with the small things in Jeddah: secretly buying me the candy I wanted even when Amma said it would spoil my appetite, calming her down when she got especially angry with me, praising me when she went overboard with her criticism.

I open my sketchbook, pausing at a page I must have drawn sometime in Class IX, when my parents and I were on vacation in India, spending time in the backwaters of Alappuzha and the Periyar Tiger Reserve in Thekkady. I'd drawn a tiger. A wolf. An elephant. A clouded leopard. A Nilgiri tahr. A kingfisher perched on a stump next to a houseboat floating on a lake of water lilies. I didn't see every animal on the trip—the clouded leopard isn't native to the state of Kerala and the wolf was from a magazine I'd found at our hotel. I'd added them to fill the blank spaces on the page, and then created a border at the edges with peacock feathers and lotuses.

Appa had admired the drawings back then, calling them clever. *Your old appa would never be able to do something like this*, he'd said.

I recall the smile on his face, the spark in his eyes—reassess them now based on the conversation we just had. Did he truly think I was good or was the compliment simply a formality? The type parents reserved for their children's efforts, no matter how good or bad.

I look at the page again. Flaws that I'd dismissed as minor back then—the kingfisher's misshapen claw, the slight disproportion of the elephant's head and body—appear magnified. Even the border, which I'd spent hours on and thought so lovely at the time, looks cheesy. Clichéd. I toss the book aside.

I text Alisha: They said no. About art school. I asked.

Barely a minute goes by before Alisha responds: I'm sorry ☹

Then: At least you tried

The lack of argument from Alisha's end (the real Alisha, not the one in my mind) and the quickness of her responses makes me wonder if there really had been any chance. If she really did think my parents would say yes or if she'd only been saying those things to make me happy. After a long pause, I type back: Yeah.

Another text pops up: Sorry, Suze. It's a little busy here with debate practice at my house. Can we talk later?

Busy. Always busy.

Well don't let me disturb you.

Alisha writes: What's that supposed to mean???

This time I don't bother responding, letting her messages flash on-screen one after another, before shutting off the phone.

Tests. Exams. Debate practice. Tutoring sessions. Perfectly legitimate excuses in Alisha's book to avoid life's stickier discussions. What makes things worse is that I understand perfectly. If I was still in Jeddah and Alisha and I had switched positions, I would have reacted in the same way, probably with a similar kind of excuse. Alisha and I have been best friends since kindergarten, but we've never been the sort of friends who put each other before school stuff—*your first and foremost priority*, our parents and teachers always told us.

For the first time in my life, I begin to wonder why.

"I can't believe this." Amma's voice rises, floats through my open bedroom door. "Another month? How many times is this going to happen? Rensil, you were supposed to be here by now!"

I tune out Appa's excuse; it's another consolation for my mother to bear. Instead of reading the next chapter in physics the way I'd been planning to, I check my emails for the tenth time that day, and then Facebook. Right below a notification for someone's birthday, an ad for an Arabic restaurant nearby pops up, bringing to mind the conversation I had this week with Malcolm. Partly out of curiosity, partly boredom, I click on it, and this leads to several minutes of googling and looking up more restaurants.

Intermittently—and again, purely out of curiosity—I type *Malcolm Vakil* into the search bar on Facebook. Several Malcolm Vakils appear, mostly in India and Pakistan. I even find one in Australia and a few others with no location or photo. There's no sign of spiky black hair or that all-too-knowing grin.

"What are you doing?"

My mother's voice nearly makes me leap out of my skin. I shut the browser and turn around, automatically positioning my head and shoulders in front of the laptop screen.

Amma is pale today, the dark circles around her eyes more prominent than usual. "What is it? What are you hiding?"

"Nothing."

"Tell me, no!" Amma gives me the wide awkward smile of adults who have suddenly realized that their children have grown older and aren't exactly sure how to behave around them.

"I was researching." Not exactly a lie.

"Was it a boy?" She waggles her eyebrows. "Were you sexting?"

"Amma!" It creeps me out that my mother even knows of the term, let alone what it means. "It's nothing like that!"

"Well, if it was nothing, you should have no problems showing it to me." Her voice grows hard.

"God!" I reopen the browser and show her the results of my last Google search. "Here! This is what I was looking at."

"Best place to eat a shawarma in Mississauga?" I swear my mother sounds disappointed. "That's all?"

"Yes," I say, emphasizing the word in a way that will hopefully underline it thrice in her head.

After our conversation last week, Malcolm and I haven't talked again even though now he gives me a half smile whenever he passes my desk in English. It's getting easier for me to smile back in return.

My mother gives me a suspicious look, but then gets distracted by something more important: my hair, which she declares is an utter mess. I feel her fingers sift through the locks, parting them better than any comb. She digs through my dresser and finds my hairbrush, running it through a few knotted ends, smoothing them out, before starting to brush my shoulder-length hair from scalp to end, the bristles stiff and soothing, her hands tugging, plaiting, but never painful.

Once, when I was five, Amma made me sit on the floor and, after picking out a variety of colorful ribbons, wove them into my hair. Back then, I could tell her anything: about the funny way my science teacher scratched her nose, about the games we played during recess. Now I have a strong urge to do what I did then: only this time I want to close my eyes and speak about how I can't sleep either. About Appa and how much I miss him. About school and how strange everything feels here. About—

"Kanna"—Amma tugs at the braid and ties it off with a plain black elastic—"I called the driving school to ask about your progress. Joseph thinks that you still need more preparation if you intend to give your road test in December. Since there's still time, I think you should book three or four extra driving lessons with him for practice."

Panic tightens my chest. Driving. Again. "I don't think the lessons are working."

"What nonsense!" The braid falls over my shoulder, hitting my collarbone. "Who said they aren't?"

"*Joseph* did! He keeps yelling at me. Half the time I'm afraid of getting into an accident!"

I think back to my lesson last Sunday: Joseph's shouts and his constant braking, his insinuations that I was not only his worst student, but also entirely useless.

"If you keep driving like this, it's just a waste of your parents' money," he told me. "Better for you to go home, tell your mother to teach you how to cook and understand how to take care of a household."

The trouble with Joseph Kuruvilla is that he comes highly recommended—*the best*, they call him, not only in the driving school's online Google reviews, but also at the Jacobite church

Amma and I attended a couple of times when we first arrived here. As furious as I am about Joseph's misogyny, a part of me—the part that worked successfully with the toughest teachers at Qala Academy and scored high grades—still wants to prove him wrong.

I didn't realize that as I worked on doing so, Joseph's haphazard instructions would settle in my brain, would affect me every time I got behind the wheel of his car. I think uneasily about the Corolla Appa bought for us before returning to Jeddah. A car that now sits in the condo's underground garage, untouched.

"Amma, I want to go home," I tell her now. "To Jeddah."

She doesn't try hiding her wince. Her mouth firms into a straight line. "This is home now, Suzy."

"But Amma—"

"The transit system is terrible here. A twenty-minute wait between buses during the weekends. You know this. Do you think I would have bothered you otherwise to get a license?"

I do know this. Yet as tiresome as it is at times, I don't really mind taking transit the way my mother does. I find that traveling by bus is the best way to watch people, to observe the slant of a cheekbone, the curve of a chin, the width of a nose. Some days, when I return home, I fill my sketchbook with these observations, play around with facial features until I understand how to distort them enough to produce another drawing, or sometimes even add one to my class portfolio for Ms. Nguyen.

"And now your father is getting on my case about getting *a job*." Amma spits out the last two words. "As if it's the easiest thing in the world."

I hesitate, not wanting to ask her how her interview went today—for an admin position at a middle school a few blocks from our condo. But she tells me anyway.

"Even today, they asked me the same thing. 'What were you doing for the last sixteen years, Mrs. Thomas?'" Her voice mocks both the interviewer's voice and the Canadian accent. "I was raising a family, you fool. That's what I was doing."

I begin tuning her out. Amma's rages are the kind that can go on for several hours, her rants long and repetitive, often leaving me with a pounding headache at the end. Instead I stare at the picture on my desk, a framed photo of my parents, taken by a friend the day they arrived in Jeddah, a year before I was born. My father wore a gray safari suit, while my mother was cloaked in black, her white cotton scarf knotted neatly under her chin, a flap of pale yellow sari peeking from between the folds of her polyester abaya, near the hem. They are not smiling, but there is something in their expressions—an innocence, maybe—that brings out the magic in that picture.

It's my favorite picture of them, not so much Amma's. "I look like such a schoolgirl in that one," she told me once. "Well, I suppose I was one at the time. I didn't even think of how limited my options would be once I got to Jeddah. Even back then a BSc meant nothing unless you wanted a teaching position."

Here her bachelor's degree means even less, especially since it's from the University of Kerala.

"Maybe if you took those night classes on Elm Drive," I begin now, trying to interrupt her rant, "or went back to university, then—"

"Night classes?" she retorts. "*University?* If I go to university, then who will take care of you?"

"I can take care of myself." I feel myself bristling. "I'm seventeen years old, Amma! If you want to get a job in a lab over here, you'll *have* to upgrade your degree and get some Canadian qualifications.

Even Edmund Uncle and Bridgita Aunty did so. There's no point in complaining about it all the time!"

When Amma's mouth trembles, I know I've said the wrong thing even while being completely right.

"So. I complain all the time, do I?" she says.

"Amma, you know I didn't mean—"

Amma walks out of the room and leaves me hanging—a tactic she often uses while playing the victim, her antics often driving Appa into a frenzy. Unlike me, however, Appa never seems to see through Amma's melodrama and it makes me wonder if love truly does turn a person blind.

I stay strong for the evening, not talking to my mother or apologizing when she looks expectantly at me once we finish dinner and the dishes.

"Good night," I say, and head for my room. I will not give in, I tell myself firmly. I was *not* wrong in telling her to go back to school. It was only the truth.

It's not until the next morning that exhaustion begins to seep in, a guilt as old as time weighing on me with a phrase that has been drilled into my head since I was a girl and that is embedded in my conscience: *How could you speak to your mother that way?*

After physics ends, I rest my forehead against the cool metal surface of my locker. Amma makes me so mad at times. But I know she is scared as well. If I am out of my element, Amma most certainly is—a woman who left behind an active life in India in exchange for the monotony of household chores in Saudi Arabia for sixteen years, only to be thrust into an active life once more in a new country where her qualifications aren't valued.

In Jeddah, my father played the role of a buffer, the water to my mother's fire, a tree that bent to her wind instead of resisting its pressure. Now, though, after nearly three months of being left alone with Amma, I wonder about Appa's insistence on us staying here while he went back to Jeddah—if there is some validity to my mother's paranoia about him trying to abandon us.

To top it off, Alisha and I are still not speaking. My anger over her responses yesterday feels ridiculous now and I said as much in the text I sent her early this morning. **I'm sorry. I shouldn't have blown up at you like that yesterday.** I check my phone for the hundredth time. The message, read almost a minute after it was sent, still doesn't have a response.

My hand seeks out and holds on to the slender gold lock hanging from my locker—one Appa pressed into my hand the day before we left Jeddah. The back of my throat pricks. When I turn around, I am surprised to find a pair of eyes on me. Malcolm Vakil.

Heat instantly flushes my cheeks, much to my annoyance.

"Are you okay?" he asks, and for a moment I remember the boy I saw from my apartment window: the boy underneath Malcolm's usual swagger.

"Yes. I'm fine. Tired," I admit before realizing how true it is.

I think back to what lies ahead—another class, another bus ride, another day spent in silence with an angry mother waiting by the computer for a father who does not call.

Rebel, a voice that sounds suspiciously like Alisha's says in my head. *Have a little fun.*

"Do you want to skip the next period?" I ask.

"What?" Malcolm looks at me closely, a tiny furrow between his eyebrows.

The surprise on his face gives me confidence and I go on. "Skip next period. We used to call it 'bunking class' in Jeddah. Not that I ever did it." Even Alisha bunked for a whole day once in Class X, slipping off with Mishal Al-Abdulaziz and several other classmates to visit a private beach, where they had a fantastic time. I'd shrugged it off back then, but now I can't help but wonder if I missed out. If, by saying no, I simply lost an opportunity to experience something I might have otherwise enjoyed.

"Oh yeah, bunking. That's what the Brits call it. Or brown people colonized by Brits." His forehead is smooth again; cocky Malcolm is back.

"Look who's talking!" I scoff. "At least India doesn't still have the Queen of England on its currency. Besides, you're brown, too, you know."

He grins at me. "Yeah, but I was born here. It's not quite the same."

It's the truth. It does not matter that Malcolm and I share skin tones. Everything about him screams Canadian, from the way he speaks to the way he dresses to the self-assurance with which he walks. Malcolm *belongs* here as much as I don't and probably never will.

"Hey!" He snaps his fingers in front of my face. "Where'd you go?"

I force a smile. "Nowhere."

"You were somewhere, all right." He taps the side of his head. "My sister used to call it Fuzzyland when she was younger. It's when you're neither here nor there."

"Limbo," I say. Neither Saudi, nor Indian, nor Canadian.

"Limbo," he agrees.

I study his face—the faint traces of a mustache over his top lip, the scar on his chin, the oddly soft wisps of eyebrows on his wide, smooth forehead, his far-too-pretty eyes. There's something about Malcolm that makes me want to trust him, a foolish instinct I catch before it takes root. I cross my arms in front of me.

The furrow reappears between his brows for a second before clearing again. "So are we skipping or what?" His voice is light, almost flippant.

My fingers twitch for a few seconds before I open my locker and dump my binder inside. All I'm carrying now is my backpack, which feels oddly light, and my wallet with twenty dollars and a transit pass.

Malcolm leads the way, taking me to a side door I never saw before. He pushes it open. "After you."

When I brush past him, I catch a whiff of rain-soaked earth, with a trace of the minty gum he always chews between classes. I breathe it in, deep, before I realize what I'm doing and then step out into the afternoon light.

Malcolm

We take the bus to Square One Shopping Centre, which is about ten minutes away from school and has a decent food court, including a chain Arabic restaurant that sells shawarma.

"This other place I was telling you about is better," I say, grabbing hold of the yellow railing, swaying in place as the bus begins to move. Susan stands about a foot away, next to a lady with a stroller near the window. "It's a Lebanese joint on Dixie and Crestlawn. But it takes too long to get there by bus and I don't have a car."

"You don't drive?" She looks surprised.

I snort. "Of course I drive. I mean I have a license and everything. But I don't have a car of my own." Susan doesn't need to know that the old man has banned me from borrowing his car ever since the Incident two years ago, or that I would consider hara-kiri before asking Freny for hers.

"Oh," Susan says, and I swear I see her shoulders droop slightly.

I grin. "Don't tell me that *you* don't drive."

Susan's cheeks instantly flush with color. "I take the transit."

"Oh, okay. Cool."

"I don't know why everyone in this place needs to drive. If more people took the transit, there'd be less traffic and it would be good for the environment."

She looks out the window, jaw clenched, her eyes narrowed into a squint against the sunlight. I watch the shadows play over her face, which has grown so still it might have been carved out of stone. The lady with the stroller reaches out to pull on the string, requesting a stop. Once she steps off the bus, I move in to occupy the space she vacated, leaning against the window, blocking part of Susan's view. Her eyes meet mine and then flick downward, focusing on my chin—probably on the scar left by an old basketball injury.

"Ahmed was terrified when he first got behind the wheel, you know," I tell her.

She looks back into my eyes. "I don't believe you."

"Oh yeah. Never seen someone that yellow-knuckled. He was crapping his pants by the time the instructor told him to turn on the ignition."

A surprisingly deep chuckle emerges from her throat. "Liar."

Maybe I am. Maybe Ahmed never was afraid of driving. But a little white lie never hurt anyone. At least it made her smile. Behind Susan, a man gets up from his seat, forcing her to move closer to me. If it was Afrin or another girlfriend, I would put my arm around her shoulders. But Susan and I are not dating. I press a hand flat against the window, my arm stuck at an awkward angle from standing this close and trying not to touch her by accident and freak her out. It's surprising how, after days of antagonizing her, I am suddenly considering her feelings. Maybe it was that drawing of the dead girl. Maybe it's because she isn't perfect and has her own failures like the rest of us. Or maybe it's as simple as the part of me attracted to Susan Thomas temporarily overcoming the part that wants to keep her away.

The bus driver takes matters out of my hands, braking so hard at the next stop that Susan falls into me, her smooth cheek against my rough one, her hands grabbing my jacket, flattening there, exactly two layers above where my heart beats. I breathe in, picking out scents that are both familiar and not—jasmine and paint and spices from a kitchen.

Small, fragrant, warm. Three more things that I now register about a girl who I sometimes pretend is a figment of my imagination before someone coughs in the back and Susan and I split apart, embarrassed. It is how we stand for the rest of the ride, quiet, four inches apart, looking anywhere and everywhere except at each other, until a robotic voice announces our arrival at the mall.

Late-September afternoons carry a lingering warmth in the air, as if a final bit of summer has reached out and is still holding on with a fading green grip. Even Susan, who's wearing a thick gray peacoat, takes it off, her face suffusing with such pleasure you'd think she'd never bared her arms to the sun before. I think of the few pictures I've seen of women from Saudi Arabia—always veiled, always garbed in flowing black—and figure that she probably hasn't as much, or that it's still enough of a novelty that it feels good against her skin.

Inside the mall, fall launches a full-frontal assault: from the overpriced pumpkin spice drinks and java roasting at a nearby coffee shop to actual pumpkins and fake maple leaves embellishing nearly every store display. It's only the air-conditioning, still on full blast, that gives any indication of the weather outside.

A boy of about six races ahead of us, LED lights flashing in the heels of his sneakers, and grabs hold of his father's hand.

He may look like you, Daulat, but mark my words, he will be like me, my father used to tell my mother when I was five. *A-plus at school, A-plus at sports.* Back then he was still Dad, a mythical being I both loved and somewhat feared, and I did everything possible to prove him right. After Mom got diagnosed, everything began slipping—my parents' marriage, my grades. *How could you be so stupid?* my father demanded when I failed a second, then a third math test in ninth grade. *You'll never graduate high school this way, let alone get into a university.* But the doctors were going to amputate my mother's leg to get rid of the cancer that year, so I stopped listening to my father. A year later, when the cancer returned, I no longer cared about the old man or his rants.

There are times, though, when I'm still a victim of memory, of habit. It's surely the only reason why, two years later, something inside me automatically clenches when the boy with lighted sneakers grins at his dad at the mall, when the father raises a hand to ruffle his curly black hair.

I avert my gaze, scanning for distractions and find one in Susan, who's staring at the display of a newly opened arts and crafts store. The mannequin in the window wears a bright yellow smock and a painter's hat.

"Someone should tell them that painters wear white, not yellow," I say.

"Chartreuse," she replies, still staring at the mannequin.

"What?"

"The color. It's chartreuse, not yellow."

"They named a color after alcohol?"

Her head snaps in my direction, a frown—always a frown where I'm concerned—on her face. "They did *not*."

"Well, chartreuse is alcohol. French stuff." I've seen bottles of it in the past, behind lock and key in the liquor cabinet at Justin's house. "Also, it's *green*, not yellow."

Susan rolls her eyes, as if she doesn't quite believe me, but says nothing in response. Instead, she looks at the mannequin again with an expression that can be only described as longing.

"Want to go inside?" I ask.

She starts and waves a hand in the air. "No, no. Besides, I don't have money to waste on a hobby."

"Did your parents tell you that?" The words slip out before I can bite my tongue.

A pause, followed by a glare that could spear through steel. "What does *that* mean?"

"Well, when a teenage girl talks like she's forty-five, a parent is usually involved. Or some form of boring grown-up." Since my foot is already in my mouth, I might as well step all the way in.

Her scowl grows deeper at that and she quickens her pace, trying to leave me behind. Too bad my legs are longer. I match her, stride for stride, and continue talking. "So you're not a teenager, right? You're really a middle-aged woman who has infiltrated our school in disguise."

"Do I look like Drew Barrymore to you? Also, she wasn't middle-aged in *Never Been Kissed*; she was in her twenties!"

Maybe it's the unexpectedly witty comeback when I expected silence from her. Or maybe it's the way Susan says it—like she could strangle me for comparing her to a movie star. I snort.

Susan's mouth twitches and seconds later shifts into a smile—a full one that lights up her whole face. And then she's laughing and I'm laughing and we're both laughing like our lives depend on it, uncaring about the stares we attract from passersby.

Susan

I take the stairs two at a time to catch up with Malcolm, who walks a lot faster than I expect him to.

Do I look like Drew Barrymore to you? I don't even know where the response came from, how it sounded funny instead of rude, the way I intended it to be. It almost felt as if there was another girl waiting inside me for exactly this moment—confident and friendly and fun.

By the time we order shawarma at the shop in the food court—him beef, me chicken—and find a table to eat at, Malcolm is talking to me about his favorite movies. It's easier to watch him while we're eating, to cast casual glances his way when he's sitting right in front of me, licking a drop of grease off his thumb.

While he makes fun of the strange-looking metal-cut chandelier hanging from a high dome inside the mall, I take the opportunity to study him. How his eyes take on a slightly faraway look when he's telling a funny story; how he wrinkles his nose when he laughs. His hair is long on top and shorn skin-close on the sides. I wonder what it looks like when not spiked with gel. If it's all waves and curls or straight and floppy. Today a faint stubble covers his chin. My cheek tingles with the memory of it brushing against my skin. The only other time I've felt a boy's cheek against mine was during a Christmas in India, several years ago, when the son of a family friend gave me a light hug and wished me a Merry Christmas. An old crush whose name I don't remember in this moment.

"So?" he asks me. "What do you think? Better? Worse? The same?"

I nearly choke on the slice of dyed-pink turnip I bite into, my guilty conscience engaging in a split second of panic before realizing that he was asking me about the shawarma and not himself.

"It isn't bad," I say after a quick swallow. "We never use these over there." I hold up the turnip. "Only pickled cucumbers and fries. But the chicken is the same. They even have the same garlic sauce. Or toum, actually."

"Yeah, they're one of the few places that use it. Others use hummus or tahini."

I grimace. "Who pairs hummus with chicken?"

"That's a no-no, then?"

"I guess there isn't exactly a no-no," I admit. "I mean, there are restaurants that serve chicken shawarma meat on hummus. And these days people mix all sorts of foods anyway. But as a dip, hummus goes way better with beef. The toum tastes better with chicken."

"Sounds like the beginning of your PhD thesis." He dips a fry into my container of garlic sauce and slathers it over his beef.

"Ha! Very funny."

He gives me a wide, toothy grin. I control my own twitching lips by focusing on my sandwich, absorbing the flavors that take me back to Jeddah. If I concentrate hard enough, I can even pretend we are at the Red Sea Mall, under the cold draft of the central AC.

"Are you cold?" Malcolm's eyes are focused on my bare forearms.

"I'm always cold. It's the air-conditioning."

He stares at me for a moment and then shrugs off his flannel shirt. "Here."

"Malcolm, I'm fine. I have a coat."

"Yeah, whatever; you can return it. It's not like I'm topless." He points out the plain white T-shirt he had been wearing under the flannel.

A part of my brain rebels. Warnings, accumulated over years of mentally rejecting boys before even talking to them, flash through my head on a marquee, until logic finally intervenes: *It's a shirt, Susan.* A temporary source of warmth.

I slip it on, rolling up sleeves that are longer than I expect them to be, but not giant size like the men's shirts I've seen hanging in stores. The cloth still retains the residual warmth of his skin. I lean back into my chair, basking in it.

Malcolm gives me a little smile and wipes the side of his lip with a thumb. "We'll need to leave in another five minutes if you want to get back to school on time," he says, crumpling his shawarma wrapper into a ball.

Reality, held so well in check by good food and a boy's flannel shirt, forces me to sit up again with a groan. A part of me wants to continue this day, prolong it with a movie or a walk through the open square across the mall that fills up every week or so with crowds for concerts and food festivals, for open-air Zumba and salsa and Bollywood dance classes.

Somewhere at the back of the square, there is a wall dedicated to graffiti art—murals of the city and random people—that Amma and I accidentally came across once when we got lost trying to find our way back to the bus stop. I could have spent hours standing there, studying the paintings, imagining one of my own on another blank patch of wall. But when Malcolm stands up with his tray, I follow suit without saying anything. Thoughts of the graffiti wall bring back thoughts of my mother and the reason I skipped school in the first place. I squash down the guilt before it begins to set in.

"Solving math problems in your head again?"

First that crack about the PhD thesis, now this. I scowl. "Do you really think I'm such a nerd?"

Malcolm shrugs, which I take to mean yes.

"At least I care about school." Even as the words come out from my mouth, I realize how nerdy I sound.

"By skipping class?"

Okay. Fair point.

"I still don't skip as much as you do," I argue.

"Actually, I've been pretty good about skipping this year. I might even graduate on time." There's a slight edge to his voice—as if my words may have unexpectedly hit a nerve. But then I wonder if I'm imagining things because he simply shrugs and in the blink of an eye, the Malcolm I know reappears. "Besides, can't get *too* many calls back home about my absences or my old man will get mad."

I feel the blood drain from my face. "They call your parents if you don't come to class?"

"For a smart girl, you sure didn't think this through."

When I don't answer for a while, Malcolm's eyes soften.

"It's a recorded call," he explains. "Your parents will get it hours after you come home. You can always pretend that your teacher made a mistake. I bet you've never skipped a class before."

My breath emerges in a sigh. "That's true."

"So why'd you do it today?" Apart from curiosity, there is something else in his voice, a genuine concern that I've had few people direct my way, apart from my parents and Alisha. "Why'd you suddenly decide to skip school?"

I had a fight with my mother. My best friend isn't speaking to me. I don't think my father will ever permanently move here.

The words appear in my head and have just slid to the tip of my tongue when loud voices echo with laughter somewhere behind me. The change in Malcolm's expression—a shutdown of every bit of the concern he showed me seconds earlier—tells me more about who might be the cause of it even before I turn around to see her staring at me.

Godafrin Irani. A girl whose name I remember because of the way Mr. Zuric butchered it for an entire week while taking attendance. Tall and beautiful Godafrin—*Aaf-reen*, she enunciated carefully for Mr. Zuric—with red highlights in her wavy black hair, and a body that could probably have Nusrat Fateh Ali Khan burst into his famous song from beyond the grave. Afrin, who sometimes shoots me dirty looks; who always seems to be staring at Malcolm even though he rarely ever looks at her.

She climbs up the steps with a pair of friends, a large cone of ice cream held in a hand tipped with varnished red nails, the bronzed flush on her cheekbones so perfect that I'm tempted to ask her for tips on contouring. She walks toward where Malcolm and I now stand, our empty trays still in our hands, waving at us as if we were waiting here for her.

Afrin's eyes narrow when they fall on the shirt I'm wearing, but the brightness of her smile never diminishes. She turns her attention to Malcolm, licks the tip of her ice cream. This time, instead of ignoring her the way he does in class, he watches, jaw tightening.

"Malc. It's been so long. How are you?" Her free hand grazes his arm.

"I'm good, thanks." Malcolm's voice is so cool, I can almost pretend that he's entirely unaffected by Afrin's presence or her touch.

Amma told me once that the line between love and hate can be as thin as a paper's edge. *It's why your appa and I get so angry with each other at times. Because we love each other so much.* The real danger, she said, is when you no longer feel anything for the person.

Indifference is more dangerous to love than hate ever is and I can see that Malcolm, whatever he may pretend, is not entirely indifferent to Afrin.

Afrin's friends, who flank her, are watching the whole exchange as if it's a mildly entertaining gossip show. Their hands will flit to their purses the moment we leave, broadcasting the exchange to everyone they know on social media, elevating a random run-in at the mall to the second coming of Romeo and Juliet.

"We have to go," Malcolm says after a pause.

And then, without warning, as if he always planned on giving these trolls more ammunition, he puts an arm around my shoulders, locking me to his side. I am pretty sure the expression on my face mirrors Afrin's. An ounce of four-letter curses mixed with a tablespoon of *When did this happen?*

It's only shock and Malcolm's hard grip that keeps me from saying anything. On any other day, the whispers that Afrin's friends break into—"He's with *her*?"—would have embarrassed me enough to set everything straight.

It isn't until after we dump our trays and leave the food court, Afrin and her posse disappearing from sight, that Malcolm's grip on my shoulder loosens. I force myself out of my stupor and push off his arm.

"What was that about?" I snap. "Why were you pretending we were together?"

To his credit, Malcolm looks a little ashamed. "I'm sorry. I didn't mean to make you uncomfortable."

"Is she your girlfriend?"

"Ex-girlfriend." He frowns. "She . . . I really don't know what she's doing. We broke up before the summer and haven't spoken since. She's even dating someone else right now. It's . . . She likes to mess with my head."

"So now you've decided to mess with hers?"

I may not always be able to tell when a boy is flirting with me, but even I can sense that Afrin is jealous over seeing me with Malcolm, no matter who else she's dating right now.

Malcolm says nothing in response. Rationally, I know my anger over this is silly. Why should it bother me if he plays a little pretense to get away from an old girlfriend? It's not like he kissed me. Malcolm and I are not dating; we are barely even friends. I stare down at the shirt I'm wearing, the warm feeling of being surrounded by his heat now replaced by nausea.

I slip it off and hand it to him. "Thanks for letting me borrow this."

Something flickers in his eyes and for a second I could almost swear he is disappointed. But then he takes the shirt back without a word.

———————————

The bus ride back to school goes by in frosty silence. We get to the school yard as the last bell goes off, Malcolm's pace slow and relaxed, mine frenetic with what must be first-skip jitters.

"Hey. Hey! Slow down," he says.

I pause a few feet from a ramp littered with tissues and ciga-rette butts and watch as Malcolm pulls a box of Marlboros out of his pocket.

"What are you doing?"

It's a useless question (clearly, he's planning to smoke) and I get an equally useless response: "Fulfilling my role in cancer research."

"By being the subject?"

He lights up, a small blue-orange flame briefly flickering at the end of the cigarette. A thin veil of smoke pours from his nostrils and mouth. "School's done. It's time to relax. Do you mind?"

He leans against the redbrick wall, looking away from me. It's the first time we've spoken at length after running into Afrin at the mall. From a window overhead, a teacher calls out last-minute instructions, fragments of her voice floating into the yard. Inside the room, binders snap, voices hum, chairs screech across tiles. On the other side of the building, where the parking lot is, where I need to be, cars and buses will have already lined up at the pickup point.

Here I am, once again in a standoff with Malcolm, who leans sideways against the wall next to the ramp as if he has all the time in the world, his shoulders jutting forward, his eyes cool, expect-ing my judgment.

"No," I say. "I don't mind."

"You don't need to lie. My sister doesn't like it either. Neither would . . ." His voice trails off and his mouth tightens ever so slightly.

I remember the passing reference Heather made to his mom in physics class and wonder now if he stopped short of mentioning her. Not that I can ever ask him about it.

"I think we'll only have a problem if you blow the smoke in my face, Malcolm."

I expect him to laugh at my little joke but he only frowns. I shift my bag from one shoulder to the other, even though the straps aren't cutting into my skin and my textbooks are still in my locker. *Bunking?* I can almost hear Amma screaming in my head. *You bunked school?*

My only consolation is that the two classes I did skip—English and art—are what my cousin Yvonne and her university friends call "bird courses," the sort you can breeze through without much difficulty. A door to my left hinges open, muted chatter from the window rising into the air in full volume.

"Malc!" A slender figure—why does it not surprise me it's a girl?—detaches from the group of students pouring out and approaches, her long brown hair pushed back by the wind, a grin on her face that mirrors his.

The resemblance between the two is beginning to sink in, along with a strange sort of familiarity—have I seen this girl somewhere before?—when she turns to me with a grin. "Hi! I'm Mahtab, Malcolm's sister. What's your name?"

I am simultaneously relieved and embarrassed at the petty thought I had about her.

I force myself to smile back. "Hi. I'm Susan."

"Nice to meet you!" Mahtab's grin widens. "Please don't tell me that my big brother has been bossing you around."

Malcolm makes a sound that could almost be mistaken for a snort.

"I don't get bossed around that easily," I say with a shrug.

"So maybe you can boss *him* around, then. God knows he needs it." Mahtab reaches out and plucks the cigarette from his fingers. Ignoring his shouts, she puts out the glowing end with the heel of her boot.

"I barely even smoked that," Malcolm mutters, watching her dispose of it in the trash.

"It's a disgusting habit and I don't want you chasing your new friend away with it."

He glances at me sideways. "Who said she's my friend?"

I watch the two banter, fascinated by Malcolm's younger sister. From the way she's dressed—jeans rolled up over low-heeled ankle boots, crop top, black leather jacket—to how tall she is (she must have at least four inches on me) to the confident way she holds herself, I would not be surprised if someone looked at the two of us and mistook her for the senior and me for the ninth grader.

"Is he always such a jerk?" Mahtab tilts her head in her brother's direction.

I think of how he is now with Mahtab and compare it to the way he tortures Mr. Zuric. "Only in English class."

Mahtab's giggles infect me in spite of my vow to hold on to my deadpan expression, and more so because of the partly exasperated, partly amused expression on Malcolm's face.

"He has been nice to me today," I say, when we recover. "Surprisingly kind."

The words slip out without intent, leaving me exposed to the heat of two stares. I study the pavement, the tiny yellow leaves gathering in the creases. Mahtab clears her throat after a pause, but Malcolm does not make a sound.

"I need to get going soon," Mahtab says. When I look up, she smiles at me. "I'm part of a team organizing a benefit concert to help the people harmed by the war in Syria. The first meeting's today."

"That's where I've seen you before!" I blurt out. "I mean, you came to my physics class two weeks ago. With a boy."

Mahtab beams. "Yep, that was me. And that was my boyfriend, Ronnie. We were thinking of heading to Joe's across the street to get pizza before the meeting. Do you want to come along? Malcolm won't." She scowls at him.

Friday, September 25. Still circled in red on the flyer tucked in the back of my school binder along with the words *Art Director*.

"I . . . I don't think I can."

"Are you sure? I mean, we haven't picked a full committee yet. There are still lots of positions available."

What's the point? For a second I freeze, thinking I've said it out loud. But Mahtab is still staring at me expectantly so I shake the cobwebs from my head.

"I doubt I could contribute much." The words taste both bitter and true. "I also have a lot to study this weekend. Tests and stuff coming up." Not to mention that Amma is probably waiting at home for me right now, ready with questions about my sudden absence from my last two classes.

"That's too bad." A small frown mars Mahtab's forehead. "Well, I better get going, then. Hope I see you around, Susan. Bye Malc!"

The sound of Mahtab's boots fades away, but I can still feel Malcolm standing next to me, his stare like a touch on my cheek.

"Why didn't you go with her?" he asks. "You wanted to, didn't you? Like you wanted to go into that art store at the mall."

When a long time passes by and I say nothing in response, he sighs. "Also, did you tell my sister that I'm not a complete ogre? I'm so touched."

"You were never an ogre." Which is true.

He steps closer, the back of his hand brushing mine. If I was bolder, I would reach out, tangle my fingers with his. Instead, I will the ground to swallow me up.

"Thanks."

This is when I screw up the courage to finally look; when I see an expression on his face I have seen only on other boys, directed at other girls, maybe only ever in the movies. Then he blinks and the moment is gone and he is Malcolm and I am Susan and he tells me to get going if I don't want to get a "brown parent lecture" at home.

———

A lecture, surprisingly, is what I *don't* get—mostly because Amma is so busy chatting with Bridgita Aunty over the phone that she doesn't even put it down when I step inside.

"Yes, poor Vineeta," Amma says. "That nose job certainly did not work well in her favor."

I raise my eyebrows. Are they talking about my father's eldest sister in Kottayam? *A nose job?* I mouth at Amma. *What?*

Don't ask, Amma mouths back and, in spite of the crappy day I've had, minus my time at the mall with Malcolm, I feel a smile breaking through. Amma smiles back and then crosses eyes at something else Bridgita Aunty says—probably again about her least favorite sister-in-law. This time a laugh bubbles out, forcing me to clap my hands over my mouth.

There are moments when Amma and I are less like parent and child and more like sisters—a thing that Alisha says comes with being an only child, one of the few parts of my life that I sense she secretly envies. Amma squeezes my shoulder now and I know, with one look into her sparkling eyes, that she has forgiven me for our fight last evening.

"I'm sorry," I whisper anyway. "For yesterday."

She breaks the conversation to press a kiss to my forehead. "What? Oh yes, Susan just got home. Bridgita Aunty says hi," she tells me. "So tell me, Bridgita, when are you and Edmund getting Yvonne married?"

I duck under her arm and make a beeline for my room. Poor Yvonne. It's like you can't turn twenty without getting a slew of marriage questions. Forget about building a career or buying a house, the modern desi girl needs to have everything to be considered successful. My phone buzzes with a text.

Alisha: It's okay. I read through my own texts again and I can see why you reacted the way you did. I'm sorry, too.

I check the time; it's a little after 10:00 p.m. in Jeddah. I type and erase my reply several times with shaking fingers before finally hitting Send: Skype?

I expect Alisha to say no, but a second later, she replies: I'll log in from my phone.

"Hi," I say, once she picks up.

"Hi."

A pause.

"How was school today?"

"It's Friday. Weekend here, remember?"

"Oh. Yeah." I completely forgot that weekends in Saudi Arabia fall on Fridays and Saturdays, not Saturdays and Sundays, the way they do here.

Longer pause.

"I bunked school today," I finally say.

She snorts. "Nice. What did you do, then? Paint graffiti on the school walls?"

"Nothing that extreme. I ate a shawarma at the mall. With Malcolm Vakil."

It sounds unbelievable, even to me. But Alisha must have sensed the truth in my words because her eyes widen and I start giggling.

"Oh my God. You're serious!"

"Taking the Lord's name in vain." I click my tongue disapprovingly. "What would Pastor Verghese say?"

Alisha rolls her eyes at our nickname for George Verghese, Verghese Madam's ultra-religious husband, who isn't a real pastor by any means, but almost always acts as if he was one. "Pastor Verghese will excuse me in this instance. Susan Thomas *did a bunk?* And is this the same Malcolm we're talking about? The hottie from your English class?"

"He's *not* a hottie!" I clap my hands over my mouth, heart hammering, hoping I didn't yell that out loud.

"Relax, your mom didn't hear. And judging by that reaction you gave me, he definitely is. Or at least *you* think he is." Alisha laughs. "I can't believe this. We don't talk for like, a day, and you actually skip school with a boy you have a crush on!"

"I do *not* have a crush!" I say as emphatically as I can without raising my voice. "It just happened. I mean, he's been a little nicer to me ever since he accidentally saw my sketch of Zarin Wadia and—"

"Wait—he saw your *sketchbook*? You drew Zarin Wadia and didn't show me?" Alisha sounds disappointed about this.

"It *wasn't* my sketchbook and I wasn't planning on showing anyone." I'm not entirely sure why I drew my old classmate's picture. Zarin and I were not friends. In our time together at Qala Academy, we barely said a few words to each other. But she was Appa's patient. The day Zarin died, he went unusually silent, spoke to no one for a whole evening—something I never saw him do before.

"It was an accident," I tell Alisha now. "He saw the sketch, we started talking and . . ." *I think he asked me out.* I bite back the words. "Then yesterday was . . . crappy. You know about the whole art school thing. Also, Amma and I had a fight. So, this morning, after physics, I was at my locker and he was there, too, and . . . something came over me."

"Oho!" Alisha bobbles her head like a cheesy dancer in a '90s Hindi movie, a knowing smile on her face. "I see what came over you!"

"Shut up." I can't help but grin. "So anyway, I asked if he wanted to skip class. And we did."

A long pause. "You so like him."

I groan, partly wishing I hadn't told her a thing. But there's this other part of me that's secretly pleased at having surprised Alisha—at having done something she'd never have thought me capable of doing.

"Tell me you have his number, at least."

"What? No! We're not—we're barely even friends, Alisha!"

"That's what she said . . . before racing off into the sunset with him!"

That's not how that joke works, I'm about to retort when there's a knock on my door. Amma pokes her head in, eyebrows raised.

"What are you doing still dressed in your school clothes? Don't you want dinner?"

"I'll be right there, Amma." I turn to Alisha. "I gotta run."

"I want details later!" Alisha shouts seconds before I sign out.

It's only afterward, when I'm eating, that I realize I never asked Alisha about what's going on in her life. *I'll do it tomorrow*, I promise myself. Or whenever we have time to chat next. I think back to the conversation we had today and grin, wondering if I've ever seen Alisha this excited before. You'd think I won the lottery or something.

"What are you so happy about?" my mother asks, a curious look on her face.

"N-nothing," I manage to stutter before stuffing a spoonful of rice into my mouth.

Like Malcolm told me, we do get a recorded call at home about my absence at school. Amma also reacts exactly the way he predicted.

"What nonsense," she mutters. "Where would you go if not to class? Don't worry, kanna, it's probably one of those computer glitches."

She does not hear the sigh that rushes out of me once she puts down the phone. *Okay, Susan*, I tell myself. No more of this skipping business. Today was a fluke. An anomaly. In fact, if his reactions after our mall trip today were any kind of indication—like he couldn't wait to get away from me—I'm pretty sure Malcolm and I will go back to not speaking during classes. Ignoring the odd tightness in my chest, I pull out the binder from my bag and get started on homework.

Later that evening, I'm typing up the conclusion to my lab report for physics when a *ping* on my laptop makes me look sideways.

And do a double take. I quickly save the draft and then, after a beat, open my email.

From: Malcolm Vakil <mvakil@arthureldridge.ca>
To: sthomas12@arhureldridge.ca
Subject: chartreuse

you were right. there is a version called chartreuse
yellow. but i'm right as well.

He has pasted a link below that leads right to a Wikipedia page
about Chartreuse—the liquor, that is, not the color. Which, as he
said, is a sort of lime green. But first . . .

My hands fly across the keyboard.

From: Susan Thomas <sthomas12@arhureldridge.ca>
To: Malcolm Vakil <mvakil@arthureldridge.ca>
Subject: Re: chartreuse

How did you get my email?

A reply pops up almost immediately: school directory.

Oh right. Arthur Eldridge assigns each student a log-in ID to
access the school computers on the first day of classes. Though I
didn't realize the school directory was public.

Before I can question him about this, he writes again: and it's
not like I had your number.

I stare at the screen for a whole minute. Did he say that he
wanted my number?

I'm figuring out how to reply, when he sends another email:
aaand. you didn't answer my previous question. was i right
or not?

Fine, yes, you were, I type back hastily. To get him off my
back.

He doesn't give up. i know i'm not as smart as you are, but i'm not a TOTAL dummy. 😜

I never said you were! I'm sorry if it came off like that!

Does the tongue emoji mean he's kidding? Or is it secretly a taunt that I'm too full of myself? Alisha calls me a know-it-all on a regular basis, but she usually means it as a joke.

My heart skips a beat when another email flashes red in the in-box. it's okay, susan. i know. He follows up with a smile emoji, which sends warmth prickling across my skin.

I tug my hair back into a ponytail, twisting it so hard that I'm sure I'll pull out a few locks. How did I go from ignoring the class troublemaker to bunking classes with him and exchanging flirty emails in the space of a couple of days?

"This is ridiculous."

I take a deep breath. Why am I overreacting? Malcolm hasn't done anything to antagonize me in these emails; he's been pretty nice. Even the word *troublemaker* no longer feels right, not the way it did those first two weeks at school. Also, simply hinting he wanted my number doesn't necessarily mean he's *into* me. He dates girls like Afrin Irani—girls who walk the school halls like they're runways, who are capable of getting good grades without burying themselves in schoolwork for hours at a time.

I think about the calculus homework I've already completed, the physics lab report that's nearly done, the English essay that I turned in yesterday, a day before schedule. Okay. Maybe I don't have to bury myself in books either. Physics aside, schoolwork at Arthur Eldridge has been fairly manageable, leaving me enough time to study *and* do other things—if I so choose.

I could join the science club, I think dully. Or try out for the qualifying exam for the Canadian Math Olympiad that our home-room teacher talked about today. I could volunteer at the library and finish the mandatory forty hours of community service I need to perform to graduate high school in Ontario. I reach back into my binder and pull out the piece of paper tucked into the back.

Art Director. The words still circled in red.

Fund-raising counts toward volunteer hours, too, right? My parents can say no to art in college, but they'll never say no to anything that could jeopardize my graduation.

Maybe there's still time, I think hopefully. Maybe Mahtab didn't get anyone to fill the spot. My fingers hover over the keyboard. I *could* send an email to the account listed on the flyer—though I don't know how often they're checking it. Better yet, I could ask Malcolm for Mahtab's number. But he'll want to know why. I glance at the flyer again. It's not like it's *that* important, I reason. Besides, today was only the first meeting. I can easily wait until Monday and find Mahtab myself to ask if the position is still open.

Coward.

Outside my window, the sky glows yellow and pink, the temperature sinking along with the sun, after the afternoon's unexpected heat wave. Outside the mall entrance, it took me a moment to remember that I was wearing a fall coat and not an abaya, that I could actually take it off without being stared at or, worse, reprimanded by the religious police.

There are days when I still grow disoriented—like today, when I forgot about Friday being a weekend in Jeddah. Fridays were when Appa usually had a day off from the clinic; when he would, without fail, drive us to the Corniche or to a friend's house or to the mall, where we would scarf down a meal of shawarma sandwiches exactly the way Malcolm and I did today.

I chalk up what I do next to the overall stress of the week. To the coffee I drank—Amma's strongest Kerala kaapi—while doing today's homework. To that pesky voice in my head that keeps telling me to *live a little*.

I type a new email. You said you wanted my number, right? Here it is. I enter ten digits before I have the time to think—or breathe—and hit Send.

One minute passes, then five.

Just when I'm cursing myself—great, Susan, now he thinks you're a despo with a crush—my phone buzzes with a text from an unknown number.

hey. it's malcolm.

It's embarrassing how quickly I save the number. Even more embarrassing how I wait a full thirty seconds before texting back: Hi.

what's up? finished your homework? applied for a phd at harvard? 😊

I send him an eye-rolling emoji in response.

hey, susan, he writes after a minute.

Yeah?

today was nice. at the mall.

It was? I'm so surprised that I nearly text him my thoughts. But I see that he's typing a new message.

i mean, before afrin and company showed up. Cross-eyed emoji, followed by a devil emoji. i had fun talking to you.

It's okay. I had a nice time, too. It's only after I hit Send that I realize it's true. I did enjoy talking to him. There were

103

several moments when I forgot to be self-conscious the way I normally am around boys. Around him.

soooo. see you at school monday?

The question mark at the end almost feels like hesitation—as if he thinks I might have not enjoyed his company as much.

Yes, I type back quickly. See you Monday.

This time, I'm the one who sends him a smiley. And I don't even feel embarrassed by it.

Malcolm

I don't know why I looked up the color. Or her email—using one of Ahmed's old hacks to sneak into the school's database. I sure didn't expect her to give me her number or myself to spend the next few minutes trying to compose a text that had the right balance of interest and nonchalance.

hey, it's malcolm.

Okay, so Mahtab got the creative genes in our family. But in the end it didn't matter. Somehow, with Susan, my usual mask slips off and I go from being cool, calm, and collected to embarrassingly sincere. It was probably why I was grinning for a good hour after she sent me that silly smile emoji.

I don't text her on Saturday. Or on Sunday. Even though there's some English homework I can probably ask her about, stuff she probably finished a year ago. On Monday, I decide enough time has passed to talk to her again without looking like a stalker—even though stalking is what I end up technically doing, when I spot her passing by my accounting classroom after second period, following the swing of her ponytail down the business studies hallway and out the side doors.

"Hey. Mind if I join you?"

Her head snaps up and she blinks, as if surprised. Like I'm a stranger and Friday never happened.

"It's cool if you're waiting for someone else—"

"No, no, it's okay!" She's suddenly scrambling to make room for me on the steps. I take a little pity on her and sit down, careful to leave a few inches between us. "You can . . . oh, never mind, you're already sitting."

Her smile's nervous, a lot more like the girl I remember from the first couple of weeks of the semester—the one who could barely look at me, let alone talk the way she did last Friday. I unzip my bag, and pull out the sandwich I packed this morning instead of going for my usual slice with Ahmed and Steve. I glance at Susan, who's fussing with her own lunch, and wonder if I made a mistake. If our connection last week was a fluke.

I'm beginning to regret this whole idea when Susan's phone rings.

"One minute," she says, before picking up. "Hello? Appa?" Her face undergoes a transformation, nerves melting into happiness. She chats for a bit with the person on the other end in a mix of English and an Indian language I don't understand. As the conversation goes on, though, her smile slowly fades. The words *blame* and *Canada* emerge and then she's silent for a long moment.

"Fine," she says, her tone clipped. "We'll talk later." She hangs up and rubs the bridge of her nose. I'm pretty sure she's forgotten I'm here.

"Is this a bad time?" I ask after a pause. "Maybe I should go."

"What?" Her eyes widen. "No! I mean there's no need for you to go." She shakes her head. "It was my father."

A minute of silence follows before I venture another ask. "You guys have a fight?"

"Not really. Well, sort of." She stares off into the distance. "Appa was supposed to leave his job in Jeddah and come join us this month. Now he's saying that he needs *another* month, that his replacement at the clinic hasn't come in from India. When I asked him if he really *had* to wait for his replacement, he said he had to go. Probably for a smoke break." She mutters the last sentence under her breath.

"Your dad smokes?" I don't know why this surprises me. ER visits were the norm when Mom was still alive and I often saw a doctor or a nurse smoking in the alley outside the hospital, breathing out the shift's stress in puffs of smoke. But it does explain Susan's reaction last Friday, the distaste on her face when she saw me smoking.

"Yeah. I mean, no one else knows. Not my mom, not my best friend. It was an accident that I even found out."

There's another long pause—the sort that I know better than to fill in with pointless conversation.

"When I was little, my dad took me to his clinic in Jeddah. He wanted me to see what it was like, being a doctor. I couldn't stand the sight of the blood." She shudders and I laugh a little. "So, anyway, I was in his office getting bored, when I glanced out the window, and there he was. Smoking a cigarette next to the garbage bin behind the clinic. My appa who, until then, had lectured me about the bad effects of smoking. He begged me not to tell anyone. Even bought me a DVD of my favorite cartoon."

She huddles deeper into her coat, though I'm not sure how much of it is because of the weather itself.

"Thanks for telling me," I say.

I know it's nothing special. Strangers are often our best outlets for secrets—especially those who never have and probably never will meet our families. But she could've easily told me to mind my own business. And for some reason she didn't.

She shrugs. "I guess I'd better get some reading done." She pulls out her copy of *King Lear*.

"Don't know how you even understand that." I begin unwrapping my sandwich. "I mean, I have a hard time understanding modern-day stuff, let alone that seventeenth-century drivel."

She straightens and, for the first time that day, looks me directly in the eye. "It's not that hard once you get used to it. What are you having trouble with?"

I would laugh if not for the cheese and meatballs stuffing my mouth—or the absolutely serious expression on Susan's face.

"It's okay." I try to chew and talk at the same time, which ends up garbling my words to something completely indecipherable. Susan's mouth twitches, as if she's trying not to laugh. I force myself to swallow. "Really, Susan. I don't—" *have any plans for this to turn into a study session*, I'm about to say, but Susan cuts me off.

"No, really." She opens the book to the first page. "I mean it. What don't you understand? Maybe I can help?"

I should get up and walk away, saying I have things to do (semi-truth: other homework I've been procrastinating on), people to meet (false: no one). I should simply say *Everything!* and pull the book out of her hands, the way I would with another girl. But one look at Susan's face, those too-long lashes blinking at me expectantly, and I realize I don't want to walk away. Don't want to break this moment, whatever it is.

I move closer, my right knee pressing against her left one, on the pretext of looking at the book with her. She stiffens and I wonder if I've gone too far. But Susan doesn't shift to the side, does not put her bag between us, the way I expect her to.

I release a breath I didn't know I was holding. "It's that stuff Zuric talked about on Friday. You know, how we needed to figure out what the passages meant and transcribe them in our own words? Everything's so convoluted that I have no clue where to begin."

"R-right." She clears her throat. "That's act 2, scene 4." She locates the passages—which she probably has memorized—and places a pair of fingers under the first one.

I stare at her hand, the long, slender fingers, the clean, stubby nails and, for a second, am tempted to cover it with my own. But that'll only scare her off, so I do the next best thing, pointing out the passage that has been giving me the most trouble, my own fingers accidentally—oh, who am I kidding?—purposefully brushing hers.

"Th-that's a t-tricky one. But look!" Her stammer suddenly vanishes. "You can figure out the meaning this way."

Surprisingly, as I listen to her, I do.

"Okay," I say. "So when Lear's talking about this *hysterica passio* stuff, he's really growing hysterical? Like he can't believe his daughters would betray him? And this part, where the Fool's talking to Kent, he's telling him that there's no benefit in serving Lear now that he's old and growing powerless?"

The sunlight, at this angle, reflects every shade of brown in Susan's eyes. They crinkle at the corners now. "Exactly! That's exactly what it means."

We go over a few more passages. Even though not everything makes sense, in the end, I end up deciphering a whole passage, with only a single correction from Susan.

"You're good at this," I tell her. "Too bad Zuric doesn't explain things as well as you do."

"He does. You don't pay attention." But her face flushes and she gives me a slight smile.

"Maybe. Then again, Zuric's not as easy on the eyes."

A full blush colors her face, which makes me grin. Susan is way too easy to embarrass. She looks away and whispers, "Umm. I think Mr. Zuric's kinda hot."

Dead silence. I'm trying to wrap my head around her words and react with something other than *What the heck?* when Susan's shoulders begin to shake, laughter pouring out of her like summer rain.

"You should see your face!" She gasps, wiping a corner of one eye. "You actually thought I was serious!"

I suddenly feel like I'm back in middle school, on my first ever date with a girl, where I spilled pop all over my clothes. I force a grin. "Good one. You got me there."

"Sorry." She grins back, looking anything but. "I couldn't resist."

"What are you planning to do later today?" I ask, changing the subject. "And don't say homework."

"I don't know. Maybe I'll watch something on Netflix and chill out."

I freeze, wondering if she's making another joke at my expense.

But this time, her face is innocent, as if entirely unaware of what she said. I bite back a grin. "Oh yeah? Who with?"

"By myself, of course."

"Ah." It's a struggle to keep my facial muscles under control. "Of course, self-love can be a good thing as well. From time to time."

"Self-lo—what on earth are you talking about?"

I pull up Urban Dictionary's definition of *Netflix and chill* on my phone and quietly hand it to her. Seconds later, Susan's face is buried in her hands, and I'm the one howling with laughter.

Saturdays at Michelle's Coffee House are always busy—something my boss, Jay Campbell, warned me about during our first interview.

"We need *dedication*," Jay told me with a giant smile on this face and a hard look in his blue eyes. "If you're not dedicated to your job, we lose money. Understood?"

"Understood," I said. "It's what always impressed me about this place. The customer service, the dedicated employees—and the coffee, of course! So much better than Tim Hortons or Starbucks!"

Naturally I didn't tell Jay that the only reason I even bothered applying for a job at Michelle's was because there was too much competition for jobs at Tims and Starbucks. Advertised as "Mississauga's café by the lake," Michelle's was located in the village of Port Credit near Lake Ontario, an area packed with restaurants, cafés, and tiny boutiques selling everything from olive oil to vintage clothing in thrift shops. Michelle's wasn't exactly *on* the lakefront—which new customers often complained about—but in a plaza across from it. The doors opened to a busy street, jam-packed with cars, cyclists, and pedestrians, and the windows offered a view of a giant No Frills supermarket, with no water in sight.

Not that this mattered once people were eating the soft, freshly made scones and drinking the frothy cappuccino Michelle's was famous for. By noon I'm so exhausted that I mess up a customer's order for the second time in a row.

"I asked for a medium cappuccino!"

The air around us reeks of bacon grease and coffee. Jay's skin has turned a deep red, which makes his blond beard appear almost white. He slams the cup next to the sink, splattering a few hot drops of liquid on my arm. "*Not* a medium Columbian roast!"

I pour out the drink without a word or a wince—waste of product, if you ask me—but Jay never lets us consume any orders we mess up, as a part of internal control.

"Any more mistakes and I'll have to take that out of your paycheck," Jay warns.

"Yes, sir." I try to keep my sarcasm in check. And fail from the looks of Jay's skin, which now matches his purple Michelle's Coffee House apron.

"Watch it, Vakil." He gives me one final glare and heads back to the cash register to tell the angry customer that I'm remaking the coffee.

I watch it. While I don't *think* Jay will fire me—our other barista, Meg, is worse than I am and *she* hasn't been fired yet—I have no intention of pissing him off any more. Ever since he broke up with his boyfriend last week, Jay has been touchier than usual, his usual strict-but-friendly demeanor replaced by a perpetual sulk. There is no telling what he'll do in this mood.

Get it together, I say to myself, while the right coffee pours into the right-size cup. It has been like this almost all morning. Me minding the cash, taking orders, making coffee, thinking about Susan.

I bite back a grin. It's been a while since I've been this distracted at work over a girl. Susan and I haven't even kissed and I'm already at risk of getting my pay docked. I force myself to focus again, and make the next few orders perfectly. I take over the cash register when Jay goes on break, my smile professional, my hands moving at record speed. Pouring coffee, bagging doughnuts and cookies, shouting orders for sandwiches to the cook assembling them in the kitchen behind me.

My smile is still in place when the next customer steps up, even though my hands freeze at the sight of him, over the topmost tray of the doughnut display case.

"Hey, Malcolm."

"What do you want?"

My rudeness does not faze him. If anything, Ronnie Mehta's smile grows wider, a benign glow overtaking his bony, bespectacled face. Ever since he and Mahtab started dating, Ronnie has been doing his best to recruit me into the ZCC, letting me know about gambhar celebrations and prayers, about volunteer opportunities I have no interest in, about nearly every charity drive in existence.

"Why can't you be more like Ronnie?" the old man once asked, which instantly made me want to be everything Ronnie isn't.

In a way, I can see why I'd be of special interest to someone like Ronnie. I am a lapsed Zoroastrian at best. Based on my father's lectures about good thoughts, good words, and good deeds, and the crap I've done in the past, I've already paved my way to securing an afterlife in purgatory (since there is no permanent hell in our religion).

To Ronnie, I am a part-afterlife, part-impressing-Mahtab project. It is probably why he shows no hint of surprise when, in response to his comment about the fund-raising concert for Syrian refugees in January, I say, "What can I get for you?"

"Malc, come on," he cajoles. "It would look great on your university applications. Besides that, we could really use your help— two of our fund-raising directors dropped out. You must have seen the news on TV, right? About the Kurdi boy?"

"I have," I admit. I'm not as well-versed in world events as Ronnie or Mahtab. But I *am* following this year's election— Ahmed, Steve, and I have placed bets on who'll win—and thanks to that, even I'm aware of the brutal civil war in Syria, the horror of which was broadcast across every news channel earlier this September with the image of a three-year-old refugee boy found dead on a beach in Turkey.

"It's terrible." Ronnie's usual smarmy tone turns grim. "Aleppo is even worse. Kids are dying there without access to medicine and—"

"Hey, *I'm* dying here!" the woman behind him snaps. "Will you hurry up with the propaganda? Some of us want coffee and don't have the time for this!"

I don't have the time for this, the old man told the triage nurse at the ER when I was fourteen, his anger stemming not from a concern over Mom's worsening condition, but over a meeting he was missing in Michigan at the time. *We've been waiting four hours already.*

Mahtab says she's not exactly sure when it happened—when his love for Mom diminished into indifference. I, alternatively, wonder if the love was ever there. If the old man had always been the sort who put himself before others, even if they were his wife and kids. For a second I stand there, frozen in a memory I was pretty sure I'd forgotten.

I force myself to snap out of it.

"Ma'am, it's not propaganda." I face the angry customer, careful to keep my voice polite but firm. "It's someone's life."

The woman's face turns beet red. She leaves the line, muttering about "rude staff."

I turn back to Ronnie who's staring at me with awe in his eyes. "Seriously now, Ronnie, you need to place your order. Can't afford to make any other customers mad."

Ronnie orders a large black tea.

"That will be two dollars and ninety cents." I hesitate before asking the question: "Why me?" Even when Mom was alive, I was never anyone's first pick for any kind of school project, let alone something important like this.

"You're good with people," he says simply. "Remember that bake sale back in ninth grade? For Intro to Business?"

"You mean that ridiculous little challenge your team won?" I grin now, even though I remember feeling pissed at the time. Losing to Ronnie, listening to his mom crow about it at every ZCC event for a whole month—it had been my nightmare come true, until Mom's cancer returned.

"We won by a single cupcake. Your team came in second." Ronnie laughs. "I was so mad at the way you hustled our customers away from us. You would've won, too, if you guys hadn't run out of time."

I fall silent. I didn't realize Ronnie knew. Or that he had even noticed.

115

"There's another meeting coming up soon." Ronnie slides the money across the counter: exact change. "The concert's in January. Think about it, Malc. You could do a lot for us."

"I thought you already had a committee in place." This much I know, mostly because of Susan, who asked Mahtab in the last week of September if the art director position was still available. When my sister said that it wasn't, something in Susan's eyes dimmed. She remained silent for the rest of the lunch period and later all the way to English, barely acknowledging my presence or my jokes.

"We do. Mahtab has this great idea of hiring this amazing high school choir from Streetsville. And renting out a hall at the Living Arts Centre." Ronnie hesitates. "But we need money for that first. Getting sponsors is tough."

"I bet." It's difficult to get people to spend a lot of money when they can't exactly see what they're getting in return. I saw that at the bake sale in ninth grade, see enough of that at Michelle's on a daily basis.

I think about what Mahtab and I have done so far: contributing our toys and old clothes to a Syrian family one of our friends was sponsoring in Toronto. It was the best I thought I could do at the time. Now, though, after talking to Ronnie, I wonder if even someone like me can do more. The back door scrapes opens—a sign that Jay has returned from break—so I quickly prepare Ronnie's tea.

"Sugar and milk are on the side. Have a nice day."

There's a break after Ronnie is gone and I take the opportunity to close my eyes for a second. When I open them again, I realize someone's watching me. At first I think it's Jay, back with the angry customer I ticked off earlier. But it's only Ronnie.

He tosses his used tea bag and stirring stick into the trash before raising his cup. "Saheb ji."

It's what my uncle Mancher says whenever he sees a Parsi friend: a greeting that men from our community have been using to say hello and goodbye for generations in India. "It's the highest form of respect, Malcko," Mancher Mama said, when I asked him about it once. It was the most serious I'd ever seen him. "Call a man *Boss* and add a *ji* to it—it's for the best men you can find."

Later, I will attribute my reaction to surprise and exhaustion. To not wanting Jay on my case for being impolite to customers. I wave back and echo Ronnie's words: "Saheb ji."

"But when will the 'good days' for India come?"

Freny's voice floats into the front hall, where I'm slipping out of my sneakers and placing them next to a pair of muddy heels.

"Fine. I won't argue with you. You live there, you know better." Freny sounds a little out of breath, a clear sign that she's pacing the living room while talking on the phone. "Oh, I miss *our* good old days, Jeroo. Back when we were still in college."

A stray leaf flutters to the floor when I hang up my jacket. I pick it up, twirl it between my fingers. A deep red, like the sweater Susan wore to school this week. I smile slightly to myself.

It has been strange how close we've grown over the past couple of weeks. We talk more frequently during classes. We laugh a lot more. We text nearly nonstop once we're home. These days, Ahmed and Steve instantly begin talking to each other when Susan turns to pass me a new handout or answer a question when I tap her shoulder. They grill me later, when I'm back at my locker, but that's okay since Susan barely uses hers anyway and doesn't see how much they annoy me with their teasing.

"We're friends," I've insisted. "Just friends, okay. I don't like her like that."

It's easier to be friends instead of plunging headlong into another relationship that'll break my heart into pieces again. Neither Ahmed nor Steve know what that's like. They've never given themselves to a girl—any girl—as fully as I have.

"Malcolm, dikra? How was work?"

Around me, Freny grows nervous, timid. Full of artificial sweetness.

I wrap my fingers around the leaf. "Okay. Work's work."

"Y-yes. Of course."

When I first took this job at Michelle's Coffee House, the main idea was to make enough money to move out when I turned eighteen. To get a place of my own, away from the old man and Freny. Of course, on minimum wage, that isn't turning out to be likely. And I can't exactly leave Mahtab here by herself.

Freny fidgets with a red bangle on her wrist. Parsi women wear them after marriage and never remove them. Mom didn't, even after she found out about Dad cheating on her.

"I've made a snack for you," Freny says. "Bhakhras. You like them, right?"

They are my favorite. Fried little circles of sweet dough, flavored with cardamom. Mom used to make them for us every Saturday morning, infusing the kitchen with the smell of sugar and masala chai.

"Not the way you make them." I relish the way Freny's face falls and stalk past her, across the living room and up the stairs. Mahtab is in her room, wearing headphones, giggling at some sitcom on

118

Netflix. I make my way to my own room at the end of the hall. Downstairs the phone rings again. Freny's voice floats up again seconds later. "Hi, jaanu. How's work?"

It still irks me that she calls my father what Mom used to call him. Jaanu. Her life. I resist the urge to slam my bedroom door shut. I rip off my black button-down work shirt and the sweaty white T-shirt I wear underneath, exposing my skin to the cool draft of air from the partially open window. When I open my closet, my eyes automatically start looking for a glint of glass at the bottom, among the mess of hangers and T-shirts. The old man's voice is ringing in my head: *He will never come to any good.*

There are days when I can ignore my father's taunts. Moments with Ahmed and Steve and Mahtab that make the Malcolm from the past feel like a distant relative I can barely remember. But then there are days like this. When Freny inserts a hook under my skin and pulls up old, buried anger. My mouth waters for a sip of vodka from the bottle I poured down the drain months ago.

Vodka, Justin said, was the mother of grief. "When love leaves, she takes over."

I lean against the wall next to my closet, feeling my skin prickle into bumps against its cool white surface. Grief, mom said once, feels like a stone crushing your ribs. Vodka, on the other hand, burns my throat and my insides; it makes me light-headed. I know that if I drink enough it will, for a few brief moments, diminish the weight of my mother being gone for good.

Mahtab's face hovers briefly in front of mine.

I pull out another T-shirt from the closet and a black hoodie. Drinking with Justin is no longer an option. So I do the other reckless thing I used to do back then. I stick an arm and a leg outside the window and grab hold of the old pipe nailed to the wall.

Susan

"Stop! Stop!"

My driving instructor barely allows me any time to shift my foot from the accelerator before pressing down on the second brake. The car jerks to a stop, nearly a foot away from the stop sign, where it's supposed to be.

"I *was* stopping," I say under my breath.

"Not fast enough. You are never fast enough. You would have rolled over the line again. In the road test, that results in an automatic fail." Joseph Kuruvilla takes off the baseball cap he always wears to these lessons and wipes off a trail of nonexistent sweat from his bald head. "How many times have I told you this? How many times?"

I say nothing in response. Joseph never compliments me on the days I do well; half the time his yelling drives me up the wall. But

Amma trusts Joseph because he talks to her in Malayalam whenever he's on the phone, almost puppylike in his efforts to squeeze out more practice lessons (and more money) to make sure that I pass on my very first attempt.

"Joseph Uncle means well," Amma told me the last time, when I complained again about his yelling.

"Stop calling him that." While I don't mind the Indian tradition of calling unrelated adults "uncle" or "aunty," Joseph isn't an adult I particularly like. "He's not really my uncle."

"Susan! How dare you speak to me that way?"

"You don't see him in the car. You don't know what he's like when we're alone."

"Well, I've already paid for these lessons with the driving school. They don't have any other instructors available during the time slot we need."

Or, in other words, I would have to deal with it the way I dealt with many other things, with gritted teeth and white knuckles, willing myself not to simultaneously blast Joseph and crash the car in the same instant.

"Move," Joseph says. "Take the next right."

He makes me parallel park behind a school bus on a hill, and criticizes how far I am from the curb.

"At least I won't fail," I snap. "Doesn't touching the curb mean you fail as well?"

Joseph's nostrils flare. "I see there is no improvement. Not in your driving. Nor in your attitude."

"Sorry to ruin your track record. What was it? Eighty percent pass, twenty percent fail like you keep telling my mother? Or is it really the other way around and you're trying to rip students off by charging for more and more lessons?"

It is the first time I have ever talked back to a teacher, to any authority figure who isn't a parent, and I think this surprises Joseph enough to shut him up for the remainder of the lesson. He doesn't wait around to schedule my next lesson and I don't ask. I step out of his Honda Civic, my shirt sticking to my skin. Instead of going into the condo complex, I walk around to the back, where the deliveries are made, and sag against the wall, watching a pair of men loading a white truck with boxes and old furniture.

The air in October is cold and carries the scent of firewood. I feel myself grow calmer when I breathe it in. I am grateful that Amma isn't in this afternoon, waiting by the door to ask about my progress, but instead out with Bridgita Aunty and a few of her friends.

"Come, Aruna," my father's cousin objected, when Amma tried to weasel out of going. "Susan is a good girl. She will be fine on her own."

Amma gave me the house key before she left, along with a lecture on not letting strangers into the condo. You would think I was seven, not seventeen.

"Sometimes I think you're seventy," a voice to my left says.

My spine tingles when I see Malcolm grinning at me, an unlit cigarette dangling from his fingers. His hair is no longer in spikes, but a mess of waves on top of his head. There's a streak of white dust on the front of his black hoodie.

"Did I say that out loud?"

He nods. "Do you make a habit of it?"

"Only when I'm stressed."

"Ah." He pockets the cigarette again without lighting it.

I ask, "Were you here to see Ahmed?" when he says something at the same time.

We both smile. He indicates me to go first and then nods. "Yeah, I was here to see Ahmed. We were planning to . . . do homework."

"Smoke weed you mean?"

He grins. "Ahmed doesn't smoke weed. And I stopped months ago."

We stand in silence for a few moments, watching the movers load the last of the furniture on the truck. It's a quiet that somehow does not feel uncomfortable. A stray draft ruffles my hair.

"The reason for your stress. Was it the bald guy? Your driving instructor?"

I shrug. I wonder how much he saw, if he could tell how badly I did at my lesson, if he was wondering why I was still struggling with something that seems so easy for the rest of the student population at Arthur Eldridge.

"He must be a jerk," Malcolm says.

"How can you tell?" I ask, even though a part of me is relieved by this assessment, that someone can see the possibility of Joseph being a bad teacher.

"Let's see: You're not a slacker and you catch on to things pretty quickly in class. I can't imagine you getting stressed over something like driving unless your instructor is a class-A jerk."

"Is Mr. Zuric a jerk to you?"

I don't need to look at him to know he has stiffened. I can hear the defensiveness in his voice. "That's different."

A few weeks ago, I might have backed off at his response or changed the subject. But today, I'm feeling a little reckless, my tongue loosened by lashing out at Joseph.

"I don't understand why you're so nasty to him. He doesn't do anything to you."

Malcolm's mouth curls into a sneer. "That's what you think."

"What do you mean?"

"He *bugs* me. I think of it like a science experiment. Testing a subject's reaction to an external stimulus. In Zuric's case, I like seeing how far I can go before he snaps."

"You're saying you really *don't* have a reason."

Malcolm simply shrugs, even though I get the feeling he isn't telling me everything. There's a strange, sad look on his face, which simultaneously puzzles me and makes me want to comfort him. But before I can say anything, Malcolm says: "Do you want me to teach you? How to drive."

The question is so surprising, so out of left field, that I am unable to form a coherent response. "You want . . . *what did you say?*"

He laughs. "I'm offering you a driving lesson. With me. See, driving's a lot like math. You need lots and lots of practice to get it right and to let your body memorize the sort of reflex actions you need to operate a car."

Another math analogy. But this one makes sense. "I don't know . . ."

"Is your mom at home?"

"No—I mean, why are you asking?" My voice comes out sharper than usual.

Malcolm laughs. "I'm not asking for an invitation upstairs—though I wouldn't necessarily say no if asked." Upon seeing my scowl, he hastily adds: "What I'm saying is that if your mom isn't here, I can teach you."

"What? You mean *now?*"

"If you're up for breaking a couple of rules. And a law or two." His tone, though not sarcastic, clearly suggests that I'm not. And while the idea of losing my license before I even get one does bother me, something else has been nagging me a lot more.

"Why are you doing this for me?" I ask him. *Why do you even care?*

"Because I want you to see driving the way I see it—not as something to be scared of, but something to enjoy."

I say nothing, surprised by how sincere he sounds.

"Besides," he continues, "from what I can tell, there is no contest. *Anyone* can teach you better than the bald guy."

I laugh. "Maybe I'm just as bad as he says."

"Oh really? Then I'm just gonna have to try my best with you." He gives me a cocky grin.

"I didn't know I was special."

"Of course you're special. You're my first."

I feel my face turn red, wondering if there's a double meaning to the statement. But instead of laughing or teasing me the way Alisha would have, he reaches out to gently tap the side of my cheek with a finger.

"My first student, Susan. And I promise I won't let you fail."

"Maybe we should go to an empty parking lot?"

"Don't be silly," he says. "How are you going to learn anything in a parking lot?"

Malcolm does not have a car. Which means our only other source of practice would have been through Ahmed, whose fancy sports car frankly scares me to death with its manual gears, or Steve, who I do not trust to keep quiet about this.

"It's bad enough that you know how terrible I am," I tell him. "I don't want everyone else to know as well."

Malcolm rolls his eyes, but does not argue. Even he knows how big a gossip Steve Patel is. Thanks to Steve, I have now caught up on various stories about most of the popular kids in school—the fights, the makeups and the breakups, even silly things like how much time some guys on the basketball team spend doing their hair.

Gossip fuels Steve the way it did my old friend Mishal Al-Abdulaziz at Qala Academy. It lights up his face, makes him blurt out things about his friends that he should have been keeping secret. Steve was the one who confirmed my suspicions about Malcolm and Afrin, with a passing reference one afternoon to Ahmed about Malcolm losing his mind when he found out about Afrin and some other guy.

It is that—sympathy, really—and the disappointment on Malcolm's face that makes me offer an alternative solution without entirely thinking it through.

"My dad got us a car before he left for Jeddah. I've never used it though."

Malcolm's eyes widen with excitement. "And you're telling me this *now*? What are you waiting for? Let's go get it."

"What? No, I can't." I try to backtrack. "I haven't really driven it and—"

"Is it automatic?"

"Yeah."

"Does it belong to Ahmed or Steve?"

"No."

"Then I don't see what excuse you can have."

"What if I crash the car? I mean, it doesn't have extra brakes. And you're only seventeen. You don't have a full G license yet!"

"So what? We're not going on the highway. Do you wanna go home and cry instead?"

I grow silent. Embarrassment and rage battle each other in my rib cage.

"Hey, Susan. Susan."

I refuse to look at him.

"Look, I'm sorry. I didn't . . ." He sighs. "Look, if you don't want to drive your dad's car, it's okay. But remember that if we're going by the law, with a G1 license, you really can't drive with anyone who doesn't have a full G *and* four years of solid driving experience. You wouldn't be this worried if it was my car, would you?"

Guilt muddies my embarrassment. It's true. What I'm really worried about is the car Appa bought for us to use here.

The movers are long gone and their space is now occupied by a brown UPS delivery truck. The driver, a woman in her twenties, leaps out with a package and gives us both a smile before heading into the building. I think of Jeddah, where women can still be arrested for driving a car, where I have seen unlicensed eleven-year-old boys chauffeuring wide-bodied Cadillacs filled with their mothers and older sisters.

Think of the opportunities you'll be getting once you immigrate, Alisha and Appa always told me. And now, here it is: an opportunity presented on a platter, boy and car combined, and I am being the same old scared Susan.

"Okay, let's do it," I say finally. *Just this once.*

"Are you sure?"

"It will probably be the most irresponsible thing I've ever done. But I think it's necessary."

"You're serious." Malcolm does not smile; he probably does not believe me. I hardly believe myself.

"Yes," I tell him. "I am."

I am not in Jeddah anymore.

Breaking the rules and the law is surprisingly less eventful than I thought it would be. Once on the road, Malcolm grows calm, taking me as promised around quiet neighborhood streets, littered with cars parked against curbs and frequent all-way stop signs.

His directions are clear and succinct and he keeps a light conversation flowing in between. As he talks to me, I feel myself relax behind the wheel, for the first time not worrying about the exact pressure I've applied on the brakes or about not handling the steering wheel gracefully.

He asks me to make a right onto a road Joseph uses fairly often during our lessons and, as always, I end up shooting too far and going a little wide. I feel the first curlicues of panic—this is the part where Joseph starts shouting at me—when all of a sudden Malcolm says, "You need to start watching hockey now that you're in Canada. The Leafs could use another fan."

"The Leafs? Don't they always lose?"

"As a lifelong fan, I take serious offense to that!"

I smile slightly, my head automatically tilting to glance into the rearview mirror. "I don't care much for sports, honestly."

"What? Not even cricket?"

"Not unless India's in a World Cup final. Besides, it's not even the national game—field hockey is. Or *was*, according to every school textbook, until the Sports Ministry made a sudden announcement a couple of years ago, saying there was no national game at all. Cricket's just more popular. And lucrative."

"Susan Thomas, the girl who knows words like 'lucrative,' do you realize that you're driving quite well right now? You haven't frozen up once behind the wheel."

My heart beats hard against my ribs. My fingers tighten on the steering wheel. "Uh-oh, you jinxed it."

"No, I didn't. You're overthinking as usual."

I wait for the jinx to take effect. But after long moments pass and my car remains steady in its lane, I can't help but feel a little proud of myself.

"So this is what it feels like to drive."

"This is exactly what it feels like."

The confidence in his voice boosts mine. With Joseph no longer yelling into my ear, my hands smoothly cross over while taking the turns Malcolm asks me to, my eyes scan the mirrors automatically every few seconds. I don't even panic when a car cuts us off without signaling.

Malcolm tells me that my biggest problem is changing lanes. I take much too long, he points out, and I know this is true. Even while driving with Joseph, I often lost opportunities to make easy lane changes because the driver behind me got tired of waiting for me to make a move.

"You know how they always tell you in driving classes not to drive aggressively?" Malcolm asks.

"Yeah."

"Well, in your case, screw that rule."

I frown. "You've got to be kidding me."

"Imagine you need to get to an exam real quick," Malcolm says. "You're late, Susan. Very, very late."

"You sound like the White Rabbit from *Alice in Wonderland*."

"Yeah, and my pocket watch tells me the Queen of Hearts is following us with an ax, about to chop off our heads."

I try not to laugh.

This time, when he tells me to take a left at the traffic lights, I decide to follow his advice. I replace the Queen of Hearts with Amma, heading back home after her spa day with Bridgita Aunty, her face fresh and glowing, only to grow pale with fear on discovering my absence.

My shoulders tilt forward. I check my mirrors and give the signal. I turn my head once more to check my blind spot. The car in the left lane almost instantly speeds up.

"Push." Malcolm's voice is soft, sure. "Move and push or he'll never let you pass."

I glance once more into the mirror and take a deep breath.

I don't know who's more shocked, Malcolm or me, when I successfully manage to change lanes without cutting the other car off and slide to a stop at the red light.

Malcolm

"What..." Freny sputters when she sees me entering through the front door again. "Where . . . ? Weren't you . . . ?"

Normally I am not this sloppy. But it's a pain skinning up the pipe and back into my room. And I'm still running on the high of Susan's smile and my own success at teaching her. I kick off my shoes in the corridor, streaking the tiles with mud.

"When did you leave?" Freny is not letting up this time. "You can't go out like that without telling me!"

I shrug. "You were on the phone. I didn't want to disturb you."

From the living room, I hear my sister's giggles, intertwining with a familiar male voice.

A vein pulses in Freny's forehead. "Malcolm—"

"Steve?" I cut her off midsentence and walk into the living room. "Is that you?"

Mahtab is sprawled over the couch, her mouth hidden behind her hands, shoulders shaking. Steve, on the other hand, looks embarrassed, the lower half of his face more swollen than usual. Across from them, a muted TV flashes with scenes from a rerun of the *Rick Mercer Report*.

"What's that?" I reach out to poke his fat lower lip. "A bee sting?"

"Hey!" He slaps my hand away. "That hurts!"

"He tried to kiss a girl and fell," Mahtab volunteers before bursting into laughter again. Steve scowls at her from the leather recliner.

I nudge Mahtab to the side with a light kick on her knee. The cushions sigh as I plop down next to her. "Need Polysporin?" I ask Steve. "A Band-Aid?"

Steve flips me the bird.

"How'd you fall anyway?" I persist. "Were you like leaning in and she stepped aside or something?"

Steve face nearly turns the shade of his swollen red lip when Mahtab begins laughing again. "It's probably good I didn't break my teeth," he mutters.

Next to me, Mahtab is wiping away tears. "Sorry, Steve. But for real: Do you want something to put on that lip?"

Steve's eyes soften, which doesn't surprise me one bit. Mahtab has that effect on people.

"I'll be okay. I was looking for this jerk anyway." He tilts his head in my direction.

"What do you mean?"

"We have that assignment for English, remember? You said you could meet today after work?"

The memory returns to me in a sudden rush. Crap. I completely forgot Zuric's assignment—a short story that we have to read and figure out the themes to, worth 5 percent of the final grade. It's not an assignment I'd care about normally, but after the D-plus I got on that horrible *King Lear* essay this week, I figure I could use the extra marks.

"What were you doing anyway?" Mahtab asks. "I called Ahmed and he said you never came over. And then you sent me some weird text about being busy?"

"Was hanging with a friend," I say vaguely.

"What friend?" Mahtab asks, her tone unusually harsh.

But before I can respond, Steve butts in, a manic grin overtaking his face. "Oh, I know! It's *Susan*! His new *girlfriend*."

"Oh, shut up."

My annoyance erases the tense lines around Mahtab's mouth. A slow smile overtakes her face.

The back of my neck grows warm. I know Susan will not like being linked with me again—she was pissed over me pretending that when we ran into Afrin at the mall—but I can't exactly deny anything without giving away her secret about the driving lesson.

"Whatever," I mutter in response, hoping they'll drop the subject.

"I like Susan," Mahtab says, not taking the hint. "She's a little shy, but she seems nice, unlike some of the other girls you've dated."

I know that by these *other girls* she means Afrin. If there's a thing such as hate at first sight, it definitely existed between my sister and my ex-girlfriend, their faces hardening from the moment they first shook hands at the ZCC, even though Afrin always called Mahtab a *sweet kid*. Mahtab, on the other hand, was less diplomatic. *There's something about her that rubs me the wrong way,* she had said. *She may be Zoroastrian, but I don't trust her.*

And though she turned out to be right, I still hated the righteous arrogance on my sister's face, the warnings she always deems necessary now, as if I'm the younger sibling and she the older one.

"Susan and I are not dating. I like her, okay? She's cool."

"Oh, he *likes* her," Mahtab tells Steve.

"She's *cool*."

"Will you both cut it out?"

My exasperation brings out matching grins on their faces. Of course I like Susan, I tell myself. Only not the way they're implying.

"Yeah, make sure you wear a jockstrap around that one." Steve guffaws. "She'll probably get you in the balls if you try anything."

"I'm glad he's hanging out with Susan." Mahtab's smile eclipses the sun. "At least he's no longer sulking."

Steve raises his hands in supplication. "Okay, okay."

I glance at the TV to avoid their knowing looks. There's a story about the Syrian refugee crisis. "Hey, Mah. How's that fund-raiser of yours coming along?"

"It's coming along great. Though"—my sister fakes a cough—"it would be better if we had *more people* to help fund-raise and get sponsors."

I stare at the news anchor, speaking silently on-screen, closed captions flashing underneath.

"One meeting," I say.

Barely a moment passes by before Mahtab begins to crow. "YASSS!"

"I'll come to one meeting and see if I can actually do anything," I say loudly, trying not to cringe at her enthusiasm. Or the *yasss*. "When is the next meeting anyway?"

"October 30. We had to cancel yesterday's and next week's meetings because of midterms."

Midterms. I try not to think about those—even though I've been averaging an A in phys ed thanks to basketball, and a B-minus in accounting and math. I'm still way behind in English thanks to the Shakespeare stuff, though only Susan knows about that.

"Is there, um, room for more people?"

"Yeah, you can bring Susan along." Mahtab grins at me, then grows serious. "I really felt bad telling her no about the art director position. But she didn't seem interested in anything else."

"I know you did." I don't know what Susan will say when I ask her. But I figure it's worth a shot. If anything, the meetings will serve the dual purpose of keeping Mahtab happy and staying outside the range of Freny's microscope. Susan's company isn't exactly a chore, either.

Steve coughs and a strange look passes between him and Mahtab. My sister gives him a single firm shake of the head. "Okay, you two. Midterms start on Tuesday. I gotta go study," she says, before leaving the room.

I turn to Steve, who's pulling out a binder from his bag.

"What's up?"

Steve looks at me, his eyes extra wide. "What?"

"You and Mahtab gave each other a look. Like you know something I don't. What's going on?"

"I swear it's nothing, man!"

I frown. "Wait, are you two—Steve, if you're messing around with my little sister—"

"I'm not," Steve interrupts. "She's dating Ronnie, remember?"

"Oh yeah? Then what was it?"

Steve hesitates for a split second. "It was about Susan."

My heart skips a beat. "What about her?"

"Maybe I shouldn't say this."

"What is it?" I must sound more aggressive than I normally do because Steve flinches.

"I heard Afrin talking crap with her friends about Susan. Nothing major or anything. I mean, what's Afrin ever done except complain about girls she doesn't like, right?"

A memory surfaces: tenth grade, Afrin's red heel jutting out from under a table, tripping a girl who had flirted with Afrin's then-boyfriend in the cafeteria, and then laughing when the girl fell flat on her face.

I push the thought aside. Afrin and I aren't going out anymore. She's probably pissed that Susan did better than her in the last assignment that Zuric gave our class.

"You're right," I tell Steve now. "It's probably talk."

Steve nods, a little relieved, and pulls out his copy of the short story. "C'mon. Let's get to work!"

Midterms in the tenth grade were a series of parties—"study sessions," people called them—held at Justin Singh's house on the border of Oakville and Mississauga when his parents were out of town. Justin and I were both fifteen years old, but there was a look on his face that always made him appear older: a weariness around his eyes, his smile as hard as flint. He wasn't known for stopping and talking to people or inviting them to his parties. Especially nobodies like me.

This year, the Monday before midterms begin, I end up having a study session—a real one—with Ahmed and Steve in the school library at lunch, the three of us actually reading the books in front of us instead of fooling around the way we normally do when we're together. Part of that credit also goes to the librarian, Ms. Mehra, who kicked us out the last time for being too loud.

"I could use something stiff," Steve whispers now, one eye on his accounting textbook, the other on the library desk. "Who came up with this stuff again? Some bored Portuguese guy?"

"Italian," I say, remembering Mr. Hill's lecture from the beginning of the term. "I think it was an Italian who came up with modern double-entry bookkeeping."

"Europeans," Steve grumbles. "Trust them to come up with more ways to bore us at school."

"Wanna do what the Arabs came up with instead, Patel?" Ahmed looks up from his calculus text and grins in a way that tells me that Steve will like this answer even less. "Y'know, *real math*, like algebra?"

I tune out their bickering and double line the totals of my balance sheet. Perfectly balanced on the first try. Accounting, surprisingly, makes sense most times. I'm guessing working cash at Michelle's sort of helps me there. English, on the other hand, continues to be an indecipherable mess, especially the Shakespeare unit that Zuric keeps insisting will be on the midterm *and* the final. A few pages into *King Lear*, I decide I've had enough of both fossils—bard and teacher—and stick it back into my bag.

I glance sideways at one of the individual study carrels, where Susan's been sitting for the past twenty minutes, scribbling away in her binder. Susan wanted to use today's lunch period to study at the library—owing to the fact that it's getting colder outside. Naturally, the moment Ahmed and Steve heard me saying that I would join her, they decided they needed to study as well. So now, instead of spending my lunch hour at a table cozied up with a pretty girl, I'm stuck with Wheels Three and Four, both of whom sported identical grins on their faces when Susan chose an individual carrel to "avoid any distractions."

I wait until Ms. Mehra's working on her computer and then pull out my phone: hey.

A chiming sound erupts from the area of the carrels, followed by the rustling of pages and a sharply whispered apology.

Susan hastily silences her phone before scowling at the screen. My phone buzzes with a reply: What are you doing? Do you want to get me kicked out?

If there was any quicksand available, I'd have gladly sunk into it. Even though the two jokers in front of me can barely hold back laughs.

sorry!! i thought you had your phone silenced!! I add an emoji with a halo. Or try to. In my haste, my finger shifts and I accidentally send her the kissing emoji underneath. Susan's head snaps sideways in a glare. I'm about to type another apology, when she holds up her phone and makes a point of showing me as she shuts it down. *Later*, she mouths, before turning back to her books.

A loud snort forces me to look around. I glare at Steve, who's shaking with silent laughter. But Ms. Mehra isn't at her desk at the moment and the tension in my muscles loosens. Ahmed's grin, though a little more sympathetic, tells me he doesn't exactly mind my embarrassment either.

I scowl at them both. Okay, so I know I messed up—something I tend to do on a fairly regular basis when it comes to this particular girl. I tap my fingers on the table for a few seconds, thinking.

I pull out a piece of paper from my binder: *Sorry. Wanted to wish you good luck. Even though you're probably going to ace everything.*

Maybe it's a little old school, sending notes like this. Cheesy, too. But the words aren't exactly a lie. Susan *is* probably going to ace everything, unlike me.

When the third-period bell goes off, I'm the first to get up and I let the folded square drop lightly on Susan's desk. This time, I wait until reaching the door before risking another glance. Susan's looking at me, too. And, in the split second before she looks away, she gives me a smile that stays with me for the rest of the afternoon.

The week after midterms end, my accounting teacher taps me on my shoulder after class. "Malcolm. A word."

I stay behind, wondering what I've done to deserve being held back, when Mr. Hill—part-time basketball coach, full-time LeBron James look-alike—looks up and says, "Have you thought of applying for a bachelor's of commerce degree at university, specializing in accounting?"

What the—*what*? A degree specializing in *accounting*? *University*?

"I doubt I could get into a college right now, let alone a university," I manage to say once my tongue unglues itself from the roof of my mouth. "I mean, don't grades count?"

"They do." Mr. Hill gives me a sudden smile that reminds me why every kid in a two-block radius instantly wants to trust him. "And, while your midterm report cards aren't out till mid-November, I can safely say you haven't been doing too badly in most of your courses. If you pull up that English grade, I think you could easily get into a university."

English. Yeah, well. Never expected any miracles there.

"I don't know. I never saw myself doing accounting," I admit. Or going to a college or university. But the idea that someone else, especially a teacher, thinks that I may, that I *can* . . .

"Think about it, okay?"

I manage a nod and step out, still feeling a little bit like I've been slammed in the ear by a basketball. The last time a teacher mentioned my name in conjunction with college or university was Mr. Kristoff in eleventh grade. I didn't take him seriously then, but now I begin to wonder if it really is so far-fetched—this idea of me going to a postsecondary institution. It would be worth it, I think, to see the look on the old man's face when I showed him my acceptance letter.

Next to my locker, I find a girl cooing at a boy, both glowing with a look that shouts Newly Hooked Up. "Poor baby." The girl touches the boy's chin. "Let me see that."

Behind the couple, I see Susan, a couple of thick textbooks in hand, the expression on her face a mix of discomfort and disgust.

"Excuse me," Susan says. "You're blocking my locker."

Neither girl nor dazed boy move from their spot. Now the girl is dabbing the boy's chin with a tissue she moistened with her tongue.

I try not to laugh. And fail. The boy and girl start at the sounds coming from my mouth and notice Susan standing behind them.

"Oh sorry," the girl says. "Were we blocking your locker? I'm so sorry."

Susan does not say that it's okay. She glares at them until they hastily move aside to the safety of a wall and then directs her gaze at me.

"What's so funny?" If those brown eyes of hers shot sparks, I would've been ablaze.

"You," I say, once I manage to control myself. "You look so . . . appalled." Susan would never call a boy her baby. Of that I'm pretty sure.

"What does *that* mean?" Susan's voice rises now, exasperated.

"Maybe you should put those books in your locker." Though I'm not sure if her arms are trembling from anger or the extra strain.

She drops the books to the floor with a resounding *thud*. Behind us, the girl detaches herself from her boyfriend and mutters something that sounds like "psycho." While the two shuffle away, I stare at Susan, fascinated by the completely unimpressed look on her face.

"It's no wonder you don't get along with everyone," I say. Susan can't be fake for one second. It's one of the things I like best about her. The moment the words slip out, though, I realize they are a mistake.

She winces and then undoes the lock. "Yeah. Thanks for reminding me why I don't have any friends in this place."

"What?" I ignore the sting of her words. I thought *I* was her friend. "I didn't mean—"

"And I never know what you mean, so thanks for that as well."

How did this go so wrong? Why is she so pissed off? The old Malcolm would ask if she's PMSing, but the new one—thanks to being gut-punched by Mahtab—knows better.

"Is everything okay?" I ask cautiously.

She sighs. "I'm sorry. I got a bad test score in physics."

"How bad?"

She kneels to pick up one of the books she dropped to the floor, pulls out a test paper from it, and hands it to me.

"B-minus?"

"Don't shout it to the world!" Color rises to her cheeks again.

I can't help it. I start laughing. "What's wrong with a B-minus?"

She wraps her arms around herself, the knuckles turning pale. "You don't get it. No one over here does."

The laughter drains out of me. This is way more serious than I thought.

"It's just a test, Susan," I tell her calmly. "Not a midterm that's like 30 percent of your final grade."

She bites her lower lip. Crap, shouldn't have mentioned midterms—didn't she tell me she wasn't entirely happy with how her physics one went last week?

"Look," I add, "I'm going to a meeting for that fund-raiser for Syrian refugees tomorrow. D'you want to come along? I know Mahtab really wants to see you again."

That's right, Malc. Tell her how excited *your sister* is to see her. I try not to wince. But this isn't exactly how I planned on asking her anyway, with her mood so off. Not like going to a fund-raising meeting is a date or anything.

She stares at me for a minute, almost as if considering it. "I don't think I can."

"Come on. It'll be good for your Nobel Peace Prize application!" A joke that, judging by the scowl on her face, falls flat. "Seriously, Susan. No one cares if you got a B-minus on a test. You're acting like you failed or something."

"Just because you're constantly failing your tests doesn't mean others don't care about their grades."

Silence. One beat passes. Then two.

I'm tempted to tell Susan what Mr. Hill told me minutes earlier, with the same amount of venom. But there's a look on her face that reminds me too much of the old man. A look that hits far too close, could cut way too deep. If I let it.

"Maybe I should let you cool off or something," I say instead, my voice cold. It ices over the sting of Susan's words, leaving behind an odd numbness. Wounds only fester if you let them, I remind myself. If you let yourself like someone way more than they'll ever like you. Afrin taught me as much.

Susan's eyes widen with something that could be shock. Or regret.

I don't wait to find out.

Susan

I know I've made a mistake the minute he drops the test to the floor and begins walking away. I raise a hand to call him back, when a soft voice makes me pause: "You said the right thing, you know."

It's Afrin Irani, dressed to the hilt as always, her pretty face oozing compassion.

"Were you listening to us?" I ask.

Afrin covers her cheeks with her hands. "I honestly didn't mean to. He doesn't even talk to me now. But you know how it is." Her airy laugh holds a note of awkwardness and for a second I almost believe she's being genuine. "You can't stop stalking his Facebook even though he's over you."

I nod, even though I've never had a boyfriend, and the extent of my internet stalking has been limited to old crushes who I never spoke to or was even friends with on social media. And Malcolm. I push away the last thought.

"Malcolm is too carefree. I mean, he's great, but he doesn't understand the sort of pressures we go through to perform well in school. My parents are, like, MIA most of the time, but the minute I come home with a B or a C, it's like they suddenly wake up and start asking all sorts of questions."

They may be only words, I think. But they resonate with me. They also partly explain why Afrin shoots me dirty looks whenever I get praise from Mr. Zuric in class. It's not only about Malcolm. We're both in a competition that goes beyond the boy I—

No. I force my train of thought away from there. I don't have a crush on Malcolm Vakil.

There is a look in Afrin's eyes, a sort of sadness and anger that makes me wonder if she can read my thoughts, muddled as they are. But then she blinks and the moment is gone.

"My friend Justin is having a party tomorrow. I know it's short notice, but I'd like to invite you. A lot of people from school will be there."

I hesitate, taken aback by the sudden gesture of friendliness. "I'm not sure . . ."

Afrin doesn't take offense. She reaches into her purse and pulls out a notepad. Scribbling an address on it, she hands it to me. "Here, in case you change your mind. The party starts at eight. Just don't show up exactly then 'cause no one will be there."

She waves as the warning bell rings, her heels clicking on the tiled floor. I slip the note into my pocket and slam my locker shut, managing to make it to art seconds before Ms. Nguyen closes the door.

Sunsets here stretch out during the summers, the sun a great fiery ball hanging relentlessly in the sky, as late as nine or even ten in the evening. As fall fades into winter, the days grow shorter and shorter, Yvonne's mother tells us, darkness falling as early as 4:30 p.m.

"Canada feels most like home to me toward the end of October," Bridgita Aunty said. "When the sun sets at around six. When the birds roost in the trees."

In the tree outside my bedroom window, crows gather each evening at sunset, their loud cries rising in the air before they slowly fall silent, black bodies huddled on bare branches. I have gotten into the habit of watching them whenever I can, sometimes even catching hold of a stray gray-black feather that floats my way against a blushing sky.

It is a scene so reminiscent of Jeddah, it is almost painful. I half expect Amma to tell me to shut the window—*Do you want a bird to get in?*—but she hasn't been herself lately, hasn't been functioning the way she normally does ever since Appa once again changed his plans to visit us. When I came home this afternoon, she was snoring on the couch, her phone resting on her belly. It has become her usual pose: a sleepless night's long bout of worrying melting finally into exhaustion during the day.

I push aside thoughts about my parents and wonder again about Malcolm and Afrin, the utter strangeness of being invited to a party by a girl whose ex-boyfriend stirs up a myriad of strange feelings in me. I glance at the address Afrin gave me today at school. Not like it matters. It's not like I'm going to the party anyway. My phone buzzes with a text. My heart races and then slows to a dull thud when I see that it's Alisha. Who else would it be?

I'm glad she can't see my face right now or know that the smile I'm sending her is a forced one. **What's up?** I type, checking the time. It's 1:00 a.m. in Jeddah. Friday already. **Any plans for the weekend?**

Sorta lol. I'm seeing the guy tomorrow, remember? Well, technically today, but . . .

I blink. **What guy?**

THE guy, remember? Didn't I tell you?

"What the—?" I nearly curse out loud. **NO! YOU DID NOT!**

Oh, no, wait that was Emerald . . .

Alisha told *Emerald Verghese* she was seeing a guy before she told me?

SKYPE!!! I text. **NOW!!!**

She must have sensed my fury because when I log on, she's the one who calls me.

"Hiiiiii." Greeting stretched out. Smile sheepish. Her natural curls flat-ironed to ruler-like straightness behind her earphones. I'm pretty sure her eyebrows have been threaded as well. "You're mad, aren't you?"

"You're meeting some *guy* and you didn't tell me?" I want to shout at her. I probably am, based on the wince that appears on her face. I lower my voice. "When did this even *happen*?"

"Last week," she admits. "My parents set it up. Everything happened so fast that I barely had time to breathe. I'm so sorry. I thought I *did* tell you!"

"You told Emerald Verghese." Verghese Madam's simpering gem of a daughter, who was always nice to my face, until I heard her call me a brownnosing loser behind my back. I find it hard to believe my best friend would ever mix the two of us up. "You hate that girl, Alisha!"

"I don't *hate* her, Susan." Alisha stiffens, her mouth flattening slightly. "I know you two never got along, but trust me when I say that she's changed a lot from how she was last year. She even asks me how you're doing! In any case, we only started getting closer over the past month or so. Her parents have set her up as well—with a guy from Kochi. She's been really helpful. Full of good advice."

"Did *she* tell you to straighten your hair?" I wonder if it's a good idea to tell Alisha that the effect is more sphinx and less Cleopatra.

"I went to the salon she goes to, yes." Alisha bristles. "They did my hair and eyebrows."

"The eyebrows look good," I say grudgingly. "I can't believe you're actually talking to a guy. For marriage."

"It's not for *marriage*. Not yet anyway. I'm not like you, Susan. I don't have the same opportunities to meet guys or date them. I'm pretty sure you have guys falling over themselves to talk to you over there."

"Guys falling—what are you talking about?" I laugh, expecting Alisha to join in. She doesn't.

"Suze, have you even looked into a mirror? You, like, don't even need makeup let alone any facial-hair removal." She says the words in such a way that I'm not sure they're a compliment.

"You don't need makeup either," I tell her, and she snorts.

"Yeah, right. Anyway, the first meeting's tomorrow and I haven't been able to sleep all night!"

I instantly feel guilty about the third degree I've been giving her. "What's he like? Have you seen his picture or talked to him?"

"Yeah. He added me on Facebook yesterday." She sends me a

link to a profile. In his picture, Isaac Cherian wears square-framed glasses and a nice smile. To my relief, he also appears to be around the same age as she is, maybe a year or two older.

"College of Engineering in Trivandrum," I read out loud. "Impressive. Cute, too."

"I know." Alisha lets out a whoosh of air. "What if I make a fool of myself?"

"You will not." I can't help but smile at her nerves. "You're head girl of the entire school, Alisha. And a class topper!"

"That's because *you* aren't here." Another compliment that feels like a jab, even though I'm not sure if I'm topping *any* class here after those midterms. English and art are pretty subjective in general, which makes it difficult to top them consistently, and I'm pretty sure I messed up the graphing section of the exam in calculus. As for physics—Mr. Franklin decided to pick this morning to not only give a surprise test (bloody B-minus), but also to go over our entire midterm paper in excruciating detail, like some of my old teachers at Qala Academy used to do. By the time I discovered that I got the fifth question wrong, I stopped keeping track.

"Well, he's not talking to me, is he? He's talking to you," I remind Alisha. "And you're way better than me at making friends anyway." Malcolm's hurt face flashes before my eyes. I didn't see him in English after our fight today and he hasn't responded to the text I sent him after school. The one time I screwed up the courage to call him, his phone went to voicemail. I didn't leave a message.

"That's true." My words seem to mollify Alisha slightly. "Hey! Emerald says I should get my arms and legs waxed for the second date. What do you think?"

Second date? She's *already* thinking of a second date? I try not to automatically glance at my own arms, which are covered with a fine dusting of hair. "Is this a thing now? Are we all supposed to do what Emerald says?"

Alisha frowns. "It's not that big a deal, you know. Many girls our age wax or shave."

"I know that!" A part of me realizes that I'm making this into a bigger deal than it probably is. But the sight of my best friend with her hair done, her eyebrows shaped into perfectly inverted check marks—

"*You're* the one who made fun of that matrimonial website," I finally say. "You always talked about not conforming to society's standards of beauty! Especially to impress a guy."

"So maybe I'm changing my mind! People are allowed to do that when they grow up. You should try it sometime."

She's mad, I tell myself. She doesn't mean what she's saying. But the words still sting.

"I gotta go do homework," I say before logging off. "I'm sure you can get all the advice you need from Emerald."

There. Let *her* see how it feels to be ditched. The satisfaction that comes with the petty thought is short-lived though and minutes later I'm feeling miserable again.

I pick up the phone and send her a text: I'm sorry I snapped at you like that. I had a bad day at school.

I wait for a few minutes, but no response. She hasn't read the message, either. I begin typing another.

I also fought with Malcolm and said some pretty mean things to him. Now he isn't speaking to me . . .

I pause and press backspace, watching each muddled thought, each letter flicker away into nothingness. What's the point of telling Alisha this? I'm the one who messed up things with

Malcolm, not her. And it still doesn't excuse the way I behaved in the face of her big news.

Even though Emerald Verghese knew about it before I did.

I take a deep breath and close my eyes. Alisha and I no longer live in the same country, let alone the same city. What's wrong if she makes a new friend in my absence? Alisha always had more friends than I did, always managed to balance her studies and social life without alienating anyone.

I think of Afrin's invitation again, reconsider my initial thoughts about not going. It isn't like Afrin is a stranger I met at the mall. I know her from my classes. I know she scored the only other A-plus on the *King Lear* essay. Not that the grade makes a real difference when it comes to trusting her.

Besides, I can always call a cab home if I don't like the party. Amma made me download the Uber app and program the numbers of every local cab company into my phone, in case there's a public transit shutdown or strike.

The door creaks behind me and my mother enters without knocking. "He never called. He said he would, but he didn't."

I look up to find Amma staring into the mirror, as if examining her face for flaws.

I hesitate for a second. "A girl at school invited me to a party tomorrow. At eight o'clock."

"Where is it?"

I dig into my pocket for the piece of paper. "Somewhere on Burnhamthorpe."

Her forehead smooths out again. "Oh, that is close."

It isn't; I've mapped it on Google. Burnhamthorpe is a long road and it will take me a little over an hour to get to the house by transit, about nineteen to twenty minutes if I take a cab. But my tongue freezes when it comes to telling my mother this. I do not trust her to say yes. I might only be a few months short of turning eighteen, but I am still micromanaged, unable to go anywhere without my mother's permission, without answering every little detail about the person I am going with.

So it surprises me when Amma does not even ask for Afrin's name. "Will the girl's parents be there?"

"Of course."

I have never been a good liar. Appa told me that I give myself away with the redness that creeps up my neck, the way I never meet anyone's eyes while telling the lie. But my mother doesn't even ask for Afrin's phone number to chat with her parents, when only months earlier she would have seen my heart beating through my chest, veins and all, the word *LIE* flashing cartoon-yellow at the center.

"That's good." Amma does not look at me. She does not even meet my gaze in the mirror. Her eyes have that elsewhere look they often do when she's thinking of other things. "It's about time you made some new friends."

I don't recognize the song that pulses somewhere in the heart of the house the taxi drops me off at. It's nearly as alien as the girl who stared back at me in my bathroom mirror this evening—one who wore skinny jeans, a cute top, and lip gloss, her arms smooth, newly shorn of hair.

"Are you sure this is the right place, miss?" the driver asks.

"Yes," I say, spotting the number on the mailbox. "This is the place."

It has to be. It surely isn't the barn we passed nearly two kilometers away, or the darkened building next door with the Zoroastrian Community Centre's logo on top.

This place, at least, looks relatively alive—a converted farm-house with lights burning in the windows, the area in front of it scattered with haphazardly parked cars. The cold pinches my ears, the winter cap forced on me by Amma securely zipped in the pocket of my coat. I speed walk to the front door and ring the bell. A boy opens it, his spiky hair so familiar that for a moment my heart skips a beat.

"Hey. Come on in."

No. They might be of the same height and build, but the boy in front of me does not have Malcolm's face, nor his trademark cocky grin.

"Susan!" a voice calls from the left. Afrin, her face shimmery with makeup, wearing a red dress that matches the highlights in her hair, and knee-high leather boots. "Let me take your coat."

I feel the boy's stare when I shrug off my coat and scarf, resisting the urge to cross my arms in front of my chest and cover up the lacy, somewhat see-through white top Amma got me for my birth-day in March, even though I'm wearing a camisole underneath.

Afrin insists on putting away my satchel as well. "Don't worry," she says, ignoring my protests. "Why don't you go get a drink?" She gestures to the boy who opened the door. "VJ can show you."

He raises a glass in my direction. "What would you like? We have beer, wine, vodka—"

"Sprite," I interrupt. "Or Coke."

VJ smirks and leads me farther inside, to the kitchen. He grabs a can from the fridge and hands it to me. "Glasses are on the table."

"Thanks."

I head back out into the living room. A chandelier hangs from the center of the sloping insides of the unfinished wooden roof, casting a dim orange glow over the bodies crammed inside. A pair of boys stand by the gas fireplace, talking.

As I move deeper into the room, I draw stares—unusual scrutiny for a girl who is used to being invisible unless her hand is raised to answer a question in class. I force myself to smile and awkwardly make my way to the couches lined up in the room's center, the brown leather cracked and peeling. I find a spot next to a boy and girl who are laughing together and nursing drinks in bright red plastic cups.

I try to concentrate on my surroundings. As far as parties go, this is worlds apart from the ones I've been to. The boys and girls aren't sitting in separate corners of the room, staring at one another and giggling. There are no adults hovering nearby, asking if we need more snacks or soft drinks. The couple next to me begins to make out. Across the room, a group of boys begin setting up shot glasses in a row across the bar.

While at other parties my fingers often sought out my sketchbook in boredom, at this one, it's really more due to nerves. My phone, my only other source of pretending to be occupied, is still in my satchel, along with the book. The realization makes me panic for a second. Amma made me promise to keep my phone with me at all times so she would know I was okay. If any texts go unanswered, I will be in big trouble when I get back home.

The chilly Sprite can sweats in my hand. I begin navigating through the living room crowd again, spying a streak of reddish-black hair disappearing into the kitchen, when my shoulder knocks into someone else, the impact sending a dull shaft of pain through the bone.

"Ho-*ly*. Susan Thomas, is that you?"

I press the still unopened can of Sprite to my shoulder and look up into Steve Patel's grinning face.

"Hi, Steve."

"I didn't know you knew Justin."

"I don't. Afrin was the one who invited me."

"Guess she's keeping her friends and enemies close these days."

"What?"

He blinks. "Nothing. Forget I said anything." He grins widely as if compensating for a faux pas.

"Is . . ." I clear my throat. "Was Malcolm invited?"

"Not by Afrin, at least." Steve laughs at his own joke. When I don't laugh in response, he sobers up quickly. "Justin probably invited him. They used to be friends, you know. Though now, with dating his ex . . ." Steve shrugs.

"So he's still not over her."

I want to slap my hands over my mouth. Or maybe use them to cover my face, which is now turning hot under Steve's gaze.

"I'm not sure," Steve says after a long pause. "Malcolm usually falls in and out of relationships pretty quickly, but I've never seen him fall as hard for anyone as he did for Afrin."

"Oh."

Steve shifts his weight from one foot to another. His gaze falls somewhere behind me. "Hey, there's Dave. I better go say hi. See you around, Susan."

"Bye, Steve."

It doesn't take a genius to realize that the conversation made him uncomfortable or that he found an excuse to ditch me. I can't blame him. I would ditch me myself. It's not like I'm that fun a person to be around.

When I finally spot Afrin exiting the kitchen, I do not ask her for my jacket or satchel. I allow her to pull me back into the living room, to the leather couch now populated with boys, and to jam a glassful of beer into my hand.

Malcolm

In a corner of my bedroom close to the ceiling, you can see the remains of leftover wallpaper, a design that involves blue skies, clouds, and cherubs—one I would have ripped up or covered with a poster without question if it wasn't for Mom, who insisted on keeping it there. "Now I can always be assured that an angel is watching over you," she told me.

A creepy, chubby angel with blue china-doll eyes and golden curls, whose beaming smile holds the hint of a sneer. After the years I've spent in this house, I've grown used to ignoring the angel for the most part. Except on days like this, when the girl I have a sort-of crush on decides I'm a loser, and the angel's sneer seems more pronounced.

Outside, the temperature has dropped by several degrees, but I open my window anyway and pull out the cigarette pack I always keep in the pocket of my jeans. Trees that I could've sworn were full a couple of days ago have now been stripped bare, the ground underneath littered with yellow and brown leaves. As the air outside my window puffs with smoke, I picture the angel's gold curls, imagine taping his mouth shut and plucking out each perfect lock.

"Hostile thought alert!" a voice sings out from somewhere behind me.

"Go away, Mahtab."

"Why? You're not doing anything. Except attempting slow suicide."

I ignore her and take another long drag. I'm pushing things by smoking in the house, especially after the old man banned it, but I know that Mahtab won't rat on me.

"Good thing it's not weed," she says. "Otherwise the room would've smelled like skunk for days."

I tap the butt into the air, allowing the ash to fall. "Quit exaggerating." I finally turn to face my sister, who is perched on the edge of my bed, right next to my unfinished math homework.

She rolls her eyes behind the wire-rimmed spectacles she wears at home when we have no company. "How come you're not out with your friends?"

I crush the last of the cigarette into the ashtray. "Ahmed has a family thing at his mosque."

Mahtab straightens and crosses an ankle over her knee. "What about Steve?"

"Steve's at Justin's. Partying." *And hopefully feeling guilty about it*, I add mentally. I know I'm being selfish, but it's not like Steve and Justin are friends anymore. Then again, Steve has never been able to resist a party. No matter who's throwing it.

"You know what's funny?" Mahtab rises from the bed. Her tone holds the sort of contempt she usually reserves for my ex-girlfriends or dictators from foreign countries. "How Ahmed and Steve actually managed to come to the meeting for the fund-raiser your sister has been telling—no, begging—you to come to over the past few weeks—" I feel the blood drain from my face as her words sink in. Crap. Crapcrapcrap. "—while her own brother completely *bailed* on her!" She gives me a shove that nearly makes me drop the cigarette butt.

"Mah, I'm sorry. I . . . I totally forgot."

Since Mom died, I've blown off people who were once my friends, messed up so many relationships that I've lost count. I've never looked back. Mahtab, though, is the one person in my life who I've never wanted to let down. My stomach clenches. Maybe the old man had it right. Maybe I *am* a screwup.

Mahtab rubs her upper arms with her hands. "It's cold in here. Will you at least close the window now that you've finished?"

A smoky smell still lingers in the room, but I pull the window back into place, cutting off the cold. Mahtab noisily blows air through her lips—the closest she can get to whistling her relief—and tucks her feet behind her. We both sit in frosty silence for a while.

"So." Mahtab breaks it again—a sign of a possible thaw. "How's your new friend, Susan?"

I remember the angry look on Susan's face and feel the pinch of her words again. "She's no friend of mine."

"What happened now? Did you two fight over crayons?" Okay, so maybe Mahtab hasn't quite forgiven me.

When I say nothing in response, Mahtab sighs. "Do you want to talk about it?"

"What's there to talk about?"

"Stop pretending to be stupid."

"She thinks that, too. That I'm stupid." The words spill out before I can stop them.

Mahtab blinks a couple of times. "Are you serious? She said that to you?"

"Well, not exactly," I admit. "But she implied it."

"Maybe she didn't mean what she said. People say all kinds of things when they're angry." But I can hear the doubt in Mahtab's voice. A doubt that solidifies the sick feeling in my gut.

"That's what Mom used to say about the old man."

Mahtab's lips tighten infinitesimally; she doesn't like it when I call our father that. In the silence that follows, I hear the disjointed laughter of our next-door neighbors. A motorcycle rumbles into someone's driveway. A police siren blares in the distance.

Mahtab lets out a breath that sounds like a sigh. "Susan is not like Afrin."

"I *know* she isn't—"

"And she's not like Dad, either," Mahtab interrupts. She has never stopped calling him that, never stopped hoping that one day things will change and that we will be a family once more. "What Susan said about you wasn't right. But she doesn't seem like someone who'd try to manipulate you or mess around with your head. I can bet that she tried contacting you after your fight. A text? A call? Something?"

I think back to the text on my phone screen: Can we talk? Followed by the missed-call notification I haven't yet managed to erase. Mahtab is right—manipulation isn't exactly Susan's game. It's impossible when nearly every thought she has shows up in her big brown eyes. Something in my face must have changed because Mahtab clicks her tongue in disapproval.

160

"Khodai!" she exclaims in Gujarati. "If I had a dime for the number of times you, Ahmed, and Steve have said awful stuff to each other and fought about it, I would be able to buy myself a new prom dress. At least let her explain her side of things. Give it a shot before you give up on her for good."

"There's nothing between us."

"But you want there to be something." Mahtab rises to her feet and walks to the door. "And I think she does, too."

———————————

I'm nearly asleep when my phone buzzes on the table. I pick up when I see Steve's face flashing on-screen.

"Hey man!" Steve shouts over the pounding music in the background. "It's your girl!"

"What are you talking about?" I ask in a groggy voice. Is he drunk already? "What girl?"

"Susan! They got her wasted, Afrin and the rest of them. She's throwing up in Justin's backyard."

A hundred questions run through my mind, centering around one: Who invited Susan to Justin's in the first place?

"Oh crap!" Steve says. "Now Afrin's snapchatting the whole thing."

I leap out of bed and grab my jacket. "I'll be right there."

———————————

"Where do you think you're going?"

My heart leaps to my throat. I had hoped to sneak out (with the car keys Freny always leaves lying around the house) unnoticed. But when I turn around, it's only Mahtab, in her *Star Wars* pajamas, scowling at me from the foot of the staircase.

I raise a finger to my lips. "Shhhh. Do you want to wake Frankenstein's monster and his bride?"

Mahtab's scowl deepens, but she lowers her voice. "Seriously, Malu, it's nearly midnight. What do you think you're doing, sneaking out this late?"

I know what she's thinking. She's remembering the other nights. The ones when I sneaked out the door, even my window, the nights when I came home reeking of booze, before my car privileges were finally taken away.

"It's Susan," I say. "She's at Justin's party. Drunk and throwing up, from what Steve told me."

"Susan's at Justin's?" Mahtab's face falls. "I didn't know she knew him!"

"Neither did I. But she's there. And Afrin's filming her right now and—"

"Wait." Mahtab pulls out the phone she always carries with her and slides her thumbs across the screen. "Crap. It's there on Afrin's Snapchat. She's throwing up."

I grit my teeth. Except for Facebook (which I deactivated), I deleted my own social media accounts earlier this summer after pics of Afrin and the other guy began making the rounds of Arthur Eldridge's gossip circuit. I don't know what game Afrin's playing now, but I don't want Susan involved in it. No matter how angry she made me today.

"I'll cover for you." Mahtab slips her phone back into her pocket.

"Thanks, sis."

"And Malc?"

"Yeah?"

"Please be careful."

Of the two of us, Mahtab takes the most after the old man.

Same brown hair. Same skin tone. Same nose and mouth, only smaller. But tonight, her lower lip trembles the way it used to when she was a little girl. The way Mom's did whenever she fretted over me.

"I will," I tell her. "I promise."

Susan

My insides churn. I feel the tug of fingers in my hair.

"I'm gonna title this one *Girl Vomiting on Grass*," I hear a voice say. Afrin. "Very artistic, no?"

In the background, her friends laugh like nails grating on a blackboard. I want to rip her hand out of its socket. I want to collapse on the grass. But I will likely end up falling in my own vomit. Somehow, I manage to stay on my knees, head angled over a bush, waiting for the world to stop spinning.

For a drinking game, it didn't even seem that crazy at first. "We call it Most Likely," Afrin explained to me. "Everyone gets a turn and they say 'most likely to do something.' Everyone points at someone else in the group. You have to take a drink for every person pointing at you."

Easy enough. I was sure none of these people would ever say

stuff like *Most likely to do her homework*. And they didn't. For a long time, my shot glass lay untouched, and I laughed with the rest, pointing fingers at whoever I thought was most likely to have had a crush on Vice Principal Han, or most likely to have gone skinny-dipping, or most likely to secretly cry during sad movies.

Then Afrin said, "Most likely to have a secret boyfriend," and seven fingers pointed at me.

Which was followed by, "Most likely to have a temper." Four more fingers.

It didn't matter what the truth was. In the game of Most Likely, results depended on the votes, and for each vote, I took a shot, the vodka burning down my throat. I never expected to be buzzing by shot four. Or dizzy by shot seven. By the time shot nine came along, I was so sick, I could barely stand.

"You're on camera, Susan," Afrin tells me now, her giggles barely suppressed. "Say cheese!"

If I was sober, I would tell her exactly what I think of her sense of humor. But I'm trying too hard to not fall right into my own puke.

A *tsk*ing sound in my ear. "Oh Susan. You should have known to eat a little before drinking so much."

"Hey, stop it, will you?" A voice that's both familiar and not, from somewhere in the distance.

"Loosen up, Steve. It's not like this is the first time you've seen someone throw up after a few drinks."

"It isn't a party without a dizzy girl," another voice says. A hand creeps up my calf, almost ticklish in its ascent. I try to kick it off.

"Hey!" Afrin's voice takes on a sudden sharpness. "Back off, VJ."

The smack of flesh on flesh. The fingers in my hair loosen, then release. An argument breaks out somewhere above. Footsteps crunch the drying leaves in the backyard and a hand tentatively brushes my shoulder.

"You okay, Susan?" For the first time since I've known him, Steve sounds scared. My vision begins to clear again and I see my coat and, thank heaven, my bag in his hands.

"Do you want a ride home?" he asks, almost desperately.

"No," I manage to say, shrugging on my coat again. Dizzy though I am, I'm pretty sure Steve has knocked down more than a couple of drinks tonight. "I'll call a cab."

"Are you sure? I can—"

My stomach lurches again and I rise on unsteady feet. "No," I insist. "I'm fine."

Well, that's a lie. But it'll be hard enough to explain the smell of booze and vomit on my breath to my mother, as is.

My mother.

I want to hurl again even though I'm pretty sure there's nothing left in me to spit out.

Steve mentions Malcolm's name. Malcolm, who's not even here. Who'll laugh when he finds out what happened, the way Afrin's friends are laughing now.

I grab my bag from Steve's hands and stumble back into the still-pulsing house.

I am not sure how I manage to find my way to the front door and outside. Or if the woman at the cab company even understood the address I slurred out to her. When I try to look at the time or the missed notifications on my phone, my vision goes blurry again. I sit on the front steps, the stone cold against the back of my jeans. A few feet away I hear laughter and the now familiar sound of

166

hacking. It makes me want to throw up again so I bury my head in my arms. It's only the feel of hands, warm and oddly familiar on my shoulders, that makes me look up, right into the gray centers of his otherwise dark eyes.

Malcolm's mouth moves before his voice reaches my ears. "Susan? Susan, are you okay?"

My heart zigs and then zags at the hard tone of his voice. If there is a spot in the ground somewhere untouched by vomit, I want to sink right through it.

"Go away, Malcolm."

Naturally he doesn't listen and kneels right in front of me.

"Did anyone hurt you?" he demands. "Susan, talk to me!"

"No." I try not to think of the strange hand creeping up my thigh. "I don't need saving, Malcolm Vakil. I'm fine."

I try to rise to my feet to make this point and promptly trip over the step's broken edge. Somehow Malcolm manages to hold me in place without falling over.

"You're not." The brush of his mouth on my ear almost feels like a kiss.

No, I'm not. I know this. But for some reason I still want to argue this point. My body, however, has other ideas and happily sinks into an embrace that smells like leather and cigarettes and boy—a sweaty musk that is uniquely Malcolm. For a long moment, I hear nothing except the sound of his breath in my ear and I am not sure if the silence around me is because of his presence or simply the result of my mind shutting down now that it knows it's safe.

"Come on," he says quietly. "Let me take you home."

I'm about to answer—yes or no, I don't know which—when a car horn sounds behind Malcolm, followed by the sound of tires on gravel. I pull away, seeing the dull glow of a roof light on a dark blue sedan.

"Taxi for Susan Thomas!" a man calls out from the driver's seat.

My mouth goes dry. I can feel Malcolm watching me.

"Are you Susan Thomas, miss?" the cabbie prods.

"No," I tell him. "I'm not."

It's not entirely a lie. The Susan Thomas I know would have never gone to a party like this, let alone get drunk. The Susan Thomas I know would be at home, fast asleep, homework complete, ahead of the class in every course.

This time when Malcolm holds out a hand, I don't resist. We trudge along the perimeter of the house, nearly stumbling over something on the ground—a can that he kicks out of the way. As we reach the car, a series of electronic sounds pound my ears. Malcolm's grip on my shoulder tightens before he reaches into his pocket for his phone.

"Hey," he murmurs. "Yeah, Mahtab. I found her. Gonna take her home. Make sure you stall in case the old man or Freny wake up, okay?"

What time is it, I wonder. Way past Amma's bedtime for sure.

The cars are covered with a film of dew. I want to rest my cheek against one and cool my hot face. Why, oh why did I ever listen to those girls?

"It happens to the best of us," Malcolm says, and I know that I spoke the thought out loud.

"How come you're here?" I ask, common sense finally catching up with me. "How did you know?"

"Steve called. Luckily, I live only ten minutes away by car. Or maybe seven minutes based on how I was driving. Good thing I didn't run into any cops. Or wake the old man and my stepmom."

There's a note of amusement in his voice that makes me want to laugh as well. But then I think of my own father and what he would say if he saw me now. "I'm sick."

Malcolm holds me close, lets me tuck my nose into his collarbone. "Let's take you home."

By the time we get home, it's after midnight, there are over twenty missed calls and even more unread text messages from my mother. Malcolm insists on taking me up the elevator to our apartment.

"Susan? Suzy?" Amma's panic would make someone think that I am on my deathbed. She helps me onto the couch and places a too-hot hand over my head. "Lord, what have they done to you?"

"She's okay, Mrs. Thomas." Malcolm's voice is soft, but sure. "I think she drank a little too much."

"Drank? My Suzy doesn't drink!"

"I'm sorry, Mrs. Thomas. I got there as soon as I could and brought her home."

"I see."

The chill in Amma's voice is unmistakable. It makes me shiver to hear it and yet I want to laugh. Wasn't this one of the few things my parents had argued about and Amma had worried over, before we left Jeddah? That I would change. That I would become Westernized and lose my way.

Malcolm says a few more things, but I can no longer decipher his words. I think I manage to murmur "Good night" before sinking deep into the couch's pillows and falling asleep.

The morning sun drills holes into my eyes, while the leftover effects of the alcohol drum through my head.

"Amma?" I say groggily. And then foolishly: "Malcolm?"

"The boy is not here. I sent him home last night."

A large glass of water appears before me with a Tylenol. "Drink this."

I wrinkle my nose at the first sip—the water has been mixed with bubble-gum flavored electrolytes. But I swallow the pill and drink the brew without complaint. It is the least—maybe the only thing—I can do right now to appease my mother who is standing over me, still wearing her flowered cotton nightgown and knitted blue sweater from last night. I take a deep breath, pick out traces of lemon Pledge, steamed rice, sugar, and coconut.

"You will need breakfast, too, I suppose."

"I can't eat." The thought of eating anything makes me feel ill.

"Oh, but you will," she says firmly. "You will start with a banana first. If you can keep it down, then I will give you some of the sweet puttu I made this morning."

Trust Amma to pour on the guilt and simultaneously offer the incentive of my favorite breakfast item.

"I'm sorry, Amma."

"Sorry? Sorry! Do you even know what you put me through? How worried I was for you?"

I rub my temple with a pair of fingers. "I'm sorry. I didn't . . . I wasn't thinking."

She sits down next to me on the couch. "Did someone do anything to you?"

"What?"

"Did someone touch you at that party? Did you do something with a boy?"

"Are you asking if I had sex?" My voice fills with anger, even though I know I have no right to be angry. "I . . . God, Amma, I haven't even kissed a boy!"

I try not to think of that boy VJ and his creeping hands. Or my tormentor-turned-savoir, Afrin Irani, who unexpectedly kept him at bay.

"What about that one? The one who brought you home?" my mother accuses. "Who is he?"

"Amma, please. Malcolm is a friend."

Malcolm, the boy who does not answer my texts when he's mad, but still comes to my rescue when I get drunk at a party and brings me home. I don't know what to make of him either.

"Those clothes he was wearing." Amma's mouth thins. "And that horrible hair. Who does he think he is, some kind of gangster?"

I curse in my head, the only way I can do so in my mother's presence. "Amma, he's not a gangster! Many boys dress like that. It's fashion."

But the words I do speak fall on deaf ears. When Amma saw Malcolm, she did not simply see his clothes and his hair. She also saw the way I looked at him and the way he looked at me.

"I don't want you mixing with these people, Susan. They are not your true friends. No real friend would treat you the way these people did."

I know she is right. And it makes me furious.

"Well, maybe I went to them because I don't *have* friends. I never did. Even in Jeddah."

"You had Alisha."

"Yeah, I had Alisha. *Only* Alisha. No one else could stand me. And you know why? It's because of you! Because you kept saying that my studies should be my number one priority. Because I was terrified of disappointing you even when I was topping my class. Well, I hope you're satisfied now. Now I have no one over here either!"

I stalk to my room, ignoring her shouts, the cloying taste of bubble-gum still on my tongue.

———————————

To my surprise, Amma does not punish me the way she would have in Jeddah—with extra housework or taking away my phone, computer, and television privileges. Neither does she tell my father about what happened. She remains silent and sullen for the whole weekend, hardly saying anything during mealtimes, even though I can feel her watching me at moments, tracking my every move.

The video of me vomiting in the bushes behind Justin Singh's house is now on YouTube. VJ and his friends make puking sounds when I pass them by in the school hallways on Monday. At the end of second period, I find a piece of paper at the bottom of my locker: a drawing of a stick-figure boy peeing on a vomiting stick-figure girl.

I crumple the paper into a ball and then uncrumple it before ripping it to shreds. Even though I'm pretty sure they slid the paper in through one of the locker's vents, I change my lock's combination. I don't see much point in vents, though Heather tells me that they exist to air out the odor left behind by gym clothes or smelly food. Most times, however, Heather says they're used as mail slots for love notes.

I think of the note Malcolm wrote me in the library right before midterms—one that, instead of throwing away, I triple folded and zipped carefully into one of my binder's many pockets. Malcolm hasn't spoken to me since he dropped me off at my house. I haven't spoken to him either, my tongue self-gluing to the roof of my mouth whenever he pauses next to his locker to take out his books, barely acknowledging me with a nod. In English class, it's even worse because he ignores me completely, not even looking at me when I pass him a handout. Whenever this happens, I inevitably find Afrin watching us both and smirking in a way that makes me want to rip out her hair.

It's good that Malcolm's ignoring me, I tell myself. His disinterest can only lead to Afrin's disinterest and, after that video, a low profile is something I should be actively seeking. It certainly shouldn't feel like someone kicked me in the gut every time he talks and flirts with another girl. It shouldn't feel like I lost a friend.

On Tuesday, Amma finally enters my room.

"Your appa is coming here in ten days! And he'll be spending Christmas break with us." Shadows circle her eyes: a side effect of the insomnia that has affected both of us.

I feel something inside me unclench. In spite of myself, I begin to smile. "Really? He's coming? For the whole of Christmas break?"

Amma smiles back. "Yes, he is. Maybe even longer. He hasn't booked his return ticket yet. It's not as good as a permanent move, but . . . look here: He sent me the ticket confirmation."

I read the itinerary on my mother's phone. Appa's flight arrives next Friday at 1:00 p.m. Right in time for the midterm report cards. I suppress a groan. I'll also be in school at the time and won't have the chance to meet him at the airport. But then—

"He will be *here*," I say out loud. "Finally!" My father will finally be with us. What else is more important?

Amma widens her eyes like a Bharatanatyam dancer. "I know, eh!" she declares in such a perfect imitation of our building's property manager that I begin giggling. Which, of course, makes Amma giggle as well. Before I know it, we are no longer mother and daughter, but a pair of girls, who have, in some odd way, made up for the fight we had last week.

"Sorry, Amma," I say, when I catch my breath. "Sorry for yelling."

"You terrified me, Susan. I did not know what happened to you. I had so many terrible thoughts."

I wince, feeling horrible again.

"I'm sorry, too." Amma sits down next to me on the bed. "It's difficult. Letting go of you. Not having your appa around to help me."

"I know."

For as long as I've known, Appa has always helped smooth out the rough patches in my relationship with Amma, always been the bond that held us together when things got tough. Unlike Amma, I've never liked talking about the empty space he's created by leaving us here by ourselves. Or about how terribly I missed him.

"I'm so glad he's coming back." I rest my head on her shoulder. "I hope he comes here to live with us for good."

It isn't until I'm getting ready for school, minutes later, that I realize it's the first time I've ever expressed a wish to stay here instead of moving back to Saudi Arabia.

———

Alisha and I became what she likes to call BFBA or Best Friends by Accident. "If we'd not been seated together that first day in kindergarten, I'm pretty sure I would've never talked to you," she always says.

I, on the other hand, feel we became friends because of AP. Alisha's Persistence. Always including me in the games the kids played during recess. Offering to trip Emerald Verghese for laughing at me when I fell down the stairs in Class II. I never knew what Alisha saw in me back then.

"You are LTAF," she said once when I asked. Loyal to a Fault.

I'm not sure how true this is, but Alisha says it is exactly why I have such a hard time making new friends. "You're afraid of growing close to people. You wall up so that you don't get hurt."

Or hurt people in return, I think. Alisha still hasn't responded to my old texts. Or the new ones I sent on Saturday, Sunday, and Monday. This morning, before my first class, I lock myself in a bathroom cubicle and leave her a long—and admittedly sappy—voicemail.

"I miss you," I say. I never wanted to lose my best friend over something as trivial as a new makeover or a new friendship.

Malcolm's still ignoring me, of course. I wish others would do the same. When I walk in the halls, girls burst into giggles behind me, boys pretend to gag and throw up—or worse, ask me for my number so that they can get me drunk.

It happens again in physics, when a boy in the front row murmurs something about how he'd like to douse me—all of me—in beer so that he can see me better. Mr. Franklin still isn't here so I allow my hand to slide up his desk, rip out the first four pages from his open binder, and—*thud*—knock his textbook to the ground.

A moment of dead silence in which I ask him, my voice feather soft: "What did you say?"

He makes his body smaller in a way I imagine boys do after

being kneed in the groin. "N-nothing. I didn't say anything." Whispers break out again, along with scattered laughter.

"Nice work," a voice says from behind me.

I turn around to face the source, and recognize the Indian girl Heather Dupuis hangs out with. Long black hair, dusky skin, a cranberry-tinted pout, and a tight sweater that hugs the well-defined muscles of her arms. I have a feeling that if this girl was in my place, it would have been the catcaller on the floor, not his textbook.

"Some boys have big mouths, don't they?" She grins, eyes crinkling at the corners. "I'm Preeti, by the way. Preeti Sharma."

"Hi," I say, when I get over the surprise of her addressing me. "I'm Susan Thomas."

"I know," she tells me. "Heather has told me about you and your super memory."

I feel my heartbeat slow to its normal pace. I smile back. "Nice to meet you, Preeti."

Her grin widens. "Wow! Finally someone who pronounces my name right on the first try. Everyone over here calls me 'Pretty.' Which isn't the worst way to say a name, I guess, but . . ." She shrugs her shoulders.

I laugh. Preeti's comment reminds me of something Alisha once said—*If you want to make friends, learn to laugh at yourself.*

I clear my throat. "Wanna hear what my old physics teacher used to call me?"

———————————

I head to my usual spot by the stairs for lunch, even though it's beginning to feel like the inside of a fridge whenever I step outdoors.

"I have some homework," I tell Preeti and Heather when they

176

invite me to join them in the cafeteria. It's not a lie, really. It's quieter on the steps than in the lunchroom. It's not like I'm hoping to see someone else here.

"No distractions," I whisper.

I'm trying to read *Alias Grace*, the novel we've been assigned after midterms, but after staring at the same paragraph for ten minutes, I decide to put it away. I pull out my calculus problem set instead . . . and end up doodling a pair of giant eyes weeping heart-shaped tears in the margins of my binder, right over a skinny, big-eyed cat that looks far too depressed to be cute.

"Ugh."

I flip over my pencil and have begun erasing the drawing when my phone vibrates in my coat pocket. A Skype-to-Skype audio call. I stare at the caller's name on-screen, fumble for a few seconds before answering, praying she doesn't hang up.

"Hel—"

"Are you trying to make me cry, you idiot?" Alisha does sound like she's sniffing a bit. Though that could be a cold. "I heard your voice message. Suzy, I'm sorry I said those things to you—"

"I'm sorry, too," I cut in. "I don't want us to be mad at each other anymore."

Which is true. But there's more.

"If I get mad at you for making a few changes, I'm only being a hypocrite." I tell her about the fight I had with Malcolm, Afrin's invitation, the party—and what happened after.

"Holy fudgy falooda." There's a long silence from Alisha's end. "I . . . have no words for this."

"I know. It was stupid."

"Maybe. But then, what's the point of being human if you can't do stupid things every once in a while?"

The knot in my stomach loosens. "Did your guy, Isaac Cherian, tell you that?"

"He's not *my* guy, yet. I mean, we barely even talked that day. He asked for my number though and we've been chatting through texts."

"Ooooooooh."

"Stop that, goof." But I can hear the grin in her voice. "We're meeting again on Friday at Emerald's house. Her mom's hosting a potluck."

After the terrible weekend I had, the annoyance I feel on hearing Emerald's name barely registers. "Will you tell me what happens after?"

"Of course! Though don't expect anything major with the chaperones lurking around. Anyway, forget about that, you need to tell me what's happening with Malcolm now. Did you two kiss and make up already?"

"We're only friends, Alisha! Or *were* friends. He isn't talking to me. I think he's still mad about the stuff I said before."

"Well, have you *talked* to him the way you're talking to me now? Texts don't count."

I say nothing for a long moment. The idea of apologizing to Malcolm the way I did to Alisha makes me feel uncomfortable. Exposed in ways I'm not used to.

"What if he rejects me?" What if he decides he doesn't want to be my friend anymore?

"Then it's his loss, isn't it—to lose the most LTAF person I know?"

I feel a smile break through. "Are we still using those cheesy acronyms?"

"Well, duh. They're too weird to use with anyone else."

"Even Emerald?"

"Especially Emerald."

Now I'm grinning fully and, even though I can't see her, I know Alisha is as well. "Oh, Alisha?"

"Yeah?"

"Try shaving your arms for the second date. It's way more painless than waxing."

Now or never. Now or never.

After my talk with Alisha, I chant the words over and over, pepping myself up to go talk to Malcolm. I write the apology on a piece of paper. Memorize it, so that I won't forget exactly what I'm supposed to be saying. I can do things differently. I can text Malcolm again. Friend him on Facebook. After weeks of not seeing a trace of him on social media, Malcolm has suddenly begun to appear on my list of People You May Know. Deep down, though, I know a typed apology isn't going to cut it.

Overhead, clouds gather, their undersides tinged gray. Lightning flashes in the distance, and I wonder if the sky is mocking me already as I slip out of the art classroom's alternate exit and make my way to what Arthur Eldridge calls a track—even though it isn't really a track at all, but a large patch of grass surrounded by a ring of mud imprinted with cigarette butts and footprints.

My heartbeat quickens when I see him, standing in the center of the field with a couple of guys I don't know, wearing his trademark jeans and a loose Blue Jays jersey under a puffy black jacket. His hair isn't in spikes today and flops over his forehead, a dark mess of waves. My fingers curl in reflexively and I almost convince myself to turn, leaving things as they are, to push back apologizing to a day when I'm better prepa—

179

His gaze locks with mine.

—too late.

As tempted as I am to run off, now that he's watching me, his features growing stiff with surprise, I know this is it.

Now or never.

I paste what feels like a smile onto my face and walk across the yellowing grass. My sneakers sink into the softened ground, make a squelching sound at one point. I grimace, hoping I haven't stepped into something gross. By the time I reach Malcolm, the other boys are watching the two of us with ill-concealed curiosity.

"Hi." I tuck a strand of hair behind my ear. "Can I talk to you?"

He frowns slightly, and for a moment I think he's going to say no and call me Vomit Girl like everyone else. But then he nods and looks at the other guys. "Later."

"Later," the boys say. One of them smiles at me before leaving.

If I thought it would get easier without two other sets of eyes gawking at us, I was wrong. Especially when a lock of hair falls over his eyes and he doesn't push it away, giving me the insane urge to do it myself. Malcolm's gaze flicks to my mouth and back up.

"You want to *talk*?" The sarcasm in his voice is enough to bring me out of my haze.

"I . . . I want to say I'm sorry. I shouldn't have said the things I told you last week. It was completely wrong and out of line." After the Vomiting Video Debacle, a B-minus on a test feels like a blessing. "I also wanted to thank you for . . . you know."

He gives me a cool look. "No. I don't, actually."

Blood rushes to my cheeks. I know he's torturing me. I also know that I probably deserve it.

"For taking me home. I don't know what I was thinking,

accepting the invitation to that party. I thought she wanted to be friends." I try to laugh if off even though I want to sink into the ground for making the assumption.

Malcolm is no longer smirking. "Did someone mix something into your drink?" he asks, a hard edge creeping into his quiet voice.

"No. No, that was me. I mean, the beer tasted bad so I didn't drink much. But the vodka . . . We were playing a drinking game," I admit.

His eyebrows shoot up.

"What?" Why is *he* acting so surprised? "I wanted to try something new. I mean, I know I'm not a fun person to be around. Afrin said the alcohol would loosen me up."

"That's ridiculous."

I feel myself bristle. "You don't have to lie. I know you think of me the same way."

"I did. For a while." Malcolm sighs. "But maybe that was a mistake to begin with. Me thinking about someone in a certain way doesn't always make it right. Sometimes it makes me judgmental."

Shame rises, hot across the back of my neck. "I judged you, too." Might as well admit it. "And I'm sorry for that."

He stares at me for a long moment, as if weighing the sincerity of my words. "It's okay. You were upset."

"There was no excuse for me to—"

"Susan." A step forward and he's inches away, his breath warm against my cheek. His hand slides around the back of my neck, gently nudging my head upward. "Stop apologizing."

Noses collide. Faces tilt. The world narrows to a pair of lips. Breath. To heat unfolding under cold hands.

The earth pauses for a brief second. Then spins a tiny bit faster.

The sky rumbles over our heads. A drop of rain plunks on my head, then two. We break apart, gasping like we've been kissing for hours, when it was probably only a few minutes. I retrieve my fingers, which were buried in his hair.

"Do you know there's a smell that they associate with rain?" I tell him.

"Really?" His nostrils flare and I would laugh at his reaction if not for the way he's staring at me. Like he would devour me whole if he could.

Before I can answer, it begins to pour down on us, the wind swirling the drops like a secret dervish. We run for cover, under the branches of a big oak on the perimeter of the field, Malcolm's wet hand in mine, his breath warm on my neck when we finally stop under the branches, not entirely out of range, but still less exposed to the elements. His other hand slides down my elbow and lightly clasps my wrist, as if feeling the pulse there. I wonder if he knows how quickly it's going. Eighty-two, maybe a hundred now that I can feel his chin resting on my shoulder.

"Yeah." My voice comes out shaky, but I'm determined to answer the question. "It's called petrichor. 'Petra,' which is Greek for rock or earth. 'Ikhor,' which means the blood of the gods. It's probably just sweat," I add. He laughs softly, then presses a kiss behind my ear that nearly brings me to my knees.

"In North India, they bottle the scent up and sell it as perfume.

'Mitti attar,' they call it." A rain scent encapsulated by the soil, by the boy whose arms now bracket mine.

His hands move up to my shoulders and turn me around. "Susan," he says.

"Yes?"

"I really want to kiss you again."

"Okay."

The word barely slips out before his lips are on mine, and I imagine that he's found a way to capture it with his tongue. It gently traces my lower lip, while his right hand slides up my neck and into my hair.

Malcolm isn't as tall his friend Ahmed, who is at least six four. But to kiss him, I need to tilt my head up, need to balance on my toes so that I can fully reach his lips. As if sensing this, he presses my back to the tree and slides his other hand under my wet jacket, under my T-shirt, resting cold against the dry skin of my stomach, which goose bumps at his touch.

When we break free, our mouths hot, nearly as wet as our clothes, he brushes a thumb over my cheek and grins. Raindrops cling to his lashes, turning them into spiky clusters.

Amma may not have punished me for getting drunk at Afrin's party. But I am not foolish enough to think I will be so lucky a second time around. Not when it comes to a boy. A boy who isn't Malayali or Christian.

As if sensing my turmoil, Malcolm gently taps the center of my forehead. "Stop overthinking," he teases. "This is not a math problem. Just go with the flow."

And when he kisses me again, that's what I do.

Malcolm

It's funny how easily we fall together after that kiss.
Holding hands. Sneaking kisses between classes. I smell hints of
cardamom, coffee, and freshly cut grass on her skin.

Susan refuses to see me outside school: "It's my parents. I'm not
allowed to date."

But I know there's more to it than that. I saw it in Mrs. Thomas's
eyes the one and only time I took Susan home, the hard lines of
disapproval on her face, which looks so much like Susan's. I can
sense it in the stiffness of Susan's posture whenever I tease her about
inviting me home as her English project partner.

So I kiss Susan every chance I get. I kiss her until her lips are
swollen and pink. I pour everything into our kisses: anger, frustration, longing, and something else, something that skips and

pulses under my ribs whenever I see Susan waiting for me by our lockers or giving me a shy smile.

When I kiss Susan, I can, for a few brief moments, forget our differences, wipe away every bad memory.

The Friday after our first kiss, we're making out (again) in the empty hall next to the art classroom. "Want to skip school?" she asks, once we catch our breath.

"Don't you have classes?" Based on how things blew up between us last week I'm surprised that she'd want to miss a single minute of them.

"It's only art. It's not that important." She frowns slightly at the wall behind us: a mural of Arthur Eldridge painted by some students years ago. "But if you have something important to do—"

"I don't. It's only phys ed." When it comes down to choosing between bouncing a basketball around the gym and kissing Susan, I'll know I'll choose the latter. Always.

"Want to come over to my place?" I ask at the bus stop. "I have a new game on my Xbox."

Okay. I have no plans for us to play video games. But everyone will be out at this time of the day and we'll have the place to ourselves to . . . do whatever. Even though I doubt we'll go any further than kissing. Unlike Justin and some guys on the basketball team, quick hookups aren't my thing and I'm pretty sure our kiss on Tuesday was Susan's first. In fact, I expect Susan to refuse me right now, but surprisingly, she doesn't.

Not that it helps because when we do reach my house, we find Freny there, standing right next to the mudroom, taking off her leaf-caked boots.

"What are you doing home so early?" My stepmother glances at Susan and then stares at me. "Shouldn't you both be at school?"

"School let out early because of a fire alarm." Susan raises her eyebrows disbelievingly behind Freny. I shrug. Someone has to say something, especially with Freny back home way earlier than I expected her to be.

"This is Susan," I tell Freny now. "My—"

"Girlfriend!" Freny's lips form an O and she claps gleefully. "Of course! I should have known from the dreamy way you've been acting all week!"

Dreamy? *Me?*

I glance at Susan, whose eyes have widened with alarm. But neither of us bothers correcting Freny. In fact, it's probably one of the few times that one of my stepmother's instant assumptions about my life doesn't exactly annoy me.

"So sorry, dear." Freny turns to face Susan. "Look at her, she's terrified of me! Let's start over again, shall we? I'm Freny. How are you?"

"Fine, thank you, Aunty." Susan, who seems to have recovered from her initial shock, gives Freny a shy smile.

The way she greets Freny startles me for a second before I remember that Susan wasn't born here. She knows that every desi adult who isn't a parent or teacher must be called Uncle or Aunty, even if they're unrelated to you.

Freny's normally nonexistent cheeks pop up like plums on her bony face. "Are you from India?"

"Yes, Aunty. I was born in Mumbai, but our family is originally from Kochi."

It's like the floodgates suddenly open and my plans of kissing

Susan dissolve into an hour-long journey of recollecting Mumbai—the markets, the food, the landmarks—even though Susan has only ever visited India during vacations and Freny hasn't been back since she married the old man.

"God, I thought she'd never shut up!" I tell Susan later, when Freny leaves the living room to take a phone call.

"Sorry we bored you." Susan's mouth trembles as if suppressing a smile. "She isn't that bad, Malcolm."

"Tell that to someone whose family she didn't destroy to make a place for herself in," I say bitterly.

There's a pause before Susan speaks again. "What happened? To your mom, I mean."

"Osteosarcoma. Bone cancer. It hit her shortly after I was born. When I was a kid, I didn't know why she used a cane or why she took so much medication. It was only later that she told me. By the time I was fourteen, though, the tumors had spread through most of her lower leg and they had to amputate it."

I'll get better, she used to tell Mahtab and me before every new treatment plan, before every surgery. *I'll beat the cancer and we'll be a family again.*

"She always blamed herself." My tongue feels too thick. "For her marriage breaking down."

Susan's fingers link through mine and tighten. Freny's voice echoes in disjointed fragments from the kitchen.

"At least I have Mahtab," I say now. Speaking of which—"Crap, it's Friday!"

"Is this a new version of TGIF?"

"No, it's my sister. She has another meeting today for that fundraising concert. I totally bailed on her last week. And . . ." I glance

187

at the date on my phone and groan. "I'm supposed to be working at Michelle's later this afternoon. I can't believe I forgot to fix my schedule this week with Jay!"

"Can you get someone else to switch shifts with you?" Susan's calm voice cuts through my panic.

I think for a bit. "I guess I can ask the other barista, Meg. She's a pain to deal with. But it's worth a try." I send Meg a text and after some negotiating—u cover for me for the whole Sunday not half, she insists—an agreement falls into place. I grimace. Not like I have much to do this weekend anyway.

I turn to Susan. "Come to the meeting with me. Mahtab says there's still room for more fund-raising directors."

Susan draws her socked foot in a line across the carpet. "I don't know. I'll have to ask my mom for permission. Besides, I'm not like you or Mahtab. I can't think quickly or talk to people the way you guys do. I'll probably only end up doing more harm than good."

"That's bull. You're, like, the smartest person I know." But even as I say the words, I know that they're not going to convince her. "I'm sure there's other stuff you can do."

Susan's still staring at the floor. "Maybe I'll come to the next meeting."

A pause before I say, "Sure."

I can tell she isn't going to come. But I don't want to get into a fight right now. Not when I've discovered what she tastes like. Or how it feels to have a girl like me for being myself—Malcolm—without any calculation.

"I should get going." Susan rises to her feet. She waves at Freny, who's still busy talking on the phone in the kitchen. Freny waves back.

I follow Susan to the door, where she slips into her sneakers. "I guess, I'll, uh, show you my video game another time."

Susan finally turns to look at me. "Malcolm."

"Yeah?"

"I think we both know I don't play video games."

Before I've had time to fully register that statement, she presses her lips to mine. The world shifts. Stops. I feel the kiss long after she pulls away and flashes me a wicked, un-Susan-like grin before running to catch the bus back home, ponytail flying behind her.

What I learn from my first meeting for the benefit concert Ronnie and my sister are organizing:

(a) There are more people on the committee than I expected—including my two best friends.

(b) The art director's Vincent Tran. Ace athlete. Ace student. Tran has so many aces up his sleeve and so many chicks on each arm that most guys I know secretly hate his guts.

(c) The committee still doesn't have the funds needed to rent a decent venue for the concert.

"Some of you have been wondering what the VIP liaison position entails." Mahtab picks off exactly where Ronnie left off, and I wonder if it's a couple thing or if they practiced this in advance. My sister grins. "I'm happy to say that we've been working with a couple of aid organizations and they've agreed to bring in twelve special guests, ten of them kids between the ages five to ten—from Syria!"

There's a moment of silence and then a "Whoa!" Laughter and applause break out.

"That is really a great idea," Vincent Tran says, his dimples flashing. "I'd love to help—if no one else wants the position!"

"That's wonderful!" Mahtab's eyes take on that sickeningly dreamy look every girl I know gets whenever Tran speaks. "In fact, I think you and Yusuf Shire would be perfect for this job!"

As she continues to talk, I notice Ronnie—normally the most cheerful person in the room—glaring at Tran. It's probably why when my sister's boyfriend approaches me a moment later, I don't react with my usual sarcasm.

"Malc. Great to see you here." Ronnie pinches the bridge of his nose under his glasses—a thing he does when he's nervous. "Mahtab's so excited."

I nod. "What do you want me to do?"

"Get more sponsors. Look, there's Isabel Abanda." Ronnie points out a pretty girl with black curls and deep brown skin. "Her mom works at the Board of Trade. She got a couple of member organizations to sponsor us and cover the fees of the high school choir and some of the admin costs. But we still need cash to rent the venue. Can you approach the coffee shop you work at?"

Talk about direct. While I'm a tiny bit annoyed that Ronnie specifically targeted me with Michelle's in mind, I have to admire him for his pushiness.

"Michelle's Coffee House isn't Tim Hortons. You'll probably not get the big bucks that you need," I warn him. Also, the owner, Michelle is notoriously stiff with money. The biggest raise I've ever seen her give anyone was Jay—a single dollar added to his hourly wage after he had worked there for five years.

"Can you ask her, though?"

"I can try."

"Great! That's all we want really." But the worry lines don't disappear from Ronnie's forehead and I'm flooded with a strange sense of guilt. I'm about to ask him if there are other places, other people he'd also like me to approach, when Mahtab calls for everyone's attention again.

"Okay, so we still need a name for the concert! A good one, please!" She glares at Steve who gives her a sheepish grin. "We need to vote on this today so that Vincent can start designing the posters."

Steve's the first to throw out a suggestion, probably trying to make up for whatever he said at the last meeting: "A Night of Music!"

"That's too generic," Isabel points out.

"A Helping Hand from Canada to Syria!"

"Too long," Ronnie mutters next to me.

"Songs for Syria!" Ahmed shouts.

"Homecoming!"

I can see from Mahtab's face that she's not entirely happy with any of these suggestions, though she doesn't strike down any of them. I glance at the newspaper Ronnie brought in again, thinking about the images that flash on our screens nearly every day. *It's not propaganda*, I told the woman in the coffee shop. *It's someone's life.*

"How about To Syria, with Love?" I say when there's a brief lull.

I know I'm on the right track when I see the smile on Ronnie's face, the nods from the others, including Vincent Tran.

"That one's perfect, actually," Isabel says. "Simple and effective."

It's Mahtab I'm looking at, though. My sister, whose beaming gaze finally meets mine when the votes are cast and my suggestion wins by a landslide.

Susan

Somewhere, I'm sure there is a rule set by the universe—or maybe it's in a chain email—where you get ten years of bad luck if you don't tell your best friend absolutely everything about your very first kiss.

A part of me still wants to hold on to the girl Alisha knows, the one who called boyfriends overrated. What's happening between Malcolm and me is so strange, so *new*, that I barely understand it myself. It's why I keep the first kiss (and the others that follow) secret for four whole days, terrified of the minefield of questions that my best friend will likely bombard me with: *Is it a casual thing or is he your boyfriend? Are you going to go on birth control? Does Aruna Aunty know?*

Amma knows nothing about the kiss, of course. By luck, I even managed to intercept the school's recorded call about my absence from art class on Friday, telling my mother it was a wrong number. But I know I can't keep such a big secret from my best friend.

When Alisha and I finally fix a time to Skype on Saturday, an hour after my morning driving lesson with Joseph, my palms are sweating, even though a part of me is looking forward to seeing Alisha's eyes bug out and her jaw drop when I tell her.

"Hey!" I say when Alisha appears on-screen. "What's new?"

"Not much." Alisha's voice, far from bubbling over with its usual energy is flat. Dull. "Oh, you know. The usual."

I hesitate before asking the next question. "How are things with you and Isaac? You met him again yesterday, right?"

Alisha's lower lip begins to tremble—usually a sign that she's going to cry. My heart sinks even further. "I don't think I'll be seeing him again."

"What happened? Did the meeting not go well?"

Alisha laughs shakily. "Something like that. I guess in a way it's my fault for getting too hopeful and thinking we were talking exclusively to each other. I found out yesterday that he's also simultaneously talking with four other girls. He told me himself. Right before he said that he didn't think we were well-suited to each other."

"What a loser!" I've never hit another human in my life, but I'm more than willing to knock Isaac Cherian's glasses off his nose right now. "'Well-suited'? What does that even mean? You had two meetings together. With chaperones!"

"Maybe that was enough for him."

I hold up my fingers to form an L against my forehead and this time Alisha laughs for real. "Let him make best use of his busy schedule, then," I tell her. "You deserve better."

"I do." Alisha grins, looking a little more like herself. "By the way, your accent's changing. Did you know?"

"What? No, it's not!"

"Yes, it is! You pronounced schedule as *ske-jule.*"

Ske-jule instead of *she-dyool. Tu-ishun* instead of *tyu-shun. Tri-go-gnaw-metry* instead of *trig-no-metry.* Alisha isn't wrong. I say twenty as *twenny* and forty as *fordy* without meaning to do so. I am careful to emphasize my *r*'s when I speak, instead of dropping them like I normally would have, so that teachers at school don't ask me to repeat myself. My relatives in India insist on speaking to me in English to hear my "Canadian drawl." They are disappointed when I give them replies in perfect, unaccented Malayalam.

"Does it matter?"

I must sound a little defensive because Alisha's grin fades. "No. It doesn't."

"It's different here," I try to explain. "If I pronounce things the way I did in Jeddah, people don't understand me. If I call a ruler a scale, they think it's a weighing scale and give me confused looks. Specifics matter a lot." I learned this the hard way—after calling an eraser a *rubber* in calculus and having a boy laugh his head off at me.

When I speak to Alisha now, though, I wonder if I'm fighting a losing battle. Especially when she says "Okay, Miss Canada," with a laugh that borders more on sarcasm than humor.

I decide to change the subject and tell Alisha about Heather Dupuis and Preeti Sharma, who I now talk to regularly during and outside physics, feeling strange, yet also pleased to see the approval on her face.

"So you sit together at lunch and everything, now?" Alisha presses. "You're not alone anymore?"

Blood rushes to my face. "No," I say truthfully, thinking back to the feeling of Malcolm's lips on mine. "I'm not alone."

It's not like Heather and Preeti don't invite me to sit with them. But lunch is the only time I get to spend with Malcolm at school outside of English. And I don't want to miss a single second of it.

"What about Malcolm? Are you friends again?"

I'm glad we're separated by a pair of screens because there's no way Alisha would miss the blush on my face if she saw me in real life. "Yeah." I know now is the time to tell her. To say that over the last week, Malcolm has become a lot more than a friend.

"I'm glad." Alisha's smile splinters. "You know I think you were right when you said that boyfriends are overrated. Friendship's better. Less painful."

I bite my lip. I can't tell Alisha about Malcolm now. Not when she's still heartbroken over Isaac Cherian. Even though Alisha is my biggest cheerleader, I know that in this moment my news will feel like salt rubbed into a fresh wound.

"You'll only say that until you find your next crush," I say, trying to cheer her up. "Someone a lot cuter than Whatshisname."

"Isaac."

"Isaac, who?"

She smiles. "I'm glad I have you, Suzy."

There's a lump in my throat. "I'm glad I have you, too."

On Monday, in the schoolyard, Malcolm tells me why he hates Mr. Zuric so much.

"I was doing badly in ninth-grade English, so Zuric called my parents to complain. It was the first time the old man came to school. Suited up, as polite as can be." Malcolm flicks a piece of lint off his jacket. "Until we were back in his car and he slammed my head right against the window. I guess he was lucky no one else was around to see."

I stare at him for a second, wondering if he's exaggerating, but the bleak look on his face tells me otherwise. "That's terrible!"

He shrugs, jaw tightening. "It's not like it was the first time."

"I can't believe this would happen here, of all places!"

"Abuse doesn't have borders."

"But you have child protective services here, the police! I mean, there are running jokes about this in India—how kids tend to have the upper hand over the adults!"

A raised eyebrow. "Stereotypes, you mean."

I slide a hand into his. "I'm sorry," I say, and it's true. Both for having made the assumption and for what he has gone through.

For long moments, we simply watch students trickling back to school, in twos and threes, hoods pulled over their heads against the wind. Even I'm wearing a cap, but Malcolm wears nothing except a puffy black jacket. Sometimes I wonder if he feels the cold at all.

"When I was fifteen, he beat me up so bad, I was sure he was going to kill me," he says, his voice eerily quiet. "It was partly my fault. I stole his car, sneaked out to a party, and got wasted. In the movies, it's usually your lip that's the first to split open and bleed when you get punched in the face. In my case, it was my tongue. My teeth cut into it. Should've shut me up then and there, but it didn't. I laughed at him. It made the old man so mad. He used to be a wrestler, you know? Every hit felt like a thunderclap against my skull."

Malcolm's hand tightens around mine, almost to the point of being painful. I don't think twice before pressing it to my lips.

"He thought I'd driven home drunk." A short sound that might have been a laugh. "I might have broken every rule in the old man's book, but that wasn't one of them. I made sure I took a cab back home. But he never really paid attention to what I said, did he? Even when Mom was alive. Kept hitting and hitting me, until Mahtab came between us. The next thing I knew, my twelve-year-old sister was on the floor, knocked out." Malcolm's mouth is drawn so tight that his lips are colorless. "The only good thing that probably came out of it was that it shook up the old man like nothing else. He's never raised a hand to me again."

I want to say something. Put words to the horror I'm feeling right now. But everything tastes inadequate. Sour like bile at the back of my tongue.

"I wanted to leave. Report him to the police. But Mahtab and Freny begged me not to. What if we were put into foster care and got separated, Mahtab kept saying." He shrugs. "So I stayed. Kept quiet. Waited for the bruises to fade."

"Did Mr. Zuric know about your dad hitting you?" I finally ask.

"No. No one did. Well, Ahmed and Steve know about some stuff. But not everything. They definitely don't know about this."

I'm quiet for a long moment. Part of me knows Malcolm should have told an adult. That it isn't exactly Mr. Zuric's fault for not knowing about Malcolm's situation at home. But then—

"When I was ten, my mom found pictures of another woman on my dad's phone," I begin. "It was a family friend of ours. One of them was of her wearing lingerie. My mother grew hysterical. She began packing bags for herself and for me to go back to India. I spent a whole week in terror, waiting for the divorce announcement. But it didn't happen. Somehow, someway, Appa convinced her to stay."

It's a story I didn't tell anyone. Not even Alisha.

I look into Malcolm's eyes. "I can't begin to understand the horrible things you went through. But I get why you didn't tell anyone. Why you didn't *want* to tell anyone. It's . . . it's . . ."

"Embarrassing," he fills in.

"Yeah. You want to put it behind you. But you can't. Not really." The air nips at my cheeks, stings when I breathe it in too quickly.

"Maybe we can. For a few moments." He slips a hand around the back of my neck; the thumb circling the skin there is warm. "Maybe we can make the most of the time we have."

And for the next fifteen minutes, that's exactly what we do.

———————————

Later that evening, I'm in the living room with my sketchbook, trying to come up with ideas for my final art project. Worth 30 percent of our overall grade, it has to be a painting in oils or watercolors, using the techniques we've learned during the semester. Which wouldn't be that bad except for the following stipulation: the painting must also represent the artist or their life in some way. "I don't want to see Da Vinci or Kahlo," Ms. Nguyen said firmly. "I want to look at the painting and be able to see *you*. Bonus points if it's not a self-portrait."

I stare at the ideas I've doodled so far, along with potential titles, each one worse than the last:

 – A pair of girls standing next to the Red Sea, friendship
   bracelets fraying under the sleeves of their abayas. *BFF*?
   Breaking Bonds?
 – A boy and a girl perched on a staircase poring over a
   book, against a background of brilliant red and yellow
   leaves. ~~Boy. Friend.~~ *Canadian Fall*?

– A girl seated at a table littered with textbooks. There's an
empty thought bubble overhead, one that I could fill
with a myriad of things: paints, canvas, a smock, a
comic strip in a major newspaper.

"Seriously, Susan," I mutter to myself. "What would you title
that? *Unfulfilled Dreams*?"

"What are you doing?"

My head snaps up at the sound of my mother's voice.
"N-nothing . . . I mean, I'm working on ideas for my final art project." As an afterthought, I add: "I thought I'd get it out of the
way so that I can focus properly on my other courses."

Amma nods. "Will it disturb you if I watch TV?"

"Of course not." It's not like I'm getting anywhere with the project anyway.

Amma switches on the television, flipping channels until she
finds a science program. The show features a female scientist
developing an app to help people with Parkinson's disease write
again.

"Clever." Amma's eyes are both critical and approving. "Whatever we say about the West in India, when it comes to technology
and modern medicine they are still far superior to us."

"Don't let Appa hear you say that," I joke. I don't know if it's
homesickness or a heightened sense of nationalism, but my father's
attachment to India has always been greater than mine—even
greater than Amma's. It's part of the reason we were both so surprised when he decided to have us immigrate to Canada for my
final year of high school.

"Do you think this would have been possible in a place like
India? There, she would've been married off and told to raise
children." A tiny nerve pulses at the base of Amma's jaw. "Or her

199

husband would've said that it's better to stay home. That two working parents would make it difficult to have a family life."

Her statement is a bit of an exaggeration; these days it's getting common to see both parents working—even in India. But I don't articulate my thoughts.

An image surfaces in my head: an old jewelry box, and inside it, a letter from my maternal grandmother in India, to Amma. It was the first time I discovered that words could burn themselves in my memory, leave an imprint even though I read them only once. I was five years old.

I know how difficult it is for a married woman, Ammachi wrote. *Once we marry, it becomes our lot as women to follow our husbands. To have children we never wanted in the first place.*

Years passed by, but the jewelry box and the letter always stayed at the bottom of Amma's cupboard in Jeddah, where I first found them. I never asked Amma why she'd kept the letter or if she brought it with her to Canada. If it was the reason she'd refused to have more children after me.

"I'm glad your father chose this place over India for your higher education," Amma says now. "Or even over Jeddah."

"I thought you loved Jeddah." She certainly never complained about it as she does about Mississauga. "That you didn't want to leave."

Her face drops a second before she fixes it with a smile. "Of course I love Jeddah. Many of my happiest memories with your father, with you"—she pinches my cheek—"are attached to that place. But there were no opportunities for me to work there unless I became a teacher or a nurse. I don't want you to end up like that. Sitting at home. Wondering how it could have been if you'd waited a little longer to get married."

200

"You can still do it, you know," I say after a pause. "Amma, you're so brilliant. Maybe even more brilliant than that scientist on TV. I know if you did a few courses at a college or university, you could get a good placement. Even in a lab."

After what happened the last time we discussed this topic, I brace myself for another scolding. But my mother's hand simply smooths out a knot in my hair. She doesn't look into my eyes.

"You're a good girl, Suzy. But this move has always been about you and your future. Right now, your father has a stable job in Saudi, but who knows about tomorrow? We are and always will be foreigners over there. As for India—neither your appa nor I wanted you to languish in a place saturated with red tape and bureaucracy. What a waste that would be—with brains like yours! It's why I'm so glad you put that art school nonsense behind you." She kisses my forehead.

Something inside me curls tight, stays balled up under my ribs. The question about Ammachi's old letter rests on my tongue. I swallow it when Amma asks me if I want the gulab jamuns she bought this week from the Indian grocery store. I focus instead on mundane conversations about life and school, the way I would have in Jeddah. I hold on to the love my mother offers: a pair of rose-brown dumplings soaked in syrup and garnished with pistachios.

Malcolm

"Come in."

Michelle Walters, owner and operator of Michelle's Coffee House, has the voice of an old country singer: slow and soothing, a tinge of melody rounding off her words. It's the sort of voice that, if taken for granted, can turn quickly, deliver the nasty surprise of reduced hours or even a dismissal—as the café's milk supplier (or ex–milk supplier) learned a couple of weeks ago.

Even in my best pants, a button-down shirt, *and* a tie—*Dress to impress*, Ronnie had advised me—I feel like I'm treading on thin ice. Especially in Ronnie's too-tight dress shoes that pinch my toes. Michelle looks me up and down. "I have exactly five minutes to spare you this morning, so make it quick."

"Of course!" Great. Now I sound like a Muppet. I clear my

throat. "I'm here to talk to you about a concert my high school's doing to benefit Syrian refugees."

I lay out the plan: the concert, the probable venue, the sponsorships we've received from a couple of other organizations.

"That's good," she cuts in. "But what do I get out of it?"

"Your name will be on the banners," I say, recalling what Ronnie told me about sponsor packages. "And on the programs."

"How much do you need?"

When I tell her the amount, she shakes her head. "No can do."

"It's a really good cause!" Ugh, why do I sound so eager? I try to tone my voice down. "It would be great publicity for the café!"

"Malcolm, this café has been in my family for three generations. I didn't keep it running by giving money away," she says bluntly. "I'm not against donating to a worthwhile cause, but I'm also a businesswoman. Who's publicizing the event? The local press? Will it be on television?"

My heart sinks. A part of me is tempted to lie and figure things out later, but I know it won't help in the long run. "I don't think so," I admit.

"Then I'm sorry, son." And she does look it. "I can give you a hundred. But that's it."

"Sure." I keep my smile fixed in place as she writes the check. "That's great. Thank you for your time."

It's only after the door shuts behind her that I allow my shoulders to sag. Sweat coats the inside of my collar. A hundred dollars—barely enough to cover dinner for a family of four at a restaurant these days, let alone rent out an auditorium with over a hundred seats at the city's most prominent arts and culture facility.

Some fund-raising director I am. I was so nervous, I didn't even try to charm her. Not that charm would work on someone like Michelle. More than anything, I hate the idea of giving Mahtab the news at this afternoon's meeting and seeing the look of disappointment on her face.

I check my phone. 6:37 a.m. My meeting with Michelle lasted a grand total of seven minutes. Which leaves enough time to change out of this Ronnie Mehta–doppelgänger outfit and into my regular school clothes. I pull my hood over my head.

When I get back, Mahtab and Freny are chatting over breakfast in the kitchen. The old man's nowhere in sight. Great, I think. There's still time to sneak upstairs, unnoticed.

"Where were you?"

I stiffen at the sound of his voice and do a slow one-eighty on my heels. Tehmtun Vakil is wearing the same suit he did the day Zuric called him to school: blue pinstripes crisply ironed, a silver tie that reflects the ice in his eyes. "What on earth are you wearing?"

"Clothes," I say breezily. "Shirt. Pants. Tie. Like you."

His hands fist at his sides and I brace myself for a hit. It does not come. "Mind your tone."

I think of sassing him again. Of saying nothing. But then I decide the truth will be infinitely more shocking.

"I was at Michelle's. Trying to raise money for the concert Mahtab's organizing."

"Don't lie to me!"

"Not lying, old man." Now I'm *really* pushing it. I've never called him *old man* to his face before. Before he can react, I hold out the check Michelle gave me. He snatches it from my hands and holds it up to the light to see if it's real. Slowly, his arms lower to his sides.

"Do you mind?" I say when his stare begins to unnerve me. "I have to give it to the treasurer at today's meeting."

He drops it in my hand without a word. I still feel the weight of his gaze as I race up the stairs, two at a time, before slamming my bedroom door shut.

Mancher Mama told me once that a romantic relationship is never just between two people. There's the girl, the guy, and what he called the *ghosts of people in between*. These ghosts could be exes or even celebrities. *Everyone has an ideal person in mind. Someone we're always measuring the people we're dating up against,* my uncle said.

Mancher Mama, however, never talked about other variables. Like parents, who, in Susan's case, hover over us like two shadows. Always watching.

Except when I'm kissing her. The way I am now, my hands brushing the soft skin of her waist. Pulling her close, until I realize what's happening in my jeans and then I'm pushing her away slightly. Her lips are swollen; a deep pink. I angle my head another way and kiss her again, harder. It's been five months since I kissed another girl, but the way I'm kissing Susan now, you'd think it had been forever. When we break apart to catch our breath, I bury my face in her neck.

She laughs.

"What?"

"That tickles."

I grin. I haven't shaved for a couple of days, and the evidence is there on her chin and her cheek, light scrapes that will leave no bruises on her skin.

I dip my head again, but she draws back. "I need to get home."

"Are you grounded?" Guilt creeps in. If I hadn't thrown that fit, Susan would have never gone to that party. Would never have gotten into trouble with her mother.

"No." She brushes a bit of hair off my forehead. "But Amma has been angry with me all weekend and for most of this week. I don't want to get her angrier. Or make her worry."

I reluctantly slip my hand out from under her shirt, even though I get the feeling she isn't telling me everything. She gives me a sheepish smile. I can't help but smile back. In a goofy way that would have Ahmed and Steve ribbing me for years if they ever saw.

I scratch the back of my head. "So."

"So."

"Want to take the bus home with me?"

"I don't think that's a good idea." With a sigh, she finally says, "My father is flying in from Jeddah this afternoon. He's probably already here."

Overhead clouds gather, as if mocking me, blocking out what's left of the sun.

Susan clears her throat. "I might not be able to see you as often."

There it is. Finally out in the open.

I force myself to smile. "We'll work around that. Like we do now."

She stares at me for a long moment.

"What?"

"Nothing." She wraps her arms around my neck and nestles her head right under my chin. It feels nice. Comfortable. "I've never done this before. This dating stuff. It feels weird."

"It always does." I think back to the first time I went out with a girl. Dahlia Lim, with her luminous brown eyes and silky black hair with bangs. How nervous I felt even holding her hand, especially in front of her grandmother who said something to her in Korean before turning around to secretly give me a wink.

"It's like you're trusting a special part of yourself to another person," I tell Susan. "That's scary."

Across from the bus stop, a pair of guys are setting up drop cloths and paint cans. "They're going to paint now?" Susan says, sounding incredulous. "That's pointless."

I shrug. "Maybe they're hopeful. The weather here can be pretty unpredictable. Those clouds could pass right over us and rain somewhere else."

"That's too much to hope for. I wouldn't be out there painting if my work could wash away."

"You need to take chances in life sometimes."

I think this is probably going to be the end of the conversation, but Susan goes on talking. "Yeah, but why waste your time doing something entirely futile?"

"Um . . ."

"I mean, is there a point?"

"Susan . . ."

"Surely they could do it in the summer when—"

"Susan," I cut in. "Are we still talking about a painting?"

Susan's skin is stretched taut over her cheekbones, her knuckles pale on fisted hands.

"You like painting, don't you?" I ask after a pause. After our previous blowup, I've been hesitant to talk to Susan about anything related to school or the future. "And art?"

"It's a hobby."

"I see."

"It's not practical."

"Is that what *you* think?" I ask her gently. "Or what your parents think?

Susan closes her eyes for a second. "Do your parents monitor your grades?"

Mom used to. Tehmtun Vakil still does, but I don't pay any attention to him.

"I guess. Yeah, they do. But I'm assuming not as much as yours."

"My parents have lots of expectations for me," Susan's voice is soft. "They get angry even if I get a 95 on a test because they want to know where and how I lost the other 5 percent."

"That's ridiculous." Even my old man isn't that finicky about grades. "Why would they care about 5 percent?"

"It's different in India. More competitive. Before our permanent resident visas got approved, my mother had planned to have me apply to every reputable engineering college in India once I graduated from Qala Academy. She told me it was better than medicine. That I would still be able to marry on time." Her laugh is tinged with bitterness.

"Well, you have a lot more options here with your grades." I try to cheer her up. "Right?"

A small frown appears between her brows before disappearing again. "Yeah. Sure. Lots of options."

"Didn't you get a hundred on the English midterm? Who does that?"

"Happy I beat Afrin?"

I grin. "Beyond words."

She smiles. "Mr. Zuric is a lenient marker. He probably curves every exam or essay."

"For dummies like me," I add. Maybe a little bit on purpose, to see her reaction.

"Are you still holding that against me?" She scowls and then sighs. "You're smart. You're just . . . uninterested."

My laughter is full, belly-deep.

"It's true!" Susan raises her voice to be heard over the clouds thundering overhead. "There's a difference between being bad at something and not being interested in it. You need to find something you love doing—that doesn't bore you to death."

Like art? I want to challenge. But then I look into her big, brown, far-too-earnest eyes and the fight goes out of me.

"Like kissing?"

She rolls her eyes, but smiles at me. "Be serious."

"Kissing is serious business."

She's about to retort when her gaze falls on something or someone behind me. And for the first time in all the time that I've known her, Susan Thomas swears out loud.

Susan

It's Amma in her deep red fall coat, talking to Mr. Zuric.
But they're not the only reason I swore. There's also someone else.
A familiar someone, his silver hair darkened to gray by the light
rain, his face both dear and terrifying in this instant.

A marquee of questions scrolls through my brain: *What are they
doing at school? Why are they talking to Mr. Zuric? Did they talk to
Mr. Franklin, too? Did he tell them about my grade on the physics
midterm?*

The grade, a B, wasn't as bad as I'd expected—realistically it
wasn't bad at all, considering the highest midterm grade (awarded
to Heather Dupuis) was an A-minus. Telling Amma about it
was a different story, though, and the first thing I did after Mr.
Franklin returned the paper was hide it at the very back of my

school binder. I couldn't stand the thought of Amma going through each question and grilling me about my mistakes—or worse, demanding to see Mr. Franklin herself to fight over any missing marks. It was easy to forget about my grades when they were out of sight, with Amma being more distracted than normal last week and Appa safely in Jeddah. Now, though, with my parents in clear view, the grade and the paper swim before my eyes like a bad vision, spinning in circles before sinking into an invisible vortex.

". . . she's an excellent student. I'm so pleased to have her in my class." Mr. Zuric is talking about me. I can tell from the look on my parents' faces: that satisfied expression I've only seen when I've met their expectations without surpassing them.

"Oh, there she is!" Mr. Zuric spots me seconds before I can hide behind a tree.

I smile weakly and wave, instantly feeling foolish for doing so. "Hi, Amma. Appa, how was your flight?"

I expect Malcolm to flee the way I would have. But he doesn't. He pastes a smile on his lips, even though I'm sure he must be terrified, and turns around to face them.

The beam on Mr. Zuric's face dims when he sees who I'm with. Amma's face is blotchy, furious, her shoulders nearly up to the hood around her ears. Appa, on the other hand, is frowning, which could mean anything from confusion to disapproval.

"That's your dad, isn't it?" Malcolm murmurs, so softly that I barely hear him.

I must have nodded or made some sound of assent because Malcolm groans.

"Time to face the music, then."

I am not sure if he's talking to me or to himself, but by the time we're standing in front of my parents and Mr. Zuric, Malcolm's frozen smile has thawed to something warm and bright, his eyes sparkling even though the sun has been blotted out by the clouds.

"Hi, Mrs. Thomas. Mr. Thomas." He gives Mr. Zuric a nod, which is a miracle in itself because he usually does his best to ignore the teacher. Mr. Zuric nods back stiffly and then returns to his conversation with Amma.

"I'm a friend of Susan's," Malcolm says. "Malcolm Vakil."

"Malcolm Lawyer?" Appa asks, raising his brows. I'm about to explain the joke—that *vakil* means lawyer in Hindi—when Malcolm laughs.

"Yeah, Malcolm Lawyer. I get that a lot from my Indian friends."

"Ah, I see." To the untrained ear, Appa's voice sounds pleasant, even friendly. But I've heard that tone enough times by now to know that the questions that Malcolm answers now will have my father judging everything: from Malcolm's family background to his intelligence and character. "Where in India are you from, my boy?"

"Oh, I'm not from India, sir. I was born here," Malcolm says. "My folks are from Mumbai, though. We're Parsis."

It's the wrong answer. I can already see the way my father's smile drops a little, the way my mother's frown deepens. I hear the hollow voices of relatives traveling all the way from India and right into their ears: *Be careful she doesn't forget where she comes from like those children in the West.*

Even though "those children" were born in the West in the first place. Yvonne took a great deal of flak for it—*a black sheep* our relatives in India call her for her accent and her supposed disdain for Indian culture and traditions. I wonder what they would say if they saw Yvonne here the way I did. Wearing a traditional white-and-gold Kerala sari at her birthday party this August, teaching her non-Indian friends to pronounce *jhumka* while pointing at the gold, bell-shaped earrings that dangled from her lobes.

I'm ready to snap if my parents say anything that might make Malcolm uncomfortable. But Appa simply responds with: "I knew some Parsis back in Jeddah. Rustom and Khorshed Wadia. Do you know them by any chance?"

"No, sir," Malcolm replies. "But maybe they're related somehow to a couple of Wadias I know at the Zoroastrian Community Centre. I could ask for you, if you like."

I release my breath, bit by bit, watching my father shift from his interrogator pose to something more relaxed, and soon he and Malcolm are casually chatting about Canada and Arthur Eldridge, and other mundane topics. I try to focus on the conversation. With Mr. Zuric now gone, I can feel the laser beam of my mother's gaze burning the side of my face. When I chance a look her way, she tilts her head to the side. It means I am in deep trouble, though I'm not sure if she has already told my father about the party and how I got drunk.

In the past, my parents would never have hidden something so significant from each other, especially when it came to me. I expected Amma to insist that Appa come here at once—or even call us back to Jeddah.

But now that I think of it, Amma no longer kept vigil by the computer everyday, even during the times my father was expected to Skype. There were days when she went off to the library by herself, returning with a bagful of romance novels, which she devoured within a couple of days. "I used to read these in college, you know," she told me with a laugh. "I used to have a crush on this handsome boy in my bio lab. I wonder what happened to him."

The whole conversation made me uncomfortable—as if we were betraying my father in some way. Amma laughed at me then, but I know there's a growing gap between my parents that geographical distance itself can't be entirely blamed for. There are days, like today, when I wonder if I am the only glue holding them together.

"Rensil," she says now in a voice that's chillier than the November wind. "Shall we get going?"

As if punctuating her words, a spray of rain hits the tree we're standing under. Screams ring out from the distance as a pair of girls race to the bus from the gym doors, trying to cover their heads with textbooks. I feel my hood being edged over my hair. Malcolm grins at me. Without meaning to, I smile back.

"Susan," Appa says.

Susan, not Suzy. The slightest shift of a syllable with which my father could change a name into a reprimand. I turn to face Appa, telling myself there is nothing to worry about. That I only smiled at a friend. But then I catch a glimpse of my reflection in his rain-speckled glasses. The girl I see there glows, her happiness unhidden from the rest of the world.

"I thought you weren't going to see that boy anymore," Amma says, the moment we're in our car.

So much for hoping Amma would keep her mouth shut.

"I'm not *seeing* him," I lie from the back passenger seat. "He's in my English class with Mr. Zuric. He was asking me about homework."

"Was he asking about homework that night, too?"

I feel the blood drain from my face. My gaze darts between Amma's angry eyes and the back of my father's gray head.

"Aruna, please," Appa says impatiently, and I wonder if he even heard her. "Let's not fight today."

I register the smell inside the car; the musty odor of sweat sticking to my father's wrinkled clothes after being cloistered for over thirteen hours in an airplane. He must have come directly from the airport. To my surprise, Amma does not launch into her usual counterarguments: *I am her mother.* Or: *You're never on my side.* Or: *I am disciplining her.*

Instead she looks at him for a long moment, her mouth drawn back into a grimace.

"Are you going to tell her or am I?"

"Aruna, don't do this."

"Let me make it easy for you, Rensil." Amma is still watching Appa. "Susan, your father is here to tell you that we are separating."

"Aruna!"

I have never heard Appa sound this furious. But he does not deny what my mother said. The brakes slam and the car jerks to a stop at the red light.

Amma's words seep in, prick my insides.

"How could you do this?" Appa's voice is soft, yet unbearably loud in the silence. "We agreed we'd wait until the weekend. Until I had a little more time."

I do not need to see Amma to know what her face looks like right now—hard eyes welling, her lips pressed thin. The slightest touch of cruelty breaking through the pain.

Malcolm

On the first day of December, I wake up to a fine dusting of snow over the driveway and the hoods of the old man's and Freny's cars. Though the sun comes out by the time I get to school, the air remains freezing as if studded with microscopic bits of ice.

It's funny watching Susan shiver when we step out for pizza during lunch, wrapping her scarf tightly around her nose. "Planning to rob a bank?" I ask her.

She mumbles something that sounds like "Very funny," but I can't be too sure. She has been in a bad mood since I saw her this morning, refusing to tell me what is wrong. It doesn't take much to figure out it has something to do with her parents and the separation they announced a couple of weeks ago, but that's a can of worms I have no intention of opening now.

Right now, back at school, I want to distract Susan as much as I can—by cracking several of Steve's slapstick jokes, and failing that, kissing away her frown in the quiet of a corner on the first floor, sandwiched between the wall and a locker facing a window. I think I'm doing a decent job—if her sighs are any indication—but then, all of a sudden, she pushes me away, pressing a finger to her lips.

"I can't wait to leave this place." The girl whose locker we're standing next to has a loud, nasally voice. "It's like living in a prison with my parents always around, hovering over me, asking if I'm okay, if I need this or that . . . *God*."

Susan's brows nearly touch her hairline. I roll my eyes. Susan presses her lips together, a sure sign that she's going to laugh out loud. I muffle the sound with a kiss.

"I dunno," another voice says from a distance, a boy. "I mean, I still need to look into scholarships and stuff."

"*I'm* applying to the St. George campus." The girl's voice penetrates my happy place, grating on my eardrums. "And every other university in Toronto. You should apply as well, Leonard. Leave crappy Sauga behind."

I pull back from Susan, no longer able to resist.

"Toronto, where the lights are bright and the rents are high!" I call out. "Downtown on Daddy's dime! Is he gonna pay for Leonard's tuition, too? Or is it Mommy who's footing the bill?"

"Malcolm!" Susan says. She looks so alarmed that it's funny.

"Whatever." The girl sounds bored. She doesn't even bother looking at me. "Let's go, Leonard, and leave these losers to their make-out session. We'll see who's talking when acceptances start rolling in next semester."

I chuckle, listening to their footsteps recede. "Poor Leonard."

My phone buzzes in my pocket. I pull it out and check the screen. There is a text. A number I deleted from my phone but not from my brain.

We have to talk. Please call me.

Yeah, right. Afrin wanting to "talk" has never led to any good in the past and I'm sure that it has no way of leading to anything better now.

I'm about to press Susan back to the wall and kiss her again, but she slips out from under my arm. "That girl was right, you know." She rubs her hands as if chilled. "We *will* be hearing from universities next semester."

"March," I point out, "which is still three months away. And I don't see why you're so worried. With your grades, you'll be a shoo-in at every single university you apply to." *Unlike me.* Even if I manage to keep up my grades in my other courses, it's the D in English that will still cause problems if I flunk the final in late January, weeding me out of the sort of universities Susan is bound to apply to. I taste something bitter at the back of my tongue. The phone in my pocket buzzes again. I ignore it.

"My father wants me to get into the medicine program at St. George. My mother told me to apply to Waterloo for computer engineering, as a backup." Susan's voice is tight, thinner than normal. "I wonder what they'll say when they discover that I completely forgot we had a quiz in calculus today. Or that physics keeps getting harder and harder. At this rate, I'll be lucky if I end up with a B-minus in that course."

"Why are you having such a tough time?" I pause, wondering if there's a way to put this without offending her. "I mean, you're . . . you're . . ."

"Supposed to be smart?"

She takes a deep breath, exhaling sharply through her nose. When she opens her eyes, they are alarmingly wet.

"Initially it was the lab work that kept tripping me up. I mean, it's not easy now either—especially with the way Mr. Franklin marks our papers—but after midterms, I thought I'd be able to do a better job. But then my parents dropped that bombshell and . . . it's like I can't focus anymore. Every time I open a book, their separation is all I can think about." A pause. "I wish I *could* ignore everything around me, you know? That I could throw myself into schoolwork like a machine, producing perfect results every single time."

I wrap my arms around Susan's trembling shoulders. She leans in, her nose brushing the side of my neck.

"My grandmother likes to say that home is forever," Susan says. "She and my grandfather live in a big old house in a village in Kerala. It has been in their family for generations, that house." She makes a sound that is part laugh, part cry. "It was probably silly to associate the same feeling with my parents, huh? To expect them to last as long as a four-hundred-year-old house? I mean, a couple of months ago my dad said that we'd roam the city when he came here, see the sights as a family. Now, hardly an hour goes by without both my parents at each other's throats."

I'm not sure how to answer that until I catch a glimpse of something on the other side of the window.

"Hey," I say, "you haven't seen snow yet, have you? *Real* snow, that is."

"What do you mean by real snow? I saw it this morning." She shrugs as if unimpressed. "It was okay."

I laugh. "That? That wasn't snow, Susan. That was a flurry. A tease."

I pull her toward the window. Glancing around to make sure no one's in the hallway or on the grounds (read: a teacher or VP Han), I pop open the latch and slide the pane across. A good chunk of snow has gathered right on the windowsill, and it falls on the sleeve of my sweater like sugar.

"*This* is real snow."

A riot of white falls from the sky like feathers from a pillow, layering over the inch already gathered on the pavement below. Ahmed, who lived in Winnipeg one winter, always says that snow here isn't heavy enough to qualify for a boast or a complaint. But for someone like Susan, who has seen only sand, whose lashes blink several times as if she can't quite believe what she's seeing, it's pretty decent. I hold out my hand, gesturing to Susan to do the same. She does better, leaning out headfirst and opening her mouth to the sky.

When she pops back in, her cheeks are pink from the cold. "I've always wanted to do that. Taste the snow."

"Wait till we get more of it," I tell her. "When Mahtab and I were little, we'd gather fresh snow in a bucket and then add maple syrup to it to make taffy. Maybe we can do that together."

It's awkward telling Susan about my childhood. About the time when my mother was still alive and healthy. When my father was still Dad and not *the old man*.

But Susan only smiles and links her hand with mine. "That sounds like fun."

Luck is on my side when I put out my hand this time, managing to capture several big, fluffy flakes, right in the center of my palm. "Look."

I know when she sees them because her eyes widen and her mouth opens ever so slightly.

"They're like crystal fractals," she says, almost breathlessly. "Look at those designs . . . Wait!" She reaches into the purse at her hip to pull out her phone—probably to take a picture—and then pauses midway, groaning. "They're gone!"

"Well, yeah." I laugh at the tiny puddle in my hand. "They won't last that long. You have to be prepared. And forget taking pictures; there'll be time for that later. Go catch your own."

And she does. Flake after flake, squealing like a little kid whenever she sees a perfectly formed six-armed crystal—a diamond in a drop of frozen water.

"Nothing lasts forever," I say. "Not this snowflake. Not our homes, not our families. But it doesn't mean you can't live in the beauty of the moment."

In my head the words sound meaningful. Profound. Out loud, they're the corniest thing I've ever said.

"That's the corniest thing I've ever heard you say," Susan tells me.

I cringe.

"Maybe you should be Malcolm Kavi instead of Malcolm Vakil." There's a twinkle in her eyes that wasn't there before. "You know, Malcolm Poet instead of Malcolm Lawyer? I should ask Mahtab if you guys have poet ancestors or—"

There isn't enough snow to make the sort of balls I normally use to throw at Steve and Ahmed. But there is enough for me to grab from the sill and stuff down the back of Susan's shirt. Her mouth opens: a half scream, half laugh. Now *I* wish I had a camera handy.

Within seconds we've forgotten everything—my sister, Susan's

221

parents, the whole wide world—as we spend the rest of the lunch period trying to stuff snow down each other's shirts before collapsing into a puddle of laughs on the waxed floor.

I'm in a happy mood that afternoon.

So happy that even Jay at Michelle's Coffee House notices. "New girl?" he asks when I go on break. "Is she as cute as the one you were going out with before?"

I think of Susan—how she attracts me without even trying—and only shrug.

It's been a good week for fund-raising as well. After my poor showing at Michelle's, I teamed up with Isabel Abanda from the fund-raising committee and over the past few weekends, both of us have scouted local businesses and stores, managing to raise a little over four hundred dollars together. Last Sunday, Isabel was busy, so I went alone to a hardware store after my shift at Michelle's. I forwarded Mahtab and Ronnie the owner's email last night along with his promise to fund us another hundred and fifteen.

When I get back home, I am grinning so much, Mahtab wants to know if I've applied to be a cartoon character at Disneyland.

"Hah, very funny." I pull out a pack of cigarettes. Mahtab's smile drops.

"What's up?" I mumble through the stick in my mouth.

"Malu, when will you stop smoking?" she asks bluntly. "You know how bad it is for you!"

I remove the cigarette from my mouth. We've had this conversation before, but Mahtab usually just makes a sarcastic comment and rolls her eyes. "Mahtab. Calm down."

"No, I will not calm down!" Mahtab's cheeks redden under her glasses. "Do you know how often I think of Mom and how she died? Every freaking day. She at least couldn't help it. But you? You're smoking those things on purpose. Even though you know cancer killed Mom, even though—"

"People die every day, Mah," I interrupt. Guilt and anger thread my insides, forming a hard knot. "It's not even the same thing. Mom had no vices. She didn't even drink the occasional glass of wine. She still died! And then there's Tehmtun Vakil, who should be in jail after what he did to me and you two years ago, *but he's still here.*"

Mahtab's face gets even redder.

"It's true, isn't it?" I demand. "If I'd called child protective services, they'd have taken us both away from here. But I didn't because you begged me not to!"

"He's still our father!" she shouts. "He's all we have left! And he's sorry about what happened. Has he hit you again afterward? Has he?"

"Yeah. Big accomplishment there—a parent who refrains from abusing their kid."

The heater in my room cuts off, magnifying the silence in the room.

"He loves you—no, it's true!" she insists when I open my mouth to argue. "But you're both so alike. Too much, really. It's why you have such a hard time getting along."

"I'm nothing like him!" My blood boils. "Mah, how could you even compare the two of us?"

"See! This is what I'm talking about!" She rakes her hands through her hair and pulls the ends tight. "You're both so *angry* all the time. You go on the offensive without even listening to what others have to say!"

I open my mouth, ready to retort, and then shut it again.

"The difference is," she continues softly, "that you *do* listen sometimes. And so does Dad. I don't think he has forgiven himself for what happened that night."

I don't need to ask which night that was. I still remember Mahtab falling to the floor. The screaming match that erupted between me and the old man right after. Freny was the one who finally put an end to it by picking up a moaning Mahtab in her arms and taking her to the car. It was the first and only time I saw the old man grow pale with fear, pacing the halls outside the ER while Freny filled in the details at the triage nurse's desk. I stare at the cigarette crushed to an unrecognizable shape by my hand.

"I haven't forgiven myself, either," I tell my sister now before tossing it and the box in the trash.

Susan

The December after I turned fourteen, Appa bought me a set of Faber-Castell watercolor pencils. Thirty-six colors packed in a tin decorated with flowers, a set that retailed for over a hundred and twenty riyals in Jarir Bookstore. My parents weren't poor, by any means, but they were frugal—especially when it came to hobbies. The box of watercolor pencils was Appa's greatest indulgence of my love of art: a fact I was so painfully aware of that it took me nearly six months to open the package and begin using them.

"You spoil her, Rensil," Amma told him when she thought I wasn't listening. "Why give her dreams that she'll never be able to pursue?"

At the time, I was hurt, even offended. Appa, who saw me

eavesdropping, joked about Amma later. "Your mother has no sense of fun."

Now, three years later, I wonder again if Amma was always like this. If she had dreams—other dreams apart from being a scientist—that were crushed somewhere along the way.

Outside, snow begins falling in earnest, gathering in the outside bottom corners of my bedroom window. Back in Jeddah, I never thought I'd see a snowflake in my life, let alone catch one: first on my tongue, and later on my hand, melting seconds after I perceived a pattern so breathtaking that I couldn't help but catch more.

I shiver, remembering the feel of the ice against my skin, Malcolm's cold hand on my back. At the time, it seemed like the most perfect thing in the world—the only thing to do when presented with a handful of my first snow. Now in the silence of my room, it seems silly and pricks me with guilt. I should have spent that time outlining the essay Mr. Zuric assigned us for *Alias Grace*. Or studying physics. Or calculus. Or—

My phone pings with the sound of a text message.

Alisha: Where ARE you??? Haven't talked to you in WEEKS.

Two weeks and four days. The exact time since Appa's arrival and his talk about separating from Amma. My mother still believes their marriage can be fixed. Salvaged through the counseling sessions they've attended over the past week or so. Even though Appa insists on sleeping on the living room sofa instead of in the master bedroom, and has done so ever since he arrived.

I haven't told my mother about the papers I found in Appa's briefcase. *Petition for Divorce by Mutual Consent*. I couldn't bear to read any further, still can't bear to think he's only here to get

Amma to sign them. For years, I did my best to overlook my father's imperfections, siding with him even when I knew he was in the wrong. However, what I've learned in the past couple of weeks—couple of months, really—has steadily peeled the film off the rose-colored glasses I always viewed him through. *I understand*, I want to tell Amma now. *He makes me angry as well.*

There've been times over the past month when I've been tempted to call Alisha or write her an email about what's happening with my parents. About Malcolm. But each time I try, my words come out muddled. Wrong. If Alisha was here, I would tell her everything. But she isn't and everything is so complicated right now that I text back: I'm here. Sorry. Have been busy with school instead.

Alisha: When are you coming to visit me?

In October, the question would have soothed my wounded ego, had me thinking of ways I could convince Appa to call us back to Jeddah on vacation. But how would things work now? My parents are barely talking to each other (if I don't count the shouting). And I could never leave Amma alone here, no matter how much she annoys me.

Not sure, I text back. And then: I gtg.

There's a pause of thirty seconds before Alisha texts a simple: okay. There are no exclamation points. No barrage of hearts and kisses. I know I've hurt her so I send back a heart. It's a poor response to my best friend, but I can't bear to talk about anything right now. Not on text nor on Skype.

On the plus side—if I can call it that—I've been driving a lot better over the past two weeks. Or at least Joseph no longer criticizes me as much. Last Saturday, he made only three critical comments during the entire lesson—a record as far as he is concerned.

Seconds later, I hear shuffling outside my room. Without even opening the door, I know it's my father, his gait heavier than Amma's, the tread audible even when he's walking barefoot on a soft carpet. A series of knocks—the sort he used when I was a little girl.

"Password?" I call out.

"Garden gnome."

I remain silent.

"No? Is it kalaripayattu then? Saudi champagne?"

He goes through a series of old passwords, finally ending at one I never even made up.

"Suzy?" My father sounds hesitant, less certain that I've ever heard him. "May I come in?"

"I'm busy," I say finally. "Studying."

"Oh." A long pause. "Of course. We can talk later." He's back to using the Doctor Voice. Calm and comforting: a tonic for a sore heart.

My mouth feels dry. I wait for him to open the door the way my mother would, shouting at me for my rudeness. *Is this how I raised you to talk to your elders?* But Appa has never liked confrontations. He walks away, heavy footsteps fading into the carpet.

"Why are your passwords so difficult?" Appa asked me during our final months in Jeddah. "Your old appa will never be able to remember them!"

My throat tightens.

It's strange, I think now, but maybe not a complete surprise that he forgot the first ever password he picked himself. *Family.*

———————————

Here, we watch the news and long segments on local weather instead of Indian soap operas. Appa tells us that we can get the

ATN channel on Rogers if we want to watch them. "You can catch up on *Naagin* and *CID*," he tells Amma in a weak attempt at making conversation.

She pays him no attention, staring instead at the TV where they're doing a news segment on refugees from Syria. A host family is preparing for the arrival of a family of four from Aleppo on December 31. The reporter waxes poetic about the guest rooms and the play area set up for the children in the basement.

". . . are welcome and Canada is a society tolerant of all differences." The reporter's smile is so wide, I'm sure it will crack her face. "For CTV News, this is—"

"I really hate that word." Amma's voice muffles the reporter's. "*Tolerant.* What are they, flies? Or some other form of annoyance?"

"Come now, Aruna. They don't mean that."

"Tolerant." Amma snorts, ignoring Appa. "Remember that politician on TV, Suzy? About how she wants to screen potential new immigrants for 'anti-Canadian values'? Tolerant, my foot."

I say nothing. It's been like this ever since we returned home after that awful revelation in the car—Amma directing her comments at me instead of at Appa, even the ones that are technically meant to taunt him.

"Of course your *father* would understand. He tolerated us, didn't he? Unwanted wife, unwanted daughter, never living up to his expectations—"

"Amma," I begin. "Amma, please—"

"I've heard enough."

Appa rises to his feet and stalks out of the room and into the corridor. A moment later, the front door slams shut.

Malcolm

It takes four tries to get Susan's attention on Monday—five if I count the fact that she seems distant even when I kiss her hello.

"What's up?" I ask.

She gives me an approximation of her usual smile. "Nothing special."

Which, these days, means another weekend of her parents fighting. A germ of an idea begins to form in my head. "Well, we can't let that continue, can we?"

A tiny frown, a spark of interest that wasn't there before. "What do you mean?"

I press my lips to hers in a smacking kiss, pleased to see her flush this time. "You'll see."

As in, I haven't got a clue. But now that I'm thinking, I know

I'll come up with something. Susan wasn't exactly wrong when she said I need projects that interest me. And, at the moment, there's no bigger project than making Susan Thomas smile.

I get my brain wave in the middle of accounting, during an otherwise mind-numbing period of balancing trial balances. After the period ends, I find Susan feet away from the lunchroom. "Come on. We're going out."

"What? Now? I was going to study with Heather and Preeti."

"Do you have a test?"

"No, but—"

"Then it can wait," I say simply. "Come on, Susan, you're going to study at home again, aren't you?"

Hesitation flickers across her face. She glances at her textbook and then looks back at me. "I don't know . . ."

"What do you want to do—spend your time doing physics or"—I flip up my collar and flex my biceps like Johnny Bravo—"go on a date with me?"

"God." She raises her eyes to the ceiling. But her mouth twitches and she puts her textbook and pencil case into the locker. "Since we're on the subject, where *are* we going?"

I grin. "To see the sights!"

Back when people drove horse carriages in Mississauga instead of cars, the corner of Highways 5 and 10 ("Dundas and Hurontario," I translate for Susan), made up the downtown area.

Now I show Susan the city's new center: two steel-and-glass buildings are the highlight, fifty and fifty-six stories each, nicknamed the Marilyn Monroe Towers because of their hourglass design, even though Steve says they look like crushed soda cans.

Susan laughs when I tell her about Steve's description. She lifts

231

up her phone over her head to get a shot. "I like Marilyn Monroe better."

"I wouldn't be too sure about that," I say. "I mean, what if you're living in the building's butt? If there was an explosion, would that mean it was a fart?"

She groans. "Now I'll have that image in my head for life!"

I laugh. My fingers twitch, itching for a smoke, but I hold off for a while longer. It's been five days since my blowup with Mahtab. Five whole days without a single smoke. Maybe I can last another hour. Another day. With Susan, though, it's easy to remain distracted, our boots crunching the leftover ice glazing the sidewalk, our breath puffing into clouds.

For the first time since I've known her Susan doesn't tell me that we need to get back to school before the next period begins. We walk down the main road, passing hillocks of snow frozen into graying ice, and fir trees weighed down by the whiter stuff. I don't know what Susan finds so fascinating about the trees, but she takes over a dozen pictures.

"I've never seen snow on trees before," she admits.

I grin at the way her face colors; it's really kind of adorable. It also gives me another one of my brain waves and I nearly smack myself for not thinking of it earlier. I quicken my pace. "Come on. I want to show you something."

We bypass the mall and cross the road to Celebration Square—a large plot of land sandwiched between the sandy-brown central library and the Civic Centre. Susan and I walk across the snow-covered Astroturf and climb up the stairs to the upper level. The fountain that kids play in during the summer has been converted into an ice skating rink. A Zamboni's parked nearby like a sleeping orange giant, ready to smooth out the cracks or imperfections in the ice every couple of hours.

Susan stares at the rink and then at me. "Malcolm. No."

"Yes," I say patiently. It being the afternoon means that the rink is mostly empty, with only a couple of stragglers, the metal of their skates sliding smoothly across the ice. It'll be easier to teach her—and to help her up when she inevitably falls.

"I don't have ice skates!" If her voice goes any higher, she'll sound like Minnie Mouse.

I laugh. "That's why we rent them." I pull some cash from my wallet—enough to cover us both—only to find the rental place opens at 4:00 p.m. on weekdays.

Susan heaves a sigh of relief. But then I have an idea. A wicked idea that will get us both kicked off the ice if a patroller catches us. I glance back at the Zamboni; the driver is nowhere in sight, and I pull Susan toward the rink.

"What are you doing?" she cries out.

"Skating," I tell her, grinning.

Or walking. And slipping. And sliding. And falling. For a small girl, Susan is pretty heavy. Or maybe it's the impact of breaking her fall while trying not to break my bones at the same time. Tears leak out of the corners of my eyes. My chest heaves up and down.

Why am I laughing even though I'm in pain?

Susan helps me up. Her face looks more confused than I've seen it: like she wants to laugh and take me to the hospital at the same time. She finally chooses to laugh and we get off the ice and onto sturdy ground.

"I wonder if those paintings are still there," Susan says suddenly.

"What paintings?"

233

"Murals. In a corridor near the library, I think. Or was it the Civic Centre?"

I can tell from the casual tone of her voice that she's lying. Susan knows exactly where the murals are. But I don't push it.

"Who knows?" I say instead. "Maybe one day you'll have something of yours up here."

Susan's hand freezes in the air. "I'm not that talented."

"Are you kidding? Your drawing of that girl Zarin was as good as any of the stuff I've seen in comic books."

There's a long pause before she responds. "You really think so?"

"Yeah," I say truthfully. "You're really good."

Susan doesn't speak again as we head to the bus stop. She simply holds my hand the whole time, her fingers laced tightly through mine.

"Hello, Malc."

I hear Afrin's voice as I get down from the bus in front of my house. Smooth, low-pitched, with a lilt that I found unbearably sexy when we were dating. Now it only annoys me.

"What do you want?" I ask.

"No hi-hello?" Afrin rises to her feet from her seat on my front steps, her long legs in jeans so tight they could've been painted on. Her hair, once black and red, is wholly red now. I hate to admit it, but the look suits her. A familiar smile plays on her lips. "You didn't call."

I stop at the foot of the staircase. "Your point being?"

"Oh, no. I'm impressed, actually." She curls her fingers inward and pretends to examine her nails. "It's a wonder you managed to last that long. That Susan girl must be good in bed."

"What do you want, Afrin?"

The mocking smile slips slightly. "I want to talk to you. My parents want me to start seeing the son of one of their *friends*." She sneers at the last word and I remember something she told me a year back. How her parents never really had friends. Only business partners or people who could place Afrin's dad in even more powerful positions than he is in now.

The news still comes as a shock. "What? But why? Your parents weren't . . . they never cared about that stuff."

"Let's say they walked in on me and Justin in a . . . compromising position."

An unwanted image flashes through my head—built on old memory and my own knowledge of both my former friends. I shake it off. "It doesn't make sense. You've had boyfriends before, Afrin. Your parents knew about that."

"They didn't," she says quietly.

"What do you mean, they didn't?"

"I mean. They. Didn't. Know. Anyone," she snaps. "Except you, of course. You were the only one I ever brought home."

"You're lying."

"I'm not!" Her shoulders hunch. She stuffs her hands into the pockets of her jacket. "I know I've never been much of a girlfriend, but I'm not lying about that part."

I think back to the first time I saw Afrin's parents. How nervous I was. I didn't realize until later that they seemed especially pleased to see me—a Parsi boyfriend, Afrin told me, was what they had always wanted for her.

"Please talk to them, Malc," Afrin says now. "They'll listen to you. They've always listened to you. It would be even better if you pretended you're my boyfriend—"

"No," I interrupt. "Afrin, we broke up and with good reason! And you know I'm with Susan now."

"Yeah. Susan." Afrin rolls her eyes. "What do you see in her? She's such a stick-in-the-mud."

"People asked me the same thing about you. Only they replaced stick-in-the-mud with stuff I'm not going to repeat out loud."

Afrin's lower lip trembles. She bites it down.

"I never thought you were any of the things they called you," I say. "I mean you really hurt me, but I didn't agree with those people. Just as I don't agree with you about Susan. I care about you, Afrin. Maybe we can be friends again someday. But I can't talk to your parents. I can't be that guy for you anymore." The guy who covered up her messes without question. The guy who always pretended he didn't care about anything other than a good time. I take a deep breath. "I never want to be that guy again."

I think I hear a sob when I turn away from her, followed by the clatter of heels on the pavement. I don't look back.

Susan

"You're seeing that boy, aren't you?" Amma throws a bomb
at me the minute I enter the apartment. "That Malcolm character."

My hands are clammy under my gloves. I slip off my shoes and
hang up my coat in the closet. As calm, cool, and collected as I
always want to be in these scenes, it never happens in real life. Heat
rises up my neck, burning my face. It takes about twenty seconds—
even though it feels like twenty hours—before I turn around and
say, "I am."

There's no point in denying this. Malcolm wanted to go back
to school after lunch today, but I told him I didn't want to. "Can
we stay out?" I pleaded. "A little longer?"

We stayed. Ate frozen yogurt at the mall. Afterward, we took
the bus to the lakeshore, where we spent the rest of the afternoon
drinking hot chocolate at a café. I'm not sure what made me act

like this today. Maybe it was simply the joy I felt at being outside—away from the world of grades and parents and broken promises. Or maybe there was a part of me that wanted to be discovered. To be looked at by my parents with an expression other than guilt or pity.

After today, even my mother must have figured out that the recorded calls she was receiving from the school about my absenteeism weren't computer glitches.

"That's it?" Amma shouts. "That's all you're going to tell me?"

"Where's Appa?" I ask, ignoring her and the guilt that begins to creep up on me.

"Stop changing the subject!"

"We're dating, okay?" I'm half tempted to add that he's my boyfriend, but Malcolm and I haven't really defined each other in those terms. Besides, that will only make things worse for my mother.

The tip of her nose goes white, the way it always does when she's angry. "Susan, I forbid you to see him."

"Why?" I ask. "Because he's not from Kerala, or Christian? Or is it because you can't stand seeing someone else's relationship work out when yours didn't?"

I want to take back the words the moment they leave my mouth. But they're out there in the open, venom dripping. Instead of smacking me the way I expect her to, she droops like a flower that has begun to wilt.

"Your father is seeing another woman," she tells me after a pause. "A nurse at his hospital."

Now I'm the one who feels small. My father? An affair? For the first time, I notice that my mother is not wearing her minnu.

"He found someone else, he tells me," Amma says in a distant voice. "Just like that. It seems you both are alike in that sense. Neither of you think I have feelings. Or maybe I have been cruel to you in the past. I must have been, to deserve such words now."

The *sorry* rests on the tip of my tongue. But by the time it comes out, Amma has already walked away and my voice dissipates in an empty corridor.

"Winter holds the highest rates for driving test failures," Joseph tells me for what feels like the tenth time that week. "Slippery streets, bad visibility—"

His voice cuts off when I make a wide right turn. As he criticizes me for this, I begin to wonder about what I'm doing. My test is this weekend. And Joseph isn't exactly wrong. Winter *is* a bad time to drive if you're inexperienced, especially when it's snowing. To fail would be alarmingly easy.

Who says you're going to fail? A voice that sounds like Malcolm says in my head. *The bald guy?*

I bite back a laugh. Adrenaline buzzes through me and, apart from that one wide turn, I follow the rest of Joseph's instructions perfectly.

"Please drive like this *during* the exam on Saturday!" he tells me, which I guess is his way of giving a compliment. "The examiners are looking to cut points in various areas."

For the first time since I've had Joseph as an instructor, I really listen to him. Even then, I can't help but remember how patient Malcolm was in comparison. How he managed to get down to the real problem—my nerves—and figure out a way beyond them.

Malcolm, who shows remarkable aptitude and skills when it comes to people, who has absolutely no idea how my stomach clenches every time he excitedly talks about raising more money for the benefit concert. It's not Malcolm's fault that I'm terrible at the very things he's so good at. I do my best to push aside the insecurity.

Once Joseph drops me home, I head straight to my room without acknowledging either of my parents. Word document and Excel spreadsheet icons nearly obscure the background of my laptop screen—a painting I made last year, of Elsa and Anna from the movie *Frozen*, one Alisha insisted on keeping when she saw it.

People in India say that when a person you're thinking about telepathically appears in real life, that person will go on to live a hundred years. Alisha might be one of these people because when I log on to Skype a few minutes later, wondering if I'll see her, I suddenly do, the gray icon beside her name going green.

I'm not sure who dials first. Maybe it's me. But seconds later, when I'm staring at my best friend's familiar grin, her hair a curly mess behind the headband, I can't help it. I burst into tears.

"Oh my God, Suzy! What happened? Okay, okay, breathe first. I'm here. I'm right here."

I press the heel of my palm to my eyes and inhale deeply. The whole story comes out: Appa's arrival, the announcement of the separation, the divorce papers I found.

"They're going to a marriage counselor now," I say, my voice dull. "When they aren't fighting about each other, they're fighting about me and what my future is going to be like. Whether I should be a doctor or a bloody engineer."

Alisha says nothing for a long moment. Then: "You know what I'm thinking?"

"What?"

"That I'm glad no one died." A nervous laugh emerges. "I mean, that's what I thought when you started crying. That there was an accident. Not that what you told me isn't serious but—"

"I know." And I do. A part of me wants to smile at her attempted joke. Only I can't. "Alisha, it feels like my whole world has turned upside down. And to top it off"—I take a breath; it's now or never—"Malcolm and I are dating. In secret."

Bug eyes, check. Dropped jaw, check. And then Alisha blurts out a word I've never heard her say in all the years I've known her.

"*That's* what makes you swear for real?" I can't believe my ears. "What happened to the food subs?"

"Even falooda can't solve this mess!"

She says it so seriously that I can't help it. I make a sound that could pass for a laugh. After a moment's hesitation, Alisha laughs as well, and a tiny bit of the weight I've been carrying around lifts.

"I know I'm a big mouth when it comes to giving advice, but even I'm coming up empty this time," she admits. "Does Malcolm know about your parents?"

"Yeah. He's been really nice about it. He keeps trying to cheer me up."

"As he should." There's a surprisingly fierce look on Alisha's face. "Suzy, have you tried talking to your parents about art school again?"

I blink. "Again? Now? They already said no!"

"Sure. But it doesn't mean it's a final answer. Look, your parents mean well. It's hard to get work as an artist. But does it make you happy, Suzy? That's the bigger question."

"It doesn't matter what makes *me* happy!" I don't understand why she can't see this. "I still have to take care of Amma. If the divorce goes through and Appa gets remarried, it won't be the same anymore."

Even though Appa has promised he will be there for me and for Amma, no matter what. But that isn't the biggest issue.

"Let's face it," I tell her. "I'm no Schulz or Seuss or R. K. Laxman. I have no idea if I can make it big as a cartoonist."

"Neither did Schulz, Seuss, or R. K. Laxman when they first started out," she retorts. "But could you live with yourself if you didn't try?"

I say nothing. It's a question that I'm still too terrified to answer.

Alisha sighs. "Never mind. Know I'm here for you no matter what."

We end our conversation a few minutes later, Alisha asking over and over again if I'm going to be okay. I pull out my school binder, divided into three neat sections by course, except for art, for which I keep a separate portfolio. My fingers itch for my sketchbook. I want to draw my anger out in flames, blue, red, and orange over an entire page.

Instead, I turn to the first tab in my binder—*Calculus*—and begin finding the derivative of a function using first principles.

———————

There's a saying that bad things happen in threes. Or multiples of threes.

Sometimes they happen in the form of Afrin Irani, who stops by my locker on the way to English on Tuesday, breezily cutting through my conversation with Malcolm.

"Malc, I want to apologize for yesterday." She gives him a slow, tentative smile. She doesn't spare me a glance. "I don't know what I was thinking."

Malcolm frowns and I almost expect him to ask, *What do you mean* yesterday? But then he shrugs, smiling back nervously in return. "It's okay." His tone is polite. Warm, even. "It happens."

The warmth isn't entirely his fault. Afrin has that effect on people. Especially when she's wearing a knee-length emerald-green sweater dress and sheer stockings, her calves encased in black leather boots that probably cost more than my entire wardrobe. Even her hair is glossy and smooth, red curls perfectly in place, unlike mine, the strands sticking up in the air or to my mouth like fine wires the moment I took off my winter cap.

"I mean it." Afrin pauses right in front of him and touches the collar of his jacket. "I really am sorry."

Malcolm's eyes widen. His breath catches, as if he's about to say more, but then he stops. This is when Afrin turns to look at me. Her smile sharpens, the rose pink of her lip gloss glistening under the fluorescent lights.

"See you around."

I say nothing in response. Neither does Malcolm. But he still turns to watch when she walks away, her heels tapping the linoleum.

"So," I say, when she's gone.

"So," Malcolm says, clear-eyed and innocent. As if it's no big deal that his ex-girlfriend walked up to him and touched him, thanking him for some conversation I wasn't even aware of.

His jacket, my mind corrects. *She touched his jacket.* But as much as I want to listen to that voice, another one continues to prod me, rears up green-faced and snarling.

"Are we going to talk about what happened?"

Malcolm sighs. "It's not what it looked like. Honestly, I wasn't even expecting her to come talk to me. Especially after the argument we had yesterday afternoon outside my house."

"She was at your *house*?!"

"*Outside* my house," he corrects. "It wasn't a social visit. She's been having some family issues. I can't go into the details, but she wanted me to talk to her parents on her behalf and I said no. I told her I couldn't do stuff like that for her anymore. That was it."

I want to believe him. I really do. Afrin and Malcolm were together long before I came into his life. But I wonder now if there are other things I don't know. Other secrets between them that I'll never be privy to.

"I'd better get to class," I say.

"Hey, Susan. Hey." Malcolm gently turns me around. "I don't love her anymore. Okay?"

His voice is quiet, serious.

"Okay," I say. Then, as he makes a move to head to English, I tell him: "You go ahead. I need to use the restroom first."

He hugs me goodbye, leaves a kiss on my forehead.

It's only when he's gone that I realize the reason behind the lump still in my throat. Malcolm said he doesn't love Afrin anymore. But he never said that he loves me.

Malcolm

In the past I've told girlfriends that I loved them. Long before I knew the meaning of the words. It was easy enough; *I love you* lost most of its meaning for me, in a way, when my parents' relationship began splintering, reducing the words to words, again.

"You're breaking me, Tehmtun," I overheard my mother say on the phone when she first discovered his affair. "Please come back. Come back and I'll forget everything. Forgive everything."

I vowed then I would never be like that over a girl. Over anyone. Until Afrin came along and I found out about her cheating on me. Ahmed told me then that there was no point in madly loving a girl who didn't love you back in the same mad way.

"The girl's gotta want to fight for you, too," he said.

"What about you and Noorie?"

"Noorie and I liked each other, but it wasn't love," Ahmed said simply. "It was pretty innocent as far as relationships go. You, on the other hand, were crazy for Afrin."

And though I know Susan and Afrin are nothing alike, I can't help but think of every bad scenario that could happen if I tell Susan I love her. What if she gets scared off or, worse, decides she doesn't love me back?

Or maybe I'm overthinking. Three days have passed since Susan and I ran into Afrin in the hallway and apart from that time on Tuesday, Susan hasn't asked any more questions about her. She has been distracted by other things—more specifically, her driving test tomorrow. I'm thinking of what I can get for her—a gift that could work for either celebration or commiseration, depending on how the test goes—when my sister races past me down the hallway.

"Mahtab!" I shout. "Hey, Mah, what's wrong?"

She skids to a stop, her sneakers squeaking against the tiles. "*Everything's* wrong, that's what!" She scowls, reminding me of the way she used to look when she was little. "I have to do *everything* and no one helps me do it!"

Trust my sister to overdose on dramatics when things aren't going her way. "So this isn't a mega-crisis?"

"It *is* a mega-crisis!" she wails. "Vincent Tran is leaving school!"

"What?" As much as Tran annoys me, this is a surprise. "When did this happen?"

"Last night! He told me his family is moving to Edmonton next week!" Mahtab looks like she's ready to cry. "He was supposed to finalize the posters for the concert. I should've pushed him to do it earlier, but he kept saying he was busy! To top it off, the events coordinator at the Living Arts Centre emailed me and Ronnie this morning, asking to see a poster for the concert—right after we made the down payment for the venue. I tried to get hold of Jen Angus, but she's booked solid with web-designing projects. The only other person who seemed interested was Susan, but I've no idea if she's any good!"

"She's great," I say confidently. "I've seen her stuff and it looks almost professional."

"Really?" Some of the stress on Mahtab's face fades. "Crap, I need to go find her—"

The warning bell rings, cutting her off. "I'll ask her when I see her today in English, okay?" I tell my sister. "I gotta go now or I'll be late for class!"

I turn the corner, barely catching the tail end of Mahtab's "Don't forget!"

I'm about four feet away from English class—twelve steps from victory—when I'm hit by a roadblock in ratty jeans, a white sweater, and bright red hair.

"It's Justin!" Afrin's nose is red from crying. "He's in the hospital!"

A drug overdose. An accident. The wrong end of a fist or a knife.

When it comes to Justin, none of these possibilities are impossible—and I hate that they run through my mind, one after another, as I drive a sobbing Afrin (and her car) to the emergency room ten minutes away from school. Afrin herself is no help, a mess of tears and unintelligible phrases when I ask her what happened.

"It's my fault!" she keeps saying. "I shouldn't . . . I . . . God, I was such a witch to him. What if he's dying, Malc? What if he's already dead?"

"Stop," I tell her, finally, through gritted teeth. "Get ahold of yourself, Afrin."

That I'm thinking the same things is probably terrible, and I need her to hang on so that I can, too, without losing myself to grief again. I have no idea if the hospital will let us in to see him either, since we're not family. Once we park, Afrin and I race toward the ER doors. I'm thinking of ways to get Justin's information from the triage nurse, when someone else crosses our path.

Justin and his mother share the same angular features, identical deep-set eyes. I've only seen the woman once in my life, at a party she accidentally crashed and threw us out of, shortly after she and Justin's dad divorced. I never forgot the look on her face—the kind that made me feel simultaneously scared and guilty—or the quiet, cold voice that hid years of pain and anger. She wears a pale blue salwar-kameez today, the same one she wore all those years ago, or maybe it's just the ball of nerves in my throat that's making me think it's the same.

"Mrs. Singh!" I say out loud. "Mrs. Singh, I'm Malcolm. And this is Afrin. I don't know if you remember us, but we're Justin's friends."

The lights pick out silver strands in Mrs. Singh's long, jet-black braid. There's a hard look in her dark eyes.

"I remember you," she tells me. "You're the boy who was throwing up until Ahmed took you home."

I feel myself go red. Ahmed's irresponsible drunk friend is not the way I want to be remembered at this time. But before I can think of something to say, she turns to Afrin.

"And you." There's no mistaking the steel within that soft voice. "I remember you as well. Aren't you the reason my son is here in the hospital right now?"

"Mrs. Singh." Afrin's voice hitches in the effort to contain a sob. "It was a mistake. I swear. My parents forced me to go out with that guy—"

"And you had to, as always, involve my son in your schemes. Telling him to beat up that other boy." Mrs. Singh no longer bothers keeping her voice down. People in the waiting area turn to stare at us.

"I didn't know a fight would break out," Afrin wails. "I even called an ambulance!"

"But you didn't go in the ambulance with him, did you? Instead you found this boy to comfort you." She jerks her head my way. "Look, young lady, I don't care what goes on in your love life, but I do care about my son. If you try to come within an inch of him again, you will have to deal with me."

Then Mrs. Singh turns, dismissing us, ignoring a blubbering Afrin. My head begins to pound. Of all the things to get involved in, this is a personal top-five worst.

"Come on," I tell Afrin softly, glancing at the stern face of the triage nurse, who looks like she'll call security on us at any minute. "I don't think it's a good idea for us to be here anyway. We'll try seeing Justin later."

If his mother ever lets us. In my pocket the phone buzzes. I slide it out for a second to see the texts on the lock screen:

Steve: why didn't you tell me you were skipping? I would've gone w/ u

Susan: Where are you? Is everything okay?

Mahtab: did you ask Susan yet?

I turn the screen black. There'll be time to answer everyone later.

The whole story comes out when we're back in the parking lot.

Afrin's talk with her parents had done no good and they'd insisted on her meeting the son of a Zoroastrian friend of theirs—a guy who was a couple of years older than Afrin.

"I went out with the guy yesterday," she says now, her voice nasally from crying. "I mean it was one date. No big deal, right? We didn't even kiss. But he showed up today at school and offered to take me out to lunch. I was so surprised, I didn't even think of saying no. As luck would have it, Justin saw us and decided to confront me about it. Then all hell broke loose."

"Why didn't you break up with Justin before dating the new guy?"

"Justin and I weren't *together*!" Afrin presses her fingers to her temples and digs them through her hair. Her nail polish is chipped and peeling. "We were seeing each other, sure. But there was no commitment. You know Justin. The moment he gets bored, he hooks up with some other girl. Since when has he ever wanted to be someone's boyfriend?"

"Were you both seeing other people at the same time, though?"

"Well, not recently, no," Afrin admits.

I try not to roll my eyes. "What do you mean by 'recently'? A week, two weeks?"

"More like a month. Or maybe a month and a half. God, you don't think . . ." Her voice trails off.

"Six weeks might mean nothing to you or me, but in Justin's books it's probably an engagement proposal," I spell out. "Do you even *like* Justin, Afrin?"

She looks up at the hospital building, staring at it for a long moment. She says nothing.

I sigh. "What now? Do you want me to take you home?"

"Not yet. I have some stuff I need to get from my locker."

We drive back to school in silence.

"Wait," she says. "Can we . . . not go back inside yet?"

I open my mouth, ready to say no, when I pause. There's a look on Afrin's face that reminds me of Mahtab when she was twelve. The times she would hide under the bed when our parents got into a fight.

"Okay," I say.

We walk to the field at the back, patches of mud visible through the melted snow.

"Remember that?" She points to the oak tree at the edge of the field. "How Han caught a guy peeing against it?"

I smile slightly. "Then Steve and I took turns pretending to unzip over there whenever Han was around, to bug him."

Seeing a smile break through the sorrow on Afrin's face, I decide to talk about more old memories. The time we came to school after a party, still smelling of booze. The time Ahmed and Steve rigged the school announcement system to play a hard rock song instead of the national anthem. Other silly things our common friends did over the years, the memory of each incident brightening Afrin's face a little more. We talk for so long that before I know it, the final bell is ringing.

"God, we were idiots!" I laugh, a little exhausted by the intensive reminiscing.

My heart sinks when I see Afrin's eyes reddening again. "Oh Malc. What am I going to do? I don't even like the guy my parents have picked for me. But Justin is so confusing."

It feels natural for me to wrap my arms around Afrin to comfort her. For her to nestle her head against my shoulder and sob. But it also feels strange. Like trying to wear a shirt that no longer fits.

"It's okay," I say now. "You need time to figure out what's best for you. Heck, it's high school. If we can't make mistakes now, when can we?"

She raises her head and looks at me through reddened eyes. "My biggest mistake was letting you go."

Then, before I can respond, she rises up on her toes and presses her lips to mine.

Susan

Malcolm disappears sometime after lunch, even though he said he would see me in English. I spend most of art fiddling with the phone in my pocket, wondering if it's presumptuous or clingy of me to text, asking him where he is. Even though another, more insistent question pesters: *Why doesn't he answer?*

"Susan?"

Fingers snap next to my left ear. Ms. Nguyen's eyelids, always a canvas of different colored eyeshadows, shimmer with gold and pink glitter today. She raises her eyebrows and gives me a look that is part disapproval, part amusement.

"I'm sorry, Ms. Nguyen," I say at once, embarrassed. "Did you ask me something?"

"I'm trying to get an idea of what you're planning for your final project."

"I'm, um, still thinking about it."

Truthfully, after Appa came here, I have given my final project little to no thought. With my driving test tomorrow morning, tests in other courses, and my parents' cold civility at home, art has taken a backseat. Something I feel deeply ashamed of now, when I look at my teacher's expectant face.

"I'm not sure if I should do caricatures or a landscape," I hedge. At least that much is true.

"I see."

I'm a little afraid of that tone of voice because I have no idea what she *does* see.

"Are you okay, Susan?" she asks me quietly. "You're not yourself these days."

At Qala Academy, I would have been scolded for my inattention in class or been sent to kneel at the back of the room. Yet, as grateful as I am for Ms. Nguyen's kindness, I don't know if I can tell her about my personal problems. It was hard enough explaining things to Malcolm and Alisha and my teacher is still a relative stranger outside the classroom. I open my mouth, ready to say I'm okay, but then shut it again.

"Know that if you need someone to talk to, my door is open, okay?" She squeezes my shoulder: a moment of warmth that disappears much too soon.

A moment later, the bell rings and I gather my stuff, ready to leave behind the general strangeness of this day. What I like best about art is that there are two exits from the room—one that leads into the hallways, and one that opens right onto the field. Today I use the alternate exit, pulling my furry hood over my head, my boots crunching the salt crystals sprinkling the concrete path. In the chilly air, I wonder once more what happened to Malcolm.

Until I see him, standing in the center of the field, his arms wrapped around a girl, bright red curls spilling out of her white cap and around her shoulders. Afrin.

He's comforting her. I tell myself. He's being a friend.

But then she raises her head and presses her lips to his. And he does not pull away.

I wait. I watch.

I move closer because I don't want to be the cliché who over-reacts to an ex-girlfriend.

When I was twelve, I came across a couple kissing in India behind a pair of palm trees on a beach in Kochi. For all the stories my mother told me about herself and Appa, I had never seen my parents do more than hug each other, let alone kiss the way this man and woman were, mouths fused together, hands on waists and entangled in hair. It had taken a few years before I understood the odd feelings muddling through me back then: curiosity and sur-prise, mingled with a funny sort of pain that I identified as longing.

I did not know back then what it feels like when the pain is compounded. How it can burn through your insides like a knife slicing skin.

When Malcolm finally does pull away, lashes blinking, Afrin giggles nervously.

Is it a consolation that Malcolm doesn't laugh in return? Is it a relief to have his eyes meet mine and to see his jaw drop in dismay?

His mouth moves, forming my name. But I can't hear anything. All I know is that I'm saying something in return. I'm saying the words I should have said a week, maybe even a month ago:

"I don't want to see you anymore."

He doesn't leave me alone for the next hour.

Phone calls that I don't take. Texts that flash across my screen—it was a mistake. it was never supposed to happen. susan, will you please talk to me?—and that I leave unanswered. An hour later, a Facebook message: i'm outside your building.

I freeze. My thumb hovers over the app, ready to delete it, when another message pops up: if you don't see me, i'm coming upstairs to your apartment.

"You wouldn't dare," I say out loud.

But something tells me he might. I may have not known Malcolm for long—not known him at all, come to think of it—but I know he is more than willing to do this and risk my parents' fury in the process. I'm still wearing my school clothes from the day so I go into the living room, school binder in hand.

"Amma, my friend Heather is downstairs to pick up some homework. Can I go drop it off?"

"Huh?" Amma looks up from the television, a little disoriented. She has been like this ever since I returned home, so out of it that I wonder if she even knows I'm here. "Oh, of course, Suzy. Of course."

I'm lying to you, I want to tell her. *Do you know that, Amma? I'm openly lying to you and you don't seem to care anymore.*

But I don't push my luck. Appa is out for the day, doing God knows what, but he might come back any moment. I pull on my winter boots and coat, grab my keys, and slip out the door. I'm not entirely surprised to find Malcolm waiting in the lobby, talking to the security guard. Like my father, Malcolm can talk to anyone anywhere, at any point in time. He straightens when he sees me approach. I force a smile for the guard and then, without another word, walk out of the lobby. I know Malcolm will follow.

The tarmac in the parking lot outside is covered with a layer of frost. My nose chills in the air, but for the first time, I welcome the cold. I lean against the wall next to a giant spherical ashtray. My skin prickles the way it always does when he comes close and then pauses a few inches away, against the wall.

"It was Justin," Malcolm says abruptly. "He was in the hospital. He got into a fight."

I say nothing. It's a tactic I have seen my mother use, her silence often pushing someone to reveal more than they originally intended.

"Afrin was a mess," he continues. "I took her to the hospital first. She and Justin's mother had a fight there. I swear I was only comforting her. I didn't mean to—"

"Did you kiss her back?"

"What?"

"Did. You. Kiss. Her. Back?"

I turn to look at him: the sharp slant of his cheekbones, the stubble over them, his funny, flat nose, those shrewd, beautiful eyes and the new shadows under them.

He licks his lips now. "Yes."

I close my eyes, my stomach roiling.

"It was more of a reflex than anything else!" A note of desperation creeps into his voice. "But I know that doesn't count. I messed up, Susan. I have no excuses."

I think of my parents. Of a relationship that was supposed to last and didn't. I think of Afrin with her beautiful face and perfect body and wonder what Malcolm sees in me. Has he already seen what he needed to? I wonder now. Did he get bored? If not, then how much longer before he does?

"It's not only about that kiss," I tell him finally. "We're not a normal couple, Malcolm. We will *never* be a normal couple. My parents will never approve of me dating anyone right now—let alone you."

"We'll continue seeing each other in secret!" he insists. "I told you I don't mind. I never did."

"You don't mind now. But you will." Once the romance of sneaking around wears off. Once frustration and disappointment begin to creep in. My parents have taught me as much. "Seeing you with Afrin today . . . maybe it was a sign."

"You seriously don't mean that."

"I think we should take a break." My mouth goes dry. "See other people."

"I don't want to see other people!"

"I'm sorry."

His face crumples for a split second before hardening again. "Fine. If that's what you want."

"Fine."

There's a tight feeling in my ribs, like a hand reached in and twisted what was left of my heart.

I wait. I watch.

I wonder if he will turn around and come back, try to win me over with another argument.

But he doesn't. After one last look, Malcolm keeps walking down the driveway and then disappears around the bend leading to the bus stop.

Malcolm

There's this trend among people in their thirties, where they write letters to their teenage selves, telling the younger version how everything that goes wrong during these years will be righted again. It appeals to romantics like my sister and to people like Freny who constantly reminisce about the good old days in Mumbai.

It never made sense to me—what was the likelihood of going back in time anyway?

It makes more sense to leave notes to your future self. The future is still a possibility, murky or otherwise. It's probably irony, or simply the universe having a joke at my expense, when I find one such note to myself while looking for a pencil the day Susan breaks up with me; the note is scribbled hastily on a yellowing, looseleaf page at the back of my school binder, written right over a badly drawn pair of middle fingers:

Dear future self—
Love still stinks.

When it comes to love, Mahtab says I'm masochistic. "You like to suffer as much as humanly possible. It's like that's the only way you know it's real."

Suffering, as the Buddha said, is caused by desire, I think drowsily the morning after our breakup. Desire for cigarettes. Vodka. Susan.

I burrow deeper into the comforter, shutting off the alarm. It's Saturday. The day of Susan's driving test. My fingers rest next to the phone on my pillow. I could wish her luck, I think, before throwing out that idea.

Or I could wallow in my sorrow. Wallow deep. Without anything to smoke or drink. I should've stocked up, I think, instantly followed by, Mahtab will kill me.

A knock on the door. "Malu! Come out of there."

Speak of the devil.

The knob jiggles. Locked. "I hate when you do this! I hope you're not drinking in there!"

My mouth waters. I close my eyes.

"That's it!" Mahtab shouts. "I'm calling for reinforcements!"

An hour later, when she knocks on my door again, I shout: "Go away, Mahtab!"

"It isn't Mahtab, it's Freny!"

This was my sister's idea of reinforcements?

"Someone is here to see you." Freny's voice is oddly cheerful.

"Who, the police?" I mutter under my breath. Then, louder: "Tell them I'm not home."

"It's your Mancher Mama!"

She's lying. My uncle is still in Bermuda on vacation. Isn't he? I squint at the calendar on my phone, trying to remember.

"Fine." I've never heard Freny sound this assertive in my life. "I'll tell your mama that his favorite nephew doesn't want to see him. Let him deal with you."

I curse, tossing the comforter off my head. "Okay, *okay*! I'll be right down."

Normally, I would never come down at Freny's request. For anything. But my mom's brother Manchershaw Bhikhaji Panday is a different story. Back when he and my father were wrestlers for the Indian Railways, Mancher Mama was known as Ek-Dus—a man who had the capacity to fight ten men at a time.

"Now you eat the food of ten men at one time," my old man once told him sarcastically.

"What, this?" Mancher Mama poked the rounded flesh bulging over his belt. "Forgot you have one, too, Tehmtun? The way you forgot your wife?"

Mancher Mama takes crap from no one and I love him for it. The trouble? *No one* also includes me. If I don't go down to the living room, my uncle will come up and probably break open the flimsy lock on my bedroom door. Mancher Mama, full-on drama. Mahtab wasn't kidding when she mentioned reinforcements.

I'm still scowling when I go downstairs. Freny jumps up from the armchair and says she'll be in the kitchen if we need her. Mancher Mama occupies most of the love seat, part Hulk, part Budai, his bulk a decent combination of muscle and fat. His face, browned even more than usual from being in a country that isn't as cold as this one, breaks into a grin when he sees me.

"Malcko!"

261

Trust adults in the Parsi community to come up with perfectly innocuous and awful nicknames. In spite of my annoyance, I feel myself smile. "Hey, Mama. How was Bermuda?"

"Hot. I miss it already. Give me a hug, gadhera."

Only Mancher Mama can call me a donkey in Gujarati and get a hug in return. Anyone else—as Steve can attest—gets sucker punched.

"So," Mancher Mama says once I'm settled in the armchair across from him, "popular with the ladies, are we? Or maybe not so popular anymore."

"Mahtab told you." I need to remind Mahtab that not everything in my life is everyone else's business.

"What, am I some stranger? Of course, your sister called me at once!"

I try hard not to roll my eyes. My mom was an excellent emotional blackmailer, but Mancher Mama has raised it to an art form with that hangdog expression, disappointment oozing from every pore. But maybe it's because Mancher Mama *isn't* a stranger, because he looks so much like Mom—and like me—that I begin telling him everything. Afrin and Justin. Susan. The whole mess of what followed.

"So yeah. I get why she broke up with me. But the thing is that I didn't even *like* that kiss with Afrin. It was truly a reflex—a douchebag reflex—but still." I rub a hand over my face. "God, how do I make her see that?"

"You don't," my uncle says simply. "You were, as you so eloquently put it, a douchebag."

I scowl. "Thanks, Mama."

"Only being truthful. But it's also true that this is not the insurmountable obstacle your teenage mind is telling you about."

"I resent that comment, but will let it pass—what do you mean *not* insurmountable?"

"Neither of you has been in a real relationship before—or at least one where there is actual give-and-take and compromise. Your mami and I have been married twenty years and I still mess up from time to time. Granted I never kissed another woman while I was married to her—"

I groan.

"—*anyway*, the point is: relationships are difficult for everyone. Plus, your girl is going through trouble at home. You need to give her time to overcome that."

"I can help her with it!"

"You can't, Malcko. Some people need time to themselves to figure things out. They don't like going to others with their problems. Your mami is like that. So is your father."

I stiffen when I hear the last word. As mad as I am at Susan, she's nothing like my old man.

"Listen to me. This is your heart." Mancher Mama holds a giant fist up to his chest. "It is not made of glass. Your heart is made of muscle, tough and resilient, meant to pump two thousand gallons of blood in a day. Two thousand *gallons*. That's over fifteen thousand water bottles! It's strong enough to weather most things, including emotional storms. Naturally, in the nature of muscle, the heart also has its weaknesses. It retains memories, good and bad. But muscle can be retrained, reshaped, can be made to learn new habits."

"So you're saying I should find another girl to, er, exercise with?"

Mancher Mama grins the way only uncles can at their nephews' bawdy jokes. "Oh, I don't think you'll be looking for other girls, or will even need to. But I do think you need to do something to occupy your time instead of turning into a Devdas."

Devdas. The brooding Bengali hero from a novel, who turned into an alcoholic over the woman he loved.

"Does it ever go away?" I ask. "The pain."

"It will." Mancher Mama opens and closes his hand. "One day your heart will move the way it used to when in pain, and you will realize it isn't pain, but only a reflex. Like that kiss of yours with Afrin."

I frown, rolling the words over in my head. "Afrin called last night. She said I didn't love her anymore." I don't tell Mancher Mama that she was trying to change my mind about it. That she wanted us to try to start over.

"You don't love me either," I told her. "But Justin? He likes you. A lot. Why are you trying to cheat on him?"

"I *am* cheating on him!" she insisted.

"Doesn't count if I'm not a willing participant."

She had no response to that.

"What do *you* think?" Mancher Mama asks now.

"I care for Afrin," I admit. "It is why I went with her to the hospital in the first place. But I don't want a relationship with her. I don't love her. Not like—"

I clamp my mouth shut. *Love.* How did that word come out of my mouth?

"From here," Mancher Mama says, pointing to his chest, and I know I've spoken the last thought out loud. "It's always from here."

"A reflex?"

"Not everything is a reflex, Malcolm."

Malcolm, not Malcko. "You're serious."

"As serious as I can be without anything to eat or drink for a whole hour. Freny, my dear!" he calls out, turning to the kitchen. "Jara chai malse ke?"

264

Chai. Brewed strong on the stove, with a secret spice mix, slices of ginger, and sprigs of fresh mint. Mom's favorite beverage.

I wonder if Mancher Mama will leave after the chai, but to my relief, he stays for lunch when Freny asks him to, and later for dinner. Mahtab is overjoyed and volunteers to bring out board games. Mancher Mama and I ignore her and play *Call of Duty* instead.

My old man is the only one who shows any sign of displeasure, but, as my uncle reminds me: "He has always looked like that."

It's only when Mancher Mama leaves that the burn in my chest, numbed by distraction and activity, starts up again. I think of Susan, wonder how she did on her test, before pushing aside the thought. My fingers shake with the need for a cigarette.

I head to my bedroom window and open it. A blast of chilly air hits, and I realize I'm not wearing my coat. I'm debating if it's worth sneaking downstairs and out the back instead of down the pipe nailed to the outside of this wall, when a city bus pauses at the stop in front of my house, hazard lights flashing. In the quiet, I hear a series of *beeps*, the *hiss* of a platform lowering to let down a woman with a baby carriage. The sides of the vehicle are, as always, covered with ads. A tax company, a TV show, a real estate agent, a new Indian restaurant. I stare at the bus for a long moment before taking out my phone.

"Hey, Ronnie? It's Malcolm." My breath rises in a mist in front of me. "Listen, I think I might have an idea to get us more sponsors."

Susan

"Reverse park between the red and white cars," the driving examiner says.

It's somewhat surprising that she's asking me to demonstrate this. Joseph made sure I began the test by reversing the car out of the lot. "If they test you on backing out the car, it's unlikely that they'll test you on backing in," he said.

My examiner, however, seems determined to make unlikely likely. She smiles at me, a shrewd look in her blue eyes that I recognize from years of being tested by teachers at Qala Academy—a look that seems certain I'm going to finally trip up. And I might, even though the test has been surprisingly smooth so far. With the exception of parallel parking, which I've always been horrible at— but even there I didn't hit the curb, which would have resulted in an automatic fail.

Be aggressive.

The words rang through my head while I was changing lanes (thankfully there was no snow or ice on the roads this morning) and vanished before I could give a name to the voice.

I nod at the examiner now, pretending this is exactly what I expected, and begin backing the car into the lot at the test center. Slow and steady, sweat trickling down my forehead and down my back inside the heavy winter coat I'm wearing. Turning the steering wheel, straightening the car in the lot. Park. Hand brake. Ignition off. My hands move through the motions automatically and I collapse against the seat, waiting for the examiner's verdict.

She grimaces at the yellow sheet in front of her. "I'm passing you for now, but your parallel parking was really bad. Your reverse parking and general driving were much better—"

"I passed?" I blurt out.

She gives me a warm smile, the human side of her shining for a brief moment. "Yes, you passed."

I tune out the rest of her words.

I passed. I passed. I passed.

Now I won't always need to take the bus. Or depend on others for rides.

I passed.

My grin is so wide I'm sure my face is in danger of cracking. While waiting in line with Joseph for my temporary paper license, I call Amma with the good news.

"Praise the Lord! I am so proud of you, kanna! What would you like? Shall I make achappam today? How about chicken biryani or fish curry?"

"Achappam sounds great." My mouth waters at the thought of

the sweet, intricately shaped rice-flour rosettes my mother makes, usually only for Christmas or as a special treat. "And chicken biryani."

"Rensil? Rensil, listen to the good news—Suzy passed her test!" I hear her say with such joy in her voice that for a long moment I forget my parents no longer want to be together.

Appa comes on the line to congratulate me. "Well done, Suzy! I told you that it was easy, didn't I?"

My smile slips slightly. There was a person who helped me do this. A person whose number I still haven't managed to delete from my phone.

"I have to go, Appa. Will talk at home."

My fingers slide across the screen, pause at the *M*s in my phone directory.

I passed my test. Thank you for your help. My thumb hovers over the Send key.

"Next!" the woman behind the licensing desk calls out.

"That's us," Joseph tells me. There's a look in his eyes that could possibly be approval. I glance one last time at the screen and then follow him, leaving the message unsent. While Joseph drives me home from the test center that afternoon, I press the backspace key, watching each letter slowly disappear.

On Monday, I do something I've never done before: I skip English by myself.

I managed to make it through most of the day without seeing Malcolm or any of his friends—even locking myself in a bathroom stall during lunch. But in English there's no way I can guarantee not seeing them.

I avoid the field and trek around the building to where Arthur Eldridge runs a small preschool and day care center, my teeth chattering in my mouth from the cold. I slip inside one of the double doors and slide down the wall and onto the floor, sighing in the relative warmth of the hallway.

Here, no one pays me any attention. Parents slip through the doors without bothering to glance around, their feet drawn to the room down the hall. They emerge moments later with a toddler bundled up in a colorful coat and hat. The sight makes my heart ache a little for reasons I don't understand.

I switch my attention to my phone instead, but even Facebook doesn't distract me today, images and status updates blurring past. A photo finally comes into focus: four girls in abayas at a restaurant, their heads uncovered, giant smiles on their faces. Alisha is one of them, her arm around Emerald Verghese. Strange, I think. How a sight that would have surely bothered me a few weeks ago barely even registers now.

"Nice picture," a voice says. "Those your friends?"

I click the Hold button, turning the phone screen black. I look up at Heather Dupuis. "What are you doing here?"

"I work here." Heather grins. "Well, technically, not work-work, but it's my day and Preeti's to volunteer at the center for parenting class." I hear a throat clearing to my left and find the other girl leaning against the wall, an amused look on her face.

I raise my eyebrows. *Parenting*, seriously? What will this school come up with next?

"Don't you have class though?" Heather's voice reminds me so much of my mother that I feel myself bristling.

"Mr. Zuric's out sick," I declare. "I figured I didn't have to sit through a class with a sub in there."

"Come on, Susan." Heather's voice grows softer. "I saw Mr. Zuric in the line for French fries in the cafeteria today. Besides, we know what happened with Malcolm."

Of course they do. Everyone who is anyone knows about the big kiss and the way I ran after witnessing it.

"I don't want to talk about that."

"Wanna hit stuff instead?" Preeti speaks up.

I blink. "What?"

She smiles at me. "Come hang out with us after school."

I open my mouth to refuse—there's no way Amma will agree—when Preeti says: "We'll talk to your parents."

"Fine, whatever."

I don't expect either of them to show up, but after art, they're right there, waiting for me outside the classroom doors.

"Are you taking the bus today or waiting for a ride?" Heather asks.

"The bus," I say. Even though I now have a license and can legally drive by myself, we still have only one car and Appa needed it today to run errands.

Amma no longer bothers asking him what those errands are. Neither do I. The rest of the weekend after that celebratory Saturday went by in relative peace, with both my parents being somewhat civil to each other instead of spending hours at a time in frosty silence. It's almost as if a truce has been reached and a little part of me can't help but hope this will be the beginning to them mending their relationship.

"Great! Then I'll drive you," Heather says, her tone allowing no room for negotiation.

True to their word, Heather and Preeti talk to my parents,

charming both Amma and Appa so well, you'd think they did this for a living.

"So," I say when we step back out of my building's lobby and into the cold. "What do we plan to do?"

"I told you," Preeti says. "We're going to hit a few things."

A few minutes ago, Preeti and Heather told my parents that we were part of a physics study group for an upcoming test.

I can't help it. I laugh.

It's only when I catch my breath again and find them staring at me that I realize they are dead serious.

The heavy bag in Preeti's garage is four feet high and weighs around forty pounds. It hangs from a hook on the ceiling like a giant sausage encased in black leather. As I move closer, I'm surprised to see an oddly familiar face painted on it.

"Is that Simon Cowell?" I ask, surprised.

"Yeah. My dad was pretty pissed with the way he treated that Indian kid on *American Idol*. I mean, it happened *years* ago, but Dad has an elephant memory about such things. Remember Sanjaya Malakar, Heather?" Preeti pulls out a pair of boxing gloves and turns to face me. "Heather had a huge crush on him."

"I did not!" Heather's face turns tomato red.

"He was on another show later," I tell them, remembering suddenly. "On this celebrity version of *Survivor* with these different rules."

Preeti's jaw drops. "Shut. Up."

"I'm serious." I laugh. "It was fun watching him. Though he didn't last long."

"What show?" Preeti asks.

"*I'm a Celebrity . . . Get Me Out of Here!*" Heather says.

Preeti and I turn to face Heather whose hands are over her mouth.

"I did have a crush on him," she admits. "Sue me."

It's strange being around two girls after months of brooding in my room or spending time only with Malcolm. It's only now, surrounded by giggles, that I realize how much I've missed female companionship. And how silly I was to isolate myself.

"Hold out your hands," Preeti tells me in a commanding voice. She removes a roll of pink cotton wraps from a box—"for protection," she explains—and begins winding them around my wrists, palms, and knuckles. Once my hands have been partially mummified, she helps me slide on a pair of bright red boxing gloves, Velcro-ing them tightly in place. I'm surprised by how heavy my hands feel, like small weights have been strapped to my knuckles and wrists.

"These weigh ten ounces." Preeti lightly taps the leather of one of the gloves. "They're pretty old—from the time I kickboxed in middle school. But your hands are small, so these should fit better. Sparring gloves are sixteen ounces and will be too much for you as a beginner. How do these feel?"

"Okay, I guess." I stare at the blobs that are now my hands for a long moment, wondering what on earth I've gotten myself into.

"Good," Preeti says. "Now, go on. Punch."

"It's better if you picture him while doing it," Heather adds.

No question who she's referring to.

I visualize Malcolm's spiky hair, the smile he gave me on my first day at Arthur Eldridge. I remember his hands cupping snowflakes and I feel my elbows drop to my waist, when another memory invades: Malcolm's hair stuck in wet waves to his forehead. Malcolm's hands lightly resting on Afrin's waist, his mouth pressed to hers.

Air rushes out of my lungs, and I swing, wild and wayward, my punch barely moving the heavy bag, let alone making a dent in Simon Cowell's nose. I feel Preeti's hand on my wrist which now smarts under the glove.

"Aim straight," Preeti says. "Like this, look. That way you won't hurt your wrist."

She shows me how to move, instructs me to keep my feet light and agile, as I throw punches, one after another. It takes about five minutes for Simon Cowell to be supplanted with images from my own mind—pictures that have me moving faster, punching harder.

I punch the space between Malcolm and Afrin's mouths. Over and over, until they break apart, clutching their jaws with their hands.

I punch the boy, VJ, who slid a hand up my thigh when I was intoxicated, picture him spitting out a tooth I broke in the process.

I punch the uncle from Kochi who asked me to come speak to him on the phone and demonstrate my Canadian accent.

My mouth opens, anger rumbling from my throat in a single sound.

I punch the line my parents have drawn in the sand, the line that split the marriage they always promised would last.

I punch. I punch. *IpunchIpunchIpunch.*

"Susan. Hey, Susan." Preeti's strong hands curve over my arms before wrapping around my diaphragm, holding me back from the last throw. "It's okay," she whispers in my ear. "It's okay."

Water burns my eyes, trickles down my chin. Preeti pulls me

back to the couch in the corner. There Heather's arms wrap around me like Amma's would have when I was small.

Alisha is thousands of miles away in Jeddah. The boy I love may still be head over heels for another girl. My parents' marriage may not last the winter. But here, amid the smell of sweat, old clothes, gas, and mildew, I suddenly feel that I am not alone.

My knuckles have bruises on them when I remove the gloves and the wrap. "Oh, no! I should've taped you first!" Preeti frets.

"It's okay." At least now I look a little more like what I feel on the inside. "I'd better get home. Lots to study."

"Are you sure?" Heather's blue eyes are wide, worried.

"Yup. These are battle scars."

"That's my girl." Preeti pats my back.

Heather and I wave goodbye and walk to her car. Unlike rain, which falls to the ground in heavy pellets, snow floats in the air like overlarge tufts of dust, feathering the front of Heather's car in white. We keep our own conversation light, discussing what might show up on the next physics test as Heather pulls out a brush to wipe the snow off her windshield.

"I wish I had your memory," Heather says, not even bothering to hide the envy in her voice. "It would save so much time!"

"That doesn't help me with lab work, though." Heather has a natural affinity for the subject that I don't, an instinct that has helped her ace every lab the teacher has assigned us so far.

"You love physics," I tell her now. I don't.

Heather peers at me from over the top of her glasses. "Do you want to talk about it?"

"About what?"

"Oh, anything. Life. Parents. Boys. Girls." Heather winks at me and I laugh.

And maybe it's that laugh that eases things between us, that lets me tell her about how much trouble I've been having in physics this year. About my parents, who can barely talk let alone decide what their future and mine is going to be. Malcolm is the only topic I leave untouched, but Heather doesn't press me about that. She listens without judgment, without interrupting me to give input the way Alisha would. As much as I love Alisha, my best friend isn't much of a listener, often cutting me short when she grows impatient with what I have to say.

"I get it," Heather says, after I grow silent. "Parents can be hard to talk to. Some even more than others. My parents got divorced when I was nine. I had the toughest time. Threw so many tantrums that at one point I was sure they'd send me away to a boarding school. But they didn't.

"My parents love me, Susan, and yours love you as well. I'm not telling you what to do—God knows, I hate when people do that to *me*—but at some point you'll have to make a decision about your life. About what's important to you. It may be your parents' wishes. It may be a different career. Whatever it is, it'll be the right decision because *you* made it."

I mull over her words for a moment. "I never thought of it that way."

Heather shrugs, turning on the car's ignition. "No one gets to pick what is right or wrong for anyone else. It's always going to be your decision, Susan. Nothing that's truly meant for you can be taken away."

"That sounds way too philosophical for someone who wants to be a scientist."

Heather grins. "Who said scientists can't be philosophers?"

It's only when I finish laughing that I wonder about those words. When I get back home, I open the curtains of my bedroom window and stare up into the sky. Here, in the city, the stars are mostly blotted out. Except for one. The North Star, with a thin sliver of moon right beside it. If I squint hard enough, I can picture Jeddah's Floating Mosque underneath: a shadowy blue jewel against the night sky.

I riffle through my bag and pull out my sketchbook. The corner is somewhat bent, probably from getting awkwardly caught under one of my other heavier textbooks. I straighten it as best as I can before turning to a blank page, where I draw the faint outline of a dome.

Here's the thing about bad grades: You can run from them, but you can't hide them from your parents. Or at least not if your parents are like mine.

The next afternoon, I find Amma and Appa sitting on the couch. Together, I note, for the first time since their talk about separating. They are also glaring at me, which, in my experience, foreshadows an ambush.

"What is it?" I ask. "What did I do?"

"What *didn't* you do is what I'd like to know," Amma begins, and then clamps her mouth shut when Appa places a hand on her shoulder.

He's *touching* her. And she's *letting* him. This must be serious.

"Susan, your mother found a recent physics lab of yours," he tells me in the Doctor Voice. "The one in which you—"

"You know about the C-plus." I should have ripped the paper to shreds instead of stuffing it in my bedroom drawer.

My father frowns. "Don't act flippant with me, young lady. Your mother was so shocked that she called the school and asked to speak to your teacher, Mr. Franklin. He said you had a good sense of the theory and the problem sets, but your lab work is weak—has been weak since the beginning of the semester. Why didn't you tell us you were having problems?"

Because I'm not supposed to have problems with academics. Because I thought I could figure things out without involving either one of you. Because I was afraid of seeing these exact expressions on your faces.

I don't put my jumbled thoughts into words. I'm not a smooth talker on my best days, and today my insides feel like a giant knotted mess.

"At this rate, you'll probably only qualify for advanced admission into general science at university." Appa's tone makes the BSc program sound mediocre. "Medicine or engineering are out of the question."

"Now *that* would put your plans in a fix, wouldn't it?" The words spill from my mouth, taste like coffee grounds.

"Susan!"

"All your plans—your *grand* plans"—I sprinkle imaginary stardust in the air—"to make me a doctor or engineer or everything I don't and never have wanted to be, are going down the toilet, right, Amma, Appa? Just like your marriage."

"How dare you—" Amma begins.

"How dare I what—exist? Isn't that what you told Ammachi in your letter, Amma? The one where you said you didn't want to get pregnant in the first place?"

My mother's mouth falls open. For the first time, nothing emerges from it.

"And you." I turn to my father who looks like he has never seen me before. "You never wanted us either, did you? We interfered with your plans to get with your nurse, so you sent us both away."

"Suzy, it wasn't like that. Please listen—"

But I don't want to listen to my parents anymore. I leave them both making excuses to the air and lock myself in my bedroom.

"Susan! Hey, Susan!"

"Mahtab?" I'm surprised to see Malcolm's sister waiting for me outside art. "Don't you have class?"

"I do, but this is more important." She hesitates. "Did, um, you and Malcolm talk?"

I feel my stomach tighten. Four days have passed since I told Malcolm I didn't want to see him anymore. A weekend, a Monday and a Tuesday. Four. Whole. Days. It shouldn't feel like time is moving at snail speed, but it does. Especially during English—which I can no longer afford to skip—where he completely ignores me *and* Afrin, in spite of the latter's hardest attempts at getting his attention.

"We're, um, not talking anymore. But I think you already know that."

Mahtab sighs, a sheepish look on her face. "Yeah. But I guess I wanted you to know that he's not with Afrin or with anyone else. And that he misses you. Badly."

I feel something pinch my insides. *No. No. I can't go there. Not now.* I'm about to make an excuse and head in, when Mahtab pulls a flyer from her bag and hands it to me.

"What I really wanted to talk to you about was this."

TO SYRIA, WITH LOVE, the flyer says. *A concert for humanitarian aid.*

"What about it?" I ask, my mouth dry.

"My art director is moving to another city. And I found out you draw really well. Like pro-level."

I swallow hard, not asking where she got that bit of info. I study the flyer again. It pretty much gives the same information Mahtab told me right now. I am about to say no—I'm already in deep trouble with my parents for ruining their dreams and they probably won't want to see me pursuing art in any way—when I begin to see places where the flyer could be improved. Like the drawing of the little Syrian girl in the corner—her hijab isn't quite right. There are maple leaves drawn all over the place, but they look haphazard and are only stenciled in.

"That's me," Mahtab says, when she sees me tracing one. "I'm not much of an artist. That little girl was the last thing I got our last artist to draw and I know she isn't perfect—"

"I'll do it."

"—either. You can also—*What did you say?*" It's not difficult to imagine Mahtab as a cartoon, her eyeballs bugging out on springs at my declaration.

I can't help but smile. "I said I'll do it."

"Oh my God, Susan, oh my God, *thank you!*"

"Don't thank me yet," I warn her. "I still have to get my parents' permission."

"They'll say yes." Mahtab's voice oozes confidence. "Have you completed your forty volunteering hours, already? No? That's perfect, then! You can tell them it's for that. I can't promise you'll complete *all* your hours with us, but we can still give you some."

As she speaks, I wonder if I'm doing the right thing. Even if my parents agree, joining the committee will only mean seeing *more* of Malcolm, who I'm desperately trying to avoid. I glance at the flyer again, at the elements that need fixing. The old Susan would back out, would make any excuse to avoid a sticky situation. The one who threw up at a party and got mocked for it, who lost a boy to another girl knows there are worse embarrassments.

I think about what Heather told me—*Who said scientists can't be philosophers?*—and replace philosophers with artists. The mosque I began drawing that night is now complete; I finished it this morning, right before heading to school.

"Sounds good," I tell Mahtab.

This isn't about Malcolm or my parents. This is about me.

Ms. Nguyen pokes her head out the door as the bell goes off. Today her hair is platinum blond. "Still want to join us, Susan?"

"Yes, Ms. Nguyen."

I wave at Mahtab who's already racing down the hall to her class. Once settled in front of my canvas, I pull out the flyer. *TO SYRIA, WITH LOVE*. I can hand-letter the words with a modern font, maybe look up some stencils online for ideas. My thoughts center, focus on the multiple ways in which I can design a new poster. In the process, I have a flash of inspiration. A warm feeling that prickles pleasantly across my skin.

I raise a hand. "Ms. Nguyen?"

"Yes, Susan?"

"I think I have an idea for my final project."

Malcolm

I sense Susan's presence before I see her in the parking lot, steps away from the cafeteria, which the school is letting us use for a couple of hours every Saturday and on the last two Sundays before the concert to organize everything. She steps out of the driver's seat of a Corolla—the one I taught her to drive in— and waves goodbye to her dad, who moves over to take her place.

She passed.

"What are you smiling at?" Ronnie's voice is cheery and way too loud.

"Nothing." It's easy enough to lose the smile when I remember I can't congratulate her. Or talk to her. Or even look at her. Either of the three will show I'm still not over her and I don't ever want to be known for *that* sort of mooning anymore.

"Need anything?" I ask Ronnie, hoping he'll give me something to distract myself with.

"Yup. Write a speech to welcome the VIPs."

"What?" Panic curls under my ribs. "I meant fund-raising."

"You're still doing that, Malc," he says calmly, not seeming the least bit fazed by my reaction. "But Vincent Tran was one of the VIP liaisons and, as you know, he's gone now. I was hoping you'd take over for him and be on the welcoming committee with Yusuf Shire."

"Why me though?" I feel my nerves kick in. This isn't some random speech or a class presentation. There'll be *kids* at the event. Kids who've faced war and death. "Why not someone like Ahmed?"

"I thought about him first, but Ahmed has been working double duty, volunteering with us and at his local mosque as well. He can't even come to every meeting. I could ask Isabel, but she's busy, too. Steve is"—we both glance at my friend, who's currently attempting to make Isabel laugh with arm farts—"Steve."

I sigh. "I'm probably going to regret saying yes, aren't I?"

"Great!" His beaming expression is instant, more overpowering than Mahtab's. "You can coordinate with Yusuf over there and make sure your speeches are the same in English and Arabic."

"Wait, Ronnie! What happened to the idea I gave you about publicity last week?"

Ronnie shakes his head. "We'll talk about that later!"

I feel my insides deflate a little. So it didn't work. It was still worth a shot. My most pressing problem right now is the speech. Sweat forms in a layer over my palms. I've done presentations at school before. A few years ago, I might have even done some good ones. But I'm so out of touch now, I barely know what I'm supposed to say. At least Yusuf, who was born in Somalia and lived in

Dubai for several years, knows Arabic. I see him now, laughing and talking to Susan, snippets of his voice reaching me two tables away.

"...I lived in Dammam for eleven years before we moved here."

Okay, so it wasn't Dubai.

Susan says something in return and they both laugh. Great. Now they're bonding over having lived in the same country.

"Wait, you have something..." He reaches out to touch her cheek, his hand resting way longer against her skin than it should, before finally holding up a finger to show her.

"Yo! Big brother." Mahtab elbows me hard, shoving a legal pad and a pencil in my hands. "Time to get started."

"Why don't you or Ronnie write your own speeches?" I tear my gaze away from Susan's happy, glowing face.

"Because you promised," my sister tells me sternly. "Because these kids and this event are more important than your love life."

The old Malcolm would flip her the bird and stalk off, finding the nearest liquor store that would take his fake ID or the nearest girl whose mouth he could bury a tongue in. I, on the other hand, take long, deep breaths until my simmering anger cools, allowing me to process my sister's words. Mahtab's right, of course. I *am* here for the kids. Besides, I was the one who messed up things with Susan. I have no right to get angry if she flirts with another guy. Or if she even starts dating him at some point.

Because it's going to happen. I've seen the boys at school, the way they've watched her since we broke up. I even caught Steve staring at one point. I can't blame them for it. Susan is a pretty girl and, now that she's started hanging out with Heather and Preeti, she has begun drawing even more attention. I try not to stare at the way her leggings hug her calves or how her long

283

sweater curves around her butt. I know I've been staring too long when Mahtab says, "Put your eyes back in your head."

I pull up a chair, focusing on the blank yellow page in front of me. After five minutes of nothing, I sigh and decide to scroll through Facebook to pass the time. My thumb pauses at Susan's name, and a photo she recently liked: a group of grinning girls at a restaurant in Jeddah.

Without really meaning to, I glance up and find her watching me, as if she sensed me looking at the picture. I'm about to say something—anything—when she turns away to focus on her own project: a giant sheet of construction paper with a pencil and a couple of markers. I turn back to my phone, swallowing the lump in my throat.

———————

It's hard enough to ignore Susan at school, but when she sits in front of me in English, the back of her neck and ponytail forever interfering with my vision, it's damn near impossible. She's doing her best to ignore *me*, though, refusing to toss me a single look, not even while passing classroom handouts back to me. One day, to spite her, I decide to brush my fingers against her desk the way I did during the first two weeks of school, earning a glare from her in response. This time, though, she doesn't look. She stares straight ahead expressionlessly; her pale knuckles the only sign that she's noticed. A part of me wants to crow in triumph (she's not completely insensitive to me) while another part wants to sink lower (she still hates my guts).

The next meeting for the benefit concert is held the Monday before Christmas Eve. I pull myself together and coordinate with

Yusuf for the welcome speeches. He really isn't a bad guy—if I ignore how he keeps eyeing Susan every chance he gets.

"Looks like I'm outta luck," he says suddenly.

I glance up and find him—predictably—staring at someone behind me. I force myself not to look.

"With what?" My voice comes out gruffer than intended.

Yusuf's smile dims for a second, as if remembering who he's talking to. Then it widens again. "With your girl."

Heat saturates the back of my neck. "Susan? She's not my girl."

"Does she know that? Do *you*?" He laughs. "Do you know how many times I've turned around to find you looking like you'd kill me?"

Now I'm genuinely embarrassed. I say nothing.

"But that's not even what bothers me. I mean, jealous exes are a part of the package when it comes to pretty girls."

I study Yusuf's strong face, his clear deep-set brown eyes, the curls cropped close to his skull. Even when he's wearing a thick sweater, you can tell the dude is ripped. If it comes down to looks, there is no contest; Yusuf wins hands down.

"But," he says, emphasizing the word, "if the girl doesn't like me back, it's a different story."

"What do . . . Nothing. Forget I asked."

But Yusuf answers anyway. "When I see a girl stealing glances at another guy when he's not looking at her, I *know* I've been relegated to the role of the lovable movie sidekick. Which, to be honest, stinks."

I feel myself grin. He smiles back.

"She's all yours," he says as he pats my back.

The relief I expect at hearing Yusuf Shire isn't my competition isn't quite there. Because Susan *isn't* mine and one day there will be competition. Serious competition, in the form of a Malayali Christian boy who won't make the mistake of kissing his ex. A boy both Susan's parents approve of. Who Susan herself may fall for. I take a deep breath and scribble something down on a piece of paper and fold it four times. Before I can think too much about it, I walk toward Susan's table and drop it on her binder. This time she looks up, right at me.

I'm the one who looks away first.

The last few minutes of the meeting are dedicated to a special announcement that Ronnie has in store.

"I've been sitting on this for a while now," Ronnie declares.

"Clearly." Isabel nods at the way Ronnie's bouncing on his toes and I smother a laugh.

"It's about publicity. And Malcolm was the one who gave me the idea for it."

I blink as Ronnie flashes me a grin. He can't possibly mean—

"He suggested reaching out to this special segment on the six o'clock news that covers local human interest stories—"

Electricity buzzes under my skin. The ad for the TV show splashed across the city bus along with the reporter's smiling face.

"—and they've agreed to publicize the event a week before the concert! We'll also get some TV coverage the day of the event!"

Instead of joining the cheering that erupts, my brain races. On impulse, I decide to text Jay, who's working at the café this morning.

hey, will michelle be in today? To my surprise, a little text bubble pops up on the other end, and seconds later, a message from Jay: **She comes in at 12. Why?**

have to ask her something important.

I rise to my feet. "Hey, Ronnie. Is it okay if I cut out a little early? The owner will be there at my café at noon. Gonna try again and see what she says."

Ronnie looks surprised. "Didn't she already sponsor us?"

"Yeah." I clap his shoulder. "But the last time, we didn't have confirmed TV coverage. Maybe I can squeeze a little more out of her. I mean, there's no guarantee she'll say yes. But no harm in trying, right?"

He smiles. "No harm at all."

Without really meaning to, I glance at Susan, whose brows are drawn together as she draws furiously on a piece of chart paper. I've never seen her draw before. Never seen her this focused, like there's an entire world locked away inside her. She looks up when Mahtab taps her shoulder and talks to her—presumably about the poster. I pull up the hood of my jacket, seconds before Susan's gaze collides with mine. The paper I left on her desk earlier remains untouched.

Susan

I hope you will find a way to forgive me someday.

A single line, etched into my brain, even though I crumpled the paper and threw it away after reading it.

Someday. Like he didn't expect it to happen immediately. Like he'll—I stop that train of thought. Even I'm not foolish enough to think Malcolm will wait for me.

"Commitment," Amma said on Tuesday morning, "is entirely impossible for the male sex."

I laughed, not because what she said was particularly funny, but because she used the word *sex* for the first time in front of me. Even if it was in an entirely nonsexual way. I tell Heather and Preeti the story before homeroom, expecting them to give me blank looks like they usually do when I try to crack jokes, but this time they laugh with me. I guess we're still first graders at heart.

Mr. Franklin surprises us that day during physics by announcing that he'll not be counting our grades on the last lab—the one on which I got the C-plus.

"Wow," a girl in front of me says amid the whispers that break out. "I know I did badly on that lab, but the class average must be really low."

"Didn't you know? Half the class failed it," the boy next to her replies. "Even Dupuis only got a B and she's, like, a genius."

"You've all been working hard this semester"—Mr. Franklin's calm voice cuts through the chatter—"and have done fairly well on average with the exception of that lab. I also realize university admissions are coming up and don't want to give your parents any reason to worry."

A few cheers break out. I feel my face turn red and avoid looking at Mr. Franklin when he hands out a new assignment to replace the canceled one.

I take the paper quietly and scan it. Relief spreads through me. This isn't lab work. With this assignment, I can probably bump my final physics grade up to something decent, which, when combined with my other courses, will probably take me right into medicine or engineering at a reputable Canadian university—just as my parents want.

I should feel happy, I think, as the relief seeps away, leaving behind a strange, hollow feeling. Right?

I don't want to be a doctor or engineer. I wonder how many desi kids have said these words out loud and withered to bits under their parents' glares.

During lunch, Preeti says I should take the easy way out. "Fail a course or two. They can't force you to go into a program if you aren't any good at it."

Heather disagrees, of course. "Only *you* could do something like that and still get away with it. The rest of us have a conscience," she tells Preeti.

As if my conscience isn't causing me enough problems, there's Malcolm as well, who never really leaves my thoughts, whose presence was strangely palpable during yesterday's fund-raising meeting, even when he wasn't looking at me. Except when I talked to Yusuf Shire. That's the only time I sensed Malcolm's stare boring a hole into my back. There was a moment when I looked at Yusuf yesterday and wondered what it would be like to flirt with him or at least pretend to. It wouldn't be difficult. Yusuf is handsome and we have quite a few things in common, both having lived in Saudi Arabia for so long.

But deep down, I know that flirting with Yusuf won't work, and my parents aren't the only reason for this.

I find a package on my desk during English. Wrapped in brown paper, it's flat and feels strangely soft to touch. I first think someone left it there by accident, but then I see my name, stuck to it on a card, along with the words *Merry Christmas*. There is no sender.

Behind me, Malcolm is laughing at something his friends said. I feel his gaze on the back of my neck when I unwrap the package, a strange, anticipatory quiet settling into the space right behind me, even as Steve and Ahmed continue to talk.

Blood pulses in my ears as I see the gift. A scarf made of a sleek rayon fabric, with tassels at the ends, in a shade that could be yellow or green, depending on your perspective. The perfect chartreuse.

I always looked forward to Christmases in Kerala as a child. Carols ringing in Ammachi's courtyard in the weeks leading up to December 25. Giant star-shaped lanterns strung over every house in the neighborhood. My cousins and I were usually in charge of making the Christmas crib in early December, constructing the nativity display out of cardboard boxes and hay before adding in the little clay figurines of Joseph, Mary, the lambs, baby Jesus, and the three wise men at the end from a set that my grandfather kept on a high shelf in a Polystyrene box.

My aunts and Amma would spend a good two days cooking for the family. Bowl-shaped rice cakes called appam with beef stew for breakfast. Kerala-style biryani and karimeen fish curry for lunch. An equally heavy dinner, followed by an array of desserts including Christmas cookies, plum cake, achappam, and caramel custard. I was seven when Appa gave me my first taste of home-made Christmas wine in a teaspoon—a taste I barely remember thanks to having spit it out seconds later.

While my cousins most looked forward to their presents on Christmas morning, I looked forward to the things I could not have in Saudi Arabia, where Christmas celebrations are banned in public. Like the giant Christmas tree inside Ammachi and Appachan's living room twinkling with ornaments and lights. The midnight mass on Christmas Eve in a nearby church, the smell of frankincense clinging to my clothes long after it was over. The laughter of my cousins and my family, the one time all year when I didn't feel the void of having no siblings.

The years we were in Saudi Arabia for Christmas, Verghese

Madam's family was in charge of organizing the celebrations, their house the only one large enough to host several families at once. Black screens covered the windows. Polystyrene and plastic cushioned the main door to muffle any sounds from going outside. "You'd think we were preparing for a war," Appa muttered to Amma, seconds before giving Pastor Verghese a broad smile and saying: "Wonderful setup, George."

The women organized a potluck dinner on Christmas Eve, bringing in traditional dishes like unniyappam and not-so-traditional ones like pasta. Men concocted illicit wine in bathtubs—stuff neither Amma nor I wanted to touch—even though Appa always chugged down a whole glass in defiance of us and of the religious police. Presents were exchanged (to be opened the next morning), followed by a group prayer at seven in lieu of a midnight mass. There were no trees or decorations, with the exception of that one year when Emerald Verghese managed to make a fir tree out of wire and carefully cut-out construction paper, glittery streamers draped around it with homemade ornaments, and even a star on top. I had to admit that it was pretty creative, lasting a full hour into the party before Emerald's drunk cousin Benjamin fell on the tree and accidentally ripped it in half. The secrecy aside, the celebrations weren't entirely terrible, if a tad boring compared to the ones in India.

Canadians, on the other hand, go all out. By the time December hits, Christmas decorations are *everywhere*: from St. Mary's church to the TD Bank outside our house. Yvonne calls us one morning to reconfirm our attendance at Bridgita Aunty's big Christmas Eve bash, an event Amma agreed to long before either of us knew she and Appa would be separating.

"Are we still going?" I ask her now.

"Of course," she says, without even looking at my father. "We're still living together." There's a challenge somewhere in that statement, but apart from his tightening lips, Appa shows no sign of having heard it.

"It will be good to see my family again," Appa says. *My* family. A reminder that Bridgita Aunty is *his* cousin and will, ultimately, be on his side when the divorce is finalized.

Amma takes the challenge in stride, putting on an emerald-green sari for the party under her coat—*Your appa's favorite sari*, she once told me—and spends a good chunk of the party with her hand inside the crook of my father's arm, laughing and joking, her fingers lightly stroking the line of his jaw.

"What's this, a second honeymoon?" my aunt teases. "Look at you two! No one would know you've been married for nearly two decades!"

Appa's smile is strained, but Amma's laughter tinkles even more than the wind chimes on the porch, her face glowing in the bright lights of the house. Yvonne, who's home for the holidays, gives me a cheeky grin. I force myself to grin back.

My mother, the consummate actress.

She keeps up the charade long after we leave my aunt's house, her voice a steady stream of chatter during the drive back home and as we go up the elevator, cutting off abruptly when Appa interrupts her to relieve himself in the bathroom.

"When is Appa leaving?" I ask, once I hear the whirr of the exhaust fan inside.

"I don't know." Now that the party is over and Appa is no longer in sight, Amma's bright facade dissolves into the exhaustion I've grown so used to seeing these days. "It's not like he tells me anything. Or like we even sleep in the same bed."

I feel something inside me break. I'm not married; I don't fully understand what Amma is going through. But when it comes to love, I've lost as well. I get up from my chair and wrap my arms around my mother who, for the first time, feels a lot smaller than she used to.

"That boy you're seeing, Suzy. That Malcolm boy?"

"I'm not seeing him anymore." Even though, for some reason, I couldn't return the gift he gave. Couldn't stop myself from touching the soft fabric whenever I got the chance.

She pulls away and looks up at me with a frown. "What happened?"

I shrug. "You were right, Amma. It wasn't going to work in the long run."

Amma is quiet for a long moment. "I always loved you, you know. From the minute the nurse put you in my arms."

I freeze, surprised by this sudden statement.

"I know I criticize you more than I should. I even say things I don't mean." She sighs. "That letter from your Ammachi—"

"It's okay, Amma—" I begin.

"No, it's not. You need to understand. I had recently moved to Jeddah with your father. You were a baby and I had no family or help like my friends back in India. I was young and got frustrated being cooped up indoors all day. Living in Saudi isn't easy for any woman, even one deeply in love with her husband. I would write of my frustrations to your Ammachi and she would write back with advice—not that I always took it. Who wants their mother nagging them, right?"

She smiles at me and I feel my face redden.

"I never agreed with your grandmother. I might have regretted

294

many things in life, including having moved with your father to Saudi Arabia, but I never regretted having you."

Tears prickle my eyes, slip out onto my cheeks before I can hold them in. Amma's thumbs gently wipe them away.

"I don't know what happened between you and that boy, Susan. But love isn't easy." She stares at the closed bathroom door. "You just need to decide if it's worth the trouble."

Malcolm

Even though we're Zoroastrian, Christmas was a festival our family always celebrated when Mom was still alive. Back then, the old man would get a real tree and string lights around it, while Mahtab and I hung ornaments on the branches. Mancher Mama and Roshan Mami came as well, with their kids, and the house would be packed and raucous for three whole days.

After Mom died, everything changed. Though my aunt and uncle still visited us from time to time, no one bothered buying a tree or stringing lights around the house anymore. Dust gathered in the living room space where the tree used to be. Eventually, Freny placed a coffee table there and layered it with books and magazines no one bothered to read. So I don't exactly blame myself for shouting an expletive this year when I come down the stairs into the living room and find a tree and our old ornaments staring me in my face, and the coffee table gone.

"Do you like it?" Freny knits her fingers together nervously. "I know I should have waited for you and Mahtab to hang the ornaments, but they were so pretty that I couldn't help myself."

"What's all the noise—ooooh!" Mahtab's gasp borders more on awe than dismay. "That is so lovely!"

"You had no right." I cut off my sister before she can offer our stepmom any more accolades. "That was our stuff—our *mom's* stuff! Wasn't it enough that you barged your way into our lives? Why couldn't you leave this alone?"

"Malcolm!" I barely register Mahtab's shocked reprimand.

Freny's lower lip trembles—a sign that she's about to flee. "I'm sorry, dikra. I sh-hould h-have asked. I'll t-take it d-down later."

I'm about to say more—like how she can't call me *dikra*, when a strong little hand grabs me by the elbow and pulls me up the stairs. Behind me, I hear slippers clattering over the kitchen tiles—Freny will be long gone by the time I turn back to confront her.

"What. Are. You. Doing?" Mahtab spits out. "Are you out of your mind?"

"What is *she* doing?" I counter. "Trying to replace Mom?"

"The tree was my idea, not hers!"

I feel my anger begin to deflate. "What?"

"But if you *hate* it so much"—Mahtab's voice grows louder—"maybe I'll throw it away!"

"No! No, wait, Mah. I'm sorry." I shake my head, feeling like a heel. "I didn't know it was you."

"What if it *wasn't* me? What if Freny decided to do this incredibly nice thing on her own?"

I say nothing. Guilt, I realize, feels a lot like the beginnings of indigestion.

"And there's no need to apologize to me," Mahtab says. "You should be apologizing to Freny."

My head snaps up again. "No way."

"Malcolm, she did nothing wrong. She was trying to be nice. And you need to face facts. Mom's gone. And it isn't Freny's fault. Or Daddy's. It was cancer."

I bite my tongue before I say something I'll regret.

"Freny was furious when he hit us that day," Mahtab says, a little more softly. "Do you know she threatened to call child protective services? Said she didn't want to live with someone who abused his children."

I frown, surprised by this bit of input.

"I know you don't like her. But for some reason, she likes *you*. You don't have to be a jerk about it."

I grit my teeth. "I'll be in my room."

In my room, fuming for nearly an hour. As I cool down, though, confusion begins to set in. I think back to that awful night, when everything went wrong. The shouts after Mahtab fell down. Freny's skinny form bent over my sister, gently splashing water on her face. She even checked in on me from time to time, though I was furious and unresponsive.

As I am now.

I trudge down the stairs into the living room, a little hesitant, not exactly sure what I'm going to do when I see Freny. The Christmas tree is still there, though most of the ornaments have now been taken off. I take a deep breath and march into the kitchen, where I smell chai brewing on the stove. Freny starts at my entrance, her fingers tightening on the mug she's pulled out of the cabinet.

"I'm sorry," I say, the words thick in my mouth. "That was a nice thing you did there. I shouldn't have made assumptions."

To my surprise, the terror melts off Freny's face, turning into utter joy. She aims that startling beam my way, making me even more uncomfortable than usual. "Oh that is fine, dear. A small misunderstanding. Why don't I make you a cup of chai? Would you like gingersnaps with it?"

Mom wouldn't have accepted my apology that easily. She most certainly wouldn't have offered me cookies and tea. Any other stepmother would've gloated, even taken the opportunity to punish me. But Freny isn't like that. She's not my mother, either. And for the first time, I have an inkling that she isn't trying to take her place.

"Yeah." I hesitate before pulling out a chair. "Okay."

"We're all set," Mahtab says. It's a couple of days after Christmas and the benefit concert committee is at the food court at the mall instead of our usual space in the cafeteria. When Mahtab first said there would be a meeting during the holidays, I doubted anyone would show up. To my surprise, with the exception of three people, the committee members arrive on time. Including Susan, who I expected to be celebrating with her family.

"I have the venue booked for the concert on January 16. I have singers—the St. Nicholas High School Choir from Streetsville! And it's thanks to Isabel and Malcolm and their fund-raising efforts!"

After some negotiation—the coffee shop's name as the main sponsor on the giant stage banner, along with spotlighting it during our interviews on television—Michelle agreed to sponsor us further, offering to cover rent for the space at the Living Arts Center.

"You don't give up, do you?" Michelle said, giving me a rare smile. "You remind me of myself."

Now the kids around me applaud. Isabel takes a bow. I grin when Ronnie thumps my back. It feels odd, but good to have done something big for the group. This is different from pulling off a dare or a dangerous stunt at one of Justin's old parties. While the rush from those acts wore off shortly afterward, I've been running on the high of raising the money for the venue for a whole week. At one point I even catch Susan watching me, but she looks away when I catch her eye.

the gift didn't work, I texted Mancher Mama yesterday. I thought I'd made progress when Susan stuffed the scarf into her bag instead of turning around and throwing it in my face. But she's made no move to approach me yet. Or even talk.

Nothing that's worth having comes easy, my uncle replied.

Initially I thought a Christmas gift was a great idea. A scarf isn't blatant like roses or over-the-top like jewelry. That I found one in chartreuse after nearly an hour of searching online made it even more perfect. But maybe I was wrong, I think, my heart sinking. Maybe the gift didn't impress her.

Right now, Susan's looking straight ahead, listening to my sister.

"Ticket sales have already started—and are going very well thanks to some early buzz. I won't be surprised if we sell out completely," Mahtab announces. "As I mentioned before, we'll have twelve VIP guests at the venue, who . . ."

I tune out as she continues speaking. Yusuf and I have been over our welcome speeches a couple of times, but Yusuf thinks I should also learn a couple of Arabic phrases, so that the kids feel more welcome.

"What if I mess up?" I asked Yusuf. "At least you know the language."

"Yeah, but you're different. You have charisma!"

Charisma won't help with my English independent study project, I think now. I picked *In the Skin of a Lion* by Michael Ondaatje, the thinnest book in the pile, figuring there was less reading to do. Only now I'm totally lost trying to figure out what the theme of the book is.

A poster catches my eye; Mahtab has been hinting around about it for a couple of days and I might have accidentally-on-purpose missed the unveiling at the end of the last meeting. This is the first time I've had the chance to see one up close.

Michelle's Coffee House presents: TO SYRIA, WITH LOVE. The title is hand-lettered in a bold, eye-catching font, followed by a line in the delicate, looping swirls I recognize as Arabic.

My mouth drops at what I see next: The rest of the poster has been divided into four panels—like a graphic novel. I follow the story of a brother and sister forced to leave after their home was destroyed by a bomb. They trudge through the countryside in the cold and then stowaway on a boat, only to be turned away by another country's barbed wire. The third panel is the most elaborate, showing the inside of a refugee camp: white tents as far as the eye can see, the boy carrying a drum of water over his shoulder, his sister cooking over an open flame, her face covered with soot. There are no words on the first three panels. There is no need. The pictures are enough to convey the story and I can't help but be impressed by Susan's talent.

The final panel consists of a group of kids wearing maple leaf jerseys standing onstage in front of a conductor. They're holding up a sign with a picture of a giant heart.

The last panel is followed by details about the event, at the bottom of the page: it's a charity concert by the St. Nicholas High School Choir, on January 16, at 3:00 p.m., at the Rogers Theatre in the Living Arts Centre. That's followed by the prices and the link to an Eventbrite page that the school helped us set up. The other sponsors' logos are printed at the bottom. I'm looking over the drawings again, marveling at the detail, when my gaze falls on one of the boys in the last panel.

It can't be . . . I squint to see if it makes a difference to the picture. It's not like I'm the only skinny, brown, spiky-haired kid in the world who wears baggy jeans. Right? I look up, my eyes finding and locking with Susan's, almost by instinct. This time, neither of us looks away.

Susan

I see his eyes widen when he catches it, that little depiction of him on the poster. I don't know what made me do it—only that one minute I was drawing, and the next minute, he appeared on the page. I was tempted to rip everything up and start over.

But Malcolm is impossible to ignore these days. With the note. The scarf. Even more so when he looks up from the poster and right at me, scattering the steady rhythm of my heartbeat. It's Isabel who breaks the spell, tapping Malcolm on the shoulder to ask him something. Isabel has shown no indication of being interested in Malcolm. But my face burns anyway when I see her bright eyes, hear her silver laugh.

It's over, I remind myself as I begin gathering my stuff. I glance at my watch. Amma said I should come home early today if I could.

That she and Appa have something important to tell me. I don't know which is worse, home or here.

Normally I can't wait to get out of a meeting, to avoid the awkwardness that might come with being around Malcolm. Today, however, I trudge past the mall's different food joints, dragging my feet more than usual. I pause in front of the restaurant where Malcolm and I first ate shawarma and, for reasons I don't quite understand, turn one last time. I glimpse Isabel smacking Malcolm on his arm. Him laughing in return.

Over, I repeat. There was nothing there to begin with.

———————

"I'm leaving for Jeddah at the end of February," Appa tells me when I return home. "I wasn't planning to stay so long, but things haven't been working as I hoped."

Which probably means my mother hasn't signed the divorce papers yet. I glance at her, but Amma avoids my gaze, making a nervous, clicking sound inside her mouth.

"I've been lucky that the clinic gave me such an extended leave," Appa continues. "But I can't stay any longer than February. Also, I think it's best . . . given the circumstances."

"Fine." I wonder if my voice sounds as brittle to them as it does to me.

"Suzy, I am still doing what's best for the family. For you." Appa looks at me pleadingly and, for the second time in my life, I can no longer see him as my father, but as a grown man with flaws.

"You can smoke in peace over there, I guess."

Appa winces. I expect Amma to be shocked or surprised by the revelation, but she only looks angry.

"You told me you wouldn't smoke in front of Susan," she says.

"But then, I shouldn't be surprised, should I? Eighteen years of marriage and I'm finding out that I don't know you at all, Rensil."

"Aruna—"

"Why do either of you care?" I ask them. "It's not like you're planning to live together anymore."

"Susan—"

"I have to go," I cut her off. "Exams are coming up. Lots of studying to do."

I want her to follow me. To shout that I have to come back and listen to what she has to say. But because she's my mother she doesn't. Nothing—not even a family breakdown—is allowed to interfere with the creation of her poster child: the daughter who never gets a bad grade. I open my calculus textbook and begin writing out equations on lined paper. I allow a single tear to fall, wiping it off before it smudges the edge of my perfect $x+y$.

The first Monday back after Christmas break, we find a substitute teacher in English. Malcolm and Afrin are missing as well—though I don't care about this. No. I'm not thinking of them at all.

"I've been told you have independent study essays to work on. You may continue doing that." The teacher's voice edges on a yawn.

Which pretty much means that I now have a full hour to get a head start on my calculus homework since my essay on *The White Tiger* is already drafted and saved to Dropbox. On another day, I would be happy about the extra time. Or about not having chosen *In the Skin of a Lion* for my independent study; it's a novel that seems to be tripping up everyone who picked it. Today, I feel resigned.

"Hey, Susan." I turn around and see Ahmed's trademark grin. "Have an extra pen?"

"Sure." Even though I fully expected them to ignore me after Malcolm and I broke up, Ahmed and Steve have been nothing but nice, going out of their way to say hello whenever they pass me in the halls or see me at meetings for the fund-raiser.

From the front of the room, the teacher calls out our names for attendance. There's a pause when she reaches the *P*s. "Sa-ma-ran Patel," she says, stumbling over the first name.

No one answers. A girl giggles up front. I glance up, wondering if there's an error as I don't recognize the student. "Smear—"

"It's Smaran!" Steve bursts out. "Smaran, okay? And I'm here!"

More laughter, which makes Steve grow red with anger.

I wait until the teacher finishes taking attendance and then turn to face Steve.

"Your real name is Smaran Patel?" I ask quietly.

Steve says nothing, even though I can tell from his scowl that he heard my question.

Ahmed snorts. "It is! It's the name on every attendance sheet."

"Shut up, A.," Steve says.

Ahmed grins. "Fine. I'm gonna use this time to pick some brains and find out the theme to *In the Skin of a Lion*." He slips out of his seat and into Malcolm's empty one to talk to the girl on the other side.

"How come everyone calls you Steve if that's not your name?" I ask.

"I ask the teachers before class every semester to call me that," he admits. "Smaran's my grandfather's name so I can't even change it without upsetting my mom."

"It's a nice name."

"Yeah, if you say it right." The tip of his pencil breaks against the paper; he's pressing so hard. "You know what, forget it. You won't understand."

Four months ago, I might have backed off. Today, I raise a brow the way Preeti does when people dodge her questions. "Oh yeah? Try me."

"*Susan Thomas?* Your name isn't even Indian. Give me one instance when you were made fun of in school because of it."

Steve's comment about my name isn't exactly new. When I was younger, I'd heard similar comments at Qala Academy—from students who weren't Christian or from states in India with large Christian populations.

"My name has more to do with my religion than my nationality," I tell him bluntly. "India is a country with plenty of Christians—which makes my name as *Indian* as any other. And that's beside the point. My physics teacher at Qala Academy called me Soo-sun. It wasn't even on purpose—just her accent—but for a good chunk of tenth and eleventh grades, the girls in class called me *Soo-soo* behind my back. That means—"

"I know what it means," Steve interrupts, looking surprised. "They really called you that?"

"People always find ways to embarrass you if they can." I think back to the disastrous party this October, the video that's now forever entrenched online. "You can't control that, but you can control your reaction."

"It's not the same. I'm not Malcolm who's so cool that he doesn't care or Ahmed, who every girl at school is tripping over. I'm the clown. That's how people know me. Imagine adding a name like *Smaran* to the mix—a name that maybe only one or two people over here can pronounce without butchering. I'd never live that down."

As much as I want to tell him it doesn't matter, I know this isn't entirely true.

"You teach them," I say after a pause. "You correct them until they start saying it right."

The teachers at Arthur Eldridge aren't like Verghese Madam, who would have thrown a piece of chalk at my head for correcting her, or scolded me for *being cheeky*.

"I'm sorry for what I said before," Steve says after a pause. "About your name not being Indian. I mean, *I* get mad at people who ask me where I'm from and then, when I say I'm Canadian, they ask again where I'm *really* from because of my last name or my skin color."

"It's okay." I accept the apology with a smile. "And I'll keep calling you Steve if that's what makes you comfortable. I just want you to know that your real name is nice, too."

He smiles back. "So, why are you still single, again?"

I'm not attracted to Steve, but the mild come-on is flattering. "Taking a break from dating at the moment."

"Yeah, I know." There's a gleam in his eyes that tells me he knows more, but then he shrugs, changing the subject. "Besides, you rejecting me is only payback for all the times I dissed desi girls in the past."

My jaw drops in mock-horror. "*No.* You, Steve?"

"Call me Smaran." He flashes me a grin and then turns both ways to make sure our convo is still private. "Only when we're alone though. I have a reputation to maintain."

I grin back. "Of course."

———————————

I look for Malcolm the next day as well, going as far as trying to spot him in the cafeteria at lunch, a place he usually never bothers stepping into during school hours. I don't see him. Afrin, on the other hand, is at her usual table, laughing with a group of friends. Someone nudges my shoulder from behind. "Hey, do you mind? You're blocking the way."

"Sorry!" I move out of the way of a pair of girls who glare at me and press my back against the wall. I take a deep breath, allowing the greasy smell of the cafeteria fries to fill my senses. Malcolm hasn't called or texted after seeing the poster. He hasn't sent me any more notes, either. Is he waiting for me to make a bigger move? Or did he finally give up on me? Maybe he and Afrin got back together. Or maybe he's with someone else now. That's what happens in the real world, the one outside teenage movies and young adult novels.

Alisha scoffs at insta-love, calls it an unhealthy trope that doesn't happen in real life. "I mean it's *literally* not possible for anyone to *fall in love* when they're so young," she told me once. I square my shoulders and head for the other end of the cafeteria, where Heather and Preeti are seated.

"So, did you bring them?" Preeti asks—her way of saying hi.

I pull out the lunch box I packed for the day. "I did. Dosas for everyone!"

"Oh my God, Heather you're going to love these. They're the South Indian version of savory crepes, but way better than any others you've tasted. You're so lucky your mom makes these, Suze."

"I made them." I can't help but smirk when their jaws drop with awe. "Hey, I don't only know how to crack open books, you know."

It had also taken several tries to make one perfectly round dosa last night, but by the time I was on my second, Amma was in the kitchen, giving instructions from the back. When I finally turned around after finishing up the sixth, she and Appa were both standing at the kitchen entrance with odd smiles on their faces.

A pair of fingers snap in the space before my eyes. "Hey, Susan, where'd you go?"

"Sorry." I blink. "You were saying?"

"I said you are so lucky to be able to eat this every day!" Heather's eyes are squeezed shut, a blissful smile on her face.

I grin. "Well, I like them, too, but trust me when I say I *don't* want to eat dosas every day."

In Jeddah, Alisha and I went out of our way to make dosas and idlis and any other South Indian staple more interesting. Alisha's latest attempt was a peanut butter and grape jelly idli sandwich, which was too experimental—even for me. A pang goes through my chest. It's during times like this that I miss Alisha the most. Times when we would be able to simply look at each other and know what the other was thinking. Now though, little holds us together during conversations, our calls ending within a few minutes, like we have nothing to say to each other.

Except for the times things really go wrong. Like Alisha's running bad luck with the boys her parents set her up with. My breakup with Malcolm. On Christmas, when I told her about the scarf he gave me, I only got a *hmmm* in response.

"You think I should ignore him."

"I'm not sure," she said, to my surprise. "I mean, if he was a two-timing jerk, I would tell you that right away, but this is different."

"You're saying he *isn't* a two-timing jerk?"

"I'm saying don't write him off completely. Besides, you have too much going on right now. Deal with your family situation first.

If Malcolm is the right guy for you, you'll get back together. Have faith."

A text pops up on my phone now—Alisha, appearing again as I was thinking of her. You free to talk? You have lunch, right?

I smile. You're going to live a hundred years. How about later tonight? Or is it urgent?

Nah. Just miss you. Tonight's good.

I send a photo of two old ladies dancing, along with the caption: When we grow up, we'll be the ones causing havoc in the nursing home.

I laugh out loud at the photo she sends right after—it's the two of us at age ten, sticking our tongues out at the camera. I tear off a corner of the dosa in my box, dip it into a small container of coconut chutney, and pop it into my mouth.

A familiar face smiles and waves at me from another table. Yusuf Shire. When I wave back, he winks. It reminds me of another boy and another wink, and I wonder if Alisha was right about the insta-love thing. If what happened between Malcolm and me wasn't love at all, but simply a precursor to it—a step that showed our hearts were capable of more than simply pumping blood.

Malcolm

The first day of school after Christmas break—exactly the day I'm planning to gather the courage to talk to Susan about her poster in English instead of sending her another note—I get held back by a case of such terrible flu that Mahtab and Freny quarantine me in my room.

"I will call the school, dikra," Freny says.

"And I'll handle anything that needs to be handled for the concert," Mahtab adds.

"That's still twelve days a"—the word gets cut off as I hack up a wad of phlegm and spit it out in a tissue—"way."

"Yeah, hopefully you'll be better by then." Mahtab grins. "See, big brother, this is why I keep telling you to get your flu shot."

"Yeah, buzz off, will you? You got the flu last year after getting the shot."

Mahtab sends me a flying kiss and leaves: a whirlwind of colorful winter clothes.

Freny gives me a smile. "I'll get you some of my special tea with haldi. That will make you feel better."

"I don't like turmeric," I croak out. Great, now I can't even speak.

"No excuses." I've never heard Freny sound this decisive before. "It will break up that horrible cough of yours. And I'll add some honey so that it doesn't taste as bad."

I groan.

But in spite of my complaints, I secretly admit it's nice being fussed over. It's been a while since that happened. With Mom being sick from her meds and surgeries, Mahtab and I had learned to take care of ourselves early on. And we'd been lucky in a way that we hardly ever got sick.

"You have your father's genes," Mom told me once. "He rarely ever gets sick either."

It's probably also why the old man never really understood Mom's illness. Or why he found excuses to get out of the house each time she wasn't well, leaving her alone to fend for herself. Mom told me theirs was a love marriage, but I wonder now if my father would have fallen for my mother if she hadn't been healthy back then.

Heavy footsteps tread in the hallway outside my room. I grip the duvet; it's been a while since Tehmtun Vakil made a trip down this hall. I look up at him when he enters, his body filling the doorway with little space left over. My father isn't as tall or broad as Mancher Mama, but he's still a big man.

"Freny tells me you're sick." His hand curls around the doorknob.

Does he think I'm faking illness to get out of school? "Yeah," I reply, my answer making me hack up more phlegm. To my surprise, the old man grabs a thick wad of tissues and passes it to me.

"Double up. It works better." His hands hover in the air for a second, as if hesitating, before he slips them into the pockets of his jacket. "And drink some haldi-milk."

"Freny's adding the turmeric to my tea," I tell him.

"Good. Good."

Just when I think it's the end of this strange conversation, my father's lip quivers under his mustache. "I didn't mean to hurt your mother. Or Mahtab."

It doesn't escape either of our notice that he's left me out of the equation.

"So hurting me was okay." My voice is hard.

"You weren't exactly an easy child to deal with. Always snapping back, never listening." His mouth pinches, as if this is difficult for him to admit. "After Daulat passed, you were even more out of control. I didn't know what to do with you."

"You're a sorry excuse for a father."

His shoulders stiffen, the tips of his ears turning red.

"You want to hit me even now, don't you?" I ask curiously. "You want me to shut up. You always hit me when you wanted me to shut up."

He closes his eyes, as if trying to compose himself. When he opens them again, there's an odd expression on his face.

"You're right," he says. "I am a sorry excuse of a father. And a husband. I took out my anger on your mother first for falling out of love with her. Later, I took it out on you for looking so much like her. For questioning me the way she would have."

314

It's the closest he has ever come to an apology. It feels so strange that I don't know how to respond.

"Malcolm, here's your tea—oh hi, dear. Shouldn't you get to work?" Freny's voice is high, bright. A clear sign she's heard everything we've been saying.

The old man nods at her. "See you," he mutters into the air, and then leaves without a single backward glance. I'm still glaring at the open door, when a mug is thrust right in front of my nose.

I glance down. "This tea is *yellow*!"

"So is turmeric. Come now, think of it as medicine and drink up."

I am thrown back in time to the dining table downstairs and another woman stroking my hair, coaxing me to eat my vegetables.

"Why did you marry him?" I ask Freny, more out of curiosity than anything else. "What in the world attracted you to a man like that?"

Freny's cheeks lose some of their color, but instead of running away, she sits on the edge of my bed. "Tehmtun's not a bad person. He's old-fashioned in some ways. It makes him a hard man, a hard father. He reminds me of my own, in some ways. I know how to talk to him, to manage his moods. It doesn't excuse his behavior with Daulat. Or what he did to you children."

It's strange hearing my mother's name out of Freny's mouth. "You knew my mom?"

"We never met," she answers. "But I knew her. We grew up in the same colony back in Mumbai. She was four years older than me. Pretty. Smart. I was so jealous of her. Even more so when she married the boy I'd given my heart to as a teenager."

I grow silent.

"Young love can be so strange," she continues. "My first husband was a friend of Tehmtun's. When he died, your father came to the funeral in Detroit. I heard Daulat was dying from cancer. He and I . . ." She licks her lips. "Well, we got back in touch again. I felt I was getting a second chance."

The confession makes me sick. But it explains a lot as well. I put the tea on my nightstand. "I'd like to be alone now."

"Malcolm, I'm sor—"

"Please." I don't want her false apologies. "You're not sorry for marrying my father."

"But I am sorry for the man he turned out to be." She rises to her feet. "I'll be in the kitchen if you need me."

I close my eyes, not opening them until I hear Freny's footsteps fade in the corridor. Mahtab tells me it's pointless to dwell on the past. Especially when someone is trying to right a wrong and make amends.

My phone buzzes on the nightstand. Can we talk?

My heart skips a beat, does a couple of leaps around my rib cage before my eyes fall on the number of the person who sent the message. My body sinks like a stone into the mattress. I've been ignoring Afrin for a whole month now. Her texts, calls, attempts to talk at school. The Afrin I knew was far too proud to chase a guy after he'd snubbed her in public the way I did in early December, telling her that I never wanted to see her again. The phone buzzes again, more messages flashing on my lock screen.

Please.

I know I shouldn't have kissed you like that in front of Susan.

It was selfish of me.

Wrong.

I need to explain myself.

Can I see you at your place after school today?

I close my eyes for a few moments. My relationship with Afrin, in a funny way, mirrors the one my mother and father had, the one he has now with Freny. For a second I have an idea of why my mother kept going back to the old man even after he messed up their relationship.

She's not a bad person. I can't remember the number of times I said the same thing to Ahmed, Steve, and Mahtab, whenever they complained about Afrin.

ok, I text back after a moment. let's talk.

I guess I am more like my mother, more like Freny than I thought.

"What happened to you?" The disgust in Afrin's voice, barely held back, almost makes me laugh.

"I am touched by your concern. What do you think, Afrin? It's the freaking flu."

"Didn't you take your shot this year?" She eyes the tissues scattered around my bed and pauses a foot away from it. She's still carrying the giant purse she brings to school and it's bulging more than usual.

I roll my eyes. "You're the one desperate to talk to me."

"You could've said you were sick. I would've come later." Sighing, she switches the bag from one shoulder to another. I almost forgot how scared Afrin is of getting sick. Or how much she hates hospitals in general. It was how we first bonded—me telling her about Mom, she telling me about her grandmother who died of pneumonia.

"What is it?" I ask now. "What did you want to tell me?"

"I wanted to apologize face-to-face." Lines appear on her smooth forehead. "I messed up everything. With Justin. With you and Susan. When you told me you didn't want to see me anymore in December, I couldn't believe—didn't *want* to believe—you. I know I'm fully to blame for cheating on you, but you wouldn't accept any of my apologies, wouldn't even *talk* to me. Then you started going out with Susan. You both looked so *happy* that I started to get mad, even a little possessive. I thought that by meddling in your relationship, I could get you back and make things right between us again. But I realize now it was a mistake. I let my ego get in the way and ruined everything."

Yeah. Maybe that's true, but—

"You weren't the only one who messed up." Pain stretches over the back of my head. "I kissed you back."

"A reflex." She shrugs.

"You knew?"

She raises a perfectly shaped eyebrow. "That wasn't the kiss of a boy who wanted me. Even when we dated, you never kissed me the way you kiss Susan."

My mouth falls open. I lick my suddenly dry lips. "And which way is that?"

"Like she's something precious." There's a strange, wistful look on her face I've never seen before.

"You were watching us?"

"The rest of us use the hallway on the second floor, too, you know." She rolls her eyes. "You two were nauseating."

I suppress a smile. "What about Justin? How is he doing now? Have you talked to him?"

To my surprise, a faint blush colors the skin under Afrin's perfectly powdered cheeks. "No . . . not yet. I mean, I *tried* seeing him in December after . . . you know . . . but no one came to the door. He didn't answer his phone or any of my texts, either. I later found out from Dave that Justin and his mom were at his grandparents' place in Ottawa and that they came back last night. Dave said Justin's doing a lot better now so today I skipped my last two classes and went to see him again. Spent an hour outside his house before I figured out he wasn't going to let me in. Or maybe it was his mom who stopped him."

I pause before asking the next question. "Are you going to try seeing him again?"

"I'm not sure I want to," she admits. "And it's not only my parents and their issues. Though now they aren't interested in me seeing that other guy anymore, thankfully. He's lucky Justin's mom didn't press charges for assault. There are times I think Justin's mom was right, you know. That I should stay away from him. Especially since I'm not sure if I can love Justin the way he wants me to."

Silence, the sort that brims with unspoken questions, settles uncomfortably between us.

"Love stinks," I mutter, more to myself than her.

Afrin smiles. "Oh, Malcolm. You always say that but your heart will never let you believe it. It's bigger than anyone else's I know. It always has been."

I watch Afrin leave the room, taking with her the scents of school and snow and perfume.

I guess I could call Susan the way I used to call Afrin after a blowup. I could beg for her forgiveness again.

Love should not be one-sided. The words echo in my head, a reminder from an old conversation I had with my mother when we first discovered the old man's cheating ways. I pull up my phone and tap into the pdf of the flyer in the fund-raiser's Dropbox account, expanding the last panel until I can see myself again.

Is it a hello or a goodbye? I wonder. These days, I'm not sure if I can tell.

"Excuse me? Sir?"

The politeness feels awkward on my tongue, the *Sir* even more so. I don't exactly blame Zuric for scowling when he looks up from the papers he's organizing in the staff lounge. "What can I do for you, Mr. Vakil?"

After two days of resting at home, I no longer have a fever, but my head still feels like it's stuffed with cotton balls. I also have exactly ten minutes before first period to make my case about my grade. Which is, I realize, more time than I had with Michelle during my first sponsorship pitch. *You don't give up, do you?* Michelle had said last week. I don't know why, but for some reason I want to prove her right.

"I'm having a lot of trouble with English this semester. I know I'm not smart enough and that it's probably too late with finals coming up this month . . . but I want to graduate this year. Go to university. I . . . I need help." It's not until the words spill out that I realize they're true.

Zuric's frown deepens. "You're not unintelligent, Mr. Vakil. That was never the problem. It's exactly the reason you can be so exasperating during classes."

Great. Now I'm going to get a lecture. But for once I keep my mouth shut instead of snapping back.

Zuric scribbles something on a piece of paper. "That said, it may not be too late. I haven't marked your independent study essay yet, but you haven't done badly with the unit on *Alias Grace*. I can set up an extra credit assignment for you. I'm also happy to tutor you for an hour every Wednesday after school. I noticed you had trouble with the Shakespeare unit during the midterm and it will be on the final, too."

Less Susan, more Shakespeare. I want to groan out loud. But with Zuric still glaring at me, all that comes out of my mouth is: "Cool. When do we start?"

Susan

Mahtab tells me the auditorium will be packed, but I don't realize how much so until I see the crowd lined up outside the Rogers Theatre at the Living Arts Centre. The air buzzes with chatter, fills with the scent of chocolate when I pass by a group of teens. A few feet away, I spot Ronnie and Mahtab talking to a reporter, a giant video camera focused on their faces.

The slim straps of my backpack, loaded with three small crates of extra programs, cut into my shoulders. It has been several months now since I've carried a full backpack the way I did at Qala Academy. I eye the table, already laid out with programs, and wonder if I can unload a couple of the crates there.

"Four dollars for one lousy bag of potato chips?" I hear Yusuf say behind me.

"You're not here to eat, Shire." Malcolm's voice sends a shiver down my spine. "Where are the VIP guests?"

"Relax, Vakil. They're who I want to buy the snacks for. They're inside the auditorium already."

"You can't take food in there!"

As they bicker a little more, I slip into the theater after flashing my volunteer badge at the usher. I can always unload those boxes later, I tell myself. I make my way down to the front rows and slip into an aisle seat for the time being, allowing my sore shoulders some respite. The twelve VIP guests are already seated. Most of them are children, but there are a couple of adults as well. I smile at a man with a little girl on his lap. They both smile back, flashing identical pairs of dimples.

"Hey, Susan! Can you keep an eye on this one?" Mahtab comes down the stairs, clutching the hand of a small boy, probably six or seven years old. "Found him wandering around outside unsupervised."

The boy raises his head and looks at me: a picture of gray-eyed innocence. There's a hint of mischief there, though, and I know I'll have to keep a close eye on him so that he doesn't wander off again.

"Ismi Susan," I tell the boy my name. "Ma ismak?"

He smiles and I wonder if he finds my accent funny. At Qala Academy, our teacher always said that we had distinct Indian accents, unable to pronounce the Arabic words as they should be pronounced.

But then the boy says, "Ismi Waleed," and I welcome him warmly, saying, "Marhaba, Waleed."

"Marhaba, Waleed! Marhaba, everyone!" Mahtab announces. Waleed and the other kids up front start giggling.

"I guess we stick out like sore thumbs with our accents, don't we?" Mahtab grins. "I mean, you don't as much, but still."

Warmth blooms under my ribs.

I have been called too Saudi for India even though I don't have a passport from the Kingdom, and too Indian for Saudi Arabia even though in my birth country I am treated like a foreigner. For the longest time, I thought I didn't fit in anywhere. Even at Qala Academy, among other kids straddling lines between two different cultures, there were times I felt like an alien. But here, in this moment, I wonder if fitting in is important after all. I pull out the sketchbook that I stuffed into my backpack at the last minute and a pencil.

"Wanna see something fun?" I ask the kids.

I settle into an empty seat again and begin tracing out a giant oval. A couple of small shadows fall over my book. Gasps emerge as I add details: a giant webbed face gazing at them with milky teardrop-shaped eyes.

"Spider-Man!"

I tear the drawing out and show it, handing it to Waleed who seems fascinated by how a face appeared within an egg.

"Me! Me!" the little dimpled girl calls out.

"Of course." I draw Kamala Khan in her Ms. Marvel costume, focusing on the hair, the mask, the flying red cape. Other requests start pouring in. I draw the Hulk and Thor and Daisy Duck. Someone says "Captain Majid!" and the kids laugh, thinking I don't know who he is. But I grin and the boy who made the request cries out with joy when I hand him the sketch of the character whose name is synonymous with soccer through most of the Arab world. By the time I'm done, each child has something of their own. I rise to my feet, electricity buzzing under my skin.

Why fit in, I wonder, when you can stand out?

Audience members trickle into the auditorium. Among them I see Preeti and Heather, both of whom had instantly bought tickets the moment I told them about the concert. I raise a hand and wave. They wave back enthusiastically. Now that the kids are occupied with swapping my drawings and talking among themselves, I make my way to the back, brushing past someone in the process.

"Susan." His voice stops me in my tracks. Malcolm takes in my face, still holding the afterglow of drawing for the kids. "You look good."

His eyes trail down to my neck, widen on seeing the chartreuse scarf he gave me for Christmas. I unglue my tongue from the roof of my mouth. "Thanks. So do you."

You look good? Seriously, that's the best you both can do? The voice in my head sounds a lot like Alisha. But it's true. Malcolm does look great today, in a black suit that I didn't even know he owned and a skinny pewter tie that draws even more attention to the gray in his eyes.

"Vakil!" Yusuf shouts from the front.

Malcolm is still staring at my scarf. He opens his mouth as if to say something, but then shrugs. "I gotta go."

Was that a dismissal? I am not sure. Malcolm and I have been dancing around each other ever since the breakup. One step forward, two steps back. Why did I think wearing the scarf would change anything?

"Hey, kids, welcome to the concert!" Malcolm and Yusuf are talking to the kids in the front row. I watch for a minute or so, see how effortlessly Malcolm manages to elicit smiles and chatter from them, even with the language barrier. My heart, silly thing, begins tap dancing.

A hard elbow nudges me from behind, forcing me into the space in front of an empty aisle seat. Raucous laughter follows. A group of older white boys march past, wearing red jackets, like they belong to a club or something. The one who elbowed me does not even glance my way, completely ignoring my glare. I jump when a hand touches my shoulder.

"Are you okay?" Heather asks, a frown on her face.

"Yeah." I force myself to smile. "I'll go tell Ronnie to keep an eye on them."

I find Mahtab's boyfriend farther back and point out the boys in red: stuffing popcorn in their mouths, allowing it to trail onto the carpeted floor, where it can be crushed underfoot. One of them tosses a piece of popcorn at an older blond woman in the front and then raises his hands in the air, as if in apology.

"Looks like the publicity got us more attention than I expected." Ronnie's normally cheerful voice grows hard. "I better let security know. They're not allowed to bring food in here."

Unease churns my insides. At the front, I notice Malcolm staring at the boys as well, his face looking like it might be carved out of stone. He steps forward as if to confront them, but is stopped by Mahtab, who says something in his ear. He turns to look at me, worry lining his forehead.

"Susan!" Isabel's voice forces me to break eye contact. "We've run out of programs!"

"I have more in my bag." We head to the auditorium entrance and begin placing the programs in neat piles on the table there.

"That's such a beautiful poster!" I hear someone say.

Isabel and I exchange quick grins. By the time the last program is handed out, the auditorium is full. Mahtab places each of us at a specific point in the auditorium and then scurries to the front, where Ronnie has started his welcome speech.

"Good afternoon, everyone! The idea for this concert began in a basement—as most great ideas usually do—"

Scattered laughter from the audience. Ronnie goes on to talk about the reasons behind the fund-raising effort.

"When news channels talk about what's happening in Syria, the first things they show are the faces of its children. And there's good reason for this. When war begins, the innocent are the first to die."

"Boo hoo!" someone shouts.

Ronnie's smile freezes on his face, but he plows through the rest of the speech, pretending he didn't hear. I scan the audience, my eyes homing in on the splash of red midway down the rows of seats. As Ronnie pauses to hand over the mic to Malcolm, who begins to introduce the choir, the boys in red begin to chant, their voices growing louder and louder with each passing moment. One of them rises to his feet and pours all his popcorn over the carpet before stomping it with his boots.

"Hey, losers! Why don't you go back where you belong with the rest of them. Go back home!"

"Go back home!"

"Go back home!"

"Go back home!"

The chanting gets angrier and angrier, even as a flurry of other voices break out:

"Stop that!"

"What's going on?"

"Where's security? I'm calling the police!"

The last voice is Ronnie's and it's nearly lost in the melee.

Malcolm's face grows harder than I've ever seen it. He places the mic on the floor and walks offstage.

"Nonono," I mutter under my breath when I see him jogging up the rows to where the troublemakers are. A red-faced security guard rushes past and, even though my brain tells me to stay put, my feet follow. By the time we get there, one of the boys is shoving Malcolm, who retaliates with a punch.

Pandemonium erupts, people screaming. A couple of older ladies crouch at the bottom of their seats up front, terrified. While the guard tries to restrain one of the red-jacketed boys, another boy has joined in to hit Malcolm. A third approaches, silver glinting in his hand.

My sporadic evenings of using the heavy bag in Preeti's garage aren't enough to have me trained to do what I want to. I am not and never will be a boxer, let alone one who knocks out a boy nearly twice my size. But my bag is nice and heavy, the straps cutting into my hands. I swing it as high as I can and slam it right between his shoulder blades.

Malcolm

Of the things I thought would happen at the concert, I never expected a fight. Nor did I expect Susan Thomas to jump into the fray, slamming her heavy backpack into one of the hecklers so hard that he falls face-first to the floor.

And she doesn't stop there, but turns to slam another boy right in the shoulder. I jump in, pushing her out of the way, taking a punch to the chest. Pain laces through my ribs and I nearly stagger to my knees. I'm about to hit back when Susan grabs hold of my arm with a grip that is surprisingly strong.

"Don't!" she tells me quietly and, for a few seconds, I don't understand why.

Then a voice booms: "Police! You are under arrest for assault."

A pair of handcuffs gleam in the hands of a burly policeman, who pushes the boy hitting me to his knees. Another officer is already marching two other red jackets to the exit.

"You okay there, son?" the officer's shrewd eyes give me a concerned look. "We'll have a paramedic look you over."

My body aches from the hits I received. But I wait patiently as a woman checks me over for injuries, finally pronouncing me good to go.

The officer nods. "You kids go ahead. I'm sorry you had to face such stuff when you were trying to do good."

It's only then that I realize that Susan never left through the whole examination process, and had stood a few feet away, watching me and the paramedic. I'm about to say something—anything to get her to talk to me again—when Mahtab rushes up to us.

"The little kids are pretty shaken," Mahtab says quietly. Ronnie and Yusuf are talking to them, trying to do damage control. "Do you think we should continue, though? I mean this incident—"

"We should," I tell her. "If we shut down the concert now, it only means they win. Besides, people already paid for their tickets. If we have to give back their money all our work be wasted."

"Malcolm's right," Susan says unexpectedly. "If the choir is still willing to perform and people are still willing to stay, we should give them a show."

"I'm staying," someone says from behind us. We turn around and see the older blond woman who the boys had heckled earlier in the evening. Another woman stands next to her. "I'm staying, too." Other voices soon chime in and Mahtab nods at me.

"Let's do it, then."

At the end, ten people ask for refunds. The rest of the audience stays when they hear that the choir is still willing to perform. Once the St. Nicholas Choir starts singing, a hush falls over the auditorium. High voices rise in an original song written by the choir for the concert. I stare at the familiar hand-lettered words on the program, skimming past the Arabic version of the lyrics and reading them in English:

> Let me give you my hand when the road is hard;
> and let the moon light our way.
>> Let the wind guide our spirits
>> and buoy what's left in our bodies.
> The road asks us to look ahead.
> Not sideways at barbed-wire walls or back
> at the home we lost to a bomb.
>> One day we will look back, you and I,
>> hand in hand.
> One day, we will find home again.

As the choir continues to sing, I look up, searching, until I finally spot a flash of bright yellow green over a dark gray coat. This time, I don't hesitate. I quietly make my way down to the middle of the auditorium, where Susan is standing with Ronnie, her hair in its usual ponytail.

She turns around, as if sensing me, before I even touch her shoulder. "Can we talk?"

"Go on." Ronnie nods at her before she can respond.

We walk out of the auditorium, the backs of our hands brushing. I expect her to move away when we step out the doors, but she doesn't.

"Why did you do that?" I ask. "You could've called the police."

"They were hitting you. I couldn't stand there and watch."

Standing, watching. We both have been doing that, more so than dancing around each other.

"If this was a Bollywood movie, there'd be a song playing in the background right now," she says suddenly. "Something by Sonu Nigam or Arijit Singh. Something deep and meaningful and depressing."

I laugh out loud. "I've missed you," I tell her.

"I've missed you, too."

Susan smiles at me and though it's tired and tentative, it's real.

"I missed your smile."

"Stop flirting."

"Okay." There'll be time for that later. "I like your scarf."

Her smile widens. "I like it, too."

Yes! I do a low-key fist pump, making her chuckle.

When the laughter fades, awkwardness settles in again. "How are your parents?" I ask.

She's quiet for a long moment. A song pulses inside the auditorium: a clapping rendition of Pharrell's "Happy."

"For years, I thought myself an expert at taking exams," she says. "Term tests, mock exams, board exams. I knew every trick in the book, never lost a mark for something as silly as not writing out the statement at the end of a math problem. Even with driving—I figured out a way to beat the system. But with my parents . . . I've never felt so helpless."

I hesitate before answering. "Your parents' marriage isn't an exam, Susan. It isn't something you can fix." I think of my own parents. How hard Mom tried to get Dad back. "It takes two people to make a relationship. If one isn't willing, then it doesn't work anymore."

She looks up at me, a little frown pricking the skin between her eyebrows. "How are things at home?"

"Freny isn't as bad as I thought she was. She took care of me when I had the flu and couldn't go to school. We talk now and then. Without sarcasm."

A tiny smile replaces the frown. "What about your dad?"

I shrug.

"Have you tried talking to him?"

"Is there a point? I'm not sure if I can forget. Or forgive him for what he did."

She looks right into my eyes, her lovely face serious. "I am not telling you to forget. Forgiving is possible though. It will only take time. A wise person told me, 'It takes two people to make a relationship.'"

I step closer, so that only a foot remains between us. "Oh yeah?"

She doesn't step back, even though her eyes widen slightly. "Yeah. You may not have a conventional father-son relationship, but you still might have a chance at something."

Now I'm the one frowning, mulling over what she said, trying to match it with the way the old man behaved recently. Always keeping me at a distance; *never* hitting after what happened with Mahtab the last time.

Yet another part of me wonders . . . is this *enough*? Has he truly changed for the better? What if this so-called good behavior of his is just a phase? I voice the last thought to Susan, who shakes her head and says, "That's unacceptable. Forgiveness doesn't mean he's given carte blanche to do whatever. He still has to earn your trust."

"Yeah," I say. Then: "Carte blanche? How old are you again?"

"Possibly middle-aged. I'm rumored to occasionally disguise myself as a student and infiltrate high schools."

We both grin.

"I guess I'll see you," she says. I wait for her to add *around*, a word that will settle things and sever the thread still somehow shimmering between us, turning us again into relative strangers. But at the last second, she presses her lips together, as if biting it back.

My heart beats a little faster, waking up again after a long slumber. "I'll see you."

I don't know who steps forward first. But out of the blue, we're hugging, my hands curling around her back, her fingers digging into my waist. She breathes out something below my ear, three words I am too scared to confirm right now.

We hug for what feels like too long and yet not nearly long enough. I feel the pulse at the base of her neck with a finger and foolishly try to sync the beats of my own heart to it. *You are not alone*, I want to tell her. And maybe she can hear what I'm thinking because that last bit of tightness leaves her shoulders and she relaxes into the hug. Into me.

Susan

I need time, I told him.

Three simple words, which might well be more important than *I love you.*

I'm not ready to start dating Malcolm again. But I don't want us to be just friends forever either. It's a truth I haven't said out loud, but something both of us must have understood on some level because when I get back home after the (very successful) concert, my phone pings with a text from him. it was good to talk to you again. can we talk more?

Yes, I text back. It's almost embarrassing how quick I am to do so. But then three big grinning emojis flash in reply nearly a nanosecond later and I can't help but smile a little.

I use the time I have to study for the upcoming finals at the end of this month and work on my final art project for Ms. Nguyen.

In some ways, I've turned back into the girl I used to be in Jeddah, focused and determined. But I'm no longer the same person. Not quite. This becomes clearer as I draw and paint with watercolors on the canvas. Somehow I never truly understand what's going on in my life until I draw it out and see it with my own eyes.

The day before the project is due, I'm in my room, placing finishing touches on the painting when Amma enters, pausing a few feet away. She stares at the canvas, starting at the upper-left corner, where the city of Jeddah is perched on a cliff, familiar landmarks like the Floating Mosque, the Red Sea Mall, and King Fahd's Fountain crowding the space. At the very edge of the cliff, a cartoon girl in a ponytail in a roller coaster car is zooming into the lower-right corner of the canvas—into Mississauga, with its curvy Marilyn Monroe Towers, the lakeshore in Port Credit, the ice skating rink where a boy circles alone, wearing a Blue Jays jersey. The roller coaster track has steep rises, sharp falls, and then a gentle descent near a building, where a man and woman stand talking, their faces in shadow, the woman's red coat the only splash of color at the end.

"*Last Days, First Days.*" Amma reads the title of the painting out loud.

"It's my final project for art."

"It's beautiful."

"You're only saying that." But my heart grows full at the praise.

"Your mother is right. It *is* beautiful." Appa's slippers lightly slap the tiles in the corridor before quieting against the carpet in my room.

I turn to face both of them, standing side by side, as they normally do these days, always a good three feet of space between them.

"We've come to a decision, Suzy," Appa says. He turns to Amma, who nods at him. "We aren't going to file for divorce. Your mother and I . . . well, we've had a long life together. But I will go back to live in Jeddah. You can come visit me on my iqama from time to time. Your mother will keep getting an allowance—"

"Until I find a job here," Amma interrupts. There's a determined look in her eyes. "I'm going to apply to those adult education courses on Elm Drive. Once I finish there, maybe upgrade my degree."

"So you are separating," I say.

"Suzy—"

"Please, Amma. I need to know." I can no longer cling to false hope.

She exchanges a glance with my father. That look tells me more about this decision being mutual than the words that follow. "Yes. We are."

A hollow truth. But at least they're no longer beating around the bush with me and that's progress where my parents are concerned.

"Suzy, I have some good news for you," Appa says suddenly. My father, who can dissect problem after problem with the human body, but can barely tolerate human sadness. "Do you know Thomas Chacko from church—Joseph's brother-in-law? Well, Thomas used to be a professor at McMaster University and knows the dean of admissions there. I told him about how much you wanted to be a doctor and—"

"I don't," I cut in.

Appa blinks. "What do you mean you don't?"

Amma says nothing, watching us both in silence.

"I mean, I don't want to be a doctor or an engineer. And I'm tired of hearing you and Amma argue about this." I realize belatedly that I've pronounced *tired* differently, emphasizing the *t*, extending the *i*, rolling out the *r* the way the others at school do. "You can't live your dreams out through me."

"We aren't trying to—"

"I want to be an artist." It's probably the scariest thing I've said out loud. "I know it's not something that may make me a lot of money. But I don't care about that. I hate science!"

My parents look at me as if I'm from another planet.

"I'll do an arts degree, okay? I have good grades—I can apply for a loan and get a job on the side if you don't want to pay for my tuition. When I graduate, I could work in graphic design or become a teacher. Ms. Nguyen said she'll be happy to advise me about scholarships. I'll figure something out."

Amma presses her fingers to her skull and I'm sure she's about to spit out *Arts degree?* like it's a swear word, but she doesn't say anything.

"*Figure something out*—that is not a career, Susan," Appa says.

"What you both have right now isn't a marriage, either," I say. "It was supposed to last. You both were supposed to be forever. But you aren't and I'm going to have to accept that. As you're going to have to accept me and my decisions."

Appa is silent for a long moment. "Think again, Suzy. Who knows if you'll even get a scholarship? There will be many people competing for the same spot. You're good, no doubt, but are you *that* good?"

I'm not sure. There's a part of me that still wonders if this is one giant mistake. But underneath the fear, there's another emotion. A slow-burning anger that, after glowing red like iron for the past several months, maybe even years, miraculously finds shape.

"I don't know," I tell him. "But I'll never know unless I try."

My father scowls. "You will have to be able to work and take care of yourself in the future. We won't be around forever, you know."

"I know."

I guess I always did.

That evening, I draw a caricature of Ravana, the king of Sri Lanka, who was reputed to be a demon with ten heads, according to Hindu mythology. Our Hindi teacher at Qala Academy told us that the ten heads represented Ravana's knowledge of Hindu scriptures: the six shastras and the four vedas. *Dashanan,* Sharma Madam told us. *He who has ten heads.*

I draw my anger into one head, my grief into another, then I add pain, and anger, more anger. Betrayal and heartbreak take up two faces, one each for my father and Malcolm. By the time I reach the last head, I am so exhausted that I am almost numb to all feeling. I leave it blank and close my eyes, resting my forehead on the cool surface of my desk. Moments later, I feel my mother's fingers in my hair, undoing the ponytail and stroking it out.

"You are not going to apply for a loan when you are still in college," she says. "Your parents are not dead yet."

I sigh and raise my head. "Amma—"

"I know I haven't been the best mother." She shakes her head. "I was thinking more of myself than I was of you."

"Well, you're *my* mother," I tell her. "And I'm still willing to keep you."

She pinches my cheek. "You will be okay. We both will."

I can tell she doesn't fully believe her words. But I don't point this out. I allow myself to accept what she says for a minute, the way I would when I was four and woke up screaming from a nightmare, only to fall back asleep after listening to my mother scare away the shadows from my bedroom.

Malcolm

I need time.

The words for some odd reason gave me hope when Susan first whispered them to me, give me hope now after she texts me an emoji with its tongue stuck out. Talking, for us, is still limited to texting. At school, we only nod or say hi, hanging out with our separate sets of friends. Which is okay, I guess.

For now.

"I don't get your logic behind not dating, though," Steve says one Saturday afternoon, while we're studying for the English final.

"I don't want to," I say with a shrug.

"Let it go, Steve," Ahmed says from the sofa, without looking up from his copy of *Alias Grace*. "He's giving her space. That's important, too."

Steve rolls his eyes. "He's not going to be a monk. There are other girls out there."

"Like Isabel, you mean?" I grin at him. To everyone's surprise, Isabel and Steve got together at the end of the concert in January. She told me that Steve made her laugh. "Maybe I should ask her out when she dumps you."

But I'm not serious and Steve, who knows this, grins back and tosses a pencil at me.

It's strange how, suddenly, everyone I know is pairing up. Ahmed, who I thought was still hung up on Noorie, is now seeing a girl from his mosque. Jay, my boss at Michelle's, has a new boyfriend. Steve told me that Afrin and Justin are getting back together. Though I don't know how Afrin managed to win over Justin's mom, the news made me smile. For real.

I haven't dated since Susan and I broke up, but I have wondered at times if I should. I've looked when a couple of pretty girls passed me in the mall, smiled when one winked at me at Michelle's Coffee House. But I've done nothing else. There's always a sort of distance now, an invisible barrier that prevents me from moving further. I've become a connoisseur of looking and not touching.

Ahmed must have a better idea of what I'm going through because he glances my way once and lightly bops Steve on the head with his book. "Quiet, you two. I need to finish reading this."

I study for finals as well, even though doing this for long hours gives me a headache. Mahtab and Ronnie email the committee members a final report, showing that we managed to raise $4,250.25 at the concert and that the school has sent the money to the Red Cross. Mahtab also sends us a list of aid organizations and community centers in Toronto that we can volunteer at, once exams are done, to further help Syrians harmed by the war. She's surprised when she finds me filling out a volunteer application form one evening.

what universities are you applying to? I text Susan a day before the exams. I copy the list she sends my way and save it in Notes. It's not like I'd get into any of those places. But what's the harm in trying?

Why? she asks.

I avoid the question by asking another one: all set for med school then?

No, Art ☺

what the . . . WHAT??

Surprised?

UH YESSSSS.

"Ugh." I switch off the caps. sorry for shouting. but how'd your parents take it?

They're not happy. They're still trying to convince me what a bad decision this is. But I'm applying for scholarships so that I don't have to rely on them for tuition. Our talk helped me a lot you know.

I blink. Then, without thinking, I press Call. After a couple of rings, she picks up. "Hello?"

"What do you mean our talk helped?" I blurt out. Then, as quickly, I realize what I've done. "Sorry, is this too soon? Should I not have called?"

"No, no, it's okay," she says softly. "I . . . I'm glad you called. And yes, our talk did help, sort of. It helped me realize that my parents weren't going to get back together. That they didn't love each other anymore. But it didn't mean that they don't love me. In a way, it helped me put into perspective that *nothing* in life has

342

guarantees. When it came to picking a career, I could go the safe route and apply for a degree in medicine or engineering. But who's to say that I'll even find a job with the degree?"

"You got that out of something I said?" I'm pretty skeptical about this.

She laughs. "Well, yes. At least it got me thinking."

There's an awkward pause. I struggle to fill it with something. Anything.

"Malcolm?" she says suddenly.

"Yeah?"

"You can call me. On the phone. We don't have to text all the time."

When we hang up, my cheeks hurt from grinning. I look at the list of universities in my Notes. This week, when Zuric handed back our independent study essays, mine had a B-plus scrawled over it, along with *Good*. The grade surprised both of us. Zuric has also been keeping my nose to the grindstone during those Wednesday tutorials and *King Lear* has finally begun to make sense.

It gets me thinking now. Hoping. If I can get a B-plus on my independent study, who's to say I can't get a decent final grade in English? Or even get into a university?

"Amazing," Mahtab mutters when she finds me sprawled out on the living room floor one evening, papers and textbooks around me. "Freny says you've been studying for four hours straight. I mean you didn't even *hear* me trying to tempt you with cookies!"

"Shhhh." I frown, but don't look up from my accounting text-book. *Why did I take this course?* I wonder for the fifth time that

343

day. It's partly my own fault for having skipped those classes about corporations and partnerships—even though I don't regret the time I spent with Susan during them. "I was trying to ignore you," I tell my sister now. Though my stomach did grumble at the mention of shortbread.

"Looks like Shakespeare was wrong. A leopard can change its spots!"

I raise my head. "'Nothing will come of nothing.'"

"What?"

"That's Shakespeare, too. *King Lear*. Act 1. It means without flattery, you will get nothing. Now buzz off."

I see a grin spread across her face before I go back to reading the section on stock dividends.

———————

When I was a kid, Mom often slipped me a cup of milk or a hot rotli, fresh from the stove, as a snack while I studied. Freny, still teetering on the edge of our newly civil relationship, does not assume such privileges, asking if I want something instead.

"Vodka would be nice," I tell her. "Or a cheeseburger."

Freny smiles. "Orange juice and cookies it is."

She's starting to get my sense of humor, too.

A day later, Mancher Mama sends me a photo of him and my aunt playing carrom with juice glasses raised to the camera. Good luck, he writes. P.S. These are screwdrivers, not orange juice. Freny must've told him.

save one for me, I text back. i'll need one after this accounting exam.

I yawn and, instead of switching off the phone, load the Facebook app. From Susan's timeline, I see that she hasn't been on since yesterday, even though I know she had a calculus exam this morning.

I text her: how'd it go?

A few seconds later, a text bubble pops up: Not bad. I think I did okay.

I roll my eyes. you mean you aced it.

I don't know that!

please.

Maybe it was better than okay. She follows it up with a giant smile emoji.

there you go. i have accounting tomorrow. gotta run. x

I stare at the last symbol. A kiss. Will she mind? Or even notice?

I silence the phone and go back to memorizing financial ratios. I'm still in the living room at midnight, half asleep, my cheek pressed to the sofa, mouth drooling over the cotton slipcover, when a pair of hands tuck something warm around my shoulders. My eyes flutter open.

"It's okay." The old man pats my head once. "Go back to sleep."

Only, after he leaves, I am wide awake again. I'm tempted to think I was dreaming, but my books, scattered across the floor an hour ago, are now arranged in neat piles on the coffee table, the old man's briefcase beside them.

———————————

There are things you no longer expect from a parent when you've been fighting with them as long as I have been with my father. Being tucked in is one. A muttered *Good luck*, right before my accounting exam is another. The sudden attention confuses me, even pisses me off at one point.

"Maybe he's taking a cue from your stepmom," Susan says when I tell her about it. "I mean, you both are talking now, aren't you?"

"Yeah," I say slowly. "But that's different." Freny wasn't around when Mom got sick. The sight of her doesn't still simultaneously weigh my heart down and make it burn with anger. "He never said goodbye," I say finally. "Never told Mom it was over. She deserved better."

"Maybe you should tell him that. No sense keeping that bottled up inside."

On a Saturday in early February, I screw up the courage to talk to the old man. I find him sitting on the couch in the living room, a mug of coffee in one large hand.

"Thanks," I tell him. "For the blanket. Um, that day when . . ."

He nods. "I used to do that for you when you were small. You weren't studying then. You always wanted to play. I had to bribe you with cookies to get you to go to bed."

I blink, thrown back for a moment into a fading memory: leaping onto a man's broad shoulders, a chocolate chip melting on my tongue.

"You wore a yellow shirt. And a blue tie."

"Yes." He looks surprised but pleased. Then, after a moment's pause: "That shirt was your mother's favorite."

Mom. Her death splintered something inside me, something that still begs to be fixed.

"You broke her," I tell him. "You broke us all."

His face, so hard and unyielding, sags. After a long moment, he says: "I know."

"Why?" I ask, years of anger encased in one word. "Why did you do it?"

"I was being selfish." The Asho Farohar pendant glints at the base of his neck. "I was trying to shield myself from the pain."

"We were *all* in pain! But what you did was beyond selfish. You ignored her. It was despicable. Mom deserved better. We all did."

He rubs a hand over his face. "You did. I was—still am—a horrible father."

I remain silent. There's nothing untrue about what he said.

"When I married your mother, it was good. Really good. Then she fell ill. I make no excuses for the way I behaved. I was young and stupid, angry with God and the universe for having taken away my wife's health." He sighs. "The first time she got diagnosed with the sarcoma, your mother was the one who said I should prepare to marry again. In case."

You're lying, I want to say at once. But there's a look on his face that gives me pause, a strange ring of truth to his words.

"She set me up with a friend of hers. Remember Coomie Aunty? You were still very young then."

Another faded memory: "She used to come over to the house. She brought me those batasas." I remember the buttery taste of the hard biscuits, the cumin infusing them. Coomie Aunty would sit on the couch, my father across from her. Mom would pull me into the kitchen, giving them time to talk. Back then, I never understood why.

"Nothing happened," he continues. "I was still very much in love with your mother."

"I don't think I want to hear this." Sickness swirls in the pit of my stomach.

"Please, Malcolm. I am not asking you to forgive me. But you need to know the truth about what happened." He closes his eyes for a moment. "I buried myself in work. I took every trip possible to keep my mind off things. I met a woman on one of these trips. A couple of years had passed since your mother had tried to set me up with Coomie. Your mother's cancer had subsided, but she was still very weak. It's ironic," he says bitterly. "How I cheated on my wife when she wasn't truly ill. But, during the course of that other relationship, I was close to your mother as well and she became pregnant with Mahtab. I broke things off immediately. I thought God had given me another chance."

I take a seat on the couch next to him.

"But Daulat didn't. She found out about what I'd done and she refused to let me touch her again. And then you were there. You weren't like Mahtab, who looks past my flaws. You were your mother's son, your uncle's nephew. You always looked at me like I was doing something wrong. I did the worst possible thing by taking out my anger on you. Hitting you. It's a wonder you didn't call the cops on me."

"I nearly did. Mahtab stopped me."

We both fall silent for a long moment.

"As I said before, I have no excuses." He raises a hand as if to touch my shoulder and drops it. "I didn't deserve your mother. I don't deserve either you or Mahtab."

No, I think. He doesn't.

"But I want to fix things." He's gripping the coffee mug so hard that the skin on his knuckles turns yellow. "Is that possible, Malcolm? Can we try to fix things between us?"

"I don't know," I tell him honestly. "I don't know if I can ever forget what you did to Mom. How you hurt me and Mahtab."

He hangs his head.

"I need time."

It's not until the words leave my mouth that I realize they are true. I do need time to think, to process everything he's told me, to see if forgiveness is truly possible. It won't be the same. I will never blindly love my father again, never forget the scars he marked my mind and body with. But I will try to be civil. Maybe someday, I will learn to accept him for who he is. If he's lucky, I might even call him Dad again.

Susan

The week before university begins, I get an email from Preeti titled *FROSH WEEK!!!* A giant poster opens up, featuring a group of smiling students in yellow-and-blue shirts. *Join us for an experience that will define the rest of your student life!*

Right above the poster, a single line of text: *OMG WE HAVE TO GO.*

I grin. Shouty caps are trademark Preeti when she's excited; I have never seen anyone else as energetic. At least, not until I arrive on the green lawn beside the pond at the University of Toronto in Mississauga and five student leaders in bright yellow shirts wave to the first years scattered across the lawn, each one at least as energetic as my extra-caffeinated friend, if not more so.

"Come on!" shouts a handsome boy with warm brown skin and long locs. "Let's split into teams!"

The next four hours pass in a barrage of activities, ranging from participating in cheers punctuated with pelvic thrusts to a water-gun battle, until a couple of kids get the bright idea to fill their guns with paint instead of water.

"I'm exhausted," I tell Preeti once the student leaders begin herding us to another part of campus, where a giant tent has been set up. As someone who avoided every Holi celebration and color fight in India, I never thought I'd be caught in one here. My shirt is splattered with purple and muddy green, and I am pretty sure the stuff got into my hair as well. So far, my university experience has included offers to hit a local nightclub, a pen with the UTM logo, a lollipop, a condom, and politely refusing a good time with an engineering sophomore who smelled like shaving foam.

"Come on, Suze!" Preeti protests, and I wonder if Alisha has taken over her for a second. "A few more minutes!"

Preeti's shirt—if possible—is even muddier than mine. She's wearing a necklace of beads and condoms and a painted smiley on her right cheek. Her face is bright with excitement, her cranberry lipstick worn off in the heat. It's strange seeing Preeti on her own without Heather, who's going to McMaster University in Hamilton. As much as I miss Heather, I know Preeti misses her even more.

"Fine!" I say with a sigh. "But only five more minutes!"

Half an hour later I wave at Preeti, who is flirting with one of the frosh leaders, and slip away from the crowd, narrowly avoiding a pair of Frosh leaders singing at the top of their voices.

Frosh week. My very own version of hell.

"I am *never* going back," I mutter to myself.

Well, not to another event like that anyway. I *will* go back for the classes. Fine Art History. Fine Art Studio. Thinking about

351

spending days studying different artists and art techniques puts a skip in my step.

"I'm not going back either." A voice jars me out of my thoughts. "Too many condoms. What's a celibate guy gonna do with them?"

I turn around and there he is. Porcupine-headed. Smiling like the sun. I almost don't recognize him through the mess of paint on his face and white T-shirt.

Warmth unfurls under my ribs. "You go here?"

"Got into the bachelor's of commerce program last minute." Malcolm shrugs. "I heard you go here, too."

"You heard? You're on my Facebook," I say pointedly. "We text and call each other almost every day." In fact, every time I asked him about his university applications, he got cagey and went silent. "Why didn't you tell me?"

"I wasn't sure if my student loans were going to come through. I only found out a couple of months ago. The old ma—my father offered to foot the bill, but I said no. I'm going to pay for my own tuition. Got promoted to manager at Michelle's though, so at least the pay's a little better."

I smile. "By the way, did I tell you I got a job?"

His eyes widen. "No way. Where?"

"Painter's Box. It's a small art supply store in Streetsville." It hasn't been too bad. The owner, Raul, is over seventy and one of the most talented painters I've ever seen. It's what keeps me going even though the pay is terrible. My mother was initially annoyed by my decision.

"How will you concentrate on your studies?" Amma wanted to know. My mother who now spends her mornings working part-time at a beauty counter in the mall and her nights poring over notes from online science courses.

"I'll manage," I told her. "Like you."

The way I managed to get into the university on a full scholarship, thanks to the application Ms. Nguyen helped me put together for the visual arts program. There was no greater satisfaction than emailing my father the scholarship letter while Skyping with him and seeing the surprise on his face. Even though, seconds later, he suggested that I enroll in a few business courses as backup.

A part of me understands my parents' fear, longs to fall back into the security net they're still offering. But another, larger part of me is more eager to prove to them—to myself even—that I can become independent and make a living, even with a degree in visual arts.

"Have you moved out?" I ask Malcolm.

"Nah, still living with him, Freny, and Mah." Malcolm smirks. "Can't afford to stay on my own."

"Same." Not that I could ever leave Amma alone after the separation. I smile. "Can't live with them, can't live without them, eh?"

He stares at me for a long moment. "You're losing your accent." He sounds a little disappointed.

"I don't think I'll ever lose it completely." I hear it seeping in now, bits and pieces of the old Susan tempering the new one, whose heart has a severe case of the flutters. "If I do, all you have to do is make me mad."

"I think I do that quite well, don't I?"

It's a joke and I'm supposed to laugh, but I hesitate. We've been edging around the boundaries of our renewed friendship for quite a while now. Though never openly enough. "Yeah, but 80 percent of the time, you make me happy," I tell him, finally taking the plunge. It's now or never.

"Eighty?" He steps closer and plucks something out of my hair: a glob of yellow paint. "Well, that's not good enough. I need to get better if I ever intend to be more than a friend."

My mouth feels dry all of a sudden.

"If you'll let me." He's really quiet now and tentative. "Maybe it's too soon for that, though?"

I say nothing. It *is* too soon. A part of me wants nothing more than to go back to where we were right before the breakup: pressed together behind a locker or against a tree, falling on our butts while trying to skate on ice without blades. But another more practical part wants to tread cautiously and take things slow.

"How about a date instead?" he says. "There's this shawarma place I heard of."

A smile pricks the corners of my lips. I crook my head to one side, pretending to study him until he shifts his weight from one foot to the other. It's fun seeing Malcolm Vakil sweat a little.

"Oh yeah?" I ask finally. "What place is this? The one on Dixie and Crestlawn?"

His eyes brighten. "You remember. Yeah, it's the same chain, but a different location. Closer to the university. A guy in my commerce program told me about it. Right after I declined his invitation to a party on campus."

Of course Malcolm was invited to a party. He probably also had fun doing those cheers today and spraying people with every color of the rainbow. It's who he is, who he always will be: able to fit in anywhere, at any time. I still don't know what he's doing here, with me. But I know I don't want him going anywhere else.

"I'm a mess." I point to my shirt and hair.

"So am I."

He flashes me a smile that has me tumbling heart-first into something that feels both familiar and new.

"Okay," I tell him. "Let's go."

Acknowledgments

My utmost gratitude to the Ontario Arts Council for funding this manuscript.

Thank you:

Eleanor Jackson—For your superstar agenting and keeping me sane book after book.

Janine O'Malley and Lynne Missen—For loving Susan and Malcolm as much as I do and helping me take this book to another level.

Elizabeth Clark and Maggie Enterrios—For the brilliant, beautiful cover.

Mandy Veloso, Melissa Warten, and Chandra Wohleber—For your thoughts, insights, and queries, and making *The Beauty of the Moment* better with each revision.

Kelsey Marrujo at Macmillan Children's Publishing Group and Sam Devotta at Penguin Canada—For being fantastic publicists.

Erika David, Bruce Geddes, Anna Priemaza, Carlie Sorosiak, Suja Sukumar, and Donia Varghese—For your friendship and enthusiasm and insightful critiques of the manuscript in its various stages.

Florence Lefebvre—You had faith in this book when I didn't. Merci, mon amie. J'espère que ça te plaît.